Buddies by Ethan Mordden
Joseph and the Old Man
by Christopher Davis
Blackbird by Larry Duplechan
One Last Waltz by Ethan Mordden
Gay Spirit edited by Mark Thompson
Valley of the Shadow
by Christopher Davis
Love Alone by Paul Monette
On Being Gay by Brian McNaught
Everybody Loves You by Ethan Mordden
Untold Decades by Robert Patrick
Gay & Lesbian Poetry in Our Time edited
by Carl Morse and Joan Larkin
Tangled Up in Blue by Larry Duplechan
How to Go to the Movies
by Quentin Crisp
The Body and Its Dangers and Other Stories by Allen Barnett
Dancing on the Tisha B'Av
by Lev Raphael
Arena of Masculinity by Brian Pronger
Boys Like Us by Peter McGehee
Don't Be Afraid Anymore
by Reverend Troy D. Perry with
Thomas L. P. Swicegood
The Death of Donna-May Dean
by Joey Manley
Latin Moon in Manhattan
by Jaime Manrique
On Ships at Sea by Madelyn Arnold
The Dream Life by Bo Huston
Show Me the Way to Go Home
by Simmons Jones
Boys on the Rock by John Fox
End of the Empire by Denise Ohio
Tom of Finland
by F. Valentine Hooven III
Reports from the holocaust, revised edition
by Larry Kramer
Created Equal by Michael Nava and
Robert Dawidoff
Gay Issues in the Workplace
by Brian McNaught
Sacred Lips of the Bronx
by Douglas Sadownick
West of Yesterday, East of Summer
by Paul Monette
Sportsdykes edited by Susan Fox Rogers
Another Mother by Ruthann Robson

How Long Has This Been Going On?
by Ethan Mordden
My Worst Date by David Leddick
Girljock: The Book edited by Roxxie
The Necessary Hunger by Nina Revoyr
Call Me by P. P. Hartnett
My Father's Scar by Michael Cart
Getting Off Clean by Timothy Murphy
Mongrel by Justin Chin
Now That I'm Out, What Do I Do?
by Brian McNaught
Some Men Are Lookers
by Ethan Mordden
a/k/a by Ruthann Robson
Execution, Texas: 1987
by D. Travers Scott
Gay Body by Mark Thompson
The Venice Adriana by Ethan Mordden
Women on the Verge
edited by Susan Fox Rogers
An Arrow's Flight by Mark Merlis
Glove Puppet by Neal Drinnan
The Pleasure Principle
by Michael Bronski
And the Band Played On by Randy Shilts
Biological Exuberance by Bruce Bagemihl
The Sex Squad by David Leddick
Bird-Eyes by Madelyn Arnold
Out of the Ordinary edited by Noelle
Howey and Ellen Samuels
The Coming Storm by Paul Russell
The Salt Point by Paul Russell
Walt Whitman: Selected Poems 1855–1892
edited by Gary Schmidgall
Baby Precious Always Shines
edited by Kay Turner
Pussy's Bow by Neal Drinnan
The Struggle for Happiness
by Ruthann Robson
The World in Us edited by Michael
Lassell and Elena Georgiou
Intimate Companions
by David Leddick
Dirty Pictures by Micha Ramakers
Half-Moon Scar by Allison Green
Troublemaker by Brian Pera
Summer's House by Eric Gabriel Lehman

Also by Eric Gabriel Lehman

Waterboys
Quaspeck

Summer's House

Eric Gabriel Lehman

St. Martin's Press
New York

www.stonewallinn.com

Library of Congress Cataloging-in-Publication Data

Lehman, Eric Gabriel

Summer's house / Eric Gabriel Lehman—1st ed.
p. cm.
ISBN 0-312-24112-7 (hc)
ISBN 0-312-27707-5 (pbk)
1. Teenage boys—New York (State)—New York—Fiction. 2. New York (N.Y.)—Fiction. 3. Uncles—Fiction. 4. Poets—Fiction. I. Title.

PS3562.E42825 S86 2000
813'.54—dc21 99-089930

First Stonewall Inn Edition: December 2001

10 9 8 7 6 5 4 3 2 1

for Ival McDermott

Acknowledgments

Novels may be written in solitude but are helped along by many. Michele Butchko generously provided me with a roof over my head and a quiet place to write. Similarly, Joseph Walton opened his home to me on several occasions so that I might work. Mark Macleod read the manuscript and provided expert editorial comment. Edwin Blesch answered technical questions.

Ulrich Müller provided much encouragement during the novel's early stages. Patrick Merla's belief in my work means much to me; I and many writers benefit from his help. I would like to thank my agent, Malaga Baldi, for all she has done and continues to do on my behalf, and I am grateful to Keith Kahla, my editor, for standing behind the book. Lastly, I remain grateful to my parents for their unstinting support and love.

Summer's House

1

Raymond

Mother played with dolls. Her room behind the kitchen was an orphanage of mute dependents. She gave them names, assigned talents, quirks, and health problems to each. It scared me to hear my mother talking to herself late at night in that room behind the kitchen, so I told myself she was memorizing chemical formulas. I wasn't supposed to know about her dolls. Mother dwelled in secrets, cloistered within walls she'd built brick by necessary brick. I found out that my father had struck a deal with her after I told her what he'd been doing. He promised to stop, and in return, he told her he wouldn't say anything to Aunt Mattie about the dolls. Mother was forever afraid of what Mattie might think. Why else would she have given me her horrible name, the one I refuse to use, if not to appease her? Mother sold my birthright, so I am to blame for what I did to her?

Mornings before her lecture at Drexel, she made my father's coffee and then took hers in that tiny room off the kitchen, cozy because of the boiler, facing the lushest corner of the yard. I wasn't allowed in. I protested—I wanted to be with her all the time—but Mother said drinking coffee alone in the morning was like praying, something she had to do by herself. Then I found out the real reason: it was where the dolls were.

I ate my breakfast in the kitchen with my father, somber as his mahogany bookshelves. The kitchen smelled like a hunting lodge because of his cologne, shoe polish, hair tonic—and from his coffee, strong enough to leave tooth marks in the air. He always dressed as if he were going to work, although he never left the house.

New Cornwall, June 25

What am I doing here? I don't need anyone's help, just someone to listen to the truth. I should go somewhere sunny to read and draw until my fury dries up. So why am I in this phony, barren place? Because I know too many secrets. Secrets are hidden truths. I've been sent here to forget. But a person's memory is their name. Without it, they have no identity. Tyrants have always tried to strip people of what they know, to rewrite them. My memories are woven into me; they'll bleed if the doctors try to tear them loose.

ONE

For as long as I could remember, my parents didn't get along. They never argued, no. The Podilacks two floors above us, now they argued. Several nights a week, Mr. Podilacks's drunken Ukrainian snarled as Mrs. Podilack hurled plates, and their noisy strife slid down the heating pipes and slipped menacingly into my dreams. Things seemed quieter in our house, but it was the stiff calm of a truce.

I was their only child, moody and intolerant as only children are, fulcrum of this delicate balance, and I soon grew aware of my power to upset it. A fork dropped at supper or a fuse blown when I fiddled with a lamp socket brightened the dullest evening. When I was older, hitting my father up for spending money brought on my mother's protest, which flamed into argument the moment he reached for his wallet. I'd leave the house, pockets full, as my mother glared. I justified my antics by telling myself that I took their minds off their domestic misery. I was as good as a marriage counselor.

Yet my motives weren't selfless; I was terrified of a breakup. For a long time, we'd been but paper-clipped together by last name. With no siblings, I sensed that our frail family tree wouldn't withstand too much of a storm. I needn't have worried. My mother considered divorce something for the irresponsible and unstable, not for decent Jewish people. As for my father, staying married was a matter of practicality or, perhaps, habit. He lived in near-biblical simplicity and claimed that he'd always be happy as long as he had a roof over his head and money coming in. This, as it turned out, was not entirely true.

Perhaps the chief source of my mother's dissatisfaction with my father was her failure to accept that her life with him would always be ordinary. Sundays she took me downtown in search of elegance. She dressed with care, hat and gloves and a new Bonwit Teller dress bought with her employee discount, and she reminded me to shine my shoes. My father never went with us, preferring to work at his drafting table in his undershirt.

"Just look at that architecture," she exclaimed before the elegant town houses near the Metropolitan Museum of Art, our destination for the day. "Those magnificent windows, the masonry." I dutifully scanned the glass polished to a blue sheen, cornucopia clustered over spandreled doorways, columns bearing Corinthian curls. Other people's luxury enthralled her.

Her face took on a reverential glow inside the museum. "I can't remember the last time I was here," she said, but I already knew: *not since I married your father*. She divided her life history into Before and After, with marriage the dark line of demarcation. The portraits of the Old Masters regarded us with severity from their heavy gold frames. My mother filed past piously, a guest in their house, and she seemed relieved when we made it to the more-recent American paintings, where the women wore recognizable clothing and jewelry.

Afterward, we stopped at a coffee shop for sandwiches.

"Don't wolf your food down," she said. She longed to stretch out our Manhattan holiday for as long as she could, but I'd already had enough, a token at the ready in my pocket, and soon we'd been back on the train, returning to our old lives.

She consoled herself over her unsatisfying marriage with

buying clothes. The worse things were, the more she bought. Like with the Queen of England's hats, I could rarely recall seeing my mother in the same outfit twice. My father, on the other hand, grew ever more spartan. For every new dress, he held onto a shirt a year longer, wearing it out at the elbows, perhaps out of spite.

But life went on. We ate together. My mother signed my report cards, and my father paid for my clarinet lessons. We dutifully attended family functions together, my father and I in our rented formal wear, my mother in yet another new dress, but once back in the house, their estrangement quietly resumed. We might have been no happier than the Podilacks, but at least no one knew.

They maintained a discreet distance from one another, my mother in her bedroom and my father in his: a corner of the living room where he'd set up camp a year or two earlier. At first my mother took pains to mask their separation and kept the room as photogenic as a furniture advertisement, the glass top of the coffee table mirror-bright, the vacuumed carpet a freshly plowed field. Early in my senior year of high school, when she ceased folding up his bedding in the morning, letting the living room look like the boarder's room it had become, I knew things had taken a turn for the worse. It wasn't long after that when we found out that my father had been having an affair.

I was never the chummy type, and I had my own opinions about things, so perhaps for those reasons, I was obliged to discover the melancholy pleasures of solitude early on. I busied myself with things best done alone: rearranging my drawers, reading magazines, and collecting postcards while my mother's mambo records blasted in the background. I shunned the playground—a nest of carnivorous local toughs lying in wait for chumps like me who didn't care about stickball. I felt safer with the shyer kids, although they, too, had their shy-person way of doing things that they also preferred doing alone. I often fell into conversation with old ladies on line in Woolworth's, mesmerized by the poignant ring of their voices. I spent undisturbed afternoons in the yard behind our building, cloister-like and fragrant with rot. The abandoned railroad station nearby drew me to its picturesque decay. Stray dogs were always sniffing their way over to me.

I'd inherited my mother's insomnia and was proud of this affliction, for it seemed the mark of the stylishly neurotic and urbane. Nights, I snuck out of the house and went for walks. Our neighborhood was bounded by railroad tracks, expressways, and the oily arm of the Harlem River. Defying prudence, I followed streets until they dead-ended and crumbled into no-man's-land. There I'd sit, waiting for the subway to churn out of the tunnel up onto the El, a deep-sea beast breaking the surface of the water with a lusty snort. I'd think of poems to write, imagining myself the subject of a curled sepia photograph, wearing a faraway and wistful expression. Mostly I waited, although it took some time before I knew exactly what I waited for.

"You and your solitude," Agatha would say later that summer. She told me I remained at too much remove from myself. "You'll never be able to love anyone that way."

"I love you," I told her.

"No, you don't, Raymond. You just like the idea of loving me. We could become good friends if only you'd get these romantic ideas out of your head." She was a good ten years older than I, which seemed to give her the right to tell me what I was thinking. But she didn't understand how necessary my solitude was. People scared me.

There was another reason why I took those long walks riverward: it kept me from going the other way—toward the park. The park wasn't like most other city parks—concrete deserts, dry boccie courts, and peeling beech trees. This park was a wild outcropping of granite, a green fortress above a moat of traffic on all sides, rising to a rocky summit flattened by a rectangular terrace set with benches. Like all such castles, it housed secrets, dangers, temptations. The terrace was reached by broad stairs that curled around the park's perimeter, turning ever inward with Yellow-Brick-Road whimsy. Missing bench slats and broken glass marked the place as a hangout, and only one of the two lamps worked, so at night, the terrace hung in shadow. I'd sit there breathing in the city's sour spirit. I imagined myself to be standing at the very top of the world, poignantly alone, except that, unlike those walks to the river, I knew that I wasn't. There was always a guy or two up there.

Guys began to be everywhere, or, more precisely, I began to notice them in a different way. They'd always been there, of course, elbowing their way around and ready to slug you if you stepped on their feet by accident. But suddenly I saw how their muscles bunched up when they bent their arms, the appealing bulge of sinew in their calves, and the enticing curve between their neck and shoulders. I became aware of their shoulders. I discovered that just about all guys looked great from the back. In short, I stopped seeing them as who they were, but as what they were. And what were they? The objects of my as-yet-unnamed desire.

About the same time, I also began to see a different kind of guy, one who walked with just a little too much edge in his step as if in a hurry, or anxious to draw glances toward himself as if by convection. Without looking at anything in particular, these guys took in everything with a microscope's precision. They often wore shoes without socks. Sneakers without socks wouldn't have stood out, but shoes? For some reason—did I attract them?—they always managed to sit themselves next to me in the subway, their butterfly net of a glance dropping over me. I enjoyed the attention, aware of the alluring power of my disinterest, but any pleasure curdled the moment they spoke or, worse, looked ready to touch me, since it implied that we were alike. I always saw it coming. A watery pleading softened their faces, and their mouths opened just enough to emit a waiting breath. I'd tell myself to change places or look away, all the while curious about what might happen next. If I didn't move, it wasn't long before I'd feel a slithery caress to my thigh or a hand darting between my legs, swift as a lizard's tongue. Then I'd flee, disgusted and full of pity. Knowing they wanted me was reason enough to find them repulsive.

But last summer I let a man from the terrace do me. He had a tattoo of a dark sun just below his left shoulder and smooth, shapely arms. He slid beside me on the bench, graceful as a dancer, and my heart sped into a trot and then a canter, and I was ready to flee. But I didn't. The light painted a delicate line down his smooth arms, and his eyes were large and deep. With his narrow face and long hair, he was, I thought, pretty, which confused me, since I'd never thought of men as being pretty. We began to talk, and all the while, I waited for the sly caress, the sneaky hand slipping onto my knee when he thought I wasn't looking. Instead, he surprised me by inviting me up to his apartment and pointed to a row of windows in a building across the street.

His lobby was brightly lit and walled with mirrors reflecting us paired together dozens of times. People looked, knowing just what we were up to, I was certain. The elevator came and disbursed a frowning old matriarch with a laundry cart. *Go home,* she seemed to say. *Go home right now, meet a girl, marry and multiply.* But the closing elevator doors sealed my fate, and we ascended.

My eyes shot around his living room, on the lookout for signs of strangeness, which I thought must mark men like him, but the sofa and coffee table appeared innocent enough, and so did the stereo. He offered me the same cheap brand of orange soda my mother bought and served it in a normal glass. But when he lowered the lights—men like him obviously had dimmer switches—my teeth started chattering. I was on the edge of an arctic precipice, and the slightest movement might hurl me into its icy, jagged mouth.

"Gotta warm you up," he said in a voice suddenly deep.

His palms worked heat into my skin. Slender fingers ivied around my wrist, forearm, and arm muscle, while his large eyes monitored my every reaction. His hands sleeved my skin in warmth, and the tattoo slithered over the muscle hardening in his forearm, its sun shooting out fiery flares. He slung his arm around my neck and pulled me close with just enough firmness to let me know he meant business. His mouth sought mine, but I wouldn't kiss him, and my face fell against his neck, whose sour-salty smell was exhilarating because it was so uniquely a man's. His hand slid under my shirt, migrating across my chest and soft belly, which I quickly tightened. He pushed my mouth against his chest, and I tasted him. This was a man, I told myself. A *man.*

He parted my knees tenderly, deliberately. His fingers worked my zipper and belt; soon my legs were exposed and, seconds later, my thing, wrinkled and puny in his hand, shaming me. His mouth swiftly engulfed it, kneading it between his tongue and lips, and miraculously it hardened. Soon—too soon for me to worry about what was happening—everything pulled out of me. I looked down to see my juice clinging to his face like fat, white tears. He grinned. It had happened. It had really happened. He went for a tissue.

I didn't stay. I feared he'd make me do to him what he'd done to me. I hurried down the hallway, its every peephole wide with surveillance. I took the stairs to avoid looking at myself in the elevator's mirrors and barrelled down the stairs until dizzy, rounding each landing with centrifugal speed to throw off what I was certain would now cling to me for the rest of my life.

I began watching old black-and-white movies on TV after school. Not surprisingly, my favorites were melodramas of rocky marriages: *Back Street, Five Finger Exercise,* and *Come Back, Little Sheba.* I began pumping my mother for details of her domestic misery, but she clung to her secrets tightly. Secrets had a long tradition in her family. A careless remark about my grandfather's youthful liaisons had all the adults in the living room *shush*ing. There was talk of my grandmother's clandestine visits to a woman in South Brooklyn to get "cleaned out" when she couldn't afford another child. And what had my grandfather said to Uncle Abe one fateful afternoon that made him storm out of the house—the very same day the Brooklyn Dodgers won the pennant—vanishing for years until turning up in San Francisco many years later? (When my grandfather's beloved Dodgers migrated to the coast, Uncle Alfred termed it divine retribution.) There were more secrets: one of my mother's cousins had been a communist; another believed that Adlai Stevenson communicated with her via the radio; still another—her name was never mentioned without a hush falling on the room—killed herself. Nothing of this was ever spoken of openly—no one wanted to risk being quoted—but passed on by word of mouth, tongues clicking like telegraphs. "Hint at, don't accuse," might have been the motto on the family crest, had there been one. When Uncle Lester landed in Chapter 11 at the end of that summer, no one in the family was surprised, since they'd already found out about it.

So many secrets. No wonder I found myself trapped in my own.

The biggest secret was, of course, my father's affair. The revelation came, sadly enough, just before Mother's Day. In an act of stupidity or cruelty, depending upon whose version you believed, Uncle Lester told his wife about it, and Aunt Rhoda in turn told my mother by phone. The question on everyone's mind was why Uncle Lester had waited until just that moment to drop this bomb. My father, it seems, had been carrying on for months.

Perhaps my mother must have sensed that something bad was about to happen, for she began confiding in me. On some of my sleepless nights, I'd creep past my father snoring in the living room and tap on my mother's door. She, too, was wide awake, propped up in bed with countless pillows before the late movie, doing her nails. My father banned, the room had become a feminine domain, soft as a tent from the many dresses hangered on the backs of doors. New blouses and a Pandora's box of scarves streamed out of drawers.

Doing her nails was my mother's sole hobby. A case held a manicurist's battery of delicately curved nail scissors, wooden cuticle pushers, emery boards asparkle with grit, as well as a large palette of nail polish and polish remover smelling of fermented roses. Somehow, my mother found something to cut, file, or polish on her nails every night. She'd claim to be ready to turn in, but it was never long before she set her nail things aside and reached for her cherished Gutenberg-sized snapshot album, its stiff black pages paned with snapshots.

"This was when your father came back from overseas," she'd say, the tip of a nail punishing the snapshot. "He still thinks that the whole world revolves around him, his mother's fair-haired boy who could do no wrong, the good one—"

As if summoned, my father passed by, ghostlike, Hamlet's dead father afoot in Elsinore. We fell silent as a pair of thieves, and the book's cover flipped closed, releasing a sigh of dust. I half-expected the door to open and for my father to thrust his head in and give his version of the story, but his soft tread continued across the carpet to thud upon the bathroom's tile.

"This was taken right after we were married," she'd continue when the coast was clear. A couple resembling my parents leaned against the railing of the Coney Island boardwalk, my mother short—"petite" was the word for it—and my father tall and lanky. He wore the baggy pants of the period, a jaunty cap, shirtsleeves rolled up like a stevedore's; she, a square-shouldered jacket, hair pulled back ballerina-style and topped with a tam-o'-shanter. Another shot showed them sunk into the mountainous cushions of my grandmother's sofa, diligently fluffed up before the next person sat down. I appeared in the pictures, wrinkly and unidentifiable at first, then defiant as I inched my way into as many scenes as I could. For the next couple of pages, we were a real family, a smiling twosome posing for the picture-taking third. I'd examine those snapshots for signs of the heartache to come, without ever finding any. The lens had captured only sunny, weekend days. But after all, only happy people had their pictures taken.

They'd met as art students, moving in the scruffy but noble bohemia south of 14th Street. Each had started out as a painter, but my mother went to work selling dresses at Bonwit Teller's, and my father quit school to draw illustrations for a technical magazine. Just before I started junior high school, Uncle Alfred got my father a job at his printing press in Long Island City. A sour cloak of ink clung to him when he arrived home in the evening, and no amount of soap erased the stain etched into his fingers.

Sometimes I went to work with him on the weekends when there were rush jobs to do. The press occupied a loft like an airplane hangar. I carried folders of material from one department to the other or hauled reams of paper, cool from the storage room. The smooth repetitions of the great hot-type machines were the calisthenics of steel giants. There at the press, cushioned by noise—and far from my mother—my father was at ease.

He lugged home an unused drafting table from the press and set it up in a corner of the living room. His dream was to design a new typeface, and he copied type specimens from catalogues with the patience of a monk. I'd find his penciled marks in the *Post*, mimicking the curves and serifs of advertisements, and his calligraphy embellished the covers of my book reports.

Nights, the patient scratch of his pen drew me from my homework into the living room. He molded each letter like a strip of wrought iron. *O* was the most difficult of letters to draw correctly, he said, all curve, hardly a letter at all. *S* was a toboggan ride. *M* was a cathedral's twin spires, *W* a valley, and *B* the side of a cliff, while *Z* was old and stooped. Strange: he spent his days around machines that spat out pages by the thousands, but he labored over individual words at night. Every second letter or so, he stopped to let the nib's proboscis drink up the shiny ink; then he'd continue and soon an entire sentence filigreed the line. *The quick brown fox jumped over the lazy dog. Let Hertz put you in the driver's seat. Yes, we have no bananas.* How important it all looked.

"What do you think?" he'd ask, holding up a sheet.

"Nice." It was what I always said. I never knew what else to say. He wasn't much of a talker, and I was shy with him. I was convinced that he didn't like me, a careful, clean-shirted boy who pleased his teachers. My loose-leaf notebook was as neat as a scrivener's ledger, my textbooks crisply covered. I'd banned all wire hangers from my closet, using only wooden ones, and I hung up my shirts with the top button buttoned. Yet even if I was sure that I was too nice for him, he intrigued me. There was something slick and seditious about the way he sidestepped my mother, and my esteem for him only grew when I learned of his affair.

The Friday night Aunt Rhoda broke the news, I'd lumbered into the apartment later than usual. My friend Stuie's dope still fogged my head.

"Where were you?" My mother's bark was whiplash to the brain. The Sabbath candles flickered with accusation in the kitchen. She sat on the sofa, still in her work clothes, stockinged feet pulled under her, an ominous sign, for she was never home for more than five minutes without changing. She told me the news.

"Your Aunt Rhoda apologized afterward for having to call me up," she said. "So why did she?" She tore a tissue from the box. "I would have been better off not knowing." She avoided my eyes; the news shamed her.

"How did Uncle Lester find out about it?"

"Your Uncle Alfred told him." She blew her nose. "It's been going on for a couple of months already."

"Who with?"

My mother glared at me. I'd asked the wrong question. I was supposed to share her grief, not be excited by it.

"Typical of Lester that he should make his wife call and do his dirty work for him," she muttered, throwing down a pulpy mash of tissue. "What I want to know is, how long did Lester know about it before he said anything?" In our family, matters were pondered, even in the midst of tragedy.

I realized that my father should have been home by now. "Where's Dad?" I asked.

She didn't know. She'd called the press. Uncle Alfred said he'd left early. We continued sitting there for I don't know how long, my mother tearing out tissue after tissue, me not knowing what to say. It occurred to me that we were waiting for my father to return. When the phone rang, my mother leaped for it.

"Oh, hello, Ma," she said in a small voice.

It was my grandmother, calling as she did every Friday night. "Ma," not "Mama," meant it was my mother's mother.

My mother began to cry. "Go," she said to me. Crying, too, had to be done in secret. In the kitchen, the Sabbath candles had burned down in their holders, shedding beards of melted wax, their yellow glow fragile. *It's a new world, and we don't understand it*, they seemed to say.

So where was my father?

One after the other, relatives called, and my mother repeated the litany. Telling the story must have helped, for she never abridged it. After eleven, their calls ceased and we were left alone with our misfortune. There was still no word from my father, and his silence deepened with the hour. The house grew empty as if someone had died.

"Go to bed," my mother told me, but neither of us would fall asleep any time soon.

He called the following evening. I picked up.

"Dad!" He seemed to be in a pay phone.

"I know you've already gotten the news," he said, calm.

"But I wanted you to hear it from me. I've been cheating on your mother." There was a pause.

"Are you coming back?"

"Who's that you're talking to?" My mother hurried over with a mad flap of her house shoes.

My father's end clicked and plunged into a buzz.

"Was it him?" she demanded. Her face had grown older in the past twenty-four hours. "What did he want?"

"To let me know what happened."

"Did you tell him that he was too late?" she said, voice trembling. "Did you tell him that he was too goddamned late?" She took the receiver from my hands and hung it up. It frightened me to hear her use profanity.

I went to my father's worktable and switched on the light. Some of his early watercolors had been tacked up on the wall. He never showed his work, so what had moved him to make this display? Perhaps the same thing that compelled my mother to pull out her snapshots: a desire to return to a happier time. There was a picture of housefronts along a city street, of an El train, of children. The drawings were softly done, even hesitant, my father unwilling to spoil the blank paper's perfection. He'd never thought much of his abilities, so he quickly agreed when my mother suggested working at the press. "If you're not going to peddle your illustrations, then stop wasting time and make some money" she'd said. After that, his images became mere letters, barely words, much in the same way he'd thinned down his life, retreating into the living room in threadbare shirts.

For the next couple of days, I was aware of being alone in the apartment with my mother and her misery. I heard when she flushed the toilet, struck a match to light the many cigarettes she smoked, and, worst of all, when she cried. She kept out of my way. My father's flight humiliated her.

Not only did he stay away from the house, he didn't show up at work. I imagined him leaving some dimly lit bar for a seedy hotel on a side street near the on-ramp to a bridge, sleeping in his clothes on soiled sheets in a narrow room with sweating walls. He'd moved into one of his drawings and become someone else, or perhaps he'd become the person he'd been all along. His lapse secretly thrilled me.

School was ending, and I had no job. The summer began, empty as a yawn. The Podilacks resumed their fighting, perhaps out of boredom. Nights, I lay wide awake on my back, the window open, imagining the mayhem two floors above. I began to think that the mere fact of people being married might be enough to make them hate each other. I missed my father, but something kept me from missing him too much, for I sensed he would've considered it sappy. He hadn't sounded sad on the phone, only worried. Mostly he'd sounded far away, too far to return at any time soon.

The racket upstairs would finally subside so that I heard my mother's movie. The emery board ground against her nails, and the persistent scrape began to sound painful, as if she'd run out of nail and hit flesh. I looked into the dark until I saw my father sweating, limbs locked around the unknown woman who'd become his girlfriend. I stared like any other Peeping Tom until my eyes burned and I knew I had to stop.

Mother skates on the Schuylkill in winter, Hans Brinker-style, muffler looping in the wind, diamond splash of sun against the blades. I call out to warn her where the ice is soft and starting to pool, but she doesn't hear me. She drifts farther away, headed for danger. My throat cramps in fear, but there is nothing I can do. I start to think that she's heading toward danger on purpose, just to escape.

Her lab was small. Mother did well in confined spaces, accepted limits. The lab's green air was fertile with algae. Slender glass vials of emerald soup filled the racks, each one a dense aquarium. "Even as a child, I loved algae," she said.

The scar on Mother's face is crescent-shaped, as if I'd tried to tear another mouth into her after her first one had kept silent for too long.

New Cornwall, July 20

There's this man here, brooding and hulking, another pampered problem child like myself. He sits alone in the dining hall bent over a notebook. Most likely he's in the poetry group. Not me. I tried it once: an hour of sticky, confessional verse and limpid little haikus. Still, when I find myself watching this huge, lonely bear, a part of me wants to protect him.

TWO

My grandfather's birthday was observed with the seriousness of a Jewish holiday, rigid with ritual, obligation, and inconvenience. It fit neatly between Shavuot in the spring and Rosh Hashana in the fall and frequently—perhaps symbolically—coincided with Father's Day. His three children—my mother and two uncles—were expected to mark the occasion with an expensive, collaborative gift and to make a pilgrimage to his house. This year's birthday, his sixty-fifth, a milestone, he'd receive a large-screen color TV.

My father had always been a dubious character in my grandfather's eyes, an "artiste." He criticized my father's lack of ambition and the cars he drove, used, held together, he said, by spit and a prayer. He avoided visiting our small apartment because of its location in a bad neighborhood. He never tired of reminding my mother that he'd favored Arthur Miller from Bensonhurst as a son-in-law, not the big-deal writer, perhaps, but a man all set to take over his father's appliance store on New Lots Avenue, and who didn't need a new toaster or a refrigerator at one time or another?

He didn't speak as much as lecture, hold forth, and orate,

the exact opposite of my father, who said little, and even then, left out more than he said. These visits rendered my father almost invisible, and he was always slipping away to some corner of the house, reappearing with the instinct of a migrating bird just before it was time to leave. "You've married a ghost," my grandmother would say to my mother.

The Sunday morning of the momentous day, my parents acted out a drama as ritualized as the birthday itself. My father informed my mother of his intention of staying home. "Informed" aptly describes his detached mode of delivery, calm and settled as sand. Seders were obligatory, he explained, but nowhere in the Bible did the Most Holy, blessed be He, require the children of Israel to journey to Brooklyn to pay homage to Lazar Loewenthal. If Lazar Loewenthal required it of his own children, that didn't concern a son-in-law, no blood relation he. My mother might go, that was fine, but wild horses couldn't drag him to Brooklyn that day. He retired to his drafting table, pen in hand, ready for a day's work on his calligraphy.

My mother pursued him. If she'd had a drivers' license, she said, she would just pick herself up and go. But she hadn't, and there was no way she was going to traipse all the way to Brooklyn by subway. Subway and bus, to be precise. My father held to his quiet refusal, growing ever calmer in the face of her ballooning rage. Things came to a head. She stormed into the bathroom, the door slammed, and she locked herself in. My father eventually relented—the apartment had but one toilet, after all—and soon we were on our way.

It had been a full week since my father left. He'd called Uncle Alfred to let people know that he was all right, but he wouldn't say where he was. The woman suspected of causing his downfall reported to work as always, but she claimed not to know of my father's whereabouts. I assumed that under the circumstances, my mother wouldn't go to the birthday party that year, but with unmistakable valor, she announced that no one was going to prevent her from celebrating her father's sixty-fifth birthday.

"We'll need a good hour and a half for the bus and train," she said.

"Can't Uncle Alfred pick us up?"

Her exasperated look told me that she'd thought of that herself, had admitted defeat, and was hardening herself for the ordeal ahead. "No, he can't," she said, biting off each word; it would mean a detour for him. "So get a move on."

A non-air-conditioned local chugged into the station, thick with the silt of human closeness. Someone had lodged their bag of cold chicken right under our noses. The car was a teenage fleshpot. Kids my age bound for Coney Island wore cutoffs and skimpy T-shirts bulging with either muscles or breasts. Girls perched on their boyfriends' laps, naked thighs pressed close, and they all looked ready to slip into a sweaty embrace. In her white linen dress and pearls, my mother might have been the math teacher who'd shown up at their party uninvited. She sat stiffly forward to avoid creasing her jacket and shifted in her seat to keep her distance from this teenage rabble. Her fixed frown blamed my father for every single minute of the indignity.

I contemplated the grim afternoon to come. My grandfather would be smoking a cigar and wearing his sleeveless undershirt, looking like a Jewish gangster. He'd worn undershirts from the days before their air conditioner, and no amount of my grandmother's arguing could persuade him to put on a shirt. He'd press a glass of seltzer into my hand, and I'd be called to sit and watch the baseball game with him. I'd drink the scratchy beverage watching a game I neither understood nor enjoyed. Gone were the days when all I had to do was behave and eat everything on my plate in order to impress my relatives; I'd have to show something for my age. I'd be grilled by my grandfather. Did I have a lady friend? What was I going to take up in college? The year before, I'd said I was thinking of becoming an architect and displayed my sketches of apartment buildings. "Another *artiste* in the family," he'd sneered.

"I only hope your uncles behave themselves today," my mother said.

They hadn't been in the same room in over four years—not since The Big Funeral To-Do.

Lester, older by several years, had been accorded all the rights and privileges my mother's family bestowed upon a first-born son. His early years had shone with the assuredness of destiny: top of the class at Erasmus Hall High School, a scholarship to NYU, quarterback on the varsity football team, and right after graduation, in the navy. He'd even managed to get himself wounded, medal, bad back and all. His Oldsmobile was never driven for more than three years. He moved his family into a big house north of the city. The sole detraction to his success story had been his inability to produce a son, but when Stevie was born at last, all seemed perfect.

If Lester was the Wise Son of the Passover story, Alfred was the Wise-Assed. Alfred shot pool with the Irish kids on Blake Avenue on Saturdays while Lester and his father headed for the synagogue. Alfred grew up hearing, "Why can't you be like your brother Lester?" Bounced from one city school to the other, he'd limped to graduation in a private school, to the dismay of his immigrant father, who'd complained that everybody in America went to school for free except for his son. He got a job hawking greeting cards, but carfare ate up the little he made, and soon he was broke. When he'd approached Lester for a loan, his brother had written out a check—and an IOU in duplicate.

Lester's outfit folded a year later. He'd just bought another Olds. He'd just gone to Vegas. He was in trouble. Meanwhile, Alfred had begun to work his way up in the greeting-card business and had just enough to lend his brother and tide him over. "Whatever you do, just don't tell Pop about it," Lester said, five thousand dollars richer.

A year passed without any talk of repayment. Another year. Two. Alfred didn't mention it, but neither did Lester. Alfred said not a word as Lester put his daughter into an expensive

Jewish day school, took more trips to Vegas, and lavished smuggled-in Havana cigars on his father. What had begun as a kind of game became a puzzle Alfred couldn't solve. Was Lester doing all this for Alfred's benefit, or was he just stupid? No. He knew his brother well enough. There could be but one reason for Lester's tactic: to mask his own embarrassment at begging, he'd make Alfred beg a little, too.

Some years later, Lester's mother-in-law died. It was my first funeral. I'd taken a peek at the deceased in the chapel. My aunt's mother was tucked into her coffin, white and primly dressed. The lace and quilted satin brought to mind a doll carriage. All that wasn't so bad, except for the makeup. I couldn't imagine someone applying lipstick to a dead person, to say nothing of that stuff my mother brushed onto her lashes. *And how did they blot the lipstick?*

The day was appropriately overcast and rainy, the grass very green, and the clothing of the mourners very black. High heels knifed into the soft, damp ground. In the midst of it all, a pyramid of earth stood heaped beside a menacing, rectangular hole. Heads turned as a black Lincoln appeared, pristine as a showroom model and almost as long as the hearse it followed. Who was this? Then Aunt Rhoda emerged, face somber behind a lattice of veil. Her daughter Deborah, a little younger than I, followed. She scowled at me; perhaps she'd counted on the privilege of being the only child there. At last, Uncle Lester got out. People began whispering. His business troubles were no secret. What was he doing with such a load? More surprised than anyone, however, was my Uncle Alfred.

The rabbi arrived soon after, a young man whose voice was pockmarked with nervousness. Perhaps it was his first funeral, too. The crowd grew respectfully quiet as he began to intone the prayers for the dead. My aunt wept softly. The occasion grew heavy upon me and I sought out the faces of those I knew, grateful they were all still living.

At some point during the service, I became aware of the drone of a man's voice thickening the rabbi's frail music.

Mourners blocked my view, but I could tell that it was Uncle Lester talking to Uncle Alfred. The more I listened, the louder and more distinct his words became. Uncle Lester was going on about his new car, ticking off its options and the cost of each.

"I was sick and tired of Oldsmobiles," spilled into a pause in the rabbi's prayer. My father turned around to see who was talking. The coffin began to be lowered into the ground. "You wouldn't believe it . . . it rides like you're on water . . ." My aunt was handed a shovel, which looked strange in her gloved hands.

". . . and those tires hold the road like nobody's business . . ."

The coffin sank still lower. Moments later, a shout shook the gathering. I feared the coffin might have dropped from its ropes or, worse, that Aunt Rhoda's shovel had plummeted, stakelike, into the coffin, but no: Uncle Alfred had barked at his brother to shut the hell up. The cemetery was quiet as only cemeteries can be. The shovel trembled in my aunt's hands. Several windy seconds passed.

If Uncle Lester had simply ignored Uncle Alfred, the incident might have been buried with the dead lady and her lipstick. But Uncle Lester wasn't the type to let things just pass.

"How dare you insult my mother-in-law's *n'shuma*, may she rest in peace!" he roared, his voice echoing biblically through the manicured hills and dales of eternity.

Alfred squared off before him. "You go on about your goddamned car the whole time they're lowering her into the ground and then have the nerve to tell me to leave?"

"Please," the rabbi said.

"And while we're on the subject," Alfred went on, "if you can go out and buy a boat like that—" he pointed to Lester's car "—don't you think it's time you coughed up the lousy five grand you owe me, you *schnorrer!*"

"Gentlemen, please," the rabbi said, gripping his prayer book.

But the damage had already been done. Everyone was anxious to hear what Lester would say for himself. Even the rabbi seemed to be holding up the proceedings in order to find out. Aunt Rhoda faced her husband, openmouthed behind her veil. My grandfather eyed his son with suspicion.

Lester's lips quivered. "W-what does one thing have to do with another?"

Alfred turned to the rabbi. "I apologize for the interruption," he said nobly.

The rabbi rushed through the rest of the service, anxious to quit the gathering. The moment the black covers of his siddur closed, the crowd broke into lively debate, and by the time the first cars pulled out, people had already taken sides. Some went with Lester. Where was someone like Alfred going to cough up five grand to loan anyone? Others couldn't believe that he'd make up a story like that and then have the chutzpa to bring it up at a funeral, so if he did, it had to be true. For the next four years, my two uncles attended alternate seders at my grandparents' house and took turns celebrating my grandfather's birthday. This year, however, his sixty-fifth was deemed important enough to declare a truce.

But the occasion was already marred. When Uncle Alfred named a store where they should buy the color TV, Uncle Lester claimed that an outlet in Yonkers sold the same model for a third less. According to my father, Lester had waited until a week before the birthday to go there, only to find a strike on, and he'd refused to cross the picket line. The strike didn't end until Friday. That morning, Lester's car wouldn't start. Alfred had to go instead, and he got stuck in the Friday-afternoon traffic, missing his younger daughter Beth's performance as Florence Nightingale in the end-of-school play. When she didn't find her father among the audience, she forgot her lines, left the stage in tears, and wouldn't talk to him for the rest of the evening. The afternoon in Brooklyn seemed doomed from the start.

My father had timed his absence well.

Our subway station finally came, and we trudged up to the bus stop, ragged as stowaways. Once at the house, we filed past my uncles' cars gleaming in the driveway, front grilles bared at each other like teeth. My mother opened the back door with her key.

"I feel like a widow," she said.

The kitchen's air was oily from a roast in the oven. My grandmother wore her usual dark dress and boxy, low-heeled shoes that barely contained her broad ankles. She wore an apron; I hardly ever saw her at home without one. The door to the living room was closed because of the air conditioning. I imagined the entire family assembled behind it sternly, like the men on the Dutch Masters' cigar box, a family portrait with my own family missing.

"Look who's here," my grandmother said when we walked in, which meant we were late. She accepted my mother's kiss to her cheek. "What took you so long?" Her face darkened with suspicion. "Where's Paul?"

My mother set her pocketbook on the table. "Don't ask."

"He still hasn't come home?"

My mother's eyes lowered. "No."

She got herself a drink of water from the sink and rummaged in her pocketbook for something she didn't find. I sensed her hesitating before going into the living room, fearing the tribunal.

"Look who's here," said Aunt Malvina as my mother and I walked in. "Raymond, you look terrific! Give your Aunt Malvina a kiss!" Her wristful of bracelets rattled. She threw a broad arm around my neck and pulled me into her cloud of perfume.

"Where's your father?" she whispered in my ear.

I told her I didn't know.

My grandfather, on the Castro before the ball game playing on the television set, sat beneath a silvery canopy of cigar smoke. He wore his undershirt as usual, upper arms lumpy with age but retaining a hint of their former heft. My uncles brooded on either side of him, gazes cemented to the television, each ignoring the other, looking like bodyguards.

"Why are you crying, Aunt Ruth?" came a tiny voice. My

cousin Gregory popped up from behind a chair.

I looked my mother's way. Yes, she was crying, just a little, but too much to hide. I'd feared she would.

"Shut the door!" my cousin Stevie shouted, spindly legs swinging back and forth under his chair. "You're letting out the air conditioning!"

Stevie, Uncle Lester's son, was . . . the word often used to describe him was "difficult." Doctors diagnosed him as hyperactive. He was about ten and attended a special school. Thick lenses left him with alarmingly large eyes, and the constant swivel of his head gave him the look of a robot.

"Stevie," said my cousin Deborah, placing a hand on his shoulder.

"But he should shut it!"

"Sha," my grandmother said, taking a large platter from the sideboard.

"Where's Uncle Paul?" Stevie asked.

"I said be quiet!" My grandmother raised her hand, platter and all, looking ready to throw it. Stevie bolted from his chair, pleased at his outburst.

The TV announcer broke into high-pitched screams as a roar rose up from the stadium crowd.

"He was safe, goddammit!" shouted Uncle Lester.

"The hell he was!" said Uncle Alfred.

"Be quiet, both of you!" My grandfather threw his hands into the air, an ill-tempered Solomon.

Uncle Lester slunk back to his side of the sofa. Uncle Alfred got up and went over to my mother.

"Hello, stranger!" he said. He put his arms around her, and she broke into fresh sobs.

"Stop that," Alfred commanded, trying to be stern.

"So where's Paul?" My grandfather's voice issued from the other side of the room, a clap of wheezy thunder. Silence followed. Even the commotion on the television screen seemed to die down. I tensed.

"Leave her alone, Pop," Uncle Alfred said.

"I want to know where he is—"

"Everybody sit down," my grandmother interrupted as she appeared with steaming bowls of soup on the platter. We had hot soup any time there was a family gathering, regardless of the weather: a golden sea of chicken broth, afloat with parsley flecks and beach balls of fat that bounced back and forth with each swirl of the spoon.

My grandfather frowned at being upstaged, but everyone was hungry and made for the table. He took his place at the head, and my uncles distributed themselves on either side of him as on the sofa.

"Did the chicken splash through the water once or twice, Ma?" Uncle Lester teased after a taste of the soup.

"Chicken, chicken!" cried Stevie.

"Sha," my grandmother said, returning from one of her many shuttles between table and kitchen.

"Chicken, chickie, chick, chick!" Stevie cried, louder than before. "Chicken, chickie, chick—"

"Stevie," Aunt Rhoda said, clutching one of his hands that had flapped up to join the other in a mad clap.

"What's with him?" Uncle Alfred asked.

"A neighbor of ours raises chickens," Uncle Lester said wearily. "Stevie likes them."

The meal seemed quieter than usual. Everyone kept silent for fear of the forbidden question about my father slipping out, all the while hoping it would. The ball game played in the background, a stadium full of happy, screaming people far from our problems.

My cousin Melanie examined her piece of chicken. "Mother, is it possible to tell whether this was a hen or a rooster?"

"I wasn't at its *bris,*" said Aunt Malvina.

Melanie, the brainy one, looked unsatisfied. "But if this is a breast of chicken, then it would have to be a female, since a rooster wouldn't have breasts?"

"He would if he worked Vegas as a female impersonator," Uncle Alfred quipped.

"Chicken titty, chicken titty!" piped Stevie.

"Eat!" commanded his father.

"Chicken titty!"

"Be quiet!" said Uncle Lester.

"I want to bite those tits of yours. Those big tits, baby—"

"Stevie, stop that!" shouted Uncle Lester.

"Those big tits, baby—"

"Stop!" Aunt Rhoda commanded.

"Gott im Himmel," said my grandmother.

"What's this?" growled my grandfather.

Stevie grinned mischievously. "You know you want it—"

"Come with me," Aunt Rhoda said, grasping Stevie's hand and leading him away from the table.

"No!" Stevie yelled as she dragged him out of the room. The door silenced his cries, but his empty chair accused everyone of his persecution. It was hard to feel sorry for Stevie. True, there might have been something wrong with him, and there were stories about his being taken from one specialist to another and about his medication. Yet he always seemed to know exactly what he was doing, which was usually trying to get a rise out of someone.

"Where did he get such a thing?" my grandmother asked.

Uncle Lester looked down. "Who knows?"

My grandfather glared at him for a moment before turning to my mother. "So where's Paul?" he demanded.

"Papa, stop," said Aunt Malvina.

"I'm asking a question, I want an answer! I want to know now—"

"You know where he is," my mother said weakly. "He's gone."

Her thin voice pulled in all directions, ready to snap apart, and my grandfather sensed that he'd gone too far but couldn't afford to show it. Like Uncle Lester, he wasn't one to let anything pass. "What kind of man lets his wife schlepp for two hours on the train alone?" he asked.

"She wasn't alone. Raymond was with her," Aunt Malvina said, winking at me.

"Such a shame," my grandfather continued. "When I had to leave Mama alone in Poland and go ahead to New York, I was worried sick the whole time before I sent her a *shiffskarte.*"

"Come on, you were fooling around with an Eye-tie girl from Mulberry Street the whole time, Pop," Uncle Alfred said with a grin.

"What's an Eye-tie?" Gregory asked.

"I want to know why Paul isn't here," my grandfather said, his fist beating down with every other syllable. The soup in my bowl trembled. *Nowhere in the Bible did the Most Holy, blessed be He, require the children of Israel to journey to Brooklyn to pay homage to Lazar Loewenthal.* My grandfather was beginning to get on my nerves.

"Maybe he just didn't feel like coming," I heard myself say.

Everyone's horrified gaze swung my way. Melanie stared. Uncle Lester shot me a disapproving glance.

"Mind your business, Raymond," Uncle Alfred said to defuse his father's anger, but his grin betrayed approval.

My grandfather took one look at me, pushed his plate away and left the table. I'd never mouthed off at a relative before. I'd crossed some kind of threshold.

"Why did you have to say that?" my mother whispered in the silence that followed. Her voice was soft and weak; it was submissive. It angered me to hear it. I didn't know why I'd said it, but I felt curiously elated. I almost felt like saying it again.

After the meal, I headed for one of the bedrooms to read the book I'd brought. Stevie came in.

"I have to tell you something," he said.

I waited.

"Not here. Come down to the basement with me."

"No," I said.

"Please."

I gave in. He was just a strange little kid, after all, and I still felt sorry about how he'd been taken from the table.

The basement had always been the best part of going to my grandmother's house when I was younger. Apartments like ours were too cramped for mystery, but that basement held all that was old, forgotten, and exotic. That first unguided dip into darkness was always terrifying and wonderful, each surge of the oil burner like the jaws of hell gaping open. But that afternoon when I turned the key left in the lock as usual, I knew the place promised adventure no more. Dusty daylight streamed in through the small windows, baring the basement's secrets and rendering them harmless.

"Come over here," Stevie said, in charge. He scurried into a corner stacked with cartons bearing the names of different relatives. His pungent, adult's smell repelled me. A chair scraped against the floor above us, followed by a muffled voice. I felt far from the gathering upstairs, exiled to Stevie's world.

"So what's up?"

Stevie smiled a slippery smile. "Guess."

"Your father's buying another new car?"

He shook his head.

"Aunt Rhoda's going to have a baby."

"Nope." His eyes glimmered terribly. "Better."

My patience was waning. "Tell me!"

"There's this guy who calls my mom up and says things to her!"

"What kind of things?"

"Dirty things."

"How do you know?"

"I've heard it."

His eyes danced. How did he know about what was dirty? Then I remembered what he'd said at the table, and I realized that he might actually be telling the truth. A band of darkness clouded Stevie's face as someone outside walked by the window. I yearned to be out of that dungeon already.

"You're scared," Stevie said with diabolical insight. "How much are you going to give me?" His hand shot out.

"What for?"

"For telling you."

"Nothing." I turned to go.

Stevie grabbed me with his spindly fingers. "Give me!" he cried. His smell grew stronger with exertion.

"Get lost," I said.

He let out a short yell and fled the cellar, throwing the door shut behind him. It took me a couple of seconds before I thought to pursue him, but too late: the key turned in the lock and was removed.

The floor above me grew quiet. I would find out later that everyone was discussing my father's absence just then. When my mother had asked Stevie where I was, he'd told them I'd gone to Church Avenue for ice cream, the little jerk.

Through the window, I saw Uncle Lester lumbering down the driveway in his shirtsleeves, red-faced. I jumped onto a chair and knocked on the pane, but he kept going. He reached into the back seat of his car and dragged out a large box wrapped in shiny paper with a huge bow like an oversized party favor. His shirt pulled from the back of his pants to reveal a white band of flesh just above the belt line. He kicked the car door closed and heaved the package back toward the house, a boy struggling with a giant alphabet block.

As soon as he was close enough, I rapped on the pane again and shouted his name. I must have startled him, for he stumbled forward and the box plunged earthward with a dense crash. I heard Uncle Lester's muffled groan, and his eyes met mine through the dirty glass of the basement window.

"I'm locked in," I shouted.

Ten minutes later, the key turned and my uncle stood in the doorway, sweating, face sagging with defeat. "You made me drop the damn set. What are you doing here anyway?"

"Stevie locked me in."

That mollified him. “Do me a favor, don’t mention anything about . . . the set, okay?”

I followed him upstairs just as my grandmother carried a large cake into the living room, the icing pierced with a ring of lit candles. My grandfather blew them with an abrupt jerk of his head, then tore off the wrapping paper impatiently, nodding with approval to see the writing on the box that identified the television’s size and make. Uncle Lester placed the new set atop the old one. Stevie yanked out the cord to plug it in. When my grandfather turned a knob, the screen lit up long enough for us to see a woman spray a bathroom wall with Lysol. Then it went dark.

Uncle Alfred looked at Uncle Lester.

“Get away from there,” Uncle Lester said to Stevie as he pulled the plug and reinserted it. “Try it again, Pop.”

But nothing happened. Aunt Malvina cast a worried glance in her husband’s direction.

“All it needs is a good whack to get it going,” Lester said.

“That only works with old sets.” Uncle Alfred began to sound on edge.

“It might have been shaken too much in the trunk,” Uncle Lester said. “Some connection must have loosened, that’s all.” He fired me an imploring look.

Melanie inspected the set’s knobs and dials with scientific interest. “Look,” she said, pointing to a dent on one side.

“They gave me a bum set, for crying out loud,” Uncle Alfred said.

I whispered to my mother about what had happened. I must have whispered it loudly, for Uncle Lester heard. Uncle Alfred heard, too. Everybody did. Uncle Alfred swung around as if on wheels and faced his brother.

“I can’t believe it.” His voice shook the room as it had shaken the cemetery four years before. “You *know* you have a bad back. You *know* you can’t lift for shit, so what do you do? You try to make like Superman and carry the thing by yourself. I asked you if you needed help—”

"Shut up!" Lester shouted.

"I haven't even started," said Alfred, sidling up closer to him. "You always have to be the hero," he yelled. "Always the hero."

"Alfred, stop," pleaded Aunt Malvina.

"I've never met anyone else in my life who talks through his ass as much as he does!"

Stevie began to wail, eyes brimming with terror. He ran toward the table. I thought he was going to start throwing things, but instead, he grabbed a handful of napkins and began stuffing them into his mouth, one after the other. His cheeks bulged like a squirrel's, and his eyes popped.

"Stevie!" shouted Aunt Rhoda. She tried to stop him, but his scissoring hands fended her off. Another napkin disappeared into his mouth.

Lester grabbed him. "Spit them out, goddammit!" he shouted, giving the boy a terrible shake. "Spit them out!"

"Dad, you're hurting him," Deborah cried.

Uncle Lester wouldn't relent. He shook the boy as he might have shaken the television set to bring it back to life. Stevie spat out a pulpy mash that splattered the screen.

"Eeeww, that's gross," said Melanie.

Aunt Rhoda wiped his mouth. "Sit down," she said to the dazed little boy.

"*Gott im Himmel!*" my grandmother cried.

Aunt Rhoda unbuttoned Stevie's shirt and combed his hair with her fingers.

"I want an apology," Uncle Lester said to his brother.

"Kiss my arse."

"I said I want—"

"I don't care what you want."

Uncle Lester lunged at his brother, landing a jab an inch or two shy of Alfred's mouth. Alfred spun sideways, ready to fall, but he recovered himself and buried a dense right in Lester's stomach.

"*Aaooh,*" Lester gasped.

"Les!" Aunt Rhoda cried. Stevie let out a fresh wail.

"Stop, please!" my mother said. She went over and wedged herself between them. Lester took another swing at his brother. His fist caught my mother on the side of her head, and she crumpled to the floor.

"Mom!" I said, rushing over to her, her face a grainy white.

"God help me!" moaned my grandmother.

"Mama, get ice!" Uncle Lester shouted.

She returned with a towel wrapped around ice cubes. Uncle Alfred held the lumpy pack against my mother's head. I knelt beside her. The disorder of her hair gave her an alarming, crazy look. Through it all, my grandfather kept to his place at the table, looking helpless, as if witnessing his house going up in flames.

The telephone rang. Melanie picked it up.

"It's Uncle Paul," she said.

"What the hell does he want?" my grandfather growled.

"Give me the phone," Uncle Lester said.

My mother's eyes fluttered open. "Paul?"

"Lie still," Uncle Alfred said, holding her hand.

Uncle Lester went for the phone, but I beat him to it.

"Dad? Where are you?" It was so good to hear him.

"That you, Ray?" he said. "I'm in Queens. You okay? Your grandfather showing you a good time, I hope?" I heard the sneer in his voice, all right.

My grandmother and my Uncle Alfred began helping my mother over to the sofa.

"Tell your father to get his ass the hell over here," Uncle Alfred boomed.

"Is that my brother-in-law?" my father asked.

"Let me go to the phone," my mother whimpered.

"Was that your mother? Is something wrong?"

By the time I turned around, she'd zonked out, stockinged feet up on the arm of the sofa, a princess put to sleep by an evil spell. My grandfather yanked the receiver from my hand.

"Where are you?" he bellowed into the phone. "Hello? Hello?" He slammed down the receiver.

But my father, always ready to take off, had hung up.

Once, in a museum, I saw a painting of a woman looking heavenward, fiery-red cloth tucked around her, hands gesturing supplication or perhaps accusation. The cloth drips with her blood. Someone holds her breasts upon a tray: a booby prize, get it? Mother steered me away from the painting to the calm Dutch landscapes and to the silvery still lifes with their perfect coils of lemon peels and artfully shattered goblets. But I bought a postcard of that painting and kept imagining the swift pain as the swordsman's blow cut off my breast, a pain both holy and delicious. I showed it to my girlfriend, Ilene Schoenberger. "Omigod!" she shrieked. "He chopped it off!" But Ilene was Jewish, so she didn't understand what joy and pain had to do with one another.

I think of seamless summer afternoons at Aunt Mattie's. A coxcomb of flesh dangles from her chin as she holds forth in a garden chair. Her cologne is strong enough to keep away the bugs. She talks about her roses: Trinidad, Helen of Troy, Galicia, Franciscan. She idolizes my father, noble and composed in his wheelchair. She asks him how his book is coming along, the one he has been writing for as long as I can remember. Perhaps there is no book at all. It doesn't matter. I yearn to go back there and smash those teacup afternoons, to pull the roses out by their roots, earth dripping like blood over both of them.

New Cornwall, August 16

The saints thought devotion meant pain, but they were wrong. Pain is rage.

THREE

It was Friday, and so my mother lit the Sabbath candles, the sole ritual in our nonobservant household. When I was younger, I was drawn to the shimmering moment when she fanned the air above the candles the prescribed three times, bundling up what mystery the flame had dispersed into the kitchen and taking it with her into the chapel of cupped hands that she pressed against her eyes. She was always teary by the time she emerged. She wept for joy to have her family with her, she said when I asked why. No wonder the Jewish religion was forever linked with sadness in my mind. Tonight the light of the candles weathered her face; she hid behind her hands longer than usual and emerged dry-eyed. I imagined her calling on the God who'd sanctioned her union with my father to heal it, or at least to make my father show up. Then she brought old-fashioned food to the table: tissuey challah, muddy-colored chopped liver, and the obligatory roast chicken.

"Eat," she said, ignoring her own plate.

During those first shapeless nights when my mother and I were alone in the apartment, she behaved as if my father were stuck in the rush hour, ready to open the door at any minute. She set a place for him at the table and cooked enough for three, so the refrigerator would soon sparkle with foil-wrapped leftovers.

Later that evening, the doorbell rang: Uncle Alfred. My mother held him responsible for my father's caprice, and she hesitated before buzzing her brother in. He sensed it; his voice pleaded through the intercom. But the moment he appeared, she threw her arms around his neck and sobbed just the same.

"Go and do your homework," he said to me.

"I don't have any. School's over in a week."

"Go," my mother said.

I went into my room but left the door open. My mother went for the schnapps.

"So, tell me, Alfred. What kind of person is she . . . this woman?" I heard my mother say.

My uncle uttered a syllable of hesitation.

"Tell me."

"A secretary," he sighed. "In Accounts Receivable. Been with us over seven years."

"How old?"

"You're asking all the wrong questions, Ruth."

"Tell me what I want to know, not what to ask!"

He said nothing.

"All right," she relented. "So what should I be asking?"

"You should be asking why your darling brother Lester decided to drop this bomb just now. He knew about it as long as I did."

Her mood flared up again. "How long?"

"Believe me, I was hoping it would stop—"

"How long, Alfred?"

"Three months. Maybe more. I didn't keep track."

"And you sat back and did nothing?" Her voice hacked at him like a machete.

"Lester did it to get back at me, not at you, don't you

understand? He's hard up again and came to me for money, so when I wouldn't give him any, he decided to stab me in the back."

"So you turn around and stab me!"

The phone rang, and I sprang for it. Aunt Malvina wanted to know whether my uncle was there.

"I hope you didn't tell her I was," he said with a smile as he got up.

"How'd you find out about . . . what they were doing?" I whispered to him as he picked up the phone. "Did you see anything?"

"Get outta here, wise guy," he said.

The story came out soon enough. He'd discovered my father and the woman one evening after the others had left the press for the day. They'd secluded themselves in a dark little room in the back where the guys snoozed on cots after overnight rush jobs. Alfred had taken one look, pretended he'd seen nothing, and left. He'd carried the secret around with him for weeks, saying nothing to anybody, hoping the whole thing would blow over. When he caught them a second time, he mentioned it to his wife, and soon the bitter truth was buzzing through telephone wires across the Greater New York metropolitan area, as if everyone had been lined up around that cot and watching.

After my uncle left, my mother asked whether he'd said anything to me. He had: the woman was from the Caribbean, a little younger than my mother, and she wasn't bad-looking for her age. But I knew better than to say any of this. Besides, Uncle Alfred had promised to brain me if I did.

"Nothing much," I said, feeling a peculiar satisfaction at having told an adult lie.

The thirsty wheels of the train squealed on the tracks, a clattering toy high above the city. Afternoon sun scorched the air, and the bricks of the Eastchester projects glowed a desert red. I imagined myself hovering in a helicopter, searching for my father.

Stuie Greenberg's mother—a short, burdened knot of a woman—answered the buzzer. Her worn dress was the uniform of someone who'd brought up two children on too little, and her face bore the tribulations of centuries. The apartment's old, dark furniture and balding carpet might have been transported from Europe on a donkey cart. As usual, a piece of fabric was held in the teeth of the sewing machine as she worked. Stuie's stereo boomed in the background, a modern intrusion.

"Tell your friend to keep the racket down," she told me, her way of saying hello.

I knocked on his door and stepped into a waist-high flood of decibels. Window shades dimmed the daylight to a sulky green, and the air conditioner filtered out any trace of weather. Stuie didn't go out unless he had to; I'm sure he'd been in the room all day. I shut the door to dam the sound.

"Hey," Stuie said. He'd been a shy, chubby kid when we first met in ninth grade, but he'd slimmed down and taken on a tough demeanor. Along with my friend Barry, who'd be over later, Stuie and I had spent a good part of high school cloistered in this room under the poisonous glow of black lights, getting high, speakers thumping beside us like giant hearts. We never met in my house: my stereo's meager wattage was inadequate. We were friends, but perhaps we really weren't all that close, if closeness meant sharing secrets, but until that summer, I didn't think I had any secrets to share. The bed's wrinkled sheets looked grimy; I pulled the bedspread over them before sitting down. Something about the room repelled me, and for a moment I was almost tempted to turn right around and leave.

"What happened to the radio?"

The guts of his old Grundig lay exposed. The radio's empty wooden case lay on its side, a fossil. The radio had been his father's, the only thing he brought with him from Europe when he fled the Nazis. It was foreign-looking, with rounded corners, gold-tone trim, and the names of European cities along the tuning band instead of numbers; WABC fell somewhere between Helsinki and Copenhagen and WNEW, near Madrid. It had reposed with certain honor on a doilied cabinet in the living room, and Mr. Greenberg had managed to make it work on U.S. current. He'd been a quiet man with a mustache who always wore a vest. He'd lean close to tune in some foreign station, the dial's gentle green glow upon his forehead, and soon the unintelligible sputter of a foreign language collected in the speaker, frail and quaint as Mr. Greenberg himself. Without its case, the radio's filmy tubes looked like balding old men.

"I'm trying to connect the radio to the Wharfedales," Stuie explained, pointing to the large pair of floor speakers. Stuie's life was his stereo. When I first met him, he spoke of nothing but assembling his dream component system, and buying it became his Manifest Destiny. He haunted audio stores. Shiny catalogues spilled over his desk. He got a part-time job at Radio Shack and saved his money. By some inexplicable twist of fate, he brought his stereo home the same day his father was stabbed to death in the building's elevator. Stuie hardly spoke of his father's death; his mammoth stereo seemed to drown out any memory of it.

There was a knock on the door. His mother stood in the doorway, grasping the knob as she might a shield.

"What do you want?" Stuie shouted over the din.

"You know what I want! Make it lower." She looked my way for support. I often found myself in the middle of their arguments. "Your sister's trying to sleep," she said.

"All she ever does is sleep."

Sharon was several years older than Stuie. She neither went to school nor worked since her father's stabbing, floating through the apartment bathrobed, a damaged fairy-tale princess. She'd been the one who found him. Most of the time, she cried. It was never long before her plaintive moaning sounded through the walls.

Mrs. Greenberg looked with horror at the dismantled Grundig. "Who told you you could take apart your father's radio?" She picked up the case, and grief manacled her eyes. She touched it with horror, as she might have touched her husband's skull.

Stuie reached for a pair of wire cutters. "He always told me I could have it. It's mine now." He snipped one of its wires and Mrs. Greenberg winced, as if Stuie had severed one of her veins.

"Put that back the way it was, do you hear me? Your father loved that radio."

Stuie gave a cruel laugh. "He doesn't care about it now."

She lifted a hand. "I'll give you." She looked at me. "Whoever heard that a child should speak of a parent that way? Do you speak to your mother like that?"

I shifted uncomfortably on the lumpy bedspread. Her helplessness was sad to watch.

"Leave us alone," Stuie shouted.

Sharon moaned.

"Turn that thing down!" Mrs. Greenberg ordered.

"No!"

Mrs. Greenberg eyed him. "God will punish you," she said, leaving.

"What's the big deal about making it lower?" I asked afterward. I imagined Sharon on the other side of the wall, softly miserable, imprisoned in her room.

"I worked for all this," he said. "It's all mine, and I like it. You know what the trouble is? She's crazy, like my father was, because of the Germans. My father once told me that he didn't deserve to live because the rest of his family got fried in the camps. Did you ever hear of anything like that? He even said that he wished they'd got him, too. No wonder my sister's crazy. I don't want to talk about it anymore. Listen. There are these guys at work who are musicians and they're looking for a roadie. I have their demo tape somewhere," he said, rummaging around his desk until he produced a small reel. He switched off the record, mounted the reel, and fed the tape through the machine. "Check this out." After some initial hiss, the tangle of an electric guitar broke through the speakers. "They're called Feelie's Wheel," he said. "What do you think? Aren't they great?"

It was too loud for me to tell, the way food that's too hot has no taste. It might have been bad Jimi Hendrix or bad Jethro Tull. Mostly it was loud, and it went on and on. I stopped listening. I thought of Mrs. Greenberg at her sewing machine, and for some reason, I began to feel very sad.

A knock startled me, and I expected to see poor Mrs. Greenberg again, but it was our friend Barry, in biker's shorts and a tight-fitting jersey. He'd pedaled halfway across the Bronx, nothing extraordinary for him, for he might hop onto the saddle of his beloved Crescent and tool the sixty miles all the way around Manhattan of a Sunday without a second thought. His forearm bore a grease smudge from lugging his bicycle up to the apartment; he'd never risk locking it downstairs.

"Hey," Stuie said.

"Turn that shit down."

Stuie did so immediately.

Barry was Stuie's opposite, his wiry body as charged as a circuit board. He was moody and brilliant; his genius let him sail into Columbia, where he'd start that fall. A cycling accident had left a jagged scar on his face that veered frighteningly close to his eye, giving him a battled look. He said little during our meetings, rolling perfect, tight joints and then staring out in Buddhalike silence as we toked. He was a mystery. The nervous bite of his lips hinted at secret worlds churning within, and he hummed with internal activity like a generator. Barry was an electronics buff, but Stuie's strobe lights and color organ were just tinkering to him; he intended to study theoretical physics. Stuie idolized Barry, but Barry once confided to me that he thought Stuie was an asshole.

"Look what I got," Barry said, producing something wooden and shoebox-sized that he set on the bed. "Hand me that screwdriver, Ray," he said and began to remove the casing on Stuie's telephone.

"Hey—" Stuie said, anxious, but reluctant to interfere. Barry's slender fingers worked with oiled precision to connect the wires from the box to the inside of the telephone. When he was finished, he lifted the receiver and announced that Stuie could now dial anywhere in the world without it costing more than an ordinary call.

"The box confuses the signal sent to the substation," he explained.

Stuie eyed the exposed telephone with its fragile appendage. "How do I know it won't cost anything?"

"You won't." Barry grinned. "Not until the bill comes."

"Can I call someone?" I asked, thinking of an old school friend who'd moved to Denver.

"If I get stuck with the bill, you're paying for it!" Stuie said.

There was another knock on the door.

"Leave us alone, Mom," Stuie shouted, giving the telephone a worried look.

The knock persisted, and the door opened. Sharon stood there, still as a statue inside a chapel, looking stiff enough to topple with one finger. She wore what looked like a wedding dress, veil and all. Satin pooled around her on the floor and sheathed her arms. Slashes of color covered her lips, and her eyes bore a frightening ring of black makeup.

"Hello," she whispered to Barry.

"What are you doing in that?" Stuie said, pointing. "Get out of here!"

"What do you think of my dress, Barry?" she asked, stirring up waves of camphor as she walked in.

"Very pretty," Barry said. He spoke to her as he might a parent.

"Don't talk to her," Stuie said. "She'll only stay longer."

"You should get out of your gown," Barry said carefully. "Otherwise you might wrinkle it."

I'd seen all this before. Sharon often appeared when Barry

was there. Barry might be impatient with Stuie, but he was always kind to her.

"Let's go for a stroll," she said. The word left her lips ripe with longing. She would never think of leaving the house, I knew, too frightened since her father's murder.

Barry played along. "Not now, Sharon," he replied with a doctor's firmness.

"Sharon, get out!" Stuie shouted.

"Look, Sharon," said Barry, motioning to the dissected telephone. "It's a magic phone now."

Sharon took a cautious step forward and Barry lifted the receiver. She looked puzzled, trying to decide whether or not she was being tricked. "Can I call my father?"

Barry was about to give her the receiver when Stuie crashed it down onto the cradle. "I want you out of here *now,*" he said, trying to grab his sister's arm. She pulled away and her arms flew around Barry's shoulders. Stuie lurched over to the stereo and threw up the volume. The razor of an electric guitar riff sliced through the room.

Sharon put her hands to her ears. "Stop that, stop that!" she cried. Tears turned her face into a stormy sea of makeup. Barry punched the power button, and the stereo fell silent, an oscilloscope hooked to a dying patient.

Stuie glared at him. "You can take your stuff and get out, Barry," he fumed.

Mrs. Greenberg threw open the door. "What in God's name is going on here?" She turned to Sharon. "Again with the wedding dress!"

"I told you to get out," Stuie said to Barry.

"Dork," Barry said to him, beginning to pack up the telephone gadget.

"Don't go," Sharon said. "Don't leave me alone with him. He's evil!"

"Come," Mrs. Greenberg said, taking Sharon's hand.

"Good-bye, Sharon," Barry said. "You coming too, Ray?"

Stuie's glance appealed to me to remain. I didn't have many

friends and Stuie had less. Barry wouldn't be coming back here again, that was for sure. Their friendship, which had always been tenuous, was about to end. Leaving with him would mean the same fate for me. I didn't know what to do.

"Not yet," I said.

Barry scowled. I had disappointed him.

"Don't go," Sharon repeated, reaching for Barry's arm.

He leaned over and kissed her, and her eyes followed him out the door. I heard the *click-click* of his bike as he rolled it out of the apartment.

"Come, angel," Mrs. Greenberg said, leading Sharon out of the room. Stuie shut the door, and we were alone. Suddenly I wished I'd gone, too. Never had I felt so close to such misery before.

"Want a beer?" he asked.

I shrugged. I didn't know what I wanted.

"I'll get us some."

The smell of camphor faded, and I was conscious of the staleness in the air, thick and caked with every joint we'd smoked in there during the past four years. I opened the window for some air. It seemed as if I'd been in that room a very long time, perhaps too long. In a couple of months, I'd be going to college. I wondered whether Stuie and I would remain friends.

He returned with two cans of Bud, which we drank in silence. I'd only started drinking beer in the past couple of months, and it still tasted bitter and metallic to me, less a flavor than a reminder that I was no longer drinking soda.

Stuie sat on the edge of the bed, staring at the floor. "I hear her at night," he began. "She talks to him. She stares out the window and talks to him. It's been going on ever since they mugged him. She's waiting for him to come back." He swallowed some beer. "It's scary."

"Who does she talk to?"

"My father."

"Your *what?*"

I imagined Sharon floating in a murky sea, her wedding dress billowing up, ready to choke her. The beer soured in my throat. I began to feel drowsy.

"I hate her," he said at last. "I hate her for being crazy. And I hate my father for letting himself get cut up like a chump." He didn't sound angry. His words emerged from somewhere deep and quiet, and for that reason, they were terrifying.

Sharon's voice sifted through the walls, light as powder. "Is that you, Dad?" she called.

"Listen," Stuie said.

"Is that you, Dad? Where are your pins?"

"Pins?" I asked.

"He was in the upholstery business, remember? It goes on like this every night. She thinks she sees him outside her window. If you don't believe me, have a look."

I lifted up the shade. Sharon stood before her window transfixed, staring out at what she alone saw. It was scary. I let the shade fall. "How come she's wearing that dress?"

"All she ever thinks about is being a bride. It started a couple of weeks ago. My mother's been bringing home bride magazines to read. You should see what's doing in her room. *Modern Matrimony. Veil and Gown. Bridal Suite. Honeymoon.* She thinks that brides are the most beautiful women in the world. My father was always telling her how happy a woman is on her wedding day."

"No, I *can't* go out, not after what happened," Sharon whispered. "Why can't I just stay here?"

There was a pause. Then: "Dad, you know I'm really not pretty. Nobody wants me."

A moment later, she raised her voice. "Stop telling me to go out on my own! You're just like Mom. Why is everyone always bothering me? Why don't they just leave me alone!"

"She really hasn't been out of the house since it happened?"

Stuie shook his head. "It's been almost four months already. She hardly goes into the living room because she can't take hearing the sound of the elevator."

"How old is she?"

"Nineteen."

Suddenly I couldn't stay there a moment longer. "I should go," I said.

The music blasted on as I closed Stuie's door. Maybe it was better than listening to his sister talk to herself. In the living room, the stop and start of the sewing machine meant that Mrs. Greenberg was back at work. Who did she make all this clothing for?

Sharon's door opened far enough to reveal no more than a sliver of face, eyes unblinking. She wanted something. I remembered how she'd thrown her arms around Barry's neck, ready to ride away with him on his Crescent. If he was no longer there, I might do. But hadn't Stuie said she was afraid to leave the house? Before I could figure it all out, she'd vanished behind her door.

My father called a week later and told my mother that he was staying with someone.

"In Astoria," my mother said. "With an old friend." He wouldn't give an address or a telephone number. The pull in her voice was unmistakable. Astoria, where was that? The last stop on a subway line I never used.

Friend.

"Why is he so all-fired vague about where he is?" my mother muttered. "What does he think, that I'll go looking for him?"

Graduation was barely two weeks away. Up until then, I hadn't cared about the ceremony one way or the other; Barry was going only because of his valedictorian's speech. But the prospect of both my parents not being there signaled our family's official falling apart, and I wasn't ready for it. Uncle Alfred intervened. A volley of last-minute telephone calls between him and my father followed; my father agreed to attend, and the day was rescued. But he'd be there only on one condition: my mother could not bring up the subject of his departure.

"One false move from me and that's it," she told me, ice in her voice. "Do you see how he's holding a gun to my chest?"

On the morning of graduation, my mother put off leaving the house for as long as she could, having me zip her into one dress after the other, only to take it off a moment later. Rejected outfits collected on her bed like so many costume changes. "Is my makeup all right?" she asked. "What about the shoes?" Her fidgeting didn't stop after we left the house, and she kept popping open her compact mirror for makeup checks during the bus ride. She might have been meeting my father for a first date. I thought of those early snapshots of them, and my heart sank a little.

"There he is," she murmured as the bus approached Fordham Road, her voice spiked with disdain. "Just take a look at him."

"Mom," I warned her.

He leaned against a building, sunny and relaxed. A cigarette hung lazily between his lips. In the short time he'd been away, he had become someone else. He wore a panama and an olive-green checked suit jacket that didn't even try to match his royal-blue pants. A dark oval of stain was crusted onto his right pants leg, perhaps the work of scrambled eggs. At first I saw nothing but that stain, almost metallic in the sun, the seal on some kind of award.

"Where did you get the hat?" was the first thing out of her mouth. I cringed. All traces of fluttery girlishness vanished, and she was my stern mother once more, ready to sweep the hat off his head. Things were getting off to a bad start.

His smile persisted. "Pretty nice, don't you think? Got it on Fourteenth Street. Two bucks. Speaking of hats, where's the cap and gown, graduate?"

I pointed to the box I carried.

"When are you going to put it on, tomorrow?" My mother

shifted her impatience to me. *This is what my father can't stand about her.*

Kids with gleaming robes billowing over their street clothes, tassels bobbing, were streaming out of the subway entrance the whole time, parents and grandparents huffing along behind them. I spilled the gown out of the carton, stepped into it, and my mother zipped me up right there on the street. My father proudly set the mortarboard upon my head. I was conscious of both of them fussing over me at once, acting like my parents once more, and I grew hopeful. I wished there was some other chore I might give them to do.

The Loew's Paradise movie theater had become a mere auditorium that day, its screen rolled up and its stage lined with folding chairs. House lights exposed all the cracked wings and chipped faces of angels that otherwise hovered so magically in darkness. I took my alphabetized place within the rows of graduates as my parents made for the noisy section reserved for families. *Stay there until I come back,* I felt like telling them. *Don't go anywhere. Just stay.*

I waved at Stuie, sitting all the way at the other end of the alphabet, plump and uncomfortable in his costume. He motioned to his watch to say he couldn't wait until it was over. We'd planned to meet afterward, and his cousin Jeff was supposed to pick us up and drive us to an Italian restaurant. Barry was nowhere to be seen, but I guessed he was being lined up to sit on the stage. Finally the lights dimmed, constellations of lightbulbs began twinkling in the ceiling, and I almost expected to see Paramount's peak rising before me on the screen. Instead, the school orchestra struck its first shaky chords, our signal to rise.

Soon it was time for Barry to give his speech. I hadn't seen him since the afternoon at Stuie's. The gown fell stiffly from his shoulders, and he gripped the edge of the podium with what looked like anger. *Barry's never happy,* I thought. His speech had to do with science battling microbes and cancer cells, with genetic research developing hybrids to feed a hungry world. His voice became the drone of a persistent fly. I imagined Sharon floating across the Paradise's cracked heaven, dress trailing cloudlike beneath her.

After the ceremony, I joined the bottleneck of people pressing into the street. My mother waited. My father was nowhere to be seen.

"He ran off right after Barry spoke," she said. "Like a thief in the night." She gripped her program tightly.

"Mom," I began, and for the first time I can remember, I had the urge to kiss her forehead. Once again, my father had slipped away.

She cut my sympathy short. "How come you're the only one still wearing your gown?"

In my rush to leave, I'd forgotten to give it in, so I pushed my way back into the theater, a salmon fighting the current. The folds of the gown trapped the heat, and the swing of the tassel teased me. I kept on the lookout for my father, hoping he might still be inside. But no.

Stuie and his mother had joined my mother by the time I returned; Jeff was yet to appear. Was Sharon all alone in the apartment, talking out the window?

"What a fucked-up speech Barry made," Stuie said to me. "Hey, where's your father?"

My mother looked my way. I swallowed. "He had to go to work," I said. I hadn't told Stuie about what had been going on between my parents. I hadn't really wanted to. Talking about it made it seem permanent.

My mother looked away, a silent partner to the lie, and glanced at her watch. "Where's your friend Barry?"

Stuie and I exchanged uncomfortable glances. Originally the plan was for Barry to come along, too. Stuie murmured something about Barry having to go with his parents, and it was my turn to play accomplice.

Battered gypsy cabs rumbled past, but there was no sign of Jeff's red Mustang. It grew hotter, and the corner began to feel deserted. Mrs. Greenberg wiped her forehead with a tissue.

Most of the crowd before the theater had dispersed, and we huddled in what shade there was beneath an awning. A damp, stray curl of hair fell across my mother's forehead, making her appear unkempt. Ordinarily her mirror would have been snapped open in an instant, but she didn't seem to notice. Little seemed to matter. It was too hot to eat. I wanted nothing but to tear off my clothes and jump into the shower. A headache drummed in my skull.

"I think I'll go home," Mrs. Greenberg said when Jeff didn't show up.

"What are you going to do now?" Stuie asked me.

He sounded like he wanted to hang out, but I imagined us back in his dank, deafening room next door to his imprisoned sister. I told him I wanted to go home.

The party split up, and my mother and I headed for the subway. With lies and disappointment, high school was over, and the long, hot summer had begun.

After supper, Mother and I put on one of her brittle 78s and danced around the living room to songs she'd known as a girl: "On the Banks of the Wabash, Far Away," "Love's Old Sweet Song," and "Goodbye, My Lady Love." I struggled to keep up with her long legs, my face pressed against clothing scented with formaldehyde like an undertaker's. Swirling around and around with her, I felt like infinity.

New Cornwall, October 15

They've just diagnosed her, and biologist that my mother is, she's asked for some of the tissue to examine under the microscope. Breast cancer, a woman's punishment, a reason to slash away at her beauty.

It's hardly five o'clock, but getting dark already. Short winter days always give me the feeling of loss.

FOUR

My mother often spoke of going to Israel. "Israel," she'd exclaim with three full syllables of enunciation, emphatic as a Moses with deserts to cross. I sensed that her travel plans were as illusory as her perennial dream of moving to an apartment with a sunken living room, and for the same reason: money. But that wasn't the primary hindrance; my father was. "Israel?" he'd say. "What's there besides sand and Jews? I can go to Brighton Beach for both." I sort of felt the same way, too.

As things worsened between them, there was less and less talk of travel, and by the time my mother got wind of my father's affair, I figured that was that. No wonder I could hardly believe my ears when, a week after the fizzle of my high-school graduation, my mother announced that she'd booked a flight to Tel Aviv.

"I originally made the reservations for two," she added, sadness in her voice. She headed for the bedroom, loaded down with shopping bags full of new purchases.

"How long will you be away?"

She'd been able to patch together all of her unused vacation time and sick leave: "Six weeks," she said. "Six glorious weeks." She began unpacking Bermuda shorts, blouses, and a sky-blue windbreaker.

I couldn't believe it. "That's almost all summer!"

"Yes," she said.

Amazing: my mother had never traveled farther than Schenectady, New York. When my father left, she'd seemed ready to mope around the house in misery for the rest of the summer, but now she was embarking on an adventure halfway around the world. She tackled a second bag: summer dresses and bathing suits, sandals, sunglasses, a Hebrew-English dictionary, even a day pack. She might have been sending herself off to summer camp.

I thought of something. "What about me?"

She'd already taken care of that. I was to be farmed out to my Uncle Alfred while she was gone. The whole summer in New Jersey! How could she do that to me?

"Do I have to go there?"

"You can't stay here alone, can you?"

Why couldn't I? Having the whole place to myself sounded great. I liked the idea of living on my own. It was what my father was doing. But everything had already been decided. I had thought that my mother's silence of the past three weeks meant she suffered; now I saw she'd been planning.

I tried finding a summer job, but had no luck. All the city jobs had already been filled. In the evening, my mother listened to Hebrew-language tapes as she did her nails, the sound of the movie on TV turned down all the way. "*Aye-foh et hatachanah?*" a reedy female Mediterranean voice intoned. "*Where is the station?*" her male British partner responded. As the day of departure drew near, my mother began covering the living-room furniture with sheets and seeding the closets with mothballs.

"Why are you doing all that?" I asked.

"It's what you do when you close up an apartment for the summer, Raymond."

Up until then, I didn't really think she'd go through with it. I wished she wouldn't leave. I wished my father might reappear and put a stop to all this madness. But he showed no signs of returning. My mother took her furniture seriously, so when the sheets appeared, I knew she meant business.

The telephone rang the morning my mother was to leave. She spoke in a cramped voice. The call didn't last very long.

"Your father sends his regards," she told me tartly after hanging up.

"Is he coming to take you to the airport?"

Her lower lip trembled. *"May I take your order?"* the voice on her tape was saying in the background. "No, he's not coming, okay?" She stepped on a bulging suitcase and zipped it. She had enough clothes to stay away for a year. "*Ma ha-sha-ah?*" She had packed enough for the two people who were supposed to have gone. *"What time is it?"*

My father hadn't wanted to speak to me, I thought, and something hard formed in my throat. He was still living in Astoria, as far as we knew, and he'd returned to work at the press. I thought of him in his panama. I thought of the stain on his pants. He seemed to be doing well without us, without me. The distance between him and my mother had normalized. It seemed ready to stay that way.

Her packing done, my mother cleaned house, just like those people in Anatevka did before they went into exile. The living room grew ghostly with its sheeted furniture, cleansed of my father's presence. The sheet over the drafting table's lamp created a snowy peak rising in the living room's chilly climate. Mothballs purged the air with a poisonous sugar.

Finally the downstairs buzzer sounded; the car-service limo had arrived. How peculiar for a stranger to be taking my mother to the airport instead of a relative. Was she really going to do this? Or were her travel plans simply a gimmick to get my father back?

"Help me with this," she said, shocking me back to reality. I hauled one of the heavy suitcases into the elevator. The driver, a young black man wearing a prominent silver cross around his neck, arranged the luggage in the trunk with the nervous formality of someone new at the job.

During the first leg of the trip, my mother filled the back of the cab with details of her proposed itinerary, the distant relatives she'd visit, the historic sites she'd see—Jaffa, the Wailing Wall, Masada—places I knew only from our Jewish kitchen calendar, a funeral parlor's promotional gift.

"Israel de promised land," the driver said in a vaguely British accent. He smiled at us in the rearview mirror, showing prominent teeth. One was gold. "Is de land of de Bible."

"Yes," my mother said, trying to smile.

"You Jewish, right?"

My mother shifted in her seat. "Yes, we are," she said, turning quickly back to me.

"Israel de promis' land," he continued, still smiling. "But not only for Jews, yes?"

I read the identification plaque near the meter. The driver's name was an unpronounceable knot of consonants, and I couldn't be sure which was his first name or which his last. The photo showed a young black man, serious and a little worried, not entirely sure of what the picture would be used for. Perhaps he came from one of those African countries that sided with the Arabs against Israel. She must have read my thoughts, for she asked him where he was from.

"St. Kitts, Miss."

"Where the hell is that? I bet they don't even have any Jews there."

His smile faltered as she took off her sunglasses to fix him in a steely glance. "There are eighty million Arabs and three million Jews. What do they want from us?"

Oh no, I thought. *Why does she have to start this?*

"They shouldn't take no land away," he said. "Should live together in peace." His smile began to look strained.

"Jewish people have lived in Israel for centuries. Who's taking land away from whom?" Her English rang with correctness against the tangled foliage of the driver's accent.

"De people who live dere, dey been kicked out, Miss."

"I'm not a 'Miss.' I'm married!"

At that point, his smile faded for good. We were on the Grand Central Parkway. Traffic began to slow. The grim terrain of Queens inched by. My mother stared ahead, a determined fix to her eyes.

"Why do I have to go to Uncle Alfred's?" I asked.

Her lips pursed. "We've been through this before, Raymond." She threw her sunglasses back on with finality. "You can't stay in the apartment by yourself, and that's that."

"New Jersey's so far from the city. What happens if I get a summer job in Manhattan?"

"Your uncle will take you in with him." I saw my face reflected twice in her dark lenses.

"But I don't want to spend the whole summer in New Jersey."

"Raymond, stop. I have a million things on my mind right now."

The driver tilted his head, listening discreetly. My mother turned away, taking my faces with her. The atmosphere in the car fouled, and we said little for the next stretch. Her worried grasp of her pocketbook made me think that she was on the verge of telling the driver to turn around. A part of me hoped that my father was tailing us—he could have gotten the departure time from Uncle Alfred—and with the timing of a Superhero comic strip, his Buick might materialize beside us at any minute and we'd be pulled aboard and freed.

As we approached the turnoff for the airport, traffic slowed even more.

"Oh-oh," the driver said.

My mother's glance snapped to her watch, agitated, even though another two hours remained before takeoff. The airport was tantalizingly near, but traffic knotted the expressway. The driver shot her a worried look in the rearview mirror. I became aware of the driver's smell, nothing more than a nervous sweat perhaps, but my mother was fanatic about hygiene, and I'm sure it didn't escape her. The smell thickened as we sat there, air conditioning and all. I could only imagine what she was thinking about him.

We finally reached the terminal and stepped out of the cab into a blast furnace of hot air. My mother barely looked at the driver as she handed him the money.

"Salaam aleikem," the man said, retreating with a little bow.

"Don't you *shalom-aleichem* me," she snapped.

The gate was crowded with passengers and the people seeing them off. Travelers in new, light-colored clothing clustered together for flash pictures. My mother's pastels might have placed her in the ranks of the happy departing passengers, but our corner was somber. Other women her age were paired with husbands, and the only women alone looked to be grandmothers. Three men in black suits with clerical collars formed a stern island of gentiles in this swirling Jewish sea. We sat near them. I kept a lookout for my father. As the time for the flight approached, my mother fidgeted, checking her passport and tickets over and over again.

Someone called out my mother's name. My heart raced. I turned, and against all odds hoped to see my father's panama and stained pants coming toward us, but the booming, slightly childish voice couldn't possibly have been his.

"Trying to sneak out of the country unnoticed, are you?" Uncle Alfred leaned down and gave my mother a kiss, tie loosened around his neck, jacket hooked on a finger over his shoulder. "How are you doing, Slugger?" he said to me.

My mother began to cry.

"Don't be so happy to see me," he said.

"Paul called," she told him. "Why did you tell him I was going?"

"He's still your husband. He should know where you are."

"Why? Do I know where he is?"

"This'll blow over, believe me, Ruthie." He put his arms

around her, and she looked like his kid sister once more.

Soon the flight was called, and the crowd started funneling toward the gate. My mother fumbled for her ticket, and as she surveyed the line forming, she seemed to be examining her fate. A moment later, she was reaching for her sunglasses, which meant she was about to cry again. When she kissed me good-bye, her sunglasses were still on, jabbing against my forehead. She disappeared into the accordioned throat of the walkway, and I was seized by the thought of never seeing her again. My fear thickened as I watched the plane pull out from the terminal to join a distant line of aircraft. The huddle of their tails became the minarets of a dangerous Arab capital, full of men like our taxi driver, plotting revenge.

"Well, we finally got rid of her," my uncle joked when the plane took off.

We headed for the parking lot. "Let me tell you in a nutshell the secret of this whole sad story of your parents," he said as we drove out, handing a stub to the woman in the booth with a Here you go, beautiful. "Your father spent most of his life trying to be a nice guy. And he succeeded. He *is* a nice guy. The nicest there is. I can't think of anyone with a bad word to say about him. Except for your grandfather, maybe, but he could find something bad to say about God. Anyway, the problem about being a nice guy is that nice guys don't always have a lot of fun because they're trying so hard to be nice. So one day your father woke up and decided that he was tired of being nice. No, let me change that. He was tired of not having any fun. So he went out and did what he did, simple as that."

"My parents never liked each other."

"How do you know? Were you there when they got married?"

"That was a long time ago. It doesn't matter now."

"I see you've become an expert on the subject of marriage, Mr. Masters and Johnson."

Uncle Alfred's appeal was that he had an answer for everything, but just then, his humor irritated, like being tickled when you weren't in the mood for it. I kept trying to think of a way to tell him that I didn't want to stay at his house. He threw the Lincoln down the highway, in a hurry to get home. The way he was driving, we'd be hitting the exit for the George Washington Bridge in no time. I had to think fast.

"My mother hates him now," I said, avoiding what I had to do.

"Your mother's too chicken to hate anyone. And that's why this thing is going to blow over by the time she comes back, mark my words. You father needed a little pepper up his ass, if you'll excuse the expression, and that's what your mother gave him by going away."

"He's the one who went away. My mother's coming back."

He shook his head as if to say that I didn't understand any of it.

"They haven't been getting along for years, don't you see?" I said, impatient. "They're two very different people." We were approaching the Triborough. *Change the subject,* I kept telling myself. *Mention not staying at his house.*

"Listen. Your father's a bit of a hermit and your mother wishes she'd married R. H. Macy. But if they've stayed together this long—"

"What about that woman?" I insisted.

This time, he said nothing. I'd hit a nerve, since I knew he felt responsible for what had happened. He braked for the toll plaza. The fortress of the mental hospital loomed up on one side, and the railroad bridge tiptoed past on the other, arch by arch. The line of cars was long, and my uncle grew impatient, looking ready to floor it the rest of the way to New Jersey.

"Now listen," he said after we were moving again. "Your Uncle Lester expects me to fire the woman. But why should I? She's worked for me for almost ten years. I like her. She's good. I'm not going to start telling people what to do in their private lives, just because of what Lester says. And for your information, that woman"—he bit down to keep her name from slipping out—"is not, I repeat, not the cause of your parents' *tsurris*. Your father's a son of a bitch to have done what he did, this I grant you, but he's still family, and it's not the end of the world. Hey, what am I doing telling you all this, anyway?"

"I'm not a kid anymore, Uncle Alfred."

A moody, purple sky began to drape Manhattan as we drove onto the Deegan. The exit for my house wasn't far. If I didn't say something soon, I'd be trapped in Jersey for the rest of the summer.

"Could we stop by the house?" I asked. "I forgot something."

"Your aunt'll buy it for you tomorrow." He kept on driving.

The ramble of warehouses near the wholesale meat market gave way to the ordered blocks of my neighborhood. We'd be getting to the next exit in a matter of seconds.

"Is it okay if I don't stay with you while my mother's away?" I finally blurted out.

"What's the matter, my house isn't good enough? Look, I promised Ruthie that I'd look after you, and I will. And if you're nice, maybe I'll even feed you."

The exit loomed just ahead. "Could I come later, maybe at the end of this week?"

"What's going to happen between now and next week?"

"Could I? Please?"

His sideways glance signaled that he'd discovered something about me that he didn't like. He turned off with an impatient pull at his lips. "Fine," he said. We drove up before the building, and I retrieved my suitcase from the trunk.

"Call and let me know when you're coming," he said. He studied me. "You're a strange kid, Raymond. Wait." He took a twenty-dollar bill from his pocket and stuffed it into my hand. "Call, you hear me?"

I knew I wouldn't be going out there. I was staying here for the rest of the summer. I was on my own now, alone. I'd do what *I* wanted that summer, just like my father and my mother were doing. We'd become a family of free spirits.

My euphoria thinned as I entered the building. The lobby was a banquet hall in a fake castle, complete with fireplace. Its sconces shed mealy colored light, and its ceilings were blistered with water damage. I'd never noticed how rundown it looked until then. I thought of the empty apartment waiting for me upstairs and felt stricken with the melancholy of Sunday evenings. The world, like the hallway, felt hollow.

The apartment was a chilly, camphored planet. It was strange how emptiness changed a place. The living room was hung with twilight gloom, its sheeted furniture a dance of shades, so I turned on a light to banish them. I stowed the suitcase in my room and yanked the sheets off my bed and desk and bookcases and threw open the windows to let in the purifying air of the street, all the while expecting to hear my father's nib against the paper or the murmur of my mother's late movie. But the apartment sighed vacantly. I had to get out of there, at least for a while.

I knew where I wanted to go.

The warm night pulsed softly with air conditioners. Darkness left the park to the muggers and drug addicts, people said, but after the apartment's ghostly chill, the place felt lush and welcoming. I climbed up to the terrace and chose a bench with enough slats to sit on. The traffic below churned like a great machine at work. I clasped my arms together, embracing myself, feeling a little chilly, or perhaps lonely, but pleased with myself for what I'd managed. I imagined the rear lights of my uncle's Lincoln driving off, heading for the stifling safety of New Jersey. I thought of that guy from last summer. I waited.

It wasn't long until I detected a figure slipping through the curtain of hedge. My legs gripped the slats of the bench. I told myself to be calm, but my limbs danced in agitation. I'd left the twenty in the apartment and had no more than a couple of dollars in my jeans pocket, no great loss in case of a mugging, I told myself. But I knew this guy was no mugger. He came closer. He wore jeans and a light-colored T-shirt, and he nodded, a peaceful gesture. Hair darkened his broad forearms and peeked beyond the collar of his shirt. He wasn't young, but wasn't old. His jeans stretched smoothly around the bulk of his legs. He chose the bench catty-corner to mine and lit a cigarette with a lighter that made a loud *pling* when he closed it. The tip of the cigarette bobbed in the dark as he moved his lips, and its glow painted the tip of his nose orange. A breeze blew my way, carrying his scent, sweetly stinging—

Old Spice. My father's brand.

I caught him looking at me from the corner of his eye, and I saw him wet his lips. His legs stretched out farther in front of him. He seemed comfortable, relaxed, *satisfied*. He was enjoying himself. Without ever turning my way, he didn't take his eyes off me. He rubbed his arm, cupping its biceps, *satisfied*. He leaned back with a leisurely stretch of his legs, his loafers gleaming with their pennies—

No socks. A crescent of light from the lamp pole limned one naked ankle bone. I was transfixed by the exposed patch of skin gently fringed with hair beneath the hem. I couldn't stop looking. He kept his feet stretched out, making sure I saw.

Without warning, he got up and sat down next to me. My heart toppled. The bench slat let out a menacing creak under his weight. His Old Spice engulfed me, and he stretched his legs out once more, tendon by tendon, an animal ready to bask in the sun, except that there was no sun. What kind of animal? A beaver, perhaps. A raccoon. Something thickish . . . and furry.

"Hello," he said, looking directly at me for the first time. "My name's Michael."

I hardly heard: my heart beat too loudly.

"What's yours?"

"Andrew." It felt exhilarating to lie to him, and for some reason I had to.

"Hello, Andrew." He offered a hand for me to shake, large around mine. It held on, I thought, a second too long.

"I'd offer you a cigarette, but I guess you don't smoke."

My defenses had clicked on by then, and resistance replaced

fear. How did he know what I did and did not do? He knew nothing about me, absolutely nothing. Kids my age smoked, lots of them—

"No thanks," I said.

"What are you doing here so late in the evening?"

"It's not so late."

"Okay," he said, backing off. He put out his cigarette, tamping it against the sole of his shoe and tearing off the remaining stump of unsmoked tobacco, which he shredded and scattered.

"I never just throw the filter onto the ground," he explained. "My old man worked for the Parks Department." He slipped the butt into a pocket.

I crossed my legs and pulled my arms in close around me.

"What are you worried about, Andrew?"

"Nothing."

"You *seem* worried." He waited a minute or two, asking for my silent permission before sliding closer, bathing me in yet more Old Spice. "No reason to be scared," he said. The engine in his voice idled to a throb.

"So why are you here?" I asked. Two could play at this game.

"My place doesn't have a balcony. Here, it's nice and cool."

"You don't have AC?"

He gave me a funny look. "No, Andrew, I don't. I guess you don't either. So is that what brings you to the park at this hour?"

"I'm just here."

His hand crept up inside his T-shirt to scratch his chest. The fabric sheathed his hand tightly enough for me to see the knuckles. His nails scratching his skin sounded like matches being struck. He watched his hand move back and forth scratching himself for what seemed to be a long time, far longer than any itch needed. I grew restless, waiting for him to stop, but he kept at it, his hand circling serenely, taking a last lazy swim across his chest and belly before coming up for air.

"Are you in high school, Andrew?"

I sensed new caution in his voice. He knew he couldn't mess with me, so I agreed to play along. "Just finished."

"I'm a teacher. A math teacher. Do you like math?"

I shook my head. I didn't believe a word he said. A math teacher who wore no socks. Did he think I'd swallow anything?

"Most kids don't like math." He looked right at me. "But I bet you don't consider yourself to be like most kids, do you? You probably think you're smarter than the other kids, right?"

I started to feel uncomfortable.

"You probably couldn't wait to get out of that school, could you? Hey, you're shaking. Cold?"

I wasn't cold. I was terrified. Something seemed about to happen, but I didn't know what. Or maybe I did.

Then he got up.

"Don't stay out here too long, you don't know who you'll meet up with," he said, a tease in his voice. And before I could figure out what he'd meant, he was gone, the firefly glow of his T-shirt dimming until the hedge swallowed it completely, a finger of Old Spice left behind.

I felt humiliated but didn't know why. I realized I was hungry. It was a good reason to get out of there.

The cafeteria was a giant diorama with customers on display in large picture windows. Fans blasting hot air around made the place noisy as a bus station. Old ladies in hats stirred their coffee without ever drinking it. Others sat crumpled over their meals as if having forgotten them. No one looked at anybody else. They all ate slowly, taking as much time as they could before having to leave.

I pushed a tray past display cases holding the kinds of food we never ate at home: ham-and-cheese sandwiches, gluey chicken a la king, and diet platters of cottage cheese ringed with brightly colored Jell-O. I claimed a lone tub of macaroni-and-cheese drying out under an infrared lamp and got myself a soda.

With the instincts of the solitary diner, I chose a far table and sat with my back to the wall in order to observe everyone else. The macaroni's skin was hot and rubbery, its slippery insides no longer warm. The fans grew louder, and soon they were all I heard. Such was the solitary life, I surmised. The cafeteria was where solitary people congregated. I'd become a solitary person myself, and these eaters of cafeteria food would be my comrades for the summer. I would return here night after night. I began to feel older.

I'd wanted to throw my face under Michael's T-shirt and taste the skin of his belly. I sensed that he'd known it, too. Knowing that he knew terrified me.

At that moment, my father walked in.

He wore the panama. The pants and jacket were the same, too. A suitcase made him look like a vagabond. He collected his tray and utensils, got himself a sandwich and a cup of coffee.

His mouth folded into a puzzled smile when he saw me. "Mind if I join you?" He clapped the side of my head. "Why aren't you in New Jersey?"

I shrugged. "Didn't want to go."

"Can't say I blame you. Your mother left?"

I nodded. "Why didn't you at least take Mom to the airport?"

"I asked. She wouldn't let me. You know your mother. Once she gets an idea into her head, there's no getting it out." He sipped at his coffee. "So she really did it," he said, more to himself than to me. "I never thought she would. Shows you your mother has guts."

My leg bumped up against his suitcase beneath the table. I recalled my trek up to the apartment with my own suitcase earlier that evening. We were both exiles. I watched him drink his coffee, looking around as I had.

"What's going to happen now?"

"Guess I'll be back for as long as your mother is away. That okay with you?"

"What about your girlfriend?"

He put a finger to his lips.

"And when Mom comes back?"

"I don't know. She'll have to decide."

"You're the one who left, Dad."

"No. It was your mother who asked me to, Ray."

"But there's that woman."

He looked right at me. "Yes, son," he said growing stern. "There's that woman." He had some more of his sandwich, then threw it down. "God, the food here's terrible. Let's go home."

Home.

Several nights later, the telephone rang just as I was going to sleep. My father had stepped out for cigarettes. A woman asked to speak with him, but when I asked who she was, she hung up.

"There's some people over," Stuie said, opening the door, his eyes lacquered with a telltale, glassy cannabis sheen.

It couldn't have been more than three weeks since I'd seen him last, yet he looked so different: he wore tight jeans, a T-shirt with cut-off sleeves, exposing doughy upper arms, and cowboy boots. Twangs of Hendrixy guitar sharp as broken bottles shot from the speakers. Three guys crowded his bed with a sprawl of limbs, boots quilting the bedding, eyes unblinking as reptiles.

"This your cousin?" one of them asked, flinging a heavy weight of hair over his shoulder.

"Ray's my friend," Stuie said. "This is Feelie's Wheel, Ray." He introduced the guys one by one, naming their instruments as a concert MC would.

"Thought you said your cousin was coming over," the one with long hair said.

"He'll be here, Graham," Stuie said, worried.

"Who's coming over?" I asked.

"Jeff," said Stuie.

Don't bet on it, I felt like saying, remembering graduation.

"We ain't got all day, man," said a guy in mirrored sunglasses. "We gotta rehearse." He spoke in a fake black accent. He and Graham were shirtless except for leather vests. His muscular arms were printed with an elaborate flaming cross and the words "Jesus, Save Me." His belly bore a hefty hang of flab.

"Shit," said someone else, pushing a can of beer to his lips. He looked tall enough to have to duck under doorways, with a sphinx's mane of dense, curly hair ready to spring out from under his baseball cap.

"This is their demo tape that's playing," Stuie explained. "Jeff promised to come over to listen to it and see about getting air time for it."

"What do you mean, he's going to *see* about getting air time? You told me he was going to do it, period," the Sphinx said.

"I . . . I just said maybe he could, Bong," Stuie sputtered.

"Shee-it," Bong said, lifting his beer to his lips. "Sounds like we done wasted our time here," he drawled.

"Quit messing with that," the other guy snarled when Stuie began to adjust the sound.

"Just trying to fix the treble, Jake," Stuie said, shooting me a nervous look.

"Treble's fine. Leave it alone."

"They're thinking of letting me be their techie," Stuie said.

"You ain't gonna be shit if you go on wasting my time," Bong shot back.

"Where'd you meet these guys?" I whispered.

"Radio Shack. Graham works there."

"You really think this stuff sounds so good?" I asked.

"You mind keeping it down?" Jake said. "I want to hear my solo." He swung his load of hair back over his shoulder. A knot of bass thumped from the speakers. "Great," he said, straightening in attention and accidentally ramming a knee into Bong's ribs.

"Damn!" Bong thundered, giving Jake a shove that nearly had him rolling off the bed. Jake struggled to stay put, as if on a raft in the middle of a lake, then countered Bong with a hefty shove in return. Bong reached over and plucked Jake's cap from his head, exposing a shiny bald spot. Jake's fringe of hair sprung free, spongy as a clown's. When he made a grab for the cap, Bong tossed it to Graham, and a second later, it was flying my way. Foolishly, I caught it. Jake leaped at me and snatched the cap, submerging me in a steamy cloud of beer breath.

The doorbell rang. Stuie jumped to get it. I expected to see Jeff, broad and top-heavy, a cigarette lodged between two stubby fingers as always, but Stuie returned alone with a pizza and a six-pack. The moment he cut the string, the others sprang from their stupor and converged upon the steaming pie. Stuie and I managed to salvage a slice each; then Bong and Jake snapped up seconds, leaving nothing more than a grease-stained box.

Bong let out a resonant belch and lit a cigarette. "You play music, too?" he asked me. I shook my head. "Music is the purest form of communication there is. Forget about words. Words are just what a bunch of dudes thought up to call things a long time ago, but they don't mean anything anymore."

"Nothing else worth doing," Graham said. "Nothing." He said it like a dare.

"Music is what is," Jake offered.

The single slice of pizza had left me hungry for more. My eyes fell to the discarded pizza box, its lid printed with a Roman temple and classical-looking script.

"My father likes to draw letters," I said, more to myself than to the others.

Graham looked at me. "What do you mean, your father draws letters? You mean he writes things?"

"No. He draws letters. A, B, C . . ."

Bong looked intrigued. "Someone pay him to do it?" When I said no, he shot me an impatient look. "Me, I don't do nothing unless someone pays."

"Put on that second tape." A fourth guy I hadn't noticed stood up from behind the bed, where'd he'd been crouching. He was slight, with a great shelf of forehead, darkly dressed in a suit jacket and black pants. He didn't seem to belong with the rest of them. There was a moment of silence as the others looked at each other.

"That song's too weird, Dwight," Bong muttered.

"Yeah," Jake said, gaining confidence. "Cue up 'Butane Beauty' instead."

"My song isn't weird," Dwight said. "It's important."

"It's weird," Bong said.

Graham shot him a look of warning.

"Shit, I hate playing it," Jake said, louder.

"You don't understand it," the suit guy said.

"Dwight, how do you know what I do and do not understand?" Jake asked, thumb jabbing into his chest for emphasis.

"Jake!" said Graham.

"You know the terms of the arrangement," Dwight continued, calm.

"If I woulda known it was this kind of shit you wanted us to play, I'd a never gone along with it," Jake blustered.

"No one's forcing you to do this," Dwight said, still calm. He produced a small mirror and a packet of white powder from his pocket. He sprinkled a bit of the powder onto the mirror and used the cover of a matchbook to shape it into a line, his narrow fingers working carefully, almost delicately. With a slender, silver tube that hung from a chain around his neck, he breathed in the powder with a thick rush of air. "Okay, Stuie," he said. "Let's hear it now."

Stuie shot Jake a helpless look and began loading the reel. A momentary arc of music shot through the speakers until the ends of the tape began whipping around frantically.

"What the fuck did you do?" Bong shouted. "You tear the goddamn tape? That's the only copy we got!"

"Best thing that coulda happened," Jake mumbled.

"It's just some of the leader," Stuie said. "I'll splice it back together." He reached for the razor, and his nervous fingers struggled with the broken tape.

Bong edged up behind him. "Don't you be cutting off too

much of that, you hear? It begins with my bass solo."

Stuie was startled, the razor jumped and met his finger, leaving an angry line of blood.

"He's getting blood all over the tape, man," said Jake.

A brilliant red dot had already fallen on the mud-colored strip of plastic. Stuie began frantically wiping the tape clean with his pinkie, face pinched with worry.

"Hey, be careful, or else you'll wipe the take right off." Jake shook his head gravely. "If you wanna work for us, you better not be messin' up like this."

"Now let's see if anything got cut off," Bong said when the tape was back on the machine. The leader hissed over the heads but no sound emerged from the speakers.

"Ho-ly shit," said Graham. "The whole thing's gone—"

"Pre-amp's not on," I said. I flicked the lever, and something hissed through the speakers.

Dwight got up. "Make it loud enough for me to hear in the bathroom," he said, and left.

"That asshole," Jake said when the door closed.

"Would you quit making trouble?" Graham said. "I've already told you. We're just going to do that gig for him at the end of the summer, collect, and then split."

"You even think he's really going to get anything off the ground? The dude doesn't have a cent."

"I already saw his place. It's huge, and we can play as loud as we want. It'll be free rehearsal space no matter what."

"Where is it?" Bong asked.

"Downtown somewhere. Greene Street."

"Where's that?" Jake asked.

The music began. Jake jumped forward and reached for an imaginary electric guitar as his heavy boots beat out the rhythm on the floor.

Life is always full with doubt,
plagued by problems unforeseen.

Predictability is what I care about.
I love the age of machines.

A knock on the wall startled him.

"Make it lower," Sharon moaned.

"Go to fucking sleep!" Stuie shot back.

"That your neighbor?" Graham asked.

"My sister."

"She nice?" Bong said with a grin.

The knocking continued.

"Quit it, Sharon!"

Bong turned up the volume even more.

I love the strength of electricity,
and the drama of routine.
I can't cope with impulsivity.
I need the strength of machines.

"Don't do that to her," I shouted. "She's sick and trying to sleep."

Bong eyed me and gave the knob another spiteful turn.

The pre-amp lever was inches away. I flicked it off.

"What the fuck do you think you're doing?" he said, pushing up close. His bare arms bulged with muscle and threat. His mirrored sunglasses told me how scared I looked. He hit the knob the other way, the music blasted back on.

Then all went dead.

"Fuck!" Stuie shouted.

"What's going on?" Bong asked.

"She took out the goddamn fuse again!" Stuie flew out of the room, slamming the door behind him.

"Get away from her!" I heard Mrs. Greenberg say in the living room.

"This place is definitely twisted," Graham said.

"Flip City," Jake added. "Let's get out of here." He fumbled around on Stuie's desk and snatched up the demo tape. "You guys coming?"

They filed out. "You little pussy," Bong said to me as he left.

"Hey, wait!" Stuie called after them, holding a fuse aloft. He raced to the fuse box, but they ignored him and trooped out. The moment the front door slammed shut, the lights came on as if the door had tripped a switch, and music burst from the bedroom once more.

Love is always problematical.
I mistrust what can't be seen,
feeling should be mathematical,
life in the age of machines.

I cut it.

"What a bunch of assholes," I said when Stuie returned to the room.

"They said I could be their techie!" he exclaimed. "They said I could go with them to the West Coast. I could start making big bucks if it wasn't for her," he said, shooting an angry glance at Sharon's room. He sank down on the bed and I almost thought he was going to cry.

The reel of tape was still wound on the machine: a second, forgotten copy.

"Let's hear the rest of it," I said. Something about the song intrigued me.

Obsolete will be the human soul.
I prefer nice things and clean.
I only tolerate what I control
in the age of machines.

Individuality I will replace.
All the world I will redeem.
I will create a master race
in the age of machines.

Misery will end.
Machines will be our friends.
Minds will be at peace.
Thinking will cease
in the age of machines,
in my age of machines.

"That guy in the suit wrote this?"

Stuie nodded. "Jake's right. It's weird. That Dwight guy's weird, too. The only reason they're doing his songs is because he's letting them rehearse in his building."

The song ended with a raucous clash of guitars. I could just imagine Jake and Bong battling it out, thrusting their instruments at each other like howitzers. Dwight had reminded me of Barry, both of them dense, contained, and maybe a little demonic, too.

I had to pee and went to the john, but when I gave the bathroom door a push, it didn't give.

"Wait." Sharon was inside. There was a rubbing sound, and a moment later, the door opened. She sat on the floor, her back pressed against the bathtub. Propped up between her legs like a baby was Dwight, face still and white against her chest. Sharon was stroking his hair, gazing at him protectively. "He's sleeping," she whispered.

"Sharon?" Mrs. Greenberg's voice barked from behind. "What are you doing on the—hey, you!" she shouted, noticing Dwight and prodding him with her space-shoed foot. "Get up!"

"Ma, leave him alone. He's asleep."

"This isn't a hotel, you!" Mrs. Greenberg said to him. "Hey!" She gave him another prod, and his eyelids flickered. Mrs. Greenberg bent over for a closer look. "Are you okay? Can you walk?"

Dwight's feeble nod might have meant yes or no.

"I'll take care of him," Sharon said.

"Help me get him up," Mrs. Greenberg said to me, shoving her arm under Dwight's. We hoisted Dwight to his feet. His limbs wobbled, a puppet with the strings cut. "Stand up straight, you!" she commanded.

He answered with a twist of his lips, turned his head, and vomited copiously into the toilet, whose lid was unfortunately down. Then he fainted.

Mrs. Greenberg uttered a syllable of disgust. "Raymond, get a rag from the kitchen!"

I peeked into Sharon's room on the way. A single lamp burned. Columns of magazines surrounded the bed. The wedding dress hung on a hanger from the back of a closet, mute and silvery.

"Dearest," I heard Sharon whisper.

A bus had been bombed in Tel Aviv in the middle of the rush hour. People had been wounded, some killed. The TV news was full of it. The camera panned a rubble-strewn neighborhood. The bus bore a great black-edged hole exposing a tangle of seats. People milled around in a daze, faces bloodied. An old man wept. I searched the screen for my mother in her pastel outfit, her sunglasses. I thought of her that evening in the airport, the last time I'd seen her. *The last time I'd seen her alive.*

My father, who was sitting at his worktable with what had become his customary glass of whiskey, ran over to the set. The phone rang: Uncle Alfred had already called up the Israeli embassy. They couldn't reveal anything about the passengers on the bus yet.

"She's hardly in the country a week and look what happens," he said, never losing a chance for a joke.

The phone rang two more times that night. First, Stuie told me that his sister had disappeared. They'd come home to find her gone. "My mother's going off the deep end," he said.

A little while later, the phone rang again and I picked up, expecting it was a relative, but a woman was at the other end.

"Paul?" she said. "Is that you?"

"Who is this?" I said, recognizing the voice from the last time. But once again the woman hung up and the dial tone flooded in.

Her, I thought. *My father's woman.*

I fell asleep seeing the bus's blackened wreck. That driver on the way to the airport had been the angel of death.

And where was Sharon?

The summer had begun to go crazy.

2

Lester

Owen, my first: slender, strong legs, and such long fingers—in my childhood bed, a deep and secret place. My maidenhead was sewn tightly inside me like the tags you're not supposed to rip off pillows. He kissed me—wet berries against my lips and face and shoulders, looking at me with unbearable tenderness. But I couldn't. It was all right to give myself to someone but not to let them take anything away. More than half the night passed before I could let him. There was a lumpy push, a hot and tearing pain, and afterward, the calligraphy of my blood on the sheets read "This is who you are now, who you are going to be." Owen noticed my St. Agatha postcard. "How can you hang up something like that?" he asked. "It's a warning," I told him. "Omigod," Irene shrieked when I told her Agatha's story. I began to cry, and she said it meant I was happy. Only a Jewish person would think that way. "No," I told her. "I'm crying because I've lost something." But maybe happiness is like the image on a cameo, discernible only against a second, deeper layer of sadness.

Mother had to know what I was doing. Nothing in that house ever happened without her being aware of it, Godlike, she was, and like God, she didn't intervene, or wouldn't. She knew I'd wanted her to know, and like any true sinner, I expected to be punished.

New Cornwall, November 18

Phyllis lives in the room across from mine, about sixty, a painter, weedy and tough. Everything she paints seems danger-

ous. She claims to be the granddaughter of a missionary who witnessed the massacre of the Herreros. Maybe that explains the way she is. Tragedy stains a person for life. She's asked me to sit for my portrait, so I showed her my postcard. "This is how I want to be painted," I said. "Giorgione, isn't it?" she asked. "Or Tiepolo." She handed the card back to me. "I used to feel that way about myself, too," she said, and laughed a little.

FIVE

Lester looked up from his paperwork to see Deborah sunning herself in the backyard on a lounge chair, bikini'd, a scallop-shaped reflector silvering her oiled face, her body slender and smooth-legged as one of Rhoda's art-deco figurines. *Languid* was the word that came to mind. Maybe just a little too languid for her fifteen years. Overnight she'd gone from girlish soft to womanly ripe. He felt like a Peeping Tom.

She shifted. The reflector dropped and a metallic glint of sunlight capped a nipple. She was topless—

The phone rang. Lester's heart tripped over itself and fell.

I'm going to work my tongue all the way down your pussy, just the way you like it.

Lester's fingers choked his pencil. Blood pummeled his temples. It couldn't be him, not at this hour of the day.

I'm going to work my tongue—

A second ring. He began to sweat. Don't answer it and it will stop.

The calls had begun at the beginning of the summer. The man spoke only to Rhoda; Lester's voice met with a stubborn click. Except once. *I'm going to work my tongue down your pussy just the way you like it.* It had notched a wound in his memory.

Neither of them could pin a name to the voice. Lester alerted the police and the telephone company, but the caller eluded taps by keeping calls short or else dialing from a pay phone. "It's that creepy Eddie Erhart," Deborah said. Mangy and discomforting, Eddie was a logical suspect. Wasn't he always telling Lester what a pretty wife he had? But somehow Lester couldn't believe it was him. Eddie was strange, but he didn't do that kind of thing.

The calls often came just after Lester returned from work, so by four-thirty, his stomach was a knotted balloon. If the man knew Rhoda's number, did he know her address as well? Would he start lying in wait for her when she was home alone? He imagined the caller's voice sinking its viper's teeth into her body, infecting her tissues with its poison. Lately he and Rhoda had been making love less frequently. She blamed it on the hot weather, and they weren't exactly teenagers anymore, but since these calls began, Lester had found himself ravenous for her, frantic with keeping her satisfied lest she have a reason to look elsewhere. "Whoa, boy," she'd say, pulling to her side of the bed to escape his onslaught.

Someone picked up. "Deborah, it's Gil!" Rhoda shouted from an upstairs window.

Deborah struggled to strap on her bikini top as she raced across the grass into the house. Gil, an oversized chunk of high-school football player who often forgot to close his mouth, was Deborah's newest consort. It pained Lester to think of her in his simian arms, to imagine the grip of his fat hands around her.

"Hello?" Her lacy giggle was silenced by a secretive door-shutting. Lester regarded the empty lounge chair sadly. His little girl.

Recently, Rhoda had begun complaining that the yard looked vacant. *Open*, he'd corrected her. No, she insisted. It needed something. Lester suggested a couple more shrubs and some flowers, but Rhoda had in mind a real garden, which, Lester knew, meant paying someone to plant it. It became clear that she was talking about more than plants, too. She wanted pudgy stone angels and naked women clutching fruit—things she'd seen in the gardens of that mansion they'd toured in Miami the winter before. She'd carted home oversized books with fold-out photographs of stately English gardens and begun talking of pergolas, walkways, and pavilions; about white gardens, bosquets, and ha-has. She marched about the yard, pencil and clipboard in hand like a foreman, note-taking. If only the developers had left the damn trees up when they'd bought the place, he thought. Then there wouldn't be any room for statues and pebbled walkways. For all he knew, the trees had been pulled down to keep the landscapers in business. Maybe there'd been some kind of deal.

The work had already begun. Just beyond Deborah's chaise, green sod had been torn up like a battlefield. Water collected in the long channels dug for pipes, and the backyard was a near swamp. A pile of glistening-white pebbles waited at the edge of the property, a dollop of cream beside the yards of muddy chocolate.

Rhoda was no stranger to renovation. In the space of a dozen years, the living room's hard Danish had made way for homier Colonial before a stint of dark, moody Mediterranean. Yards of perfectly serviceable carpeting had been pulled up and furniture, just as good, banished to the basement. The white-enameled kitchen walls were papered over with green latticework, only to be masked by a color called Fresh Apricot. ("What's next?" he'd asked her. "Canned Peach?") The present furniture was of a gray, weathered wood that might have been barn planking. The windows bore drapes of plain canvas, and the floors were covered with itchy sisal. Heavy earthenware vases held bunches of weeds, replenished daily, and piles of rocks and pinecones cluttered the coffee table. A series of old wash buckets lined one wall. "A grouping," Rhoda called them.

One day she came home from a flea market with a large ceramic pot that she placed on a side table.

"But it's broken," he said.

"I know," Rhoda said. "It's an artifact."

Lester turned his attention to the stacks of bills spread before him, the unlucky lay of a fortune teller's cards. He'd been sitting there for almost two hours, getting no more done than arranging the papers into neat piles, as if that alone might bring order to his finances. Once upon a time, his gourmet food-supply business had done well—before people knew what a quiche was or that vinegar didn't have to be colorless. Now even corner groceries stocked two kinds of grainy French mustard, *biscotti*, and vacuum-packed pesto. He picked up one of the outstanding invoices, almost too weighty to lift, so he put it back down again. A mortgage statement eyed him, its portly, two-figured balance trailing a stubborn trio of zeroes, a rattle of cans behind a newlyweds' limousine, except that his limousine was going to fall apart around the next corner.

"Les?" Rhoda stood in the doorway. Daylight deepened the lines around her mouth and under her eyes, but she was still a slender, handsome woman and looked good in jeans and one of his old oxford broadcloth dress shirts. "Did you remember to call Roger?"

"Roger?" But he knew exactly what she was talking about. He'd remembered to forget all about it. Roger Henderson, the landscaper, had revised the estimate he'd given them after hitting groundwater closer to the surface than expected, a consequence, Lester was sure, of the subdivision's brutal deforestation. Roger's suggestion? A reflecting pond. The cost: another two thousand bucks. "Turning disadvantage into ornament," was how Rhoda put it, using the cutesy vocabulary of her architecture books. Two thousand for a reflecting pool? What was there to reflect in their backyard but Mort Abromowitz's mammoth barbecue grill?

"He's waiting for an answer, Les." She'd always been the

yes/no, is-it-or-isn't-it type who stacked the forks in the drawer tine upon tine. A mousetrap memory enabled her to keep score mentally when they played Scrabble. It galled him to think that his business might be in the black if she were running it, and he suspected that she thought so, too. She never got angry at Lester's foul-ups, but her reminders could be thorned. Since she'd begun showing houses for a real estate outfit—they needed the extra income—she seemed less patient with his slip-ups.

"I thought you were going to call him," Lester mumbled, knowing otherwise, and knowing that *she* knew otherwise, too. Not only was Roger Henderson Rhoda's landscaper, he was also one of the men Lester would be playing cards with later that evening. It had seemed natural enough for her to have turned to him for help with the backyard—it might have been awkward if she hadn't—but how could Lester tell him that he wanted to forget about the whole thing *because he couldn't afford it?*

She sat down opposite him. "Talk to me, Les."

"What's to talk about?" he said, fumbling with a pencil. "You know this hasn't been the best year for me."

"You said that last year.

Les shrugged. "Last year wasn't great, either." *So maybe we should lay off the garden stuff for another year.*

"Sure, Gil," Deborah said, emerging from behind a door, carrying the telephone. "Around eight. What's that? Gil, *stop!*" Deborah hung up the phone.

Lester squeezed the pencil. "The man hasn't called this week, has he, Rho?"

She looked down. "Yesterday. Just before you got home."

Lester threw the pencil down. "Why didn't you tell me?"

"I didn't want to upset you."

"Upset *me?*"

"I know how you feel about Eddie."

"You have no proof it's him, Rhoda."

"Who else could it be?"

"You're just like everyone else around here who'll use any excuse to run him out of the subdivision."

"You mean the guys you play cards with every month? Oh, and while we're on the subject, I'm still waiting for them to replace my box of chocolates like they promised."

"Rhoda, you don't even eat chocolates. It's why you're so thin."

"That's not the point. They were Godiva chocolates, and they were a present from a client. I opened the box and found nothing but the wrappers. And frankly, I'm getting tired of cleaning up after them month after month. The game used to rotate. How come we always get stuck with it now?"

"It's good that we have them over, Rhoda."

"Good for what?"

"Artie and Moe know people. They have pull." Artie was president of the synagogue's Board of Governors. Moe was friends with local politicos. When Moe and Lester got to talking at an Israeli bonds dinner and Moe asked him whether he felt like playing cards with them, Lester hadn't given it a second thought. It seemed like the chance he'd been waiting for to join the subdivision's inner circle.

"Artie and Moe are slobs, plain and simple," she said. "Besides, you don't even like poker. And you're not too good at it, either." She looked at her watch and stood up. "I have a showing in half an hour. So tell me. What are we going to do about the backyard?"

Lester picked up the pencil and threw it down once more, wishing it were made of glass so it might break. He yearned to destroy something. "Rhoda, stop badgering me."

"I'm not badgering you. I'm asking—"

"We have to do something about that caller first."

"He's probably some poor slob coming home from his job to his wife and kids and a mortgage. He's probably bored and looking for a little diversion before supper, that's all."

Her tolerant, social-worker scenario irked him. Why wasn't

she crying out for protection, a private detective, round-the-clock surveillance? Did that mean—his mouth soured with disgust—that a part of her actually *enjoyed* those calls, just a little? Did they flatter her? Only a woman trapped in a marriage gone sour would take obscene phone calls so calmly. Something was wrong between them. Maybe she, too, was up for some diversion. Maybe she'd meet the guy one day, invite him over. Perhaps one afternoon Lester might come home to discover him and Rhoda on the sisal rug—

He got up. Any time they talked about this, Lester found himself getting aroused. He went to the sink, splashed his face with cold water.

"What's wrong?"

"Nothing's wrong!"

"We can leave the garden for now, Les," she said softly.

Lester tensed. At times like this, even her stubborn calm could be trying. Whenever they talked about the yard, he yearned for her opposition, a stiff shoulder of resistance, an excuse for the tantrum he'd been wanting to throw since he'd let her start tearing up their perfectly serviceable backyard in the first place. A reflecting pool? Make it deep enough to throw him in wearing lead boots. A reflecting pool? Just the thing to set off their fifteen-year-old daughter to best advantage splayed out half-naked in the backyard. Maybe Stevie would figure out a way to drown himself in it. And only one reflecting pool? Another four thousand would buy a pair of them, or perhaps a waterfall, a canal, a frigging isthmus.

It was all his own fault. Only a fool would have waited for the brink of financial disaster to throw away money on landscaping. It had been Rhoda's idea, yes. But he'd gone along with it. In fact, he'd encouraged her. And why? The answer consisted of four words: Moe Fleischer's new pool. Lester had been jealous, pure and simple. Who was Moe Fleischer to have a pool and not Lester Loewenthal? The trouble was, Lester didn't want a pool, he hated swimming. So when Rhoda had approached him with this pie-in-the-sky idea of a landscaped garden, he'd jumped at the expensive proposition. Some might have pools, but no one else's yard in the subdivision was going to have statuary that *pish*ed water. No one else was going to have pergolas and ha-has—whatever they were—including Moe Fleischer, whose yard had run out of room. Moe Fleischer had made his wife the star of the subdivision. Lester Loewenthal would do even better for Rhoda.

"The holes won't go anywhere," Rhoda said. She came up behind him, pressed her face against his back, and he thought he might burst into tears. Her smooth fingers brought to mind a plant's tendrils. Since she'd begun building her garden, everything reminded him of plants, soil, and pebbles, of mounds of earth moving like deadly glaciers that would one day bury him alive.

"Go ahead and call him," he heard himself say. "Just do it." *Quickly,* he thought. *Before I change my mind.*

"Are you sure?"

"Yes, my love."

"Mom, I don't see Stevie anywhere," Deborah shouted from upstairs.

"What? Isn't he in his room?"

"No."

"I'll check the basement," Lester said, sprinting toward the rear of the house. "See if he's in the garage."

Stevie went to day camp five days a week, leaving weekends dangerously vacant. He was always darting off somewhere far away, slippery as mercury, impossible to keep in one place, and he terrorized the whole house until found. The basement and garage were his favorite hideouts.

Lester trundled down the steps. The basement was a museum of the house's history, crammed full of furniture exiled from the living room. He scanned the jungle gym of chairs and end tables and lamps, waiting for a pair of eyes to peek out from behind somewhere. Why couldn't theirs have been a normal boy, a runny-nosed, clumsy brat? *Normal?* Lester could just hear Rhoda sneer. And what was *that?* She'd read somewhere that there was no such thing as normality among children, and it had become her credo. Stevie was, as she put it, his own person. Unique. Special. *Oh, he's special, all right,* Lester thought, checking behind the dryer. Stevie's normal state was commotion. His hands fluttered around him, birds trying to escape, and his legs always looked ready to take him somewhere, even when he was sitting down. In Stevie's presence, things fell, spilled, or broke. They got torn, trampled on, or otherwise damaged. At the very least, they disappeared. Stevie fashioned chaos out of thin air the way a lens sharpened sunlight into fire. Though skinny and hardly taller than the living room's ficus, he rattled his surroundings with his very being, a pair of fists forever punching their way out of invisible paper bags. Was all that normal?

They'd taken him to doctors. There were tests. Hyperactivity, the doctors said, a function of glands or diet, or perhaps of allergies. No one knew for sure what to call it. Lester remained skeptical. Hyperactivity didn't sound like a real disorder but just a high-priced name for bad behavior. All boys ran around like crazy; did that make Stevie a freak? No, a doctor told him. On the contrary: Stevie was very intelligent. They'd eventually found a special school for him and medication that kept him under control, and so things went.

Lester had consoled himself. It could have been worse: children were born blind, flippered, or dead. Some grew up nasty, or even dangerous. Stevie was basically a sweet kid, only impossible. Lester sought an explanation, so he worked out a theory. Stevie had been conceived around the time of Lester's anxiety and humiliation caused by Alfred's stunt at the cemetery. Lester's misery had sunk deep into the unborn boy's tissues, warping him. It was possible; junkie mothers birthed addicts, didn't they? Illness was often genetic. His brother Alfred was as much to blame for Stevie's condition as anyone else. It hadn't been Lester's fault.

Lester returned to the kitchen just as Rhoda did. "He's probably over at Eddie's," he said.

Rhoda frowned. She didn't like Eddie, a bus driver in a subdivision of lawyers, doctors, and successful businessmen, an outsider who shot off his own July Fourth firecrackers. Eddie's wife had raised chickens in the backyard and sold the eggs in the Ramapo farmer's market. After she died, Eddie kept the chickens, increasing his stock and building a larger coop. He let Stevie play with the chickens, and the two had become friends.

"Even before all this phone business began, I told you I didn't want Stevie going over there," Rhoda said.

"Eddie loves Stevie. He would never lay a hand on him."

"Eddie's not stable, Lester. Look at what happened to those poor kids—"

"Those poor kids had no business fooling around with Eddie's chickens. Nothing would've happened if they'd stayed off his property. They went there to do damage, and they were caught."

"So what if they roughed up a chicken or two? Was that call for him to try and shoot them?"

"He only wanted to scare them."

Two weeks earlier, Eddie had walked onto his porch to discover a chicken fluttering in a pool of its own blood. He'd brought it to Lester's house in the middle of the night, the bird stiff in his grip, and he'd looked as frightened as if he carried one of his own children. He caught two kids trying to pry their way into the coop a week later and went after them with his shotgun, which fired accidentally, leaving one of them with a bleeding foot.

"Look, it's bad enough that he comes over here, but I don't want Stevie going over there anymore." She paused. "I think it's time we let Eddie know. I think you should tell him."

Lester pulled back. "No. I can't do that. I won't."

"Then I will."

"Rhoda, please. I'm the only friend Eddie has. And Stevie loves him."

"They both should find someone their own age to play with."

"Okay, okay. I'll take care of it." Lester's head began to reel. He couldn't quite imagine Rhoda going over there in her tailored jeans and broadcloth shirt. On the way out, he grabbed two aspirin tablets from the medicine cabinet in the downstairs bathroom and swallowed them without water. He caught sight of Stevie's pills on the top shelf. No matter what Rhoda said about normality, it was those pills—and Eddie's friendship—that kept Stevie under control.

Once outside, he was conscious of walking where people drove. The subdivision hadn't been laid out with pedestrians in mind: there was no sidewalk, just the asphalt's torn pie-crust edge bordering a property line. He stopped to consider his own house, yellow with white trim, bright and sugary in the sun. A forty-by-sixty lot. Paint job about six years old. Shrubs. Terracing. A pair of coach lamps flanking the entryway. Automatic garage door. New gutters. He tallied up what each had cost him. What if one day a natural disaster wiped it all away? Some law of nature dictated that the universe had come into existence with a set amount of matter that neither increased nor decreased but merely changed form. The house would change too—becoming a river perhaps, a dog, a clump of topsoil. It was already happening in the backyard, where swampland was swallowing everything. He imagined the beginnings of some cataclysm—paint cracking and peeling before his eyes, the roof shedding its shingles, the lawn beginning to rumble, shift, and spew lava, carrying the plantings away with it, and the house listing to the side, ready to sink into a bubbling ooze like nuts in cake batter. Maybe the best thing to do would be to abandon it as soon as possible, to jump ship before everything fell apart, to simply let it all go. And he'd throw his business in, too.

Eddie Erhart's place lay just beyond the subdivision, a simple clapboard house built when the area was still rural. The developers had offered to buy Eddie out and when he refused, they simply built the subdivision around him and didn't hook his house up to the water or sewage systems, just for spite. His was the only septic tank for miles, and the county's sole working well.

During Lester's second winter in the subdivision, Eddie had appeared on his doorstep one cold morning. His pipes had frozen and burst. Stalactites hung from his living-room ceiling. He was without water, without heat. Before the day was out, Eddie and his wife were bedded down in Lester's living room, and Lester had arranged for someone to look at the pipes. Eddie never forgot it. Ten o'clock on a Sunday morning, he might appear with a basket of eggs still warm from the coop. He'd show up with a six-pack in the evening, and Lester felt obliged to join him as he drank and smoked, leaning back carelessly in one of Rhoda's prized vintage bistro chairs. Lester discouraged his visits but was reluctant to refuse Eddie's companionship entirely. Pity was only part of it. In Lester's superstitious code of ethics, if he remained civil to someone as hard up as Eddie, the Good Lord might look down favorably upon him and spare him what he'd always most feared: being desperate enough to have to borrow money from anyone, especially from his brother Alfred.

The road took an unexpected bend. It would have gone on straight if Eddie's house had been razed as planned, but it wasn't, so the developers were forced to curve their new road around him. A gradual curve would have eaten up too much land; the road's tighter curve left room for another two lots, but it became a danger spot on dark winter nights. The house was nestled in an unruly grove of spruce bordered by smooth, treeless lawns. Stern cyclone fencing, its barbed-wire cornices slanting toward Eddie's house like drawn swords, separated his property from his neighbors'. Old cars, firewood, and pyramids of bald tires littered the front yard. The damp coo of chickens was the property's heartbeat.

"Hey, Loewenthal!" Eddie shouted from his porch. He wore a baseball cap, red-striped Bermuda shorts topped with a checked shirt, blue-canvas shoes, and argyle socks. His legs were a pasty, shapeless white furred with dark hair, and his clothing looked slept in. It was easy to imagine him making those calls to Rhoda, Bermuda shorts rolled down to his knees, the receiver moistened.

Was that a rifle he was carrying?

"Hey, Eddie," Lester shouted back. He always felt just a little uncomfortable at Eddie's, a tax collector poking around in the backwoods. He knew he'd have to stay and talk for a while before getting down to business, but that evening he was too tense for socializing. The guys were coming over in less than two hours, and he'd neither showered nor set things up.

"Have you by any chance seen Stevie?"

"What's the matter, Rhoda throw you out of the house?" Eddie said, grinning as if he'd just heard a dirty joke.

Lester wasn't in the mood.

"Eddie, have you or haven't you seen—"

"Take it easy, Loewenthal." His eyes sharpened. Eddie took things at his own pace and didn't like to be rushed.

Lester tried to relax. "What are you doing with that?" he asked, pointing to the gun.

"Just finished cleaning it. Works great. Here, let me show you," he said, suddenly taking aim at Lester.

Lester backed off. "Put that down, for Chrissake—"

Eddie pulled the trigger, there was an ominous click, and Lester's face went white.

"Eddie!"

He laughed. "Scared you, didn't I?"

"You shouldn't go around doing that. Especially not now." The petition had been started by Artie Strauss right after the shooting incident. Rhoda had been among the first to sign it; Lester knew he wouldn't. Eddie had more of a right to be there than anyone else in the subdivision. He'd been there first. He'd left the trees growing around his house. He wished no one any harm. *But why did he always have to go out of his way to make people uncomfortable?* Lester knew why: outcasts didn't worry about making others uncomfortable; they were uncomfortable enough themselves.

Eddie lowered the gun. "So tell me. Do you really think they'll run me out of here?"

Lester knew he wasn't guiltless in Eddie's eyes: Moe and Artie played cards at Lester's once a month. As far as Eddie was concerned, Lester was one of them.

"I didn't sign that petition, Eddie."

"I know. And you won't, will you?" Lester shook his head. Eddie brightened. "You still haven't been inside the new coop, have you? I have a new feeder. Come on." He led Lester to the back of the house, where the cluck and flutter of the chickens grew louder. The coop was almost as long as Eddie's house and in better shape. Other people in the subdivision built conservatories or converted their garages into guest rooms; Eddie had his coop. Lester knew that more than Eddie himself or his dilapidated house or his firecrackers, it was those chickens that incensed the subdivision. "We're not farmers in goddamn Iowa," Moe complained at cards one night. Lester said that his father used to raise pigeons on the roof. "Fine," Moe shot back. "Let's pack Eddie off and send him to Delancey Street."

The coop's warm air felt dirty. Eddie's appearance signaled the approach of a feathered, cross-eyed army. "Just installed it," he explained, pointing to a feeding trough that followed the perimeter of the walls. He pulled a lever, and grain poured into the trough. He flicked a switch, a motor whirred into action, and a conveyer belt within the trough began to move. The chickens cackled with terrible excitement as they abruptly changed direction and pushed toward the trough, trampling each other on the way. Some chickens ignored the trough and pecked at the ground, at Eddie's shoes, or at the hem of his pants, so caught up in the process of pecking that it hardly mattered where. Their frenzy was frightening. What drew Eddie to these ridiculous animals, unless it was their mindless devotion?

Lester checked his watch. "A pretty nice setup," he said, eager to quit the coop.

"That's quite an operation you have going there in the backyard, too, Lester," Eddie said when they were back outside.

Lester smiled uncomfortably, hearing envy in Eddie's voice. "It wasn't my idea, believe me."

"How much is it going to set you back?"

Lester dug his hands into his pockets. He disliked talking to Eddie about money. Eddie's question was more than curiosity; it was information falling into the wrong hands. Eddie hated people with money, for they held power over him, even if their power fascinated him just the same.

"I found someone in Nyack who gave me a decent price," Lester mumbled.

"Well, how much? Three grand? Four?"

"Two and a half," Lester said quickly. "Without the materials. Between you and me, I think it's a crazy idea."

"You and your wife must be doing pretty well," Eddie said. "Hear she's been selling houses. What kind of a commission does she get, six percent?" He looked right at Lester. "How much do you think she could get for my place?"

Lester tensed. Eddie figured that Rhoda was in league with the petitioners, ready to pounce on the property the moment he was forced out. Lester was aware that Eddie was still holding the gun. "I told you I didn't sign that petition, Eddie."

"She might do all right for herself, an old house on a big lot. People like old houses these days. Fixer-uppers, they call them."

"Eddie, Rhoda's not selling your house, so stop it!"

They walked toward the road. "How's that poker game of yours going?"

Lester's lips clamped together. "Fine," he said. Eddie chafed at not being part of the game and never missed a chance to bring it up. Lester reached into his pocket for some tissues and wiped his forehead. "I have to get back now, Eddie."

"How about if I bring some eggs over a little later?"

Lester knew Eddie wanted another chance to press his nose

against the shop window of their card game, to gawk at Artie and Moe, five-dollar cigars between their fingers as they ate Lester's paté and oysters.

"I'll come and get them tomorrow."

"You'll break 'em."

"I'll be careful."

"If you don't want me coming over, just say so—"

"I have a lot on my mind, so how about if we forget about the goddamn eggs for now, okay?"

Eddie glared at him. Lester realized he'd made a blunder.

A terrible squawking erupted from within the chicken coop just then. Eddie ran inside, and Lester followed. At the far end, chickens were clustering, a foaming wave of heads and wings. In the midst of it was Stevie, strewing seed in all directions.

"Get out of there!" Eddie cried, stamping toward him, gun waving in his hand.

"Leave him alone, Eddie!"

Eddie had already come upon Stevie, hustling him away from the chickens. Feathers clung to his socks, and his sneakers were smeared with dirt. The rifle's tip jabbed at the air.

"What did I tell you about that?" he said, shaking the boy.

"I just gave them something to eat. You make them hurt each other that way!"

"I said to leave him alone!" Lester pulled Stevie away, sheltering him in his arms.

Eddie's glance shot at Lester. "You really are like the rest of them. You think I'd lay a hand—"

"I'm sorry, Eddie. I lost my head."

"Go over there and clean yourself off, Stevie," Eddie said, motioning to the sink.

Lester remembered what Rhoda had asked him to say to Eddie.

"I didn't mean that about the eggs, Eddie," he began.

Eddie nodded without taking his eyes off Stevie, who was splashing water on himself at the deep plastic sink along the wall.

"Rhoda thinks . . . it might be better if Stevie didn't come over here for a while. At least not until the whole thing with those kids blows over. You know what I mean, don't you?"

Eddie faced him. "You really think I'd hurt Stevie, don't you? You really think I'd lay a hand on that boy."

"Eddie, I'm not saying that—"

"And why does Rhoda think it might be better? You mind telling me that? Or maybe it's really you who thinks it might be better?" Eddie threw up his hands. "That's fine, Lester. You don't have to worry about nothing. I'll leave your boy alone. I'll leave you alone, too." He held the door open. "Come on, Stevie. Time to go."

"See you tomorrow," Stevie said.

"Eddie?" Lester began, but Eddie turned and walked back toward the crazed welcome of flapping wings.

Lester and the others sat around a card table in the den. A garden of exotic foods glistened before them in separate dishes: marinated artichoke hearts, sultry, purple-black Kalamata olives, dark circles of Genoa salami, shiny curls of fantail shrimp, a crock of fois gras, and calamari. A tumble of empty shells remained of the snails. Ever since their monthly card game had settled at Lester's, the proceedings began with a smorgasbord from his warehouse. The spread grew more and more elaborate, and it might be nine o'clock before the first deal.

"This stuff is incredible," Artie said, spearing a shiny chunk of squid onto his fork and ferrying it to his mouth. A tear of oil fell to the tablecloth and blossomed into a dark oval.

"Rhoda'll kill me, Les," he said.

"Don't worry, she's not here," said Moe, winking at Roger with a full mouth of paté.

Lester got a sponge and worked at the stain. Artie was right. Rhoda would notice it from ten feet away, and she'd use it as an excuse to tell him once more how she wished the card games were held somewhere else. There was a time she'd helped set up for the games, but no longer. Now she always arranged to be out of the house when they came. Tonight she'd gone off to a summer stock production with a group of women from the subdivision.

"What are squids anyway?" Artie was saying, returning his fork to the plate. "Fish or mammals?"

"Squid," corrected Roger. "Always singular." He carefully poked an olive with a toothpick. The olive fell off, and he tried again, flustered. His lumpy college ring gleamed on his finger. When the olive was finally captured, he said, "To answer your question, squid are cephalopods."

Artie's lips pulled together. "Thanks, Roger. I'm glad you set me straight on that."

"We won't tell anyone if you eat the olives with your fingers, Roger," said Moe.

Roger smiled uncomfortably, unsure of whether or not Moe had made a joke.

"Les, aren't you hungry?" Moe asked.

"Still full from supper," Lester lied, nursing his double scotch. The restless mix of vapors wafting up from the platter assailed his nose, too varied to be appetizing. He'd long ago stopped enjoying what he sold. Instead of shrimp and paté, he saw filthy, vinegared, vacuum-packed scavengers and the ground guts of forbidden animals. There were times he imagined the contents of his warehouse returning to life one day and squirming in their cans until they burst out of the cartons, a zoo of vengeful creatures as frenzied as Eddie's chickens, pecking and biting him to death as he scurried down the aisles. Other people hawked tennis rackets, washing machines, soybean futures. Lester Loewenthal? Vacuum-packed cephalopods. "My son, the canned-goods seller," his father sneered. Alfred called him a high-priced grocer. Artie and Moe gorged themselves, praising everything, but Lester was sure that they were secretly laughing at him.

I'm going to work my tongue all the way down—

The call had come an hour before the game began. Rhoda

had folded the last of the wash, Deborah was soaking in what had become her protracted pre-date bathing ritual, and Stevie was safely back in his room. Lester had begun gathering up his paperwork when the call plunged a dagger into their undefended domestic heart. Seconds after Rhoda picked up, Lester could tell by the tense crook of her arm who lurked at the other end.

He'd grabbed the receiver from her and listened—*all the way down your pussy, just the way you like it.*

"I'm going to shove the phone all the way down your throat if you don't stop—"

The line clicked back into a dial tone. Lester poured himself a drink and sat hearing the voice repeating in his brain.

He considered his guests. Artie: chunky, with a shiny, chubby face bearing the droopy wings of a Zapata mustache—a silly face, when you came right down to it. Artie's thick gold bracelet clunked against the table like a handful of piasters. He was an investment banker, the most successful of their quartet, complete with Mercedes ("To hell with what Rabbi Kleinfeld thinks!"). He bragged via complaint: the food in such-and-such hotel in Aruba was bad, the girl—their maid—broke a piece of Waterford just the other day.

Tall Moe walked with the gawky swagger of an overaged teenager. His gum-chewing, wrinkly shirts and dirty sneakers announced to the world he was a freethinker, even if he was the regional manager of a discount drugstore chain. He drove a Chevy, rebelliously beat up, but his wife's Buick Riviera was in pristine condition, and that swimming pool took up half the yard.

Lester recalled the party Moe had thrown to celebrate its completion: at least fifty people under a garden tent, music, good eats, booze. The water's gentle rippling mirrored Moe's tranquil affluence. Lester had assumed there'd be swimming, but he and Rhoda were the only ones who'd come in bathing suits. They fled the dinner jackets and linen dresses, and later, Lester sat in the dark in the middle of his empty lawn while the flickering lights of Moe's party taunted him from a distance.

"Think I'm ready for another cephalopod," Artie said.

"Too late," Moe said. "All gone."

"Snails aren't kosher, are they?" Roger inquired.

Artie tossed an empty shell in with the others. "No, Roger, they're not. You're not going to tell on us, are you?"

Roger was the only goy among them. Besides his nursery-and-landscaping business, he was rumored to be writing a novel. He wore the herringbone blazers and corduroy pants of an undergraduate. He did his best to inject humor into his talk by Yiddishizing it with the occasional *schlepp* or *kvetch,* but a Midwestern accent planed out everything he said as smoothly as a hymn. His wife, everyone knew, had had a colostomy. Lester felt sorry for him, sure that the only reason Roger was invited to play was because his wife was the town supervisor's sister. Lester had started to feel closer to Roger during the past couple of games, perhaps out of sympathy. He and Roger seemed out of Artie and Moe's league, although for different reasons. Roger was a nebbish, and Lester was a disappointment, a traitor to the cause of obligatory Jewish success.

"Looks like you're putting in the Hanging Gardens of Babylon behind the house," Moe said.

Lester's toothpick snapped as he tried to poke an olive.

"What have you got planned there for him, Roger?" Artie asked.

Roger glanced at Lester. "Nothing special," he said. "Just some plantings and a statue or two."

Lester thanked him silently for his Christian tact.

Moe wasn't to be put off so easily. "Seems like a major undertaking. Your yard looks like mine did when they were putting in the pool."

The jab in his voice was unmistakable. *Your yard, my yard.* He'd recognized Lester's plans for what they were: one-upmanship. Lester popped the olive into his mouth, mashing it between his teeth until it tasted like a clod of earth.

"How about us playing some cards?" he suggested and immediately sensed a dull pain in his chest. Rhoda was right; he didn't really care for poker, since he was no good at it. Poker was like surfing: you stayed afloat until a tidal wave knocked you down. He winced at every lost dollar and camouflaged his anxiety with more reckless betting. "You bet with your crotch instead of your head," Artie once told him.

Lester had begun liking Artie less and less. During the last game, he'd joked about Lester's old Mercury. Roger, innocent of any subterfuge, as usual, remarked that his very first car had been a '59 Mercury, and Artie asked him if he'd sold it to Lester. Moe got a charge out of that, and Roger the nebbish had apologized. Roger was frequently apologizing, even if he didn't seem to know what for. But Artie's dig wasn't lost on Lester and confirmed his worst fears: people sensed that Lester was slipping. He yearned to be released from the obligation to play cards, but pulling out would have meant admitting defeat. Worse, it would have consigned him to the ranks of Eddie Erhart. No: losing money was the best way to save face. Recklessness was bravery. He reached for his drink.

I'm going to work my tongue—

The man's voice had fascinated him, tantalized him. It had control, authority. It knew what it wanted. The caller was no hunched-over, greasy-haired borderline alcoholic in a furnished room diddling with himself, but someone savoring his pleasure from a leather chair in air-conditioned comfort. He spoke well, with poise. He spoke clearly. He knew just what he was doing. No hasty, nervous click had cut the voice short—only a serene push of the finger. The caller had felt neither shame, guilt, nor fear when Lester came on, just inconvenience.

The doorbell rang. Lester lurched forward, and a shiny arc of scotch shot from his glass onto Moe's wrist.

"Hey," Moe said, reaching for a napkin. "Take it easy."

A racket of footsteps upstairs meant that Stevie was running to answer the door. He wasn't supposed to leave his room at this hour, but with Lester occupied and his sister getting dressed, he had free rein.

Gil stood in the doorway. "Hello. Is Deb here?"

"Debbie," Stevie's voice rang out. "It's for you."

Lester rose. "Back upstairs, you!" he shouted, giving Stevie a gentle push in the direction of the stairs. Gil was only seventeen, but he carried a grown man's bulk and topped Lester by an inch or two. His shirt clung to a gymnast's body, and his goyish face was a stocky cube.

"Deborah!" Lester called up the stairs, using her full name deliberately; she was still his child.

"Be right down, Gil."

She's ignoring me, Lester thought. He was no longer important in her scheme of things. Girls like Deborah didn't wait long. They didn't have to; they knew what they wanted. The same thing that made them attractive made them want to . . . to use their attraction. Maybe it had already happened. *I'm going to work my—*

He forced himself back to the table. Had it already happened? With him?

Moe dealt, and a fresh round began. The moments before Les collected his hand were terrifying. Each new deal meant being abandoned to the foul winds of chance. You never knew what you were getting. It was almost like having to go through childhood over again and finding out the basic things about yourself—whether you were any good at sports, whether you could draw, or if people liked you. The cards felt greasy, ready to slip from his grasp at any time. The complicated designs on their backs were the gears of an infernal clock. How long would he keep on playing like this and losing his shirt? How long would it take until his world collapsed?

Artie grew serious. Roger calmly rearranged his cards, a tidy, if luckless, player, often the first to fold. Moe was a bluff artist. Artie, the real pro, played hard, bet confidently, and often won. Lester's hand consisted of a pair of eights and assorted diamonds: nothing with nothing.

"Hit me," he told Moe.

Lester would borrow a little to get him over the summer,

he thought. Things would pick up come fall. But going into new debt to pay off the old? No bank would look at him. Borrowing from Rhoda's brother Maury? Cheaper than Maury they didn't come. His brother-in-law Paul? Not good for much, the poor slob, although he was such a softie that he couldn't say no to a child-murderer. But Rhoda had said that Ruth was furious with both her brothers after what happened. That Paul—who would have guessed?

"Hey-hey," Moe said as Deborah descended the stairs.

Everyone turned. Deborah walked down like a model on a runway. Her dress clung to her as if the fabric were alive, brilliant white against the luscious creme café of her skin. Her hair was pulled back, dark, shiny, as grooved as a record. Gil waited for her, ready to possess, to devour her the moment she was out of Lester's sight.

"When are you coming home?" Lester said, weak.

"Dad!" she said, firing him an exasperated look. Moe and Artie exchanged grins.

"I mean, don't come home too late."

"Oh, Mom told me to remind you that there's a plate of brownies in the refrigerator," she said. "Let's go, Gil."

"Wait!" Lester lurched up from his chair.

Deborah stopped without turning around.

"Do you have a driver's license, Gil?"

The young man stopped and reached into his pocket.

"Dad, what's going on?" Color rose in Deborah's face.

"Don't worry," Roger said.

"Have fun," Lester said meekly, giving up, and the front door closed.

"The kid looks great," Artie said.

"Like a million dollars," Moe added.

Lester tried to smile, but all he saw was Deborah, gleaming and naked in the yard behind her tanning reflector.

The game dragged on. Moe hit both Artie and Lester with second cards, then Lester showed with two pairs, leaving the ante to Artie and his four of a kind.

Lester threw his cards toward the center. "I'm out."

"Lester, you haven't signed the petition yet, have you?" Moe asked suddenly.

"No, Moe, I haven't."

"Don't you think you should?" Artie said.

"Those Roman candles of his almost set his little forest on fire the last time," said Roger.

"There were plenty of people watching them," Lester pointed out. "No one complained."

"Listen, I got nothing against the man personally," said Moe. "But those chickens of his are always running loose. I almost hit a bunch of them the other day when I drove past. The place is a dump, it smells. It's ruining the whole community."

"Milt Goldfarb's rabbits once escaped and nobody started a petition against him," Lester said.

"Rabbits? We're talking chickens, Lester," Artie said. "Dozens of them. Every time I drive past his place, I feel like I'm in the Ozarks."

"I'd like to know the last time he had his septic tank cleaned," Moe said.

"If they'd hooked his house up the way they should have, he wouldn't *have* a septic tank!" Lester said. "Taking care of that would be the easiest way of solving the problem."

"And who do you expect to pay for this?"

"Who paid for our connections? The developer."

"Why's someone like you sticking up for Eddie Erhart anyway?" Artie demanded. "He's probably the one calling your wife."

Lester blanched. Having it mentioned out loud like that in front of everyone was like being branded a public cuckold. He cursed himself for ever having mentioned it. "Rhoda's heard the guy, and she says it doesn't sound like Eddie."

"He probably disguises his voice."

"How long has it been going on?" Roger asked.

"Since the beginning of the summer."

"You can't just let this kind of thing continue," Artie said.

Lester's ears burned. Everyone was talking about it. Everyone knew. He imagined the whole subdivision waiting for the next bit of news about Rhoda's dirty caller to emerge from the card party. *For a good, time call Rhoda Loewenthal. . . .*

Moe's straight took the pot.

Roger dealt next. Lester watched Roger's careful, freckled hands circling the table. There was something reassuring about Roger. Maybe it came from working with plants all day.

"And the police still can't do anything?" Moe asked. "They usually can trace these perverts."

Roger's chair scraped against the floor.

"We've already changed our number twice, but the guy always gets the new one," Lester said.

"Put a tap on the line. That'll do it," Artie said.

Rhoda had suggested that, too, but Lester had refused. No one else had to know his business. He tried to concentrate on his next hand, but the cards looked like the flags of obscure countries. The stained-glass design of the jacks became the windows of a drafty church. He felt Stevie watching him from the top of the stairs.

"I see you," he said without looking up. "So don't try anything."

Heads turned to see the little boy perched on high, still as a bat. Stevie had crept out of bed once more. Lester sensed him ready to pull one of his stunts: a terrifying roll down the steps.

"I'll let you come down for a little bit if you promise to behave yourself," Lester said, still burning from the talk about Rhoda's caller.

The little boy scrambled down and sat on a chair beside Lester, hands in his lap, a gesture of good behavior, toes curled in excitement. The game went on in silence for a while.

"What's a pervert?" Stevie asked at last.

"Not now, Stevie," Lester whispered.

"Tell me!" He started banging the arm of his chair rhythmically and chanting. I am a per-vert, I am a per-vert—"

"Stevie!"

Lester threw his arms around the boy, either to hold him or to silence him, and in that moment, his cards fell to the table for everyone to see.

"Nice hand," Moe said. "Best one you've had all evening."

"Back to bed now!" Lester roared at Stevie. His hand rose and Stevie winced as he fled upstairs.

"Take it easy, Lester," said Artie.

"Let's break," Moe said.

"What did I hear about fudge brownies?" Roger asked.

"Brownies?" Stevie said from the stairs.

"You can have one tomorrow. Now go to sleep."

Lester went into the kitchen for the platter, and the doorbell rang once more.

"I'll get it," Moe said.

Lester fell against the refrigerator. He'd almost struck Stevie in the face, and Stevie had sensed it. Lester had sown fire in Stevie's eyes, perhaps hatred. He was losing control. The way things were going, something bad was about to happen. Maybe he should be the one taking pills, not Stevie. He removed the platter from the refrigerator and pulled its veil of plastic wrap from the dense blocks of brownies.

"Can I help you, Eddie?" Moe was saying.

Shit, Lester thought, heading for the den. What was Eddie doing here? Maybe he'd brought his gun to bump them all off. He'd hold them hostage like some crazed airline hijacker.

"What's up, Eddie?" He set the platter down on the table.

Eddie still wore his plaid Bermuda shorts, wrinkled T-shirt, canvas shoes, and argyle socks.

"I got those eggs you wanted," he said, holding up a plastic bucket.

This was his apology for earlier that afternoon. Moe made one of his faces. Lester could see it now: the others were going to get a lot of mileage out of Lester and his eggs.

"Who's winning?" Eddie called into the den.

The men exchanged glances to reach a consensus over a reply.

"No one yet, Eddie," said Roger.

"Uncle Eddie!" Stevie cried from the top of the stairs, and a moment later, Stevie's feet were flippering down the steps. He squeezed past Eddie and through the front door. "Let's go play with the chickens!" he shouted, running down the lawn in his pajamas.

"Uncle?" said Moe.

"Get back inside!" Lester called. The others looked on with a mixture of fascination and pity. Lester took off after him. The scotch thickened his legs, he panted, but Stevie showed no signs of stopping, even when a pair of headlight beams shot around the dangerous curve in the road. Lester's head exploded with heat, sweat, and misery. He hated the little boy just then, hated Rhoda for having left him alone, hated the lawn for being as large as it was, and the road for being so unsafe. He hated the entire subdivision for being there.

Stevie's mad roller-coaster pulled him along, and Lester was powerless to stop it. Stevie skirted the road, looped onto the neighbor's lawn to bang on the sign saying "The Schlossbergs," which he set to swinging crazily on its chains. Elvis Presley, the collie in the next house, started barking. What kind of name was that for a dog, anyway? Lester finally caught up with Stevie as a second car whizzed by, screeching to a halt and barely missing him. He grabbed the boy by the shoulders. Stevie laughed, sweating and delirious.

"I told you to stay inside! Why don't you ever listen?" He shook him. He shook him and couldn't stop.

Stevie started crying. One neighbor's door opened, then another. Lester was conscious of standing on someone else's front lawn, his misery for all to see. Stevie pulled away toward the house. Lester limped after him and got back to find Stevie bawling in Eddie's arms as Moe and Roger looked on.

"It's all right, Stevie," Eddie was saying.

"Go upstairs, Stevie," Lester said.

"I hate you! Leave me alone!"

"Go, Stevie," Eddie said softly, and the little boy trudged away.

" 'Night, Uncle Eddie."

" 'Night, Stevie."

Lester waited for his good night from Stevie, but none came.

"Don't forget the eggs, Lester." Eddie pointed to the basket. He left.

"Eat," Lester said, pointing to the brownies, eager to escape the hothouse of stares in his direction. Eddie had been able to calm Stevie, who'd spurned Lester in front of them all.

Roger was the first to plunge in with a schoolboy's glee, and the others followed.

"This tastes funny," Moe said. He grinned. "Maybe I need another one to figure out why." He reached for the plate.

"Holy shit!" Artie shouted, and spat out a mouthful of pinkish brown pulp onto the tablecloth. "This is like dog food!"

"What are you talking about?" Lester said, viewing the spray across the tablecloth in horror. "Rhoda got them from a client."

"You don't believe me? Have one yourself!"

"Oh my God," Artie said, looking at the platter. "They're Dog Yummies! These are the ones we give to Miranda!" He ran to the bathroom. Moe followed.

Lester took a bite. Artie was right.

Roger spat nothing out but carefully placed an uneaten half on his napkin.

"What the hell's going on here?" Artie shouted on his way to the bathroom. "What in *hell*'s going on?"

The game broke up soon after that. Moe and Artie left, and Lester sat at the empty table, the brownies growing more fragrant on the platter.

"I'll help you clean up," Roger said.

"She did it," Lester said, still staring at the wasteland of the plate. "She did it to get back at them."

"What do you mean?"

He picked up one of the brownies, ready to throw it, but found himself squashing it in his fist until bits of the soggy mix pushed out between his fingers. "I'm finished around here," he said to himself.

After everything was cleaned up they had a drink. "A colostomy changes everything," Roger said.

Lester nodded.

"Before, just about the only thing that went down was this special formula," Roger continued. "At least now she can eat like a normal person."

Lester nodded again. He'd wondered how it worked after that kind of operation: the bag, the smell. And with sex. But he couldn't ask about that. Roger sipped at his drink. His calm camouflaged a sea of troubles. Everyone had their own row to hoe. It seemed Roger trusted him if he'd mention this. *Maybe we'll become friends,* Lester thought. He hoped so. He'd be needing a new friend or two pretty soon.

Lester couldn't sleep, so he got out of bed and went downstairs, pausing as he passed the den. Moe and Artie weren't going to let him get away with this, he was sure. Tonight something irrevocable had been set in motion, a glacier grinding his way, ready to crush him. He walked out onto the front steps. Only when he was there did he realize that he wore nothing but underwear, so he switched off the front light. It was strange standing in front of your own house with nearly nothing on, but it was pleasant. The wind cupped his shoulders and the sides of his legs. The entryway's cool brick stone refreshed his feet. He recalled his very first night in the house. Light from his neighbors' windows, still without their drapes or blinds, had reminded him of the cabins in sleep-away camp. The newly planted saplings were spindly, awkward as teenage boys. Deforested, the subdivision had looked like a trailer camp at night.

What had made him buy this house, anyway? His father, of course. Lazar Loewenthal hadn't come right out and told him to buy it; it wasn't his style to say anything directly. Instead, he dropped hints as did a king when he wanted something done: if he, Lazar Loewenthal, made the jump from a *stetl* in Galicia to a semi-detached house in Brooklyn, the least any son of his could manage was to leave Flatbush.

Lester had first seen the area in early fall, the chill in the air scented with pine and mud. The model house nested in a wood along a dirt road, and this bit of wilderness had thrilled him after his growing up where trees sprouted from square openings in the concrete. By the time their moving van pulled up several months later, however, the forest had been flattened by identical white houses and gridded with asphalt streets. His house was stranded on a dirt lot like all the others. What had happened to all the trees, for God's sake, he'd wanted to know. What had they done to the goddamn *trees?*

Something caught his attention just beyond Eddie's house. More than once, Lester had regretted that first act of kindness toward Eddie Erhart, for it had bound them together ever since. He went to see where the light came from. (In his briefs? So what?) Seconds later, something began to whizz, like the blades of a fan. A blur of metal appeared around the curve: a bicycle. At this hour? On this road? It was going at a terrific speed. He hoped the cyclist knew that a bend was coming up. The bicycle passed with a momentary buzz—it was some young kid—then sped by cleanly before the curve swallowed it.

Just as Lester made it back to the house, the phone rang.

"Hello?" Stevie had picked up.

Lester raced up the stairs. "Who is it?" he shouted. Stevie put down the receiver and fled.

"Deb?" a voice said when Lester picked up.

Lester wanted to scream into the receiver and ask what right he had calling at this hour, what right he had going out with his daughter or thinking that he had the world coming to him.

Instead, he set the phone down and knocked on Deborah's door. "For you," he said.

"Hello?" he heard her say as he returned to his bedroom. "Yes," she whispered. "It was really nice, Gil," she said.

He walked toward Stevie's room, anxious to speak to the little boy, or at least to look at him, but he got only halfway before turning around and heading back to his own room.

3

Jerome

New Cornwall, November 22

Aunt Mattie called today. Mother is sicker. She will probably have to quit work. There'd been a grace note of triumph in Mattie's voice as she told me this. She'd made God's revenge her own. I returned to my room and shut the lights. I thought about the time she'd had that operation. It was supposed to have cut away everything. She even showed me the gristly scars. Everything was science to her, her own mortality included. What a hack job. How could she lose her beauty and not be angry? But she wasn't. Slowly I understood. Mother took sick in this way to keep herself for herself.

So my father came to me instead.

That man is always watching me. Stalking me is more like it. He hardly seems to change his clothes. A schlump, to use Irene's word. Avoid.

SIX

Jerome awoke to the musky breath of kerosene, to the mean rank of history plastered into the walls like the cat in the Poe story. His room breathed age, loneliness, and infirmity. Desperation, too. Misery was by nature solitary. How many dim existences had been lived out in this house down a forgotten Williamsburg street, how many shades ferried over the East River's Lethe to two-story oblivions like this one? How many beleaguered souls had preceded him here, wretched refuse from Manhattan's teeming—if sorely missed—shores? He'd been exiled, and like his namesake—Christian imagery, often offensive, could be apt—banned to a metropolitan desert, forced to be among not skulls, but empty heads. Outcasts always mourned, said Wilde, and Jerome's dreary diaspora of the moment was certainly a reason to grieve. Still, it had the virtue of costing no more than eighty a week.

Fremde Geige, gehst Du mir nach?
In wieviel fernen Städten schon sprach
deine einsame Nacht zu meiner?

Jerome balanced a notebook on his knees to write these lines. Rilke hadn't had to worry about accommodations; there was always a castle on a coastline or a mountain villa with a spare bedroom for him and his nuts and seeds and elegies. Jerome's feet sank between the mattress springs. The lumpy bed was like . . . Rilke had a line, something about standing on fishes. Or was that by someone else? Who could remember it all, anyway? Too much that had already been written, too many pages, too many words. Maybe writers would be better to just stop, himself included, so that people could catch up. Maybe one day they'd reach a limit. No more books would be able to fit onto the universe's bookshelves, not another paragraph squeezed in, not even a punctuation mark. Writers would have to find something else to do. It might be the best thing.

Damp, wooly air collected beneath the blanket over his legs, so he kicked the cover away. His room felt cramped. Life felt cramped. He'd been exiled into a stuffy corner of the world that closed in on him like the walls in that other Poe story—he scribbled down the allusion right away, it might be useful.

Warum bin ich immer Nachbarn derer, die sich bange zwingen zu singen, he continued. Ah, the sweet weight of German.

und zu sagen: Das leben ist schwerer
als die Schwere von allen Dingen.

Indeed, why *did* life have to be the most difficult of all things? (Come to think of it, what did Rilke have to complain about?) But Jerome knew the answer to that question, which explained why he'd wound up in Mrs. Kroszak's rooming house: low cash flow. One had to pay for solitude and peace. Still, Kroszak's suited him, at least for the time being, even if Rilke's violins would have been preferable to Mr. Rose's volcanic snoring that rippled the thin wall they shared. Snoring worsens with age, he'd once read. A muscle in the nasal passage grows flaccid, an indignity added to that of Rose's long, droopy ears sprouting pussy willows of hair. But the snoring, too, was reassuring, carrying with it the abiding tranquility of anything old and venerable.

He found himself thinking about Miriam. His sister had been coming to mind more frequently during the past couple of weeks, and never without a tap to his heart. Inevitably when he thought of her, it was the sister of his childhood—barefoot, wearing the dresses that girls still wore then, starched for special days, her thick strawberry-blond pigtails almost bursting rubber bands and defying barrettes. It seemed she'd never worn shoes during their whole childhood—they were only a year apart in age—and she was always coming home with stubbed toes, punctures from rusty nails, and blackened soles. She would slip off her shoes under the table when the dining room filled with people on Thanksgiving, and even during their cousin Joel's bar mitzvah, when she danced in her stockinged feet amongst all the chiffon and rented formal wear, arms up in the air as she balanced on the half toe. She'd also been a model for Jerome—*ur*-anarchist, nonconformist, rebel. She'd smoked and taken drugs and had sex without trying to hide any of it from their parents, and she'd committed the truly unforgivable sin of never having Jewish boyfriends. She'd also been the one at the other end of Jerome's late-night phone calls from college, and the name on the checks sent him when he had to count nickels before going to the A&P. Now she was the upwardly mobile wife of a sporting-goods mogul and never spoke to him. She had sold out, capitulated.

The snores from down the hall brought him back to Kroszak's, and he sighed. Mrs. Kroszak's SRO had once been a graceful row house on a quiet street one subway stop from Manhattan, a four-postered idyll of Sunday dinners of shiny ham eaten in lace-curtained dining rooms. Then Kroszak moved in and threw up the thinnest of walls to create profitable cells like Jerome's, the ceiling molding brutally halved, the parquet's octagons lopped in odd shapes. The room brought to mind the drafty, crumbling mansion on the Upper East Side where he'd been sent to private school, a fifth-grader felon who'd defaced one too many books in P.S. 84. The room had no doubt been beautiful while still intact. Yet beauty wasn't always innocent: its pursuit had unleashed at least as much misery in the world as the pursuit of God.

You shouldn't despise something simply because it's lovely, Jerome—

"Fuck!" Jerome's Sheaffer pen flew down at the blanket, planting a blue splotch of ink on the sheet that blossomed wildly. Blood, he thought; blue blood, like Agatha's, the blood of that raised-letter family with its tennis and monograms, its murmurs and handkerchiefs, its suburban pathology. Wasn't it just like her to rhapsodize about old houses, even if she'd fled just such a house, a stifling, hot-air-registered, ball-in-clawed Chestnut Hill prison lorded over by a wheelchaired tyrant of a father?

Agatha was impinging on his soul yet again, colonizing him, claiming him with a flag planted in his very heart. She never failed to seep into his all-too-porous mind. But that wasn't all, for not only did she still possess his heart, but most of his things, too: clothing hustled off the racks of self-righteous Salvation Army stores or bought for quarters along Houston Street where bums sold their shoes for a drink, a desk missing drawers but noble in years, a curmudgeon of an office chair that launched into a tirade of creaks when sat in. His precious books, too, rescued from the trash, from the punishing commerce of shops or even—it shamed him to admit it, but they'd probably never even miss them—spirited off the shelves of the New York Public Library.

The most unspeakable loss of all, however, was his journals: twenty honest, grade-school notebooks with marbled covers, pages of kindly blue lines and stern red margins. Each was the panel of a quilt stitched day after day, a workshop, a laboratory, a playhouse. They chronicled the time right after he and Agatha had left that place, when they both had sought to start life anew—lines written in joy or in joy's absence, urgent jottings, days translated into words, periods and commas, crumpled thoughts hammered into some kind of sense. She had the journals now, and as long as she did, his life was in escrow. But he would get them back, every one. And he would get her back, too.

The walls of his stomach began to buckle—they always did when she came to mind, and when she did, her very jaws felt clenched around his middle, gnawing, chewing, causing pain. He closed his eyes, took deep breaths, imagining the air drawing the pain from his body, but the internal sting persisted, a three-dimensional pang of conscience, a gastric aginbit of inwit. "Please," he murmured to whichever deity might appease his ulcer's wrath, but it was always the jealous God of the Hebrews that came to mind. (Stomach ulcers seemed a perversely Jewish ailment; emphysema, clearly goyish.) He put off capitulating to the horrible Maalox—Mint Chalklate, he called it. He closed his eyes—darkness seemed to help—took deep breaths again, and the spasm slowly passed.

Agatha, he thought. *This can't go on.*

Memories of her clouded his tranquility like turbulence in a pond. And speaking of ponds, that aquarium of hers. He'd been against it from the beginning. Ornamental fish were useless slivers of flesh and cartilage gurgling after food, slimy links of the Great Chain of Being. With their droopy fins and bulbous eyes, they brought to mind storefront palm readers with too much makeup, lobes hung with garish earrings. Seeing the tank with its sunken treasure chest and fluorescent-colored gravel at the foot of the bed each night was like being the prisoner of a television with a single working channel. Was there anything more ridiculous than an aquarium? Golf, perhaps. Or macramé. But one of Agatha's old-lady friends in the building had given it to her, she reminded him in that blue-pinafored, good-girl voice she could turn on. And gifts could never, ever, be thrown out.

Those fish pursued him on nights when he couldn't sleep, when the desire she awakened within him but could not, would not, quench left him turning from side to side on sheets gone waxy in the summer heat. A breeze might sharpen the points of her breasts through her nightshirt while her legs fluidly drifted apart as she slept, but the temptation always proved dry and hollow. The moment his touch awakened her, she snapped shut tight as a trap. *No, I can't, don't make me.* And as if that weren't enough, he'd had to endure a tankful of miserable little fish witnessing his humiliation. Night by night, he'd grown more desperate. One night it came to him why he loathed this soup of defenseless creatures who bothered nobody: their helplessness and dependence on Agatha reminded him of himself.

His chance came during the two weeks she went to visit her sick mother in Philadelphia. He didn't feed the fish. At first it had been laziness, then a bit of mean fun to watch them dart around, anxious as they gleaned for some mushy tidbit, mouths puckered shamelessly against the glass. But negligence darkened into revenge. *You don't want to put out? Okay. See what happens.* The fish skimmed the surface of the water but finding nothing, they sucked at air. It wasn't long before the larger fish turned to what Jerome always sensed aquarium fish, for all their colors and flounces, were capable of: cannibalism. Soon even the few survivors were floating on the surface of the water, belly-up and cardboard-gray beside shreds of mangled fin. He might have cleaned everything up before she came back and told her they'd died of natural causes. He might have bought replacements. But he took credit for the deed. *This is what you get for torturing me, Agatha.*

"You've killed them!" she'd screamed the moment she returned.

"It's just some *fish,* Agatha," he'd said, hearing the dire consequence in her voice that told him he'd made a big mistake.

He was about to volunteer to go down to Woolworth's to restock the tank when she told him to get his things the hell out of there and leave. He didn't, so she scooped up an armful of clothing, books, and papers, ran to the window and let it all fall. Then she ran and got more. He'd flown out of the apartment and down the steps. Children were already playing in the mess by the time he got outside, and the skeevy man who never budged from his first-floor window of the building across the street reveled in the spectacle from behind a hedge of snake plants, Madame Defarge in a yellowed undershirt, cigarette glued to his lower lip as he savored Jerome's infamy.

Jerome had rescued a solitary journal and run back upstairs only to find Agatha's door imperturbably shut. He left the building and began walking, flimsy with shame and sadness. Sidewalk cracks knifed his shoes, and each curb was another cliff to scale. At Spring Street, he slunk into a bookstore where a reading was about to begin. He put down a dollar for a Styrofoam cup of acid red wine as a woman at a front table opened a slender volume with anemic fingers and began to read. A snowfall of snores began to fall in a back row where a tiny old man in a blue-serge suit was blissfully asleep: Mr. Rose. By the end of the evening, Jerome sat beside him on the train to his rooming house in Williamsburg where, Mr. Rose said, there was a vacancy.

That was three months ago. He hadn't seen Agatha since.

He flipped back to the first pages of his journal, the same one he'd plucked from the garbage that fateful night.

June 12

I am here on this stoop and it is my reality. It offers me its space, its chill, I must be humble in its damp presence. I shall remain here to learn patience.

The next entry was a minute description of getting up in the morning, including a page-long rendering of the dust kitty just beyond the edge of the mattress. *(A tiny, dry galaxy.)*

August 6

This still day, when the sky sent down a cloud of death, when watches burning into wrists stopped. My heart beats out the time robbed from the children of Nagasaki . . .

Come to think of it, he'd never really thought too much about children. Agatha vowed never to bring any into the world. Parenthood meant victims raising victims, she said.

September 3

The will of the people is the dream of the masses. The ultimate aim of any revolution is the elimination of hierarchy.

September 4

Woman of glass
when I look into your eyes
I see only me.
Everything passes through you.
You hold nothing . . .

He tore the pages out, crumpled them and tossed them across the room. Agatha had been right. Most everything he wrote was navel-inspired. But that was still no reason for her to throw him out and keep his things. His stomach lining rumbled once more, but this time it showed no signs of relenting, continuing instead like wallpaper curling up over the steaming broth of acid in his stomach. It worsened, leaving him to jackknife over like a man hit by shrapnel and lunge for the Maalox, putty for the burning cracks in his gastric walls. *A stomach ulcer is a sickeningly bourgeois ailment,* he thought, collapsing on the bed.

The travel alarm on the floor beside his bed said almost nine. Too late to bother going to work. Work meant burrowing into the ozone guts of the subway to drive a delivery truck through Brooklyn, Queens, and Nassau County. It meant loading and unloading cartons of Scottish kippers, tins of almond *biscotti,* Belgian chocolate, Gulf shrimp, Beluga caviar, and Japanese smoked eel—all of it overpriced and unnecessary, all of it for people like his brother-in-law.

A breeze through the window stippled his arms and chest with gooseflesh, and Jerome rubbed his skin. He still had the muscles left over from prep-school wrestling, he noted with some satisfaction, and all the lifting he did at work kept him in reasonable shape, but he'd softened without Agatha. Love tautened you, it toned the sinews and charged the limbs. *You're so strong,* she'd purr. *You're a real man.* Yet the truth was, men terrified her. But why? He'd struggled to find out. Things haunted her, she'd told him. What kind of things? But she'd never say. He'd found out anyway, and that was the real reason she threw him out, and not because of a tankful of dead fish, either.

When he felt better, he got up and went naked to the window, Kroszak be damned. People from across the street had already complained about him, and Kroszak demanded that Jerome draw the curtains, but he wasn't ashamed. His view through the window was unchanging: one half of a street of identical houses sheathed in aluminum siding, teeth of a spiteful zipper, a street of tax accountants, recipe clippers, and bacon fryers. The front yards were chain-linked swatches of grass cropped like regulation army haircuts, their cyclone-fence gates topped with a circled letter proclaiming the homeowner's last name. The four houses he passed on the way to Bedford Avenue spelled P-A-R-K or, starting at Kroszak's, K-R-A-P.

The swish of curtains from a second-floor window across the street caught his eye, and he pulled back. So someone *had* been watching him, some neighborhood defender of the faith, some starched homemaker, or else some aging, unmarried son. Maybe it was the one who taped those unsigned missives to his letter box written on Pooh Bear stationery and reeking of a nose-killing essence of tulip. *I saw you again this morning,* they usually began in their adolescent scrawl, i's dotted with fat circles. The letters had started coming the month before, more ardent by the week. *You stood for a long time. I thought you might have been looking at me. It seemed like you were talking to yourself, or maybe you were talking to me. What were you saying? I love you.*

The strident flop of house shoes coming down the hall alerted him to Mrs. Kroszak's approach. She was anyone who might appear at one's door unwanted: the black-booted secret police, the killer with a stolen gun, the process-server. She knew how much hot water requiring how much gas each tenant used in the hall bathroom, and how much current flowed through her wires into their lamps and radios. She knew when Jerome plugged in his electric heater. All the building's cables and pipes ran through the gauge of her steel-plated heart, a woman who, if she could, would bottle air and charge for it.

"Bernstein!" she barked.

It was useless to pretend he wasn't there. If he didn't open the door, she'd use her own key.

"Leave me alone. I'm dead."

There was a nervous shuffle of feet. He smiled in satisfaction. She hadn't expected that.

"Open up," the voice insisted. The knob jiggled. She fumbled for her keys, pockets jangling like a merchant's. The lock turned.

"Oh!" she cried, seeing him stark naked. The door slammed shut. "For God's sake," she said from outside. "Put something on, Bernstein!"

The door inched open once more, just wide enough for him to see her. Her shift, once plum-colored, was now a muddy brown. The sleeves of her orange sweater had long ago given up trying to reach her wrists, and a fruit-bowl of curlers weighted her head.

"Trying to play the White Rock girl, is that it?" she said, nodding at the sheet he'd pulled around him.

"Leave me in peace," he said. "I'll pay you next week." All it took was money to turn burghers into cannibals. She was but a charwoman with a title deed. She held herself like gentry, but her currency was scouring powder and soup greens.

"Put off your spring cleaning, I see. And what did I tell you about that?" A pointed finger found the hot plate. "You're just the type to set the whole place on fire. I don't know how I ever let that Maurice Rose talk me into letting you move in here."

She had all the charm of a pair of pliers. "I said I'll pay you next week!" he repeated.

"If I don't see that money, you're going to be out on your nose." She left.

Those encounters with her always left him feeling ruined, and he retreated back to the bed, steeling himself for another gastric attack, which, mercifully, didn't come. One thing was clear: he needed money, and fast. Miriam had helped before, but her crud-faced husband wasn't going to let her do it again. Brother-in-law hated Jerome just because of a vase. Jerome had taken it. No, borrowed it: he'd planned to buy it back from the pawn shop as soon as he was solvent. Miriam's living room was dark with knickknacks, and he never thought one would be missed. How was he to know that this particular three-legged *chachke* had been brought over from Lithuania by his brother-in-law's mother in nineteen whatever, surviving not only steerage but forty-three years in a Bronx apartment? Who ever heard of an immigrant fleeing poverty and religious persecution clutching a vase? It had paid for a good three weeks' worth of groceries.

Another knock, this time frailer. Jerome slipped into his pants and went for the door without worry.

"Hello, Mr. Rose," he said, opening the door.

Maurice Rose, who'd given him refuge when Agatha threw him out, was a stick figure of a man in his middle seventies with forests of eyebrow and sad, caved-in cheeks. He wore his only suit—blue wool, single-breasted, pants cuffed—in all weathers. His old-person odor of potatoes, fruited with the cough drops forever clicking in his mouth, was overpowering. Jerome doubted whether the man owned a change of underwear.

Long ago, very long ago, Rose had been married and had worked as an editor. He'd experienced the mighty post-war pantheon firsthand—John Crowe Ransom, Tate, Ellison, and Mailer, whom he once telephoned. He'd heard Elizabeth Bishop read, and Marianne Moore, too, wearing one of her notorious hats. He once had lunch with Phillip Rahv. Delmore Schwartz he knew—clearly a maniac, he said—and Malamud he'd played cards with. Then his wife died, he started to drink, and he lost his job. His eyesight failed, and without children—the great tragedy of his otherwise happy marriage—to help him, his savings declined, and rent control be damned, the landlord managed to evict him.

"I just wanted to ask you if you cared to come with me to Carnegie Hall tonight," he said. "Serkin's playing Chopin." He smiled, revealing a scary jumble of large teeth.

The days of Mr. Rose's concert-going were long since past, Jerome knew, except in memory or imagination, both interchangeable. But rarely a week went by when he didn't ask Jerome to go with him to the symphony or the opera. Jerome always played along. "Sorry, not tonight," he said.

"Aren't you going to work today?"

"I don't feel like it."

"Perhaps you'd like to stop by with something for me to read now?"

Rose was Jerome's faithful reader, perhaps his only one. His work came back from Rose stained with faint tears of tea, the paper rippled from tumblers of vodka or smudged with the fingers Rose didn't get quite clean.

"Sure," said Jerome. "Maybe just a poem or two. Let me get washed first."

Rose retreated nearly silently down the corridor's worn carpet, and for a few moments, Jerome was held in the spell of Rose's voice. Why wasn't the old man angry at the world, why not bitter because of all that had happened? Why did he never see himself a victim of some bad cosmic joke? But he didn't. Rose's drinking helped him bear his bleak days; the tea was a genteel fiction, and Jerome willingly suspended his disbelief to see Rose sober, since it would be only a matter of time until he passed out after the vodka he begged from Olga Tabachova from down the hall. Perhaps vodka was his sole concession to an unjust world.

Not long ago, Jerome had decided to take Mr. Rose on an outing. It took much convincing, and only after several weeks was Mr. Rose ready for it. Their destination was the Brooklyn Public Library, not as grand as the library on 42nd Street, perhaps, but nearer. As they'd made their way to the subway station, Jerome became aware of how small Rose was, how colorless his skin and hesitant his walk, and how daylight left him squinting. He kept touching the sides of buildings or the railing outside the library, keeping close to what might support him. With a shock, Jerome realized that Rose probably hadn't been outside since that time they'd met in the bookstore months ago. Yet as they stood before the hieroglyphics flanking the entrance to the library, Rose had seemed supremely alert. "Look at how the doorway forms an open book," he'd said, pointing, proud as the architect who'd designed it.

Jerome went down the hall to wash. The bathroom's chubby porcelain water faucets and octagonal floor tiles always reminded him of that place his brother-in-law had forced him to go after Jerome set fire to his den: a sleep-away camp retrofitted for the maladjusted from good families. He hadn't minded leaving college, although it meant saying good-bye to his crazy friend Dwight for a while. The place in New Cornwall swarmed with citizens of private, obscure universes and refugees from invisible war zones. The beautiful, dark-eyed Nana claimed to have escaped Brazil's secret police, only to fall into the hands of Maoists camping out in the rain forest. Mr. Schlingelseif continually relived a flight from Nazi Germany ending in a New York swarming with Heydrich's men who congregated in a Swabian pastry shop in Yorkville. (He'd tried to bomb it.) And there was Agatha, who'd tried to cut up her mother.

She and Jerome had left that place together, Adam and Eve quitting a dubious paradise. They went to New York, and she found an apartment for them on Avenue B. Mornings, there were fresh bagels from 14th Street and spaghetti suppers. They crowded into the kitchen's bathtub for hour-long soaks. But she'd made him promise: no sex until she was ready for it. She'd been through some bad things, she said. What things? he'd wanted to know. But she would never tell him. *Give me time: and I'll be all right. Just don't make me tell.* There were ripe, perfect days, at least for the first year and a half. But nights when he reached for her, she screamed, and he let go of her—maybe not right away or not soon enough, and she flounced away from him, bricking herself up in a tower of silence.

"Who's in there? Bernstein?" The doorknob rattled. "I must take shower!"

The massive Tabachova: stout and Slavic, with a carnivore's jaws and hands large enough to hunt her prey and eat it raw. She pressed close, and the will of the entire Russian people strained against the *kulak* of a door and its feudal lackeys, the hinges.

"Be right out." Jerome quickly brushed his teeth, then opened the door to Tabachova's great buttery face.

"Bernstein," she said, shaking her head. "Something with you not right."

Maurice Rose served weak tea brewed on a hot plate, filling grimy cups with brownish water that might have come straight from Kroszak's rusty tap without the benefit of a tea bag. Jerome liked Maurice best in the mornings, since the old man rarely drank then. The narrow sleeve of a room had just enough space for a bed and a dresser, a tiny table and a chair—a doll's room to hold a miniaturized life. Jerome handed him three pages.

"I haven't been writing much these days," he explained.

"Of course not. You're worrying about her. It's pointless to write when you're miserable."

"Dostoyevsky did."

"It's how he stayed down. Sit down." Rose motioned to a corner of the bed. "Read to me." He leaned back perilously, and his feet lifted off the floor, Humpty Dumpty on his wall. Jerome began.

"Too heavy," he said when Jerome was finished.

"That's a strange comment from someone like you. Didn't you once tell me that most of what people write today is so light it wouldn't print through toilet paper?"

"True."

"You've never had it so easy yourself. So why should I shy away from confronting my reader?"

"Since when is the reader a social worker? Who cares about whether the author has woken up on the wrong side of the bed? If life were art, novels would be no more than shopping lists or prescriptions. You can't just pour your life wholesale into what you write. You have to learn to sift. Flaubert, Henry James, Kafka—they sifted. Refined. They *rendered.* Thomas Wolfe and that guy who typed on butcher's paper—"

"Kerouac?"

"Yes. They poured. Spilled, even. Orange juice is nice, but who wants only the pulp?"

Jerome fidgeted. Rose was the last of the old order, too concerned with appearance to worry about truth. James rarely went above a whisper, and Kafka was too timid to even finish what he started. Today a writer had to be fearless, relentless, even cruel. Life demanded it. Each day was a provocation. "The pulp is part of the juice."

"It just gets stuck in your teeth. Listen to what I'm telling you, Bernstein. You have to learn to sift!"

"Writing is explosion!"

"*Feh!* Writing is control. It's . . . it's premeditation. Sift, Bernstein! Sift!" He thought for a minute. "Maybe instead of writing, you should be trying to get that woman back."

"She doesn't want me. And besides, art is more important than life."

"Where'd you get that from, some French poet? You know, you never told me why she threw you out."

"Yes I did: because of the fish."

Rose shook his head. "No one makes a lover leave on account of goldfish."

Jerome looked down. Rose was right. A week after she'd thrown him out, he wrote, begging to see her again. She'd sent the letter back scribbled over with her answer *How dare you ransack my dreams* . . .

"I think I frightened her a little, too," he said.

"Maybe you should ease up on the art for a while."

"What? You always said that when an artist stops working, he stops breathing."

"Take my advice. Forget about the art for a while. Find the girl instead. Tell her you'll behave this time. You can be a poet a month later."

The telephone rang as soon as he returned from Rose's room: Della, the woman from work.

"The big man say that if you don't come within an hour, you can forget about coming—" He heard the receiver being pulled out of her hands.

"That you, Jerry? Where the hell are you?"

"It's my stomach again, Mr. Loewenthal."

"If you don't get into work, you won't have to worry about your stomach because you'll be dead."

Jerome dressed, angry at himself for giving in. He owed Loewenthal nothing. He'd spent his first six months at work despising himself because he was working for someone like Lester Loewenthal, an older version of his brother-in-law, both of them money-grubbers with oversized guts. Jerome imagined them paired off in lounge chairs, smoking cigars beside a Miami Beach hotel pool, gloating about the terrific deal they got on a video camera. Yet Loewenthal had grown on him. There were evenings when Jerome pulled his truck into the parking lot of Seven Wonders Gourmet Imports at the end of the day to find

Loewenthal in the front seat of his car, alone, staring out ahead of him, paralyzed by what seemed to be the image of some private misery, and suddenly Jerome had felt sorry for him.

One evening Loewenthal asked Jerome whether he needed a lift to the subway. He didn't, but something in Loewenthal's eyes beseeched him to accept. Loewenthal began giving Jerome a ride once or twice a week. Jerome soon understood why: the man needed to talk. He described his time in the navy, his first job after college, his first car. He talked about his daughter, the teenage sexpot, as he called her, and his wife, the mad gardener. But it was never long before his son's name came up, when Loewenthal's face would darken. Stevie was his burden, his ordeal, a riddle he had to solve, a punishment meted out, who knew why. "He let my neighbor's chickens out of the coop again," Loewenthal said that first time. "They were all over the road. Cars were honking. It was a madhouse. Stevie went after them and ran right into the road. He could have been killed. There are times he makes me so mad, I . . . I hate him," he said. His voice pulled low. "It's a crime to hate your own flesh and blood, isn't it?" Yet beneath Loewenthal's misery, Jerome detected wonder at the boy, joy as well as dismay. "Stevie's been given to me for a reason," Loewenthal said just before Jerome got out of the car. "Of that I have no doubt." Without ever having met Stevie, Jerome grew fascinated with him, an outlaw of the spirit on the lam in Loewenthal's tidy suburban domain, a nascent poet, a cosmic force.

Jerome finished dressing and was halfway out the front vestibule when he saw it: another envelope with a Pooh Bear motif taped to his mailbox. Kroszak's door cracked open in ambush—she had geiger-counter ears—so he ran down the steps and hurried to the subway. *K-R-A-P*.

He waited until he was on the train, safely out of range of the letter's sender, before tearing open the envelope. He already knew what awaited him: a sticky declaration of post-pubescent devotion, hopeful as a training bra. But wait—a shiny Polaroid picture fell into his lap: Jerome, in his birthday suit before the window. He swallowed. She'd not only seen him that morning, but now she'd blackmailed him. His furry belly, chunky arms and red eyes gave her the appearance of a dazed stuffed animal. This was teenage madness! This was adolescent desperation! He flipped the photo over. "Love me," it demanded. He could almost feel the moist press of the girl's palm upon the page, the soft pucker of her lips as she reread her words aloud. The very paper seemed impregnated with spores of desire ready to cling to him and take root. He hesitated to stuff the envelope in his pocket, fearing infection, infestation. As soon as he left the subway, he threw it in the first sewer grate he passed, picture and all.

Later that day, Jerome pulled into the lot after his shift, threw the truck into park and let his head rest on the wheel. There were cases to unload and papers to drop off with Della, but he did nothing more than sit there as Loewenthal might, eyes closed, limbs sinking into a quicksand of fatigue, still blinded by the glare of Sunrise Highway.

The back door of the truck had opened on the way to a place in Roslyn—had he been too preoccupied to lock it securely?—and several containers of live South African rock lobsters had lurched out. The plastic lids popped open, and the frenzied creatures flew out onto the scorching pavement to a wild blare of horns. They clawed the hot roadway, delirious with fright, until they were cracked under the oncoming cars. It occurred to Jerome that the puddles of fluid on the asphalt were blood. He'd tried to piece what remained of the shipment back together, all the while avoiding the maddened snapping of the survivors. The beasts were using their last moments of life to punish him. It was horrible, horrible.

Jerome roused himself from the wheel's ribs, his face oily with sweat. A putrid reminder of the accident clung to his fingers. He unloaded what had to be taken into the warehouse and punched out. But instead of leaving, he returned to the warehouse, looked one way and the other, then began juggling handfuls of cans and packages into his backpack, provisions for the next week.

"Hey, Poet," Loewenthal called, pronouncing the word as if written with a fat "w" in the middle. He was perched halfway up a short flight of stairs leading to his mezzanine office, though Jerome couldn't see him, since he was blocked by one of the tall metal shelves.

Jerome's stomach went off like a midday siren, and his fingers locked. Loewenthal was supposed to have left early that day to pick something up. The cans bulged in his backpack. The very seams strained audibly, ready to rip.

"Think you can give me a hand out back in about fifteen minutes?"

"Sure," said Jerome, swallowing the knock of his heart.

As soon as the coast was clear he dumped one or two more cans into his backpack and slipped outside to wait.

Loewenthal emerged from the rear entrance a little later, locked in a dance with a white stone statue. One of its feet wobbled on a dolly while the other arabesqued behind. One arm reached heavenward, the other clutched a caduceus.

"Take it for a moment while I get the trunk ready, will you?" Loewenthal said. "It's for my wife," he explained, unlocking the back door of the station wagon. He pulled out an inflatable wading pool. "I was thinking I'd use this as a cushion." He brought the nozzle to his lips. The limp pool draped down like an enormous tongue.

"You have Mercury here," Jerome said, sizing up the statue's winged sandals and helmet. "The Romans' messenger of the gods. Also the god of commerce, thievery, and science. The Greeks called him Hermes."

"A real Renaissance man," Loewenthal said, pausing redfaced, his finger over the nozzle. "Tell me, if you're so smart, what are you doing wasting your time working for me?" He went on blowing. The wading pool took shape only slowly, the mermaids on the plastic unfolding grudgingly. When the pool was finally blown up, they rested the statue on it.

"I think he'll be all right," Loewenthal said, giving the door a haphazard slam shut that narrowly missed hammering off one of Mercury's fingers. "My wife's decided that what we need is a garden in the back of the house," he said as they got into the ear. "But we're not talking just bushes and grass, oh no. She wants walkways and flower beds like they have in Europe. She wants *bosquets*. You know what a *bosquet* is? I didn't either until two weeks ago, and it'll cost me a bundle to put one in. It'll ruin me. But in her mind, if it doesn't have a statue, it ain't a garden. Don't ask me why a lawn with a couple of chairs and some rosebushes wouldn't be enough. Hey, what did you say that statue guy was called? Herman? So I can show her I know."

"Hermes. Or Mercury."

"Mercury I'll remember," he said, patting the side of the car.

Loewenthal offered Jerome a lift into the city.

Yes, Jerome thought. *Maybe tonight. Just long enough to see her building.*

He listened to the details of Mrs. Loewenthal's mammoth garden project, which, even unfinished, grew as fast as crabgrass, or at least its plans did. He learned about how she'd enlarged the pool to the size of a pond, which also meant excavating even more of the yard. Loewenthal reeled off the price of sod, seed, and concrete, of flagstone walkways, cupolas, and ornamental bridges. He talked fencing and pebbles, drainage and elevation. Like his son, the garden left him feeling helpless.

They were about to enter the Queens Midtown Tunnel when Loewenthal said, "It's a girl, right? That's why you've been clamming up so much lately, right?"

Jerome's stomach rippled ominously. A solid block of red lights up ahead plugged the end of the tunnel. Traffic came to a stop. This was going to be a long ride. He felt trapped.

He nodded yes.

"She dump you or something?"

Jerome nodded again.

Loewenthal threw up a hand. "All right, I can see. You don't want to tell me nothing. I thought we were friends. Guess I was wrong."

He'd said it with a smile, but Jerome heard his disappointment and was ready to protest, but didn't. Saying something meant getting Loewenthal's advice. Rose had been no different. Most people listened to you so they could talk about themselves.

"I'm okay," Jerome said.

"You're okay, I'm okay," Loewenthal muttered.

Once in Manhattan, they turned onto Second Avenue, heading south. Jerome's limbs tightened as the street numbers dropped, as they passed the hospital where Agatha went after falling on the ice that time, past the fruit stand where they'd bought a dripping hunk of watermelon one scorching night and gone to Stuyvesant Square to eat it, where she'd first told Jerome about her family. At 14th Street—mere blocks from her apartment—Jerome's insides tore and puddled.

Would he really go over there? What if she saw him?

"So, would you at least tell me this? Did you two have a fight, was that it?"

"She threw me out."

Loewenthal waited.

"She thinks I . . . listened in on her."

"On the phone?"

"No, in her sleep." Loewenthal looked confused. "She used to talk in her sleep."

"So what'd you hear?"

Jerome sensed Loewenthal driving slower to stretch out the remaining time before Jerome would get out. "Nothing really important," he said.

"Come on, tell Uncle Lester."

Jerome's mind reeled. Suddenly he was back in Agatha's

bed and Loewenthal stood beside the fish tank, watching everything. "I was hoping she'd say something about me. I wanted to see whether she really loved me."

"You still love her, I can tell," Loewenthal said as they reached Jerome's corner. "Here you go." He turned off the ignition. "Wait. I have to ask you something, Jerry," he said.

Jerome tensed, feeling the backpack full of stolen goods like an accusing chorus.

"I want you to answer truthfully."

Jerome nodded weakly. *I'll put it all back, just don't fire me.*

"Do you believe in God?"

Jerome gripped the straps of the backpack. "I don't know. I don't think about it."

"It's time you did. You're a grown man. Adults believe in God. And you're a Jew, right?" Jerome was about to say something when Loewenthal raised his hand. "Don't give me any of that secular-Jew nonsense. A Jew's a Jew, and Jews believe in God, period."

"Okay." Jerome was anxious to leave, but Loewenthal's hand came down on his shoulder. It touched the edge of the backpack, too. Jerome flinched. Where was this leading?

"Looks heavy. Full of books?"

"Yeah." Jerome's hand went to open the door.

"Maybe you can recommend something for me to read. You know, I used to be quite a reader. The classics, biography, you name it. I still have all my books from college. But who has the time for that anymore?" He thought for a moment. "What was the name of that book about the guy who turns into a roach?"

"*The Metamorphosis*, by Franz Kafka."

"He was Jewish," Loewenthal said quickly, as if to prove a point. He grew silent. "Sometimes things happen to you and you don't know why, but they happen for a reason," he finally said. "Remember that."

Jerome tried to smile. He yearned to be out of the car, but Loewenthal showed no signs of finishing.

"Sometimes when I look at Stevie, I think he's some kind of angel, pure, and very good. I know this sounds crazy, but the other day when he was futzing around with those chickens, I almost imagined him having wings, too. Okay, I can see you want to get the hell out of here. Go." He gave Jerome a friendly shove.

Jerome pushed on the door handle, and he slipped out of the car to a slight clatter of cans. He walked eastward, anxious to shake the gloom that had collected in his chest during the drive. What had gotten into Loewenthal? Forty minutes of pure and unadulterated *weltschmerz* was too much. From now on, Jerome would take the subway.

Every step down First Avenue rhymed with those he'd taken with her during that first year in the city, and each corner unfolded like a readable page of memory. He'd planned this for days, weeks, but had been afraid to do it. Frightening her would ruin any chances of a reconciliation. He couldn't just show up on her doorstep, either. *Jerome Bernstein is hereby notified that any further attempts to visit the above-mentioned party will result in a summons before a court of law* . . . The backpack seemed too heavy to carry, intent upon keeping him from where he was going. He stopped. No. The only way to see her would be by accident on a public street. Maybe one more block? He slipped into their old bodega—was she there?—bought a container of orange juice and a roll and continued eastward past Tompkins Square Park, scanning the rows of benches. Summer had left the leaves pale and needy. The straps of his backpack chiseled into his shoulders and thickened the vessels of his arms. There was her building. He stopped. The blinds were drawn, the gate locked. The windows' blank stare might have been hers. He decided to wait a bit and sat down on a stoop across the street. *I am here on this stoop and it is my reality. It offers me its space, its chill* . . .

"Hey!"

A voice barked from behind. He didn't bother turning around. It was that cretin in the ground-floor apartment behind a spiky wall of snake plants in a window box, the kind Miriam never tired of cutting off and setting in water to root, tendrils white as baby teeth.

"Get off my stoop!"

Jerome wiped his forehead, pulled open the juice, and drank. His eyes zigzagged up the fire escape to Agatha's window. He recalled those first unbelievable days in the city when he'd wandered around, quietly delirious at being away from New Cornwall, free, reborn, and purified. The two of them had found the apartment one day and moved in with their shopping bags the next. They painted everything, and Agatha hung a Chinese paper lantern in the kitchen.

"Hey, you hear me?"

His heart ached to be so near her once more. *I am here on this stoop and it is my reality. It offers me its space, its chill. I must be humble in its damp, chilly presence. I shall remain here to observe the change of seasons and learn patience.* She'd freed him to work, to create. He reached into his backpack, took out a can of sardines and cranked it open. But he'd learned insomnia up in that apartment, too, for his frustration wouldn't let him sleep. He'd light a candle and sit up in bed with his journal. One night, very late, she'd begun to speak, whispery sputters, hardly more than sighs, a sleepy oracle in the ozone blue of the fish-tank light, and the sighs soon condensed into words. *He is everywhere, even when I don't see him, even when I know for sure that he can't be here. He is calm and imperturbable, a forest creature invisible in the cool shadow of a leaf, jeweled lizard eyes holding me in their liquid gaze . . .* It made sense as music did, not as individual notes, but as an accumulation. She remained deathly still throughout, except for the hand that crept up over her breasts. He'd heard more every night, staying awake just to listen, and soon her dictation filled his journals. At first he'd told himself that he was trying to understand her by writing it all out. Then a thought had overtaken him. *I could use this. I could get a book out of this.* He knew it was wrong, but he couldn't stop.

The sardines glistened in their oily casket—shiny, fat goldfish. *You fake, you monster, a stealer of secrets . . .* She'd found out. One night she'd wakened as if summoned and pulled the journal from him, wide-eyed and possessed. She left to visit her mother the next day. "Don't be here when I return," she'd warned him. A follow-up letter arrived a couple of days later. *You've robbed my dreams because you have none of your own. You've robbed me, just like him. You've taken what's not yours. I hate you. Leave.*

An arm of icy water hit him in the back.

"You shithead!" Jerome shouted, spinning around, feeling the old fury seize him. He plucked up one of the snake plants just as the man slammed the window shut. A reflection in the glass froze him: a woman with short blond hair, in a skirt and sandals and carrying a shopping bag, walking down the other side of the street. He turned around, his heart large in his chest—

The woman, a stranger, continued on her way.

"Put that down!" the man shouted, his voice muffled by the glass.

Jerome dropped the plant and flung the can of sardines at the window instead, hitting the glass with a greasy sludge down the pane.

"Hoodlum!" the man shouted.

The man's shirt caught Jerome's eye: red stripes with black boxes. He looked closer. Yes. The bastard had pulled it from the pile of what Agatha had tossed out the window.

Jerome brooded all the way back to Williamsburg. Agatha had been right. He was a mere copyist, a scrivener, a hack. They'd been her memories, not his. She'd seen right through him. He was some deep-sea invertebrate, a scavenger, a bottom feeder.

P-A-R-K.

Kroszak's dogs filled the backyard with barks like squeaking hinges, writhing around on the dirty floor of the yard the way sparrows bathe in dust. Like Agatha's fish, the dogs served no purpose other than to consume food and metabolize it. Kroszak neither walked nor petted them; she merely fed them. They'd pounce on Jerome in clumsy welcome when he brought his garbage down, sending foul clouds of breath into his face as they pawed and licked at him. He'd return from the yard with their smell plaguing his nose, a smell, he thought, of desperate affection.

That evening, the dogs waited under a buzzing halo of gnats, springing up the moment he entered the yard, their breath simmering, paws pressed against his shoulders, as if seeking an embrace. Jerome fell backward, pulled down by his backpack. The dogs scurried away, ashamed of what they'd done, and Jerome lay there, dazed and hurting. One by one, the animals lumbered back, sniffing cautiously in apology. He told himself to get up but couldn't. The backpack was too heavy, holding all the weight of the world within it. All that talk of God with Loewenthal had transformed Jerome's thieving into a millstone. Every can was another felony. He looked up into the lightless eyes of the dogs, each orb a universe above a loose flap of tongue. What did dogs know? What did they need to know? What did he, Jerome, know? And what did it matter?

One flight up the back stairway, the lights went out; Kroszak's air conditioner was always blowing a fuse. But darkness suited him just then. He made it to his room, sat down on his bed and took a swig of Maalox. He pulled off his shirt and threw it across the room. *You stink,* he told himself. *You stink to high heaven, so get up and wash.* But he was too tired to wash. He kicked off his shoes, stripped down naked, and opened the window. A breeze fingered the sweat on his forehead. His hand slid to the knotted flesh of his nipple, and his fingertip began to tease it absentmindedly into hardness. How nice it felt.

He sat back down on the bed, and his hand explored the

damp undergrowth between his legs. *Please, let me, please. Just once, gently. Please.* He parted his legs, his fingers caressed his wrinkled scrotum, and his nails shot tiny sparks through them. Hairy as gooseberries, she'd joked. But she wouldn't, never. *I can't. Not yet.* He stroked, getting hard and then harder, his legs parted further, and his body grew taut with expectation. Those nights beside Agatha, he'd do himself discreetly, urgently, eyes pressed to her curves, nose attuned to whatever wisp of delectable sourness a breeze might carry away from her, then shooting into her immaculate sheets. Beating off was such easy, obvious pleasure, like reading mystery novels, he thought, working his rubbery firmness. But beating off would have to do just then. He let himself down on the lumpy mattress, and the springs emitted a suggestive squeak. He stroked, head back, harder, faster, his leg muscles tensed, everything inside him pushing and ready to break—

A stretch of skin slithered against his own. His legs scissored shut, and he bolted up.

"What the fuck!"

There was a giggle, the cover sheet shifted, and a form rose before him: a girl, smooth and gauzy, a modest, dark patch between her legs, a painfully sweet navel, and two small, patient breasts.

"Hi," she purred.

"Who are you—" But in that moment, he knew. *Love me.* She'd been writing those letters. She'd sent that picture! "How the hell did you get in here?" He fumbled for his underwear, but she snatched it from him, still giggling.

"Give that back."

"Come and get it," she said, stuffing it between her legs.

"Jesus God," Jerome said, his voice cracking like a teenager's. "You have to get out."

She moved close. "Relax, darling."

He pulled away. "You have to—"

"Jerome," she said, growing serious. "I came here tonight

for a reason." She let a hand drop down the side of her neck to caress her breast. Her voice sank half an octave. "And you know why."

"I don't care why you came. You have to get out."

"Can I call you Jerry? Jerome's too nerdy."

"You're crazy and you have to go," he sputtered. The people from across the way would grind him up for sausage if they knew she was there. They'd drag his remains down the street for everyone to see, house by house, K-A-R-P . . .

"How did you get in here, anyway?"

"The same way you always do. Around the back. And the door to your room was open." She giggled. "I closed it so you wouldn't suspect anything when you returned."

"The door was *open?*" It meant that Kroszak had been snooping around. "How did you know I wasn't here?"

"Oh, I knew. I watch you. Every day. I've *been* watching you for weeks." She gave a private chuckle. "I know everything about you, Jerry. *Every*thing." She flung his underwear over the side of the bed and pressed against him. Her breasts were as round and firm as apricots, her pubic hair tickled, and a fruity smell clung to her. She closed her eyes. "Kiss me, Jerry."

Footsteps approached in the hall. A moment later, Kroszak's knock drilled at the door.

"Bernstein, you in there?"

Jerome pushed the girl under the blanket and ducked in beside her.

"Oooh," she giggled, wrapping her arms around him, her breath pooling warmly against his face.

A key turned in the lock, the door opened.

"Look at this pigsty," she muttered.

The girl's head slid between Jerome's legs, and a moment later, she took him in her mouth.

"Oh my God!" he gasped.

"Who's there?" Kroszak said. She switched on the lights and tugged at the blanket.

"Jesus help me!" she cried, seeing the two of them before looking away. "Linda? Now you get dressed and go—"

"You're disturbing us, Mrs. Kroszak. Leave."

"I want you out of here right now," Mrs. Kroszak said, heading for the door. "If you're not both out of here in ten minutes, I'm calling the police." Her voice sounded ready to fall over an edge and shatter.

"We can't stay here, Jerry," said Linda after Kroszak left. "She's going to go to my house. My father has a pistol. We have to hide. Let's see . . ."

"A pistol," Jerome moaned.

"Get dressed," she said, assuming authority. She tossed him his shirt. "Maybe we can go to my girlfriend Heather's. Her mother's never home."

"I have no place to go," Jerome said to himself.

"Sure you do," Linda said, stepping into her pants, a merry jiggle to her breasts. "You're coming with me. Now hurry! You don't want to be a sitting duck. My father is a raving Catholic. If he sees me here, he'll shoot us both, and then you'll have my blood on your hands. Come on!"

She seemed as confident as a Girl Scout. He struggled into his clothes as he surveyed the room for the last time. He couldn't help being a little sad about leaving it, yet returning was out of the question. Once more he was being banished, exiled. Would Kroszak toss his things out the window, too?

A bar of snoring tripped him as he passed Maurice Rose's door. His heart grew heavy. Who knew when they'd see each other again? He thought of the tiny man in bed asleep, dreaming his sepia-colored dreams. Memories faded; perhaps Rose's had already begun to decompose, old movies flaking into bits inside their cans. How could Jerome leave Rose without saying good-bye? For one thing, he'd just given the old man another sheaf of his poems. But there was no time to get them back now.

"Where are you taking us?" he asked the girl.

"To my house."

Jerome stopped short. "You said your father—"

"We'll go up to the attic. No one ever goes up there. It's where we keep all my brother's stuff since he got run over. I'll get food for you." She smiled. "We can be alone there." When they reached the stairs, she said, "Kiss me."

"Not now!"

"Kiss me!"

"Okay, okay," he said, planting a hasty kiss on her lips. They reached the yard, Jerome fearful of a canine ambush, but the dogs remained miraculously silent, sensing his emergency. They dashed across the street and went around to the back door of her house. A television blared unwatched in the living room, the sole sign of habitation. He saw Kroszak's house through the living-room window. *I've gone through the looking glass,* he thought. They crept upstairs, she lifted down a collapsible ladder from the ceiling, and they ascended into the dusty heat of the attic. She pulled on the light and flopped down a mattress from against the wall, sending up billows of dust.

"I'll get some sheets and a pillow," she said, hardly flagged. "If you wait an hour or so, you can use the bathroom. My father always goes to bed at ten. I'll be up as soon as I can with something for you to eat."

"Why are you doing all this for me?" he asked, reaching for her arm.

"A woman must help her man."

"I'm not your man."

"Not yet. But you will be."

From below came the sound of a toilet flushing.

"Listen, I have to be in my room so that when Mrs. Kroszak comes, I can tell my mother that I've been there the whole time. She'll believe me, not her. Everyone knows Kroszak's crazy. I'll be back up after that." She winked.

He fell down on the mattress immobilized, dizzy, unbelieving. The bare bulb was an all-seeing eye—Kroszak's, Loewenthal's, Agatha's, the face of that man behind the snake plants. Or one of the doctors in New Cornwall. For as long as he could remember, he'd been under surveillance. He couldn't be trusted. Agatha knew that a madman lurked inside him, and that was why she'd banished him. The air was musty and dead from not being breathed. A crib, a pile of dolls, an old hi-fi, cartons, more cartons—the detritus of family life was heaped around him, civilization building upon its predecessors. His eyes fell on a pile of sports equipment: ice-hockey sticks, skates, padding. The dead brother's. He swallowed. He thought of his own sister, hopelessly cut off from him. The attic began to feel too closed in. He climbed down the ladder and peeked into the room where the girl sat at her desk, patiently awaiting her interrogation, looking up from a book to gaze out the window. She'd pulled back her hair to a teenage ponytail, and with a pencil in her hand, she might have been a studious, dutiful daughter poring over an algebra lesson. From where he stood, he could make out what had been his window, dark except for light streaming from the hallway through his open door. This was what the girl saw, he thought, and he pictured himself as he'd been that morning, naked and half-awake, and he wondered what she'd seen in him to adore, what about him she sought to cherish.

He heard footsteps and raced back up to the attic.

Down below, the front doorbell rang, and his stomach pinched together. *No Maalox*!

A little later, the girl returned with a tray of food and some bedding.

"Kroszak tried to tell my mother what happened," she calmly explained, setting the tray before him. "You should have seen it. Kroszak and my mother come into my room and Kroszak says she saw me naked in bed with one of her tenants. Her *ex*-tenant, she said. My mother turned to me. I was sitting at my desk, doing my homework, so I just looked Kroszak right in the eye and asked her why I'd want to be in bed with one of *her* tenants, since Mr. Schwab at the end of the block has much cuter guys living there. You should have seen the look on her face! The old crow. Eat." There was an open can of lima beans, a drumstick, and two slices of white bread. Jerome went for it greedily, and she watched with maternal satisfaction. "Enough?"

His stomach was ablaze. He'd eaten too much too quickly. "Yes," he gulped, trying to swallow the pain. "But really, why are you doing this?"

"I already told you. There's also another reason, but I won't go into that yet. Finished?" He nodded. She set the tray aside and began stepping out of her pants, and when she was completely naked, she said, "Now you."

He motioned toward the light.

She reached up, pulled the cord, and the attic went dark. "Better?"

He thought quickly. "I have no protection."

She produced two condoms. "They're my father's, but he'll never miss them." She slid down beside him.

"There's something else," he said, pulling away. "I need something for my stomach."

"You mean like Milk of Magnesia?"

He nodded meekly.

She was up in a flash. "My dad drinks that like water. Hold on."

He'd taken off his clothes by the time she returned. She slipped in beside him.

"What was that other thing you wanted to tell me?"

Her face loomed close, a blur in the dark as she pressed a rubber into his hand. "Go easy," she whispered. "You're my first."

"Just tell me one thing. How old are you?"

"Should I lie or tell you the truth?" She stroked his chin.

"You're sixteen."

"Okay, I'm sixteen."

"You mean you're younger!"

"Shhhhh." She put her arms around him. "Come on. What difference does it make? I'm ready."

Afterward, lying on his back, it wasn't Agatha's name that spilled from his lips unwittingly, but Miriam's.

"Your mother probably never told you that your father's parents died in a plane crash while en route to Las Vegas," Aunt Mattie said in that square, Eleanor Roosevelt drawl of hers. No doubt she would have preferred them to die more respectably of a heart attack smack dab in the middle of mass . . .

Johanna Mathilde Sprague was your archetypal aging buzzard stuck in a house too large for her and with too much time on her hands. I was used to her jibes at Mother, whom she considered frumpy and naive. I was the obedient granddaughter who'd been given her name, and as long as I could remember, I'd vowed to change it. I drank the hot milk she'd made—I'd slipped some of her coffee liqueur into it—and as she droned on, I began cruising on a soft cloud of alcohol, peering down into dusty St. Margaret's Church, staging my own version of my grandparents' death. I can just see it. Grandfather's pacemaker goes on the fritz just as he receives communion, his heart sputters, and he keels over, wafer pasted to his tongue like Melba toast. Grandmother faints at the sight of the mushy, half-dissolved Savior, a sacrilege, after all, as does the organist, who slouches forward and slams against the keyboard with a magnificent noise, a fanfare for the Antichrist—

"Your mother probably didn't tell you that your father was on that plane, too," Aunt Mattie nattered on. I imagined him seat-belted into a wheelchair hurtling earthward, a fallen angel crated in chrome, asteroids of broken wing plunging into the Atlantic.

"It was a miracle that he survived," she said with much

moment. She wanted me to be in awe of him and his pain. Pain is a mystery, and all bearers of mysteries are considered powerful. She wanted me to feel sorry for him.

She wanted me to love him.

Fat chance.

New Cornwall, January 9

I asked him why he was here, always the tricky question. Even funny farms have their etiquette. He finally told me during another of our long, long walks around the grounds. He could plod on for hours without tiring, wearing nothing but a T-shirt under his parka. His mammoth grudge against the world kept him warm.

The air was glassy and cold. Numbness thickened my feet. His brooding was loud enough to hear. Like a Norseman with a saga to declaim, he told me everything. "The bourgeois cartoon of a man my sister married put me here because I rubbed his nose in his own mediocrity," he began. He had been living with his sister, and his brother-in-law complained that he was a slob. But obsessive standards of cleanliness didn't interest him, so when BIL told him to look for other lodgings, he set the den on fire. BIL gave him a choice: New Cornwall or Bedford Hills—treatment or a jail sentence.

Then he kissed me and said he loved me, and the snow on his beard chilled my face.

SEVEN

"My big man," Linda whispered as they made love. She'd clung to him as he entered her, brave, determined, nails pincushioning his shoulders. "Thank you," she said afterward, a little teary. Silently he'd thanked her, too, grateful to have gotten laid at long last.

He escaped while Linda went downstairs to get his breakfast. Near the subway station, he headed for a pay phone. He'd run into his old college buddy Dwight in Gray's Papaya a month ago. "Any new projects?" Jerome had asked. Dwight was a kind of Zen Busby Berkeley, putting together peculiar extravaganzas involving large groups of people doing obscure things to represent abstract ideas. No, he was idle at the moment, he said, but ripe for a new project. He was living in a building on the corner of Prince and Greene. "The epicenter of the soon-to-be-art-as-commerce mecca," he said. There was plenty of room. He'd scrawled an address down on a napkin—there was no phone in the place—and told him to come by. And now where was that napkin? He dug into one pocket after the other. The obscene taste of a papaya-orange drink teased his tongue as he struggled to remember.

Jerome swung up the flabby torso of the telephone book, thinking to reach someone who knew Dwight to get the address. Twice a flat, recorded message told him that the number he'd dialed had been disconnected. Meanwhile, a man in a suit and carrying a briefcase appeared outside the booth, eyeing him impatiently. What urgent business could anyone have in Williamsburg on a Saturday morning? Raindrops began to stipple the glass. The man's stare deepened. For all Jerome knew, Linda might be rounding the corner. He had to get out of there. There were only four corners on the intersection of Greene Street and Prince, he reasoned. One had to be Dwight's.

The train came, and Jerome slumped into a seat. Exile's rub and chafe were beginning to wear on him. The car was half-empty, as weekend trains tended to be, and without a load of rush-hour commuters to hold it down, it seemed ready to bolt the tracks and crash into oblivion as it picked up speed. A woman opposite him huddled over two bruised shopping bags bulging with ragged possessions, yet another unshowered soul sheathed in the grimy patina of the street. Her many layers of clothing might have been the national costume of some obscure ethnic group.

These days they were everywhere. Lucky ones found doorways and vestibules to sleep in or slipped inside the four walls of a refrigerator carton. Others learned to sleep on foot or sitting up, or perhaps they didn't sleep at all, dreaming as they trudged along. On Houston Street, a man in rummage-sale attire calmly steered a shopping cart piled high with refuse, pitching like an unwieldy galleon. It made Jerome think of a Depression-era jalopy headed west, strapped with mattresses and cooking pots. But more than their dress or what they carried, Jerome noticed how they were always talking, lecturing to no one, preaching to the averted, the disinterested and annoyed, declaiming to the wind. No matter how hungry or tired they looked, they still found the strength to orate. Words spilled from them, gallons of talk flowing without paragraph or punctuation. Their language was arbitrary, a salad of talk, gasoline surging through the hose the moment the trigger was squeezed, and as volatile. They took both sides of an argument, speaker and listener.

If Dwight couldn't be found, Jerome would be joining their ranks. His throat went dry, he grabbed his middle, and his stomach erupted. *Please,* he thought, appealing to some unseen deity. The pain made him want to pull open the doors and throw himself on the crushing mercy of the tracks. Linda appeared before him, breakfast tray in hand, angry, and the hot pulse of his stomach quickened. The woman opposite him reached into the folds of her clothing and produced a roll of antacid pills that she offered him with purple-nailed fingers. "Terrible, these ulcers," she said, calm as an executive beside him in a midtown elevator. "Try this." He accepted two pills and quickly chewed them to bits, anxious for relief. The spasm abated, leaving him tired and light-headed, his tongue sweet and pasty.

"Who is your mother?" the woman asked.

"Huh?"

"Do you know?"

Here it was again, he thought: *the catechism of the lonely, the solitary call-and-response.* The woman was inching closer, ready for conversation. He looked out the window at the shifting grime of the tunnel's walls, urging the train's progress so that he'd be able to escape. Then the train came to a stop.

"Mothers are hated for their power. That's why men leave us. It's why children leave us." Her bushy eyebrows arched like the backs of cats. She raised a skeleton arm through several layers of sleeve.

Jesus fuck, he thought.

"Your mother suffered to have you. She suffered because of you."

"She suffered because of my father," Jerome said, irritated. That was another thing about those people: like all of the oppressed, they had constant bones to pick, cosmic grudges on their shoulders. They blamed, accused, and criticized, as any zealot did.

"One day your mother will take back all she's given you," the woman called out after him as he fled the car when his stop came. He reached the street, flushed and weak. The woman might have been Linda's emissary, come to punish him for his abandonment.

One building on the corner of Greene and Prince was girded with scaffolding, and plastic sheeting billowed from its window openings: Jerome recalled something about the building's renovation. He found a steel door wheat-pasted with the posters of a hundred concerts and performances and knocked. An old man in ratty clothing appeared, his face stiff and scabby.

"Oh, you mean the kid, Governor," he said when Jerome asked for Dwight. The man spoke in the kind of clear, 1940's speech Jerome associated with the city's Caucasian down-and-out. "Okay, Phil," he said, motioning to another old man dressed in shreds and patches, carrying a length of twisted lead pipe on his shoulder. "Just bring it in for now, we'll get it downstairs later." Phil heaved the pipe onto a large pile of scrap metal with a ringing crash.

"I'm Louis," the first old man said, extending Jerome a hand.

"How much more does he want?" the man named Phil asked.

"More and more," was Louis's answer. "More and ever more."

The steel door closed them into gloom except for slivers of light that clipped through cracks in the cinder-blocked windows. The air was a crowd of smells damp, spongy, and foul. Almost every inch of floor space was occupied by someone in layers of ratty street clothes nesting on an improvised bed of newspaper, cartons, and, for the lucky ones, blankets and mattresses.

"Straight ahead until you reach another door, Governor." Louis pointed toward the rear. "Should be open. Elevator's locked, only the kid has the holy key, so mere mortals have to hoof it."

"The kid?"

"The Master Builder. The Prime Mover. The Big Cheese." He retreated to his own pile of blankets and mattresses near the door, his station. As Jerome made his way to the rear, his eyes adjusted to the subterranean darkness. Candles flickered. Some of the people talked or read, but most of them slept or lay still in their bulky clothing. It might have been a Civil War infirmary; Jerome expected Walt Whitman to appear with a basin of water and a roll of gauze.

"When you see my son, tell him I have to talk to him about something." A woman's voice rose from the huddle. She spoke as if they'd known each other for years. Jerome looked closer, worried that the woman from the subway had followed him here. She'd arranged her mat with care, ragged blankets just so, an upturned milk carton like a night table beside her, adorned with plastic flowers. She might have been someone's grandmother in the living room of a Brooklyn apartment. Jerome's stomach rumbled with discomfort. What was going on here? Was Dwight running some kind of homeless shelter?

He was about to open the door at the rear when the place exploded with a rhythmic boom, followed by the curdling shriek of an electric guitar. Soon the whole building shook with an infernal music. No one seemed to notice.

"Keep on going," said a man in a ski cap looking up from a page of newspaper as he motioned with a gloved hand. "And don't stop until you reach the penthouse."

"Greetings!" Dwight said, opening a door at the end of a dim corridor. Sunlight blinded Jerome after the long ascent in darkness.

"I wasn't sure if this was the right place," Jerome panted. "I lost the address."

Dwight led him into a rubble-strewn moonscape of broken brick and shards of plasterboard. Electric cables dangled from above. A breeze set sheets of plastic flapping at the large windows. Dwight had grown near-skeletal and was still dressed in the purposeful black Jerome recalled from college: suit jacket despite the heat, black pants and black shoes, with the green tape holding his eyeglasses together the only relief. His skin was very white. There was something submerged and hidden about him.

He'd never had much money and rarely a fixed address but lived by the laws of thermodynamics: set into motion, he kept moving, who knew how? In college, he'd practiced what Jerome termed Severe Solitude, holing himself up in a room to read all of Proust or Ayn Rand or Johann Herder in bleary-eyed twenty-four-hour stretches, swallowing amphetamines and the occasional Devil Dog. "Domino Theory," his first spectacle, had been staged in an abandoned factory on the riverfront. He'd lined up dozens of old file cabinets domino-style in a series of curves and then let them rip while videotaping the crash and bang. "Serenade" consisted of people staying up all night to hammer out the 623 fourteen-bar repetitions of Erik Satie's "Vexations" on fourteen old pianos in a condemned school building. Once he'd organized a hundred people to sit in rows of ten, gave them each a telephone book to read along with an amplified tape of Gregorian chant. ("The End of Eternity" was the name of the piece.)

But Dwight considered "Hike" to be his crowning opus. Crowds of people had walked up and down the echoing length of an old machine shop to equal the distance from London to Scotland covered on foot by Ben Jonson in 1618, all the while slides of auto wrecks were projected on the walls to the sound of car crashes. Jerome had watched him crouch in a far corner during the event, spellbound at his creation. *Does anyone care about what Ben Jonson did in 1618?* he'd thought. Yet that wasn't the point. "Art," Dwight was fond of saying, "is one-tenth inspiration and nine-tenths organization." Bringing order to crowds of people pleased him. "People crave putting themselves on display," he said. He had few friends: he preferred people en masse and in the abstract rather than individually and in the flesh. He'd never had girlfriends. He wasn't asexual, but nonsexual. People thought he might be either brilliant or deluded, and Jerome couldn't be sure of which.

"You didn't tell me that you were a super, Dwight," Jerome said.

"A real-estate speculator gutted the building to make luxury lofts but ran out of money. This whole neighborhood is going to change real soon, he says. Before long, there are going to be all these expensive stores here and people paying through the nose to live in buildings like this. I'm supposed to make sure nothing happens to the place until he gets more cash." He grabbed two beers from a bucket of water. "Not cold, but de-warmed," he said, offering one to Jerome. "The only electricity's in the basement and elevator. Let's go onto the fire escape and talk." He led Jerome over the windowsill onto a large black tub of scrollwork strapped onto the building high above the street. Jerome hesitated. It looked fragile and unsubstantial, ready to pull from the masonry, teeth from weakened gums.

"What are all those people doing downstairs?"

"They help." Dwight lifted the can to his lips, and his bony wrists and finger joints looked polished in the sunlight. "I'm thinking in terms of a kind of sculpture. A sculpture of waste, of excess, of detritus."

"A junk heap?"

"A junk *piece*, I've been thinking. A civilization should be judged less by what it builds than by what it throws away. Things in this city were built to be torn down. What does that mean?"

"That people aren't sentimental?"

Dwight shook his head. "That they're obsessed with creating waste. They build knowing that what is constructed will become rubble. In effect, the modern city builds ruins. It generates its own archaeology."

Manhattan as the Island of the Dead, Jerome thought. A necropolis metropolis. Perhaps there was something to the idea, but only someone like Dwight would find it interesting. Jerome remembered the guy carrying the pipes. "So all the scrap metal—"

"I'm using it to build my ruin. Those people downstairs help me haul stuff in."

"They don't really look like they're in any condition to be hauling scrap metal around." *Most of them looked ready to kick the bucket.*

"You'd be surprised. Fate has toughened them."

He spoke like the director of a nineteenth-century orphan asylum. "Do you *make* them work?"

"I *let* them work. In return for giving them a place to stay." He paused. "They fascinate me. I want them to be part of the sculpture as well."

"Because they're junk, too?"

"No, Jerome," Dwight said tartly. "Because they, too, are the excessed, the wasted."

"What was that I heard coming up the stairs?"

"The band. Feelie's Wheel. They're part of the project, too. I was in Radio Shack getting flashlight batteries, and a young kid who works there started talking about this band. It gave me an idea." He'd struck a deal with the band: they'd be in on his project in return for rehearsal space deep in the subbasement. "They're really not all that good, but they're loud and kind of manic and they get me some nice coke."

"What's this sudden interest in homeless people?"

"Catastrophe and decline have long fascinated me, you know that. I've always found decay poignant. And urban decay is the new American romanticism."

"You? Romantic?"

"I'm talking collective romanticism, of course: Blake, not Colette. Archetypal. Jungian maybe."

Decay. Romanticism. Old men schlepping scrap metal. It left Jerome uncomfortable.

"What's this sculpture going to look like?" he asked.

"Some kind of tower, I think. I like towers. Taut's Monument to the Fourth International, or the Jones Beach pylon. There's something about towers. Being up high is clarifying. It reduces things below to their essences. New York doesn't have enough towers—"

"Skyscrapers?"

"They're *functional*. Mine will be totemic. I'm thinking of having some kind of lookout on top of the tower. Maybe a kind of podium where people could speak . . ."

"And where are you planning to build this lookout?"

"In the subbasement."

"A tower in a basement?"

"A tower rising out of a basement. A tower that turns the idea of a tower upside down, so to speak. Feel like seeing it?"

As he spoke, something unwieldy began to animate him. Jerome sensed gears starting to turn within, pistons shooting back and forth, and some indeterminate mechanism grinding into motion. *The Master Builder. The Prime Mover*. High above the rabble in his preserve, Dwight had become the master of this grubby universe.

"The elevator doesn't work without a key," he said, leading them into the corridor. "Gottlieb—he's the owner—doesn't want anyone using the elevator, so he's locked it, but I got a key made anyway. I'll get you a copy. I never let the band use the elevator. They can get out of hand and might wreck something." The great hulking elevator came, large enough to accommodate a small truck, lit by a feeble yellow bulb. Dwight threw the accordioned cage door shut, pushed a lever forward, and they descended, pulleys and cables sighing, resentful of having to work after so many years in service. Like the fire escape, it seemed ready to break free at any moment.

"That's as far as she goes," Dwight explained when the car shuddered to a stop. The cold air was thick as chocolate, and they followed the tenuous circle of Dwight's flashlight toward a door that led to a landing high above the subbasement's vast concrete box. The air was damp, and a far wall bore large splotches of moisture like writing. In a distant corner, three guys stood in a pool of harsh white light, and a moment later, an explosion of sound shook the walls.

"That's them," Dwight said, shouting over the din. "The band." They started down a long staircase.

"How come there's electricity down here while the rest of the building is dark?"

"We pirate it from the next building," Dwight answered and motioned to a thick black cable running along the floor. The air grew damper as they walked down the stairs that ran along the wall, and Jerome expected to see water at the bottom.

The music suddenly stopped, leaving a ringing silence behind. "Hey," a guy with long hair said, waving up to Dwight. The two guys with him looked up and nodded: a burly drummer bare-chested but for a leather vest, and a bass player whose wooly hair was pulled down to twin Mickey Mouse ears with a baseball cap.

"Got a new piece for you, Graham," Dwight said, his voice sheathed with echo. "Feel like doing it sometime?"

"Sure." The music cranked up again.

"Here's what I was talking about," Dwight said, moving to the opposite end of the space. A large platform had been assembled from rubble lashed tightly together with wire. "The base of the tower," he explained. "It's going to reach all the way up there by the time I'm finished." He pointed to the ceiling, looming a good fifteen feet above them.

"Gottlieb isn't coming back any time soon, is he?"

"Not until the end of August, so I have until then. You'll help too, won't you? I mean, if you stay here?"

Jerome rubbed the chill from his arms. He'd consider it, sure, but it was hard to think of anything at all while the band's rumble coursed around them. There was something just a little odd about employing an army of homeless people to put together whatever it was Dwight had planned in this spooky underground cavern. Dwight, always a little strange, had grown even weirder, more disconnected from simple, ordinary, three-dimensional, everyday *things*. Jerome had learned from being around those people in New Cornwall that if you strayed too far from those kinds of *things* for too long, it was hard getting back. But he did need a place to live. And Dwight seemed to want him to stay.

"Sure," Jerome said. But only until his life assumed a more tenable course, he told himself. Until he got back to where he knew he was. Until he could speak to Agatha and make her understand so that she might love him again.

The band seemed to practice all the time, an army drilling for an invasion, and its amplitude's menace found him no matter where in the building he was. *Fremde Geige* yet again, he thought, but this went way beyond what even a hundred violins might do. Where to sleep? Jerome needed to be as far from the band as possible. Dwight slept alone in his loft, so Jerome settled in a windowless cubicle on Dwight's floor. At least the door closed securely, but the mattress barely softened the concrete, and the sound of the band was never far. He was glad to get up in the morning and leave for work. *No, I won't stay here too long,* he told himself. *Just for the summer.*

An unending flow of people laden down with rusting junk were forever tramping into the building. The city was a bottomless reservoir of scrap metal that Dwight's eager assistants fetched homeward, and the ground floor's ceaseless activity brought to mind some miserable English factory town with its chartered streets, marks of weakness, and all other signs of woe. The oldest and most feeble-looking of the minions might be seen lugging a car door, the shell of an air conditioner, or a pair of file-cabinet drawers, sweating and panting in their rags. *Slaves, slaves, all slaves,* he thought, *but no one complains.* On the contrary: all seemed happy for their space in Dwight's hostel. Jerome kept away from the basement and didn't ask Dwight about the project, but he felt he had to do something to contribute, so in a weak moment, he volunteered to steal food from the Seven Wonders warehouse.

Loewenthal began giving Jerome a lift home regularly, and for most of the drive, he himself talked.

It had been one thing when the ride had lasted only until Williamsburg, but now Jerome had to listen to another twenty minutes of Loewenthal's litany of woes, and by the time they reached Manhattan, his head bulged with his boss's misery. But Jerome went along with it. There was the practical standpoint of saving a token. The Olds was spacious and beat the subway. Loewenthal gave him beer. But little by little, Jerome sensed that Loewenthal needed someone to talk to, and he found himself wanting to listen.

"Last night we were eating supper and out of nowhere Stevie starts imitating that guy who's been calling up my wife," Loewenthal said one evening. They wound past cemeteries perched on the hillocks alongside the Interboro Parkway. "You wouldn't believe the filth spewing out of a ten-year-old's mouth. He's done it before, too. At first I thought he'd picked it up at school, then Rhoda says, 'Oh my God, that's him.' If this keeps up, I'm really going to lose my mind."

Jerome nodded sympathetically. Sometimes he thought that Loewenthal secretly admired the caller's nerve and the reckless pursuit of his desires.

"Maybe I'm thinking about it too much," Loewenthal said. "But it's almost like he . . . he's already had her. My blood boils each time the phone rings. I want to kill him."

But one evening it was hard listening to Loewenthal. The band had practiced all night. It'd felt like sleeping atop a cyclotron, and Jerome hadn't dozed off for more than an hour at one time. Dwight's idea of relaxing after work on the tower was snorting a couple of lines, sitting close to the speakers and getting blasted away. Jerome's gaze wandered over the lush green of the cemetery grass. The contemplation of death countered life's pettiness. *Sic transit gloria mundi,* he reflected, and speaking of *transit,* maybe he should start taking the subway again.

Loewenthal's hands choked up on the wheel. "I'm beginning to think that he always manages to get through to her because . . . she . . . because maybe she likes listening to him. Maybe she actually plans to be there when he calls. Maybe she *wants* him to call because she thinks . . . because maybe . . . she thinks she'll get from him what she's not getting from me." He paused. "We haven't exactly been very passionate lately."

An awkward silence ensued. Jerome saw Loewenthal's fleshy torso spangled with points of sweat, churning over a naked woman's body, his hefty rear wobbling as he ached toward climax. Jerome forced the image from his mind by studying the tombstones. *Entries in a ledger, solemn as a New England churchyard.* Goldsmith. Robert Lowell and E. Dickinson. *Because I could not stop for death.* (Enough with the references, he heard Rose say.) A dirgelike hexameter sounded in Jerome's ears, the slow progress of a funeral cortege.

Granite slabs
to mark the debts of unnumbered lives
known only as nine digits to
their creditors.

No: too stiff. (Get it?)

"Maybe I'm getting jealous," Loewenthal said, chugging down the last of his beer. "Imagine, a guy jealous of his own wife. Tell me, Jerry, you ever get jealous over a woman? I mean, really jealous? Hey, Jerry, wake up. I'm talking to you!"

"Sorry," he said. "Can't the police put a tap on your phone to figure out who's been making those calls?"

Loewenthal fired him a look. "You haven't even been listening to me. I should make you get out and walk. Hey, you've been pretty quiet today. What gives?"

"I'm tired."

"Burning the candle at both ends, is that it?" He grinned at Jerome. "So what's keeping you up?"

"Not what you think."

Suddenly they were turning off at the next exit. "I want to show you something," Loewenthal said, and soon they were driving through a cemetery gate topped with wrought-iron Stars of David. Gravel spit out from under the tires.

What was this? Jerome had long ago severed himself from the harsh canon of Jewish law, and he couldn't remember the last time he'd been in a cemetery. *Lustbader, Greenblatt, Richter, Schumacher.* The many silent names engraved in granite formed a procession, a litany that might have been an appeal. *Come back,* they whispered. *Come back because you're one of us. You were born a Jew, and a Jew you will die.* Once he'd believed, fingers caressing the lines of a siddur's Hebrew during a junior congregation Sabbath service, words that through their very inscrutability formed a mystical chain. If he only held on, he might pull himself forward to some celestial other side, like that ferry in Boy Scout camp propelled by tugs at a guy line across Lake Ranachqua. But no more. Religion—it mattered little which—was just one more voice saying no, not, and never. *Greenberg, Silverman, Freund*—names Germanized, like his own. Jerome Brynstyn. Who gave the Teutons the right to remake someone's last name in their own linguistic image? *Auf deutschen Wesen soll die Welt genesen.* What a crock of *Scheisse.*

They drove on. How vast the dominion of death, and how complacent. Come to think of it, the very concept of death seemed German, too. Mann's *Death in Venice.* Schubert's *Death and the Maiden.* Schoenberg's *Death and Transfiguration.* Bach's *Christ Lay in the Bonds of Death.* Boecklin's *Isle of the Dead.* What, nothing about birth? *Jawohl: The Birth of Tragedy.* Well, so much for life. Germany? *Feh!*—except for Rilke and Kafka, but they were Czech.

Mandlebaum, Nudelman, Katz. The Jews were by and large a gentle people, he thought. The goyim were always violent:

Christ-militant. "A Mighty Fortress is Our God." The Salvation Army. Praise the Lord and pass the ammunition. Holy wars. Crusades. The Jews would have been content to spend the centuries indoors reading books and eating pot roast. They were stubborn, proud, petty, and obsessive, yet ultimately harmless. There were plenty of assholes among them—his brother-in-law, for example. Roy Cohn. Plus some others. But by and large, most Jews were probably okay. And Lester Loewenthal wasn't that bad, either.

They pulled up beside a large tombstone, one much larger than any surrounding it. Loewenthal kept the engine running. "Silver" was chiseled severely upon it. Its granite gleamed in the sun, hard-edged, angled, calmly immoveable. *Beloved Husband, Father and Grandfather,* Jerome read. The words were like commands.

"Here was I disgraced," Loewenthal said. "Here was I laid low by my very own brother in front of my whole family and my child." He turned off the ignition. The throb of the expressway quieted to a tranquil hum. "Come, Jerry."

They approached the grave and stood there for a long time. Then Loewenthal reached down and picked up a stone, smoothing it between his fingers. Jerome expected him to place it on the grave, but instead, he hurled it. "Goddammit!" he cried. "My life is shot. My whole life is shot!"

"What's the matter, Mr. Loewenthal?" There was probably some Jewish law against throwing rocks at graves.

"Everything's shot, goddammit. Do you hear what I said? Everything! My marriage, my business, my life. Everything! And this is all that's waiting for me." He picked up another stone and threw it.

"Mr. Loewenthal—"

"What are you going to tell me, that everything's going to work out okay? That everything'll be fine? Why should things work out any differently than how they already are?" He spoke like water coming to a boil. "You're too young to understand what I'm talking about." He went for another stone.

"You shouldn't do that."

"Why shouldn't I? Do you think God will come down and strike me dead? Let him! In fact, I'd *love* for him to. It'll save me the trouble of filing for Chapter Eleven. And I'll tell Him what I think of Him! Then He'll finish me off and they can bury me in my wife's garden." He let the stone fly and thrust his face skyward, his arms outstretched. "Okay. Come and get me!"

"What did you mean when you said you were shamed here?" Jerome asked softly.

Loewenthal didn't seem to have heard but stared at a row of shrubs that bordered the plot. "Privet," he said. "That's what she wants around the perimeter. Nine dollars and twenty-three cents a shrub, one per foot along the three sides of the yard, so that makes . . . two hundred, which brings the total up to . . . Wait, I forgot that she wants to alternate it with something else. What was it? Whatever it was, she said it costs a dollar more per shrub." He began kicking the shrubs. "Pri-vet at nine dollars twen-ty-three a god-damn *piece,*" he barked, marking each syllable with a vengeful thrust of his foot.

"Mr. Loewenthal," Jerome said, eyes darting around to see if anyone saw.

Loewenthal thrust his hands toward the foliage, wrenched out a bush, hurled it through the air, roots trailing a lacy spray of soil, and it landed like a wedding bouquet in the neighboring plot. He went for another, sending it flying.

Someone was honking at them. "What you doing?" shouted a voice from behind: a man in a truck from the cemetery.

Another shrub arced into the air.

"Hey!" the man shouted.

"Let's get out of here," said Jerome. The vandalized hedge border resembled a row of broken of teeth.

A Hispanic man was coming toward them in bright orange overalls. "What you doing? You crazy?" He picked up one of the shrubs.

Loewenthal faced him, and a strange smile curled his lips.

"What am I doing? I'm gardening. I'm *weed*ing."

"You get out of here," the man said. "I call security."

Loewenthal laughed. "See that tombstone? I paid for it. I paid for each one of these goddamn hedges, too. And I'm paying for them again, so I can do what the hell I please with them." He reached into his pocket for his wallet, pulled out a handful of bills and threw them toward the man. "Here. Go and plant."

Later that evening, Jerome set down the heavy backpack and stepped gingerly onto the fire escape, beer in hand. Dwight was nowhere to be seen. Jerome's stomach growled with hunger. He and Dwight had fallen into a routine of eating together, except that Dwight always kept him waiting.

There's something I have to tell you, Jerry. I don't even know how I'm going to make it through the end of the summer. I might have to let you go . . .

Shee-it, as one of those guys in the band might say. Jerome understood it now: the whole scene in the cemetery had just been a scam, a way to soften Jerome up for the bad news. But if he really gave Jerome the ax, then what was going to happen? Jerome had held on by a thread all summer as it was, and the thread was the job. It was dependable and simple and punched each day into shape, boxes unfolded and flaps secured. Much else had proven precarious and slight, but the job was there each morning. Having it meant not having to think about what came next. It got him away from Dwight's bunker. Best of all, it left him too tired to think about Agatha. *I think you're a great kid, and if there's anything I can do to keep you on, you know I will . . .*

"Sorry I'm late," Dwight said, appearing at the window, a loaf of Italian bread under his arm. "You didn't eat, did you?"

"No, Dwight." Jerome was ready to lose his job and Dwight worried about dinner plans. For someone who barely lived on the material plane, Dwight's gourmet tastes were suspect. He produced a pair of candles that he fixed to the slats of the fire escape with melted wax.

"What do you have for us today?" he asked, lighting them. "Not baby shrimp again, I hope." Cooked, veined baby shrimp from Thailand had become something of a staple that summer; the small cans packed in cartons of twelve were easy to lift. Jerome never bothered to look very closely at what he tossed into his backpack, terrified that Loewenthal might catch him.

"Don't complain," said Jerome, grinding open a can as fast as he could. He was famished, and he pulled out a dripping fistful. The shrimp gurgled in his mouth as he chewed. He passed the can to Dwight.

"Great, you got jumbo shrimp this time." Dwight speared one of the dripping morsels delicately with a fork and savored the shrimp as if tasting it for the first time. "Oh, what do we have here?" he asked, eyeing another can. "Stuffed grape leaves!" He opened the can and popped one of the dark green packets into his mouth, then stopped. "Turkish olive oil," he said with a dissatisfied twist of his nose. "I bet that's what they used for these. It's coarser, *stickier* than Greek olive oil." He checked the label. "*Aha.* Just what I said: 'Product of Turkey.' " He set the can down. "You might want to tell your boss to get only the Greek kind."

I'll special order it, Jerome thought, hooking more fistfuls of shrimp into his mouth as quickly as he could. At first he'd been only too glad to steal from Loewenthal, a kind of redistribution of the wealth. But as the summer went on, the thieving increased, and Jerome began to feel uncomfortable. He was about to reach for another helping when he cut himself on the sharp edge of the can.

"Shit," he said, sucking on the wound. The thumb smarted with brine, and the flat taste of blood mixed with the juice's spice. Was this how human flesh tasted when cannibals marinated it?

"You're getting blood into the shrimp," Dwight complained, pointing to the candy-cane trail around Jerome's finger.

He pushed the tainted can toward Jerome. "You finish the rest of this." He opened a fresh can.

"I won't infect you, for Chrissake!"

"You're certainly in one foul mood," Dwight said.

"How come you were late?"

"I found a bunch of copper tubing and it took me a long time to get it home."

"Well, while you were worrying about your little *art* project, my boss told me that he might fire me."

Dwight studied him. "You don't like what I'm doing, do you?"

"I'm too tired to think about art tonight."

"My project makes you uncomfortable."

"You're right."

"You think I'm exploiting all those people on the first floor."

In college, Dwight had conscripted other students into his life-size designs, but since most people in the real world didn't work for free, he'd had to fall back on homeless people. They were marionettes, and he their puppeteer, Blake's architect, compass poised to blueprint the world, a Great White Father in black.

"Maybe."

"You've hardly been down there since that first day."

"Correct." Jerome had seen the Feelie's Wheel boys swaggering in through the ground-floor door at all hours, boots clunking against the concrete floor, startling the people on their blankets like a pack of centurions before a row of peasants. That was all he needed to see. They were nothing but urban rednecks, dangerous and frightening.

"I already told you, Jerome. Those people downstairs don't have to do it. They're all volunteers."

"If they don't work, they know you'll kick them out. And where are they going to go? If I didn't bring home all this stuff from work, you'd kick me out too, wouldn't you?"

Just then a woman appeared in the window. Paned behind

glass, her face had the untouched quality of a plaster saint upon a shelf. Long hair draped her shoulders, and she wore a long dress of soiled white satin.

"Hello, Sharon," Dwight said.

Jerome had seen her floating through the building, always in that same dress. She'd followed Dwight back to the place a week or two ago. She was quite pretty, but any time Jerome had tried talking to her, she'd vanished like a forest sprite, bits of song escaping her lips, Ophelia-like, a fairy-tale princess in Dwight's gutted castle.

"Come on out here and have something to eat, Sharon," Dwight said.

She remained before the glass.

"Did you see my father out there?" she whispered.

Jerome looked at Dwight. He gave Jerome an I'll-explain-later expression.

"Is he out there?" she asked.

"No, he isn't, but why don't you just come out here and have something—"

She disappeared.

"She's shell-shocked after some guys stabbed her father in a building where she used to live," Dwight explained.

"Does she actually believe he's here?"

"I'm not really sure what she believes. She said her father used to speak to her from outside her window after he died, whatever that means. I worry about her being here, but she says she won't go back home."

"Once I tried to talk to her, but she ran away."

"She's scared of her own shadow. I'm terrified of coming home one afternoon and finding her facedown on the sidewalk." He took another stuffed grape leaf. "The Greek kind really are much better, you know."

Jerome threw himself over onto his side in his windowless, cinder-block chamber. The room baked when the door was closed, but it was the best way to escape the band, even if their poisonous rays rose through the floor. Heavy metal, heavy water, heavy ions—all toxic. Rehearse. Re-hearse. It was like dying again each time they plugged in their amps. He squinted into the pitch black of his cubicle, trying to make out his own hands, but in such utter darkness, nothing could be seen, nothing existed. A room without any light was enough to turn one crazy. His stomach gave a rumble of warning. These days it took little to send him into a panic. Subway tracks were gleaming, long-haired sirens, luring him to their sleek third rail. Produce stands on Second Avenue were heaped with suspicious-looking apples. The token guy at the Prince Street station was ready to sell him a slug and alert a transit cop. Agatha haunted him. In Williamsburg, a river safely between them, the prospect of a bleary-eyed subway ride always chastened his yearning for her. Now a mere ten-minute zigzag of streets separated them. Ever since she evicted him, the universe rattled with loose screws. The whole city fidgeted, one monstrous, amputated limb.

How dare you go and ransack my dreams?

Yes, he'd eavesdropped, he'd transcribed. And yes, he might have read a line or two in her diaries. More than one or two lines, actually. A lot more. But it was just research. Agatha wouldn't listen. *You've probably lifted from other people, too. I knew you were a hack, even in New Cornwall.* That had hurt. Yet she was doing the same thing by keeping his journals. Maybe she was rummaging through them this very minute.

It would serve him right.

The other night, he'd seen her turning onto First Avenue. He'd longed to throw himself at her, the same black passion aroused that might just as easily love or destroy. He ducked into a doorway. Then he saw. Someone was with her, some kid. Jerome pulled back, enraged. Who the hell was this little protegé? They passed close enough for him to reach out and pull the kid like a snapping turtle yanking a duck under water. He followed them, watched them climb her stoop and go inside.

He imagined her cooking their supper, the two of them taking their baths—did she still love bathing as she used to?—and then their going to bed together—

He began to sweat. Trying to sleep was pointless. He had to get out of there, so he threw on some clothes and left. Ghostly wings of plastic flapped in the windows of the main room. Dwight's room was empty; no doubt he'd already coked up and would spend the rest of the night working on the tower. Jerome took the freight elevator—Time's winged chariot?—all the way down.

Music flooded the ground floor, and each step down to the subbasement immersed him deeper into the chilly ooze. He opened the door.

Why is life always full with doubt,
Plagued by complications unforeseen?
Predictability is all I care about.
I love the age of machines.
I crave the strength of electricity
and the drama of routine.
I can't cope with impulsivity.
I need the strength of machines.

Sound scraped the walls. Dwight sat directly before the band, an audience of one, locked in a deep-freeze of cocaine, blasted by a high-decibel wind. His sculpture brooded in darkness. Since Jerome had moved in, it had grown perilously high.

Individuality I will replace,
all the world I will redeem.
I will create a master race
in the age of machines.
Misery will end,
machines will be our friends,
minds will be at peace,
thinking will cease,

in the age of machines—
in my age of machines.

The music stopped. "Yes," Dwight said. "Very nice . . ."

Jerome slipped back outside.

"Help me," said a voice on the landing. Sharon's face pooled before him in the darkness.

"I'm afraid," she said.

"What's the matter?"

"Please." She took hold of his arm and they went up the stairs together. But just as he was about to unlock the elevator, she took off.

"Hey!" he called after her.

She kept on going, and he had no choice except to follow her.

But he couldn't catch up.

4

Raymond

There were many of them, more than there should have been, perhaps. One with deep-set eyes almost too painful to look at, another with a face heavy with memory far exceeding his age. College students, mostly. Salesmen. A man in his late fifties, mustache and hair the shiny, damp color of silverfish. The cheesy motel had a bed with a furry, orange spread, old-fashioned beer-ad labels reproduced on mirrors. He looked almost sad as he pulled off my bra. His mouth tasted like sour apple juice, and his skin was soft and powdery. He mounted me, and I carried him until a storm gathered across his face and he moaned and shivered and sighed.

One night after Owen left, I noticed an empty space between two shingles. Had it always been there? I strained to be sure and looked until I saw a crack, one large enough to peek through. Then I began to remember. There were times when creaking sounds sifted through the noise of my pleasure. I'd assumed it had been the floorboards. But it had been him. The monster. Watching.

New Cornwall, June 30

The warm weather has loosed wildness within me. I feel as Phyllis must when she paints. My bitterness matures, ripens, gaining fat and fragrance like a good, hard cheese. I savor its putrescence. I could almost belch.

I hope I leave here furious.

EIGHT

That summer I began sleeping in the nude. Mornings I awoke with my own fuzzy smell funneling around me, stuck like melted chocolate to the sheets. But discomfort or no, I was determined to get used to it. My new self-image deemed pajamas with their stripes, paisleys, and oversized buttons ridiculous. I wanted to become the kind of person who slept in the nude. People who lived in hotels and didn't get up until the middle of the afternoon slept in the nude. People who breakfasted out—or who used the word "breakfasted"—slept in the nude, too. Most important, people who had a lot of sex slept in the nude, and that, more than anything else, had me enduring those sticky morning sheets. Sex was almost all I thought about that summer, just as I had last summer, except that this summer I not only thought about it but was aware of thinking about it. I knew everyone around me was thinking about it, too. I was soft and untested, wallowing in horniness as nineteenth-century poets did in consumption. My virginity tightened around me like a skin I was eager to shed.

Oh yes, it was everywhere that summer, sex was, bulging,

entwining, oozing through the humid streets of the city. The proof of guilty pleasure branded everyone, its marks visible to my newly sharp eyes. I'd fix a couple sitting opposite me on the subway in my sights and rummage through their glances until I saw the grip, tussle, and push of their night before, until I smelled the rumple of their bed and heard their last moans fading away. Shiny-haired Puerto Rican women, dresses tight as bodices, clicked their way through the lobby of the building where I worked, their high heels setting off sparks of desire. Even subway conductors hid randiness beneath their baggy uniforms. Everyone seemed on the verge of a bump and a grind—everyone, that is, except me. It was maddening.

Every night I turned out the lights and with ritual solemnity stepped out of my clothes. I stood before the open window for a moment before dipping down into the still pool of the sheets, willing some embodiment of passion to materialize, a naked and randy genie from some forbidden bottle. It never did, of course, so I had no choice but to rub myself hard and wet. I was copious: I rubbed it into my hands until my skin was sticky as a child's with a Hershey bar. I fell asleep breathing the lush and bitter smell of guys.

Guys. The ones around where I lived were clumsy and not too bright. You never knew when they'd substitute a punch at you for an answer. They spread out in the hallways, traveling in unwieldy clumps, monster cells swallowing everything in their path. But downtown, I discovered men: the crisp stride of a businessman in a suit, the open pleasure of a guy in shorts and a T, or a sanitation worker thick with muscle as he heaved trash cans. Men swaggered, slouched, or slid down the street. They chugged and hunched, swung and surged, and when they turned their heads, veins pumped their limbs with current. Even my father began to look different. Before, he'd been a stick figure bent over his drafting table, but that summer he was fleshed out into three randy dimensions, all the world's restless fornication coalesced into his.

* * *

Since school was out, I had no schedule to shape my days. I still had no job. It was hot, and the sole room in the house with an air conditioner was my mother's, camphored and off limits. The air was seeded with grit swirling up from the gutter, the subways vacuum-packed. The neighborhood pool filled up like a fish hatchery by midday. Summer was like the blinding white on the screen at the end of a home movie. I got an uneasy taste of what it meant to have absolutely nothing, nothing in the world to do.

I went downtown to see about a Parks Department job. I was hardly alone. A thick braid of dark-skinned arms and legs crowded the grimy corridor of a city office building, dank in spite of air conditioning. Kids hooted to friends, drank soda, and played radios to bursting. Their sidelong glances told me I didn't belong. The line advanced inches at a time. People snuck ahead of me, but I knew better than to complain, for most of the guys looked springy with belligerence. I asked the guy in front of me what kind of jobs there were. He was about my age. A large gold cross dangled over his tank top.

"Pickin' up junk, mostly." He took a closer look at me. "If they ask you where you want, better tell them Central Park, otherwise they might send you someplace bad."

Shortly after eleven, a man announced that all the jobs had been filled. An angry chorus of "Shee-it!" and "Damn!" broke out. Somebody picked up a chair and hurled it in disgust. Someone else kicked the water fountain so hard that water began to shoot out. Security guards appeared, and the crowd pressed toward the emergency stairway.

"Follow me," the kid with the cross said, heading for a second stairway.

"Those people up there was crazy," he said when we were on the street, and I detected a trace of embarrassment at me having seen his people behave badly. We turned a corner onto

Madison Avenue, cool and shaded by awnings. Expensive stores lined the block, windows polished as glassware. Women in summer dresses strode by, distant behind sunglasses. Men looking prosperous in suits threw a bitter mint of cologne to the staccato of shoe taps. The kid eyed them all, wary, his cross like an amulet to ward off any menace in this alien territory.

"What are you going to do this summer?" I asked as we reached the subway.

"Don't really know," he said, slipping down the stairs with a bounce in his step. "Catch you later." The gold cross and chain disappeared into the electric dark of the subway, coins lost through a sidewalk grating, and the rest of the day yawned before me.

With my mother away and her room sealed off, my father and I became roommates in a smaller apartment, GIs bunking in the same barracks, boarders in a rooming house. My mother's disapproving spirit hovered close; we both lived in her house without her knowledge. It felt as if we'd begun a new life, each of us without a past. I hoped my father might say where he'd been and what he'd done, but he didn't, and he seemed to wait for my report. For the time being, I too kept silent.

At first we tried to preserve the domestic routines of cooking meals, eating together, and washing up. But soon each of us was fending for himself: hamburger from the freezer, things you added water to or heated up from a can. I'd come home to find several rubbery slices left over from a pizza that I'd wash down with the beer my father had begun keeping in the refrigerator. My mother's clean kitchen yellowed with the grime of the bachelors we'd become. Housekeeping only made sense for a family, not for transients like us. He worked at his drafting table as before, but most of the time I'd see him idly drawing, a can of beer at his side. Like me, he seemed unsure of what he was supposed to be doing.

One Saturday my father decided to take me swimming.

"Hurry up and get changed," he said, unbuttoning his shirt

beside me in the locker room of the public pool. He stood, nearly naked in his underwear, pink and somewhat frail, despite the muscle of his arms and legs. She saw him like this, that woman. *Paul, is that you?* All around us, guys monkeyed around, carrying on as though they were in their own bathrooms, underwear startlingly white against dark thighs and coffee-colored bellies. The black kids had strong, adult bodies. The PRs were shorter and gentler-looking, with bittersweet-chocolate eyes, thick necks hung with delicate gold crosses, appealing but for their oily skin and stubbly mustaches. I felt transported back to the Parks Department office. My father and I were outnumbered; the only other white people were mean-looking Irish kids who brooded amongst themselves in one corner, plotting to wrest control of the locker room.

I put off undressing, hoping that if I dawdled long enough, my father would give up making me change and I'd be free to leave. In high school, I always took pains to get assigned a locker in a far corner, gaining at least two walls of privacy if I couldn't have four. No matter what, gym class was unbearable, the heartless revenge taken on the smart kids. We loped around on the edges of the gym like elders, waiting for the indignity to end, while basketballers dribbled smoothly past us. Barry alone enjoyed gym, throwing himself over the horse and parallel bars, sweating profusely, face burning, arms roped with veins, savoring, I thought, the discomfort.

"What's the matter?" my father asked, setting his shirt on the hanger he'd brought with him.

Guys were the matter. Their nakedness at arm's length was disconcerting. I yearned to take a finger to the shiny curve of their biceps or to the bulge of muscle that hardened in their thighs as they walked. I yearned to press against them and feel their human pulse. But I knew better than to try.

My father stepped out of his underwear, shyly turning toward his locker for cover, completely naked. His skin let off a cloud of musk—he'd stopped using deodorant since coming home—and his body was strong and wiry, youthful and less wrinkled than his face. Beside him, I felt soft and only partially formed. He turned, and then I saw it. It loped forward, playful, bearing a smooth, shy head. Large, too, and ruddy as a drunk. Had it always been this large? Had it grown larger since the last time I'd seen it? *Since he and that woman . . .* One thing was certain: mine was never going to be as big. He gave himself an audible scratch between his legs, the skin of his balls pulled tight, and his thing's head pushed forward in what seemed a smirk. *Never as big as me,* it said. *Never. Too bad.*

I'd taken off one sneaker when two Puerto Rican kids charged past us in a snarl of Spanish. They nearly toppled my father, poised storklike on one leg, about to insert his other leg into his trunks. He tumbled against the lockers, his flesh jabbing against a sharp metal corner, and he looked ready to fall.

"Hey!" he cried out, struggling to right himself. His thing loped forward, a passenger on a train coming to a sudden halt.

"Sorry," one of them mumbled, slipping away.

"I knew we shouldn't have come here," I said.

My father pulled on his bathing suit and gave the drawstring an impatient pull. "You've been acting like a shit all morning."

Maybe he was right, but it was his fault for bringing me here in the first place. My mother would never have thought of doing something like this. And I had another reason to be belligerent: I wanted to know exactly what was going on between him and that woman. I wanted to find out who she was. I wanted to meet her.

When I'd finally changed, we made for the deck, carrying our beach chairs and ice chest. The turquoise pool was surrounded by a dark and tangled landscape planted with the colorful flowers of beach umbrellas. The air shook with Spanish music and the bass boom of the soul station from radios the size of farm animals. People played cards, ate, changed their children's diapers, and argued. Chunky women with gumdrop-colored nails wore full makeup and complicated hairdos more suitable to a wedding than to a swimming pool. Two little black girls splashed each other in the water close by, bobbing up and down to cries of delight each time one netted the other with a veil of water. My father and I were crashing a party in full swing where we knew no one.

"This is nice," he said, setting up his chair. He reached for a can of soda and stretched his legs, content. I sank into my beach chair, feeling exposed in my bathing suit. "Why don't you go in for a swim?" he asked.

"Too crowded."

"Soda?"

I accepted the can he'd pressed my way but set it down on the grass without opening it, knowing that would annoy him.

"Are you going to tell me what's eating you?"

"Who's that woman who picked up the phone when I called the other night?"

He uttered a little snort of surprise. I let my question sit. Soon his lips betrayed the hint of a smile. Unlike my mother, he never stayed angry about anything for too long. "Well, who do you think it was?"

"That woman, right?"

"Maybe."

"What's her name?"

"None of your beeswax."

"Tell me." Something had begun to take hold of me—anger, salted with satisfaction at having discovered a weakness in my otherwise perfect father. Uncle Alfred was right: my father had always been the good guy of the family, impossible to blame, flawless as a teacup. Now he was beginning to show hairline cracks. Only then did I have some soda, savoring his discomfort.

"You fucked her, right?" I said.

The little girls in the water turned around.

"That's enough," my father said through gritted teeth.

"You fucked her!" I repeated, louder, words popping out

of my evil jack-in-the-box mouth. More people looked our way.

"Shut up!" He lifted his arm, looking ready to strike, and I jerked back. The can of soda flew from my hands, and a second later, there was a scream.

"Hey, you!"

A tall black kid pushed up in front of me, eyes lit with fury. His large bare feet bumped against my toes. The two little girls clung to each other in the pool, frightened. The soda can bobbed nearby in the water, a tiny buoy oozing orange.

"You almos' hit my little sister!" the kid said.

My father stood up. "Can I help you?"

The kid was taller than my father, and more powerfully built. I pushed closer to my father, anxious, and within seconds, a crowd of people pressed around us. Dark eyes turned our away, accusing. It was the Parks Department office all over again, only worse.

"I ain't talking to you, Mister. I'm talking to this chump that wanted to hit my little sister—"

"I didn't want to hit your damn sister!" I mumbled.

"Your sister's fine," my father said to the kid.

"Hey, this is between him and *me,*" the kid said to my father, plugging an angry thumb against his naked chest.

"Darryl, I gotta go pee!" the shorter of the girls said.

Her brother threw me a look of disgust. "You best keep your cans out my way." He threw a fist toward me, more to frighten than to hit. I ducked. To my shame, my father saw.

"Darryl, she makin' in the water," the second girl cried, paddling away.

We stayed for an hour, no more, then collected our things and left. My father said almost nothing on the bus ride home.

"Come into the kitchen, you," he told me, taking out a six-pack from the refrigerator. "Sit down." He slid one can over to me and snapped open the other. He chugged down his beer, leaning back in his chair as he let out a belch of satisfaction. I could almost hear my mother ordering him to sit up straight so the chair leg wouldn't dent the linoleum. "Drink," he said.

I drank. The beer tasted cold, sour and bitter, as beer always did.

"You can be a shit sometimes, do you know that?"

He'd never spoken to me like this. He wouldn't have if my mother were there.

"I'm not a shit," I said.

"So why'd you pull that little stunt at the pool?"

I shrugged, satisfied and embarrassed at the same time.

"I want to tell you one thing, Ray," he said. "Whatever happens, I love your mother. We might not always get along, but I love her." He clutched his can. "And I don't want you mouthing off like today again."

"That woman irons your shirts, doesn't she?" I said. I'd seen a stack of them in the living room.

"I didn't ask her to. She just did it."

"Mom once told me that a woman ironing her husband's shirts was a sign of true love." I thought of Saturday afternoons when freshly ironed shirts hung in the foyer like banners in a castle hall. "So does that mean you love her?"

"It might mean that she loves me."

"Well, does she?"

He looked down. "Maybe."

He was quiet. I felt him letting me share his silence.

"This is all new to me," he finally said. "Speaking of your mother, you got a postcard from Israel, didn't you?"

It had been mailed to my uncle's house, where my mother assumed I was, and he'd slipped it into an envelope and mailed it to me. Everything in Israel was magnificent, moving, and wonderful, she wrote. The Wailing Wall, the Dead Sea Scrolls, the old city of Jaffa—all of it. She'd included a phone number. The other side of the card showed a panorama of Jerusalem. The city looked congested and very hot.

She hadn't mentioned my father, not one word.

"So what do you think of this little excursion of hers?"

Sarcasm thorned the question. He finished his first beer and snapped open a second.

"She always wanted to go to Israel," I said.

"She was just running away, Raymond."

"She made two plane reservations."

"Who told you that?"

"She did. One for each of you. Then she canceled the second one."

"I didn't realize you and your mother were such confidantes," he said. "Such . . . bosom buddies." He studied me. "Guess you found more to talk about with her than with me."

It was true: I never knew what to tell him, and not telling him didn't seem to matter. My father was like a tree: if it didn't rain or if the sun didn't shine, all he did was drop a few leaves.

"Let's retire to the drawing room," he suggested, picking up what was left of the six-pack.

In the short time my mother had been away, the living room, like the kitchen, had been transformed, becoming my father's domicile. Wallet and reading glasses, a pile of change, and his watch lay on the glass-topped coffee table. Shoes lined one wall, and shirts were hung on the backs of chairs or strewn over the sofa. He sat down at his desk, took out a T-square, a pencil, and a sheet of paper, that he began to line.

"How come you like lettering so much?" I asked, thinking of that guy who'd been over at Stuie's house.

"There was a time I wanted to be an artist," he said above the whisper of the pencil. "I wanted to be a painter. I took my little sketchbook with me all the time wherever I went. I wanted to draw everything. I thought I could capture everything." His eyes followed the pencil. "You get these kinds of ideas early on, but soon you forget them."

"What kind of ideas?"

"Delusions of grandeur, they call them."

He blames the whole world because he didn't become an artist, my mother had said on one of those nights before the TV set.

"You could still do it."

The T-square moved down the page at even intervals, and before long, the paper bore a series of roads for the traffic of letters about to roll. "If you're a painter, you think you can hold onto what you see. Or else you think you can change it. Maybe it's not that much different from being married, in a way—but sometimes things shift or slip away. They move, and anything that moves, changes, and you can never be sure how they'll wind up." He looked my way. "Did your mother happen to tell you when she'd be coming back?"

Your mother. He made it sound like they weren't related. "In about five weeks."

"Five weeks," he repeated and reached for his pen. The nib made a delicate scratching: *oaobocodoeofogo* he wrote in a stately blue to begin his writing warm-up. Alphabet necklaces, he called them. "Maybe if she'd told me beforehand about her plans . . ." he began, his thought left incomplete.

"She was always talking about going there."

"She said it so often that I never really thought she'd do it."

"Sounds like you wished you had gone with her."

"Maybe. But no matter what, she should have said something." He took another swallow of beer, and his strong grip drained the color from his knuckles. Letters began leaving his pen in an impatient line: *omonopo*. He bent over the table closely, deciphering his lettering as much as composing it: *oqorosoto*. "What gives her the right to just pick up and leave?"

"You didn't tell anyone where you were going when you left," I pointed out.

The pen stopped. "Your mother knew from your Uncle Alfred where I was," he said, bite in his voice. "At least a couple of days later."

"Mom decided to go to Israel for sure only after she found out about you and that woman."

"What does that have to do with anything?" *ouovowoxo*. He spoke to the can of beer, not to me. *ozoaobocodo*.

"You're in love with her, aren't you?"

His eyes narrowed. "Who said anything about love?"

"Well, are you?"

"You never answer my questions," he said, suddenly gruff, beer in his voice. "Why should I answer yours? You never tell me where you go at night, for example. I've kept an eye on you."

Had he really watched? Seen? The apartment's windows faced the park, but the terrace was obscured by trees. Suddenly every limb of my body began to heat up.

"You haven't told me where you were that other night," I said, trying to bounce the questions back to him. I'd come home to find the apartment empty. "Did you go to that woman?"

He laid down his pen. "Yes," he said. "Yes. Does it bother you that I went there? Does it surprise you? Did you think I slept under a bridge?" He threw back the last of his beer. "So tell me. What do you do in the park at night? Bird-watch?"

For a moment I imagined telling him everything—about the man last summer, the explosion in his mouth, or about this other guy from last week and his muscles and how his stomach sounded when he scratched it and how I thought of both of us naked and wrestling. I glanced over to the letters on my father's worktable. *ouovowoxo*. The lines seemed the code for a message I might decipher—*ozoaobocodo*. My thoughts became a ball of pure white light that lit up the room, and for those few seconds, all became clear, obvious, and inevitable. I knew what was important for me just then, and I could almost hear myself explaining it. But something clamped around my chest, the light flickered and faded, and I said nothing.

"Looks like we have more to talk about than you thought," he said. "Here—" He pushed another beer my way.

"Just tell me one thing. Do you love her?"

"Love!" he boomed. "What do you know about love? Who do you love? Did anybody ask your mother if she loved me? And if she did, then how come she never told me about that second plane ticket? Love! It's none of your business. It was none of anybody's business and it would have stayed that way if your Uncle Lester had kept his trap shut." His voice wavered, and he went for his pen.

"Can you at least tell me her name?"

"I don't want to talk about it anymore." He jabbed the pen into the bottle of ink and resumed lettering. The ink slashed across the page, hurting it.

"Before, it sounded like you wanted to talk to me."

"You're just like your mother. You don't talk, you cross-examine. All of a sudden everyone's interested in my business. Why don't people mind their own goddamn business for a change!" His pen kept on, writing more quickly until something snapped. "She-ite!"

A fractured nib lay in a tiny pool of ink on the paper. He crumpled the paper into a tight ball, nib and all, and tossed it into the wastepaper basket but missed. He reached down, not to pick it up, but to pull out a bottle of whiskey. He pulled off the cap and took a swig. I rarely saw my father drinking anything other than beer, but it looked like he'd had that bottle there for a while.

"What I want to know is how come you're so damn interested in me and Le—" His speech began caving in. He kicked at one of the crumpled balls of paper. "Oh, just go to bed," he said, waving me away with a sloppy motion of his hand.

I went into my room without putting the light on, and I undressed. The night air was heavy and uncomfortable. I wasn't a smoker, but I took out a cigarette from an old pack, lit it, and sat naked by the open window. I switched on the radio, squeezed a blues station from Chicago and listened. My father knew things, I realized. I'd always thought his quietness was shyness, but I began to see it as a kind of disguise, a camouflage, a survival mechanism.

The Podilacks were at it again, but their strife was moderate, perhaps because they'd begun to realize it was useless, or else it was just too hot. A second cigarette left a scratchy membrane inside my throat. *No matter what, the Podilacks stayed together,* I thought. *They fought, but they stayed together.* I heard my father snoring on the couch.

Le. Lena? Leonore? I'd find out.

What do you do in the park at night? Bird-watch?"

How much did he know?

Michael was sitting on a bench on the terrace when I got there several nights later, smoking a thoughtful cigarette. The lamppost floated gleaming crescents onto his ring and naked ankles bones. My father hadn't come home that night again. The house had felt too empty, and I'd had to get out. Midway down the hall to the elevator, I realized I was angry with him. Maybe he thought he could pull this on my mother, but I wasn't about to let him get away with it. I wanted to know who this woman was.

"Hello, Andrew," he said when I sat down next to him. His aftershave slipped over me like a sheet.

"Hi." The false name let me think that someone other than myself was there with him.

"How come you're always here when I am?" I asked.

"It's only the second time."

"I think I know why, Andrew."

"No, you don't!"

"It's too hot to argue," he said.

We sat in silence for a minute or two. Then I said, "My father's messing around with this woman."

"Is that what's bothering you?"

"No. Let him do what he wants!"

"Sounds like it does bother you, Andrew." His gaze drew me in deeper. "Don't you think people should do what they want?"

"He's not 'people,' he's my father."

"What about sons, Andrew?"

Each repetition of my name was a tiny pinprick. I thought

I caught him grinning, as if he were on to my lie. Then he lay back and looked away, relaxed, legs stretched out in front of him. His thigh massed close to mine, and he buzzed with that same submerged power I sensed from men passing by on the street. He grew growing broader and denser, ready to engulf me.

"I feel bad for my mother."

"Your *mother*'s far away. Your *mother* doesn't even have to know about it."

"She knew before she left."

"Families," he sighed. He finished the last of his cigarette, tore off the filter and put it in his pocket, then began stripping the rest as before. Small bits of paper swirled away in a breeze. "You know, you still haven't told me why it is you come up here."

"I thought you knew."

"Is it because you want something, Andrew?"

"I don't want anything."

"What if I put my arms around you? What'll you do?"

I had no idea of what I'd do. My heart grew large enough to choke me. A second or two passed, each one heavy as stone, and then his arm reached around my shoulder, a great, warm weight. I didn't move, turning to steel in his embrace until his arm retreated.

"Andrew," he said, shaking his head. "Poor Andrew." He pulled an inch or two away then slipped his hand under his T-shirt to scratch his chest. The shirt pulled up to reveal an inky tangle of hair curling over his belly. He made long, leisurely strokes, fingernails sharp against his skin, the strop of a barber's razor. He glanced over to see whether I watched and saw I did, and the hand circled his belly once more. A second or two later, it emerge from under the shirt and settled on its furry nest before dropping onto the bench like a small animal leaping down from the trees. There it rested.

I'd just begun to recover when I caught it moving my way, advancing toward my naked leg—I wore shorts—a large hand, heavy, and strong enough to give the whole world a spin as if it were a toy globe. He gripped my leg and squeezed it like a biceps.

"This is why you come up here, Andrew," he said in a tremolo voice, his grip unrelenting.

I shook the hand off. "Don't think I'm like you," I said. I spat out the words.

"Well, who *are* you like?"

"Not like you!"

"You come up here for one reason, Andrew: to meet me. Or someone like me. Don't pretend any differently." Pepper flecked his voice. He grabbed my shirt and pulled my face close to his. I struggled, but he held me tight, and as my hands pushed against the wet grip of his fists, I imagined I fought against myself. His hot breath singed me with a sting of tobacco.

"The easiest thing in the world would be to hurt you right now," he murmured. "I could slam you from one end of this park to the other and not a goddamn person in the world would know or care."

"Leave me alone—"

"And do you know why I'd do that? Because I hate liars!" He pushed me away. "I better not see you up here again, you hear me? This is my place, not yours." He got up and left, pushing into the bushes like the swinging doors of a tavern, and a moment later, he had gone. I caught my breath, ashamed, feeling like I'd been thrown into deep water and left to make my way back to shore. I kept hearing his voice, deep as carpet, rough and smooth at the same time.

My father wasn't home when I returned from my first day in the mail room—the job had come through after all. I'd gotten used to him staying over at that woman's house. It was Friday. Friday afternoons once meant the smell of chicken dripping from the rotisserie spit for the Sabbath meal, when the air took on a faint silvery glow from the invisible Jewish world my mother invoked when she lit the candles. But that evening, I was alone. The house felt dusty and uncared-for. A note was taped to the back of the door: *Will be back later. Your father.*

The telephone gave me a jolt when it rang.

"Feel like coming over?"

Barry never wasted time with preliminaries. "Where are you?" A passing bus churned haze into the receiver.

"Yonkers. I had something to take care of." Barry worked as a messenger, but in Yonkers? He sounded agitated.

"What's going on?"

"I'll tell you when I see you. I should be there by around eight. You coming or not?"

I said I would. I'd seen little of Barry that summer since the incident at Stuie's. Barry was working all the time, trying to make as much money as he could before starting college. I'd missed him. He fascinated me but scared me a little, too. After four years, I wasn't sure I really knew him. I got ready to go. Underneath my father's message, I scribbled, *Me too*.

A Puerto Rican girl sat near me on the train in a magenta pool of perfume. Grey light sifted through the dirty windows. I thought of the empty apartment I'd just left and realized how sad I was feeling. What were my father and his girlfriend doing right at that moment? The Puerto Rican girl crossed and recrossed her legs with a whizz of her stockings, stirring up eddies of fragrance. I imagined her naked, her bottom pressed against the molded-plastic seat, breasts balanced like servings of custard. The anxious tap of her heels startled me as she left the train, perhaps in a hurry to escape my obscene daydreams just as a black guy came in dribbling a basketball with a sharp *pong-pong-pong* against the floor.

Barry came to the door in an undershirt, pale skin glistening with sweat.

"Just got in," he said. The Crescent stood slender and weightless on newspaper in the living room beside a rag and a can of oil.

"You rode all the way from Yonkers?"

He shook his head and knelt down before the bike, taking a rag to the rims until they shone. "Farther. I came all the way from my brother's camp." He glanced at the odometer on the handlebars. "Sixty-three point five miles there and back. Did it in a little over three hours. I'm trying to get in shape for later this summer." He took a brush and worked gunk from the chain. Egg-shaped mounds of muscle hardened in his upper arms. Dirt disturbed him.

"Where's your dad?"

"Stepfather," he corrected. "Stein isn't my father."

I grit my teeth. I'd made that mistake before, and Barry never failed to correct me. Barry's father had been a blustery, chaotic man whose shirts always flapped free of his pants, a tall version of Barry's disorganized brother Felix. He'd died right before Barry and I met in freshman year, and his mother had married an accountant, stern, meticulous, and very smart. Barry was miserable. My theory was that he and Mr. Stein were just too much alike. To make matters worse, Felix loved the man. Last year, Barry's mother had died when a blood vessel burst inexplicably in her brain, and Barry felt left with someone he considered a stranger for a father.

"Stein's working late tonight, and that's fine with me," he said as he tossed down the rag. He led me into the room he shared with Felix, three years younger, a wobbly cherub of a boy who wanted to be a cellist.

He and Barry couldn't have been more different from one another. Felix never drank without dripping down his shirt. He'd slap a music folio onto the stand and use his bow to turn the pages, often throwing the score to the floor in the process. I once saw him use a glass to bang a thumbtack into the wall. Felix's half of the room was a shuffle of books and papers. Clothing and magazines layered the floor. The bed was never made. Records lay open, rainbowed where light hit them. A sleek, chrome music stand rose nobly above the clutter. Barry's side of the room was clinically neat. Squared-off piles of magazines were stacked on bookshelves, and his desk was as orderly as graph paper. Barry had straightened everything up in Felix's absence, so both halves of the room were now symmetrical.

Barry was completely devoted to Felix, tolerant of him as of no one else, but if he loved him, he terrorized him. He considered Felix his responsibility and was eager to supplant his stepfather's influence. He held Felix to an iron practice routine and checked Felix's homework. He rose early enough to rouse the dawdling Felix, and he hid cookies from him so he wouldn't overeat. Felix suffered under his brother's attention. Worry curdled his pudgy face whenever Barry cranked up the metronome or halted him at a mistake. His nervous breathing clouded the rests, and after too many of his brother's corrections, Felix's bow jabbed at the strings, each a bar of Barry's prison he was eager to break. He once showed me a mark on his arm left after Barry had struck him for making too many mistakes. "Tell him not to," Felix pleaded.

"Ray, put on some music."

I chose the first thing I saw—composers' names meant nothing to me—and soon arcs of music spanned the room. I sat down on Barry's neatly made bed, imagining that Felix played, his paunch crowded behind a sleek cello gripped with doughy fingers. I almost expected his mother to appear, a broad-shouldered woman with pudgy arms like Felix's and who, with a certain irony, had been hard of hearing. Her many needlework birds and flowers x-ed out with thread were framed on the walls. Her speech had been the bark of those with hearing problems, tongue paddling her words into sludge, and Felix always played extra loudly for her. Barry made me swear never to say anything about her to Stuie.

"Why did you go up to that camp?"

"To see how long it would take."

I thought for a moment. "You went up there to spy on him, didn't you?"

"I went up there to prepare."

"For what?"

"For when I visit him. Stein told me he didn't want me to.

But to hell with him. I know Felix doesn't even want to be in that camp. Stein made him go, and not because of the music, either. He just wanted to get Felix away from me, don't you understand? But Stein can't stop me. I'm going up there by bike to see him. Why don't you come, too? It'd be great."

"My bike's only a three-speed. And that place is too far."

"You can take the train part of the way."

"If Stein really told you he didn't want you going there, then maybe he told that to the school, too. Maybe they won't let you in—"

"No problem. The fence around the place isn't that high. We can sneak in. Hey, let's get high." He took a small plastic bag from a drawer and began rolling one of his perfect joints, and we smoked. His strong toke pressed the color from his lips, and his boxy chest labored. Barry turned everything into work, even pleasure.

"Stein had no business sending Felix to that camp," he said with a gasp, shoving the joint my way. "He just wanted to split us up. Felix could just as well have practiced here. Stein thinks I'm a bad influence. He says I control Felix, that my feelings for him aren't healthy. He says I'm going to damage Felix's ability to form sound relationships in the future. He says I stifle him. That bastard! What does he know about anything? He's always been an outsider in this family. He doesn't understand Felix the way I do! No one does!" He took another long toke, which he held until his face reddened, gathering anger. "But that's not the real reason he sent Felix away. The real reason is that Stein knows I don't like him and never have. He knows how close Felix and I are, so he wants to get back at me."

Felix had been excited about going to the camp. Everyone had their own practice room that looked out into the woods, he said. There was a swimming pool. Each Friday there was a concert. It was going to be great.

"Felix told me he really wanted to go."

Barry's face hardened. "Don't you believe it. Felix wanted to go only because he knew Stein wanted him to. He can boss

Felix around because Felix is too weak to defend himself. All this stuff—" he gestured scornfully toward Felix's records—"they're from Stein. He's tried to buy Felix's love. But Felix really doesn't love him. He just goes along with him. Stein tried to buy me off, too, said he'd pay for my tuition if I didn't get a scholarship, but I didn't fall for it. I'm not going to take a penny from him."

The joint passed back and forth. Barry grew harder, bonier, beside me, as if the dope had drained his juices. Dope condensed his anger, concentrating it. He was like those people who believe a conspiracy killed JFK, always sure that anything bad is premeditated and deliberate. Today was Friday: Felix was probably going to be playing in a concert in that camp, far from his brother's obsessions. I, too, yearned to be somewhere cool and green. Like Stuie's room, Barry's had begun to feel confining.

My eyes fell on a piece of needlework above the bed. I pictured their mother's fingers plunging the needle in and out of the cloth to create pictures as thick as her speech. Felix had been with his mother when she died. They'd been clothes-shopping and she'd just unpacked his new shirts when she turned to him and said, "Felix, where are your socks?" in the clearest voice he'd ever heard from her before she slumped onto the bed. Felix had loved her, someone who hardly heard his music and talked like a child, yet maybe that was preferable to Barry's relentless attention and precise commands.

The joint had become no more than a roach, which Barry held in an alligator clip and ignited. "I'm hardly going to see him anymore," he said, breathing in an oracle's burst of smoke.

"You'll see him when he comes back."

Barry shook his head. "Stein's sending him to this private school in New Hampshire starting in the fall. He's taking him away from me."

He sounded ready to cry. I felt like throwing my arms around him, but Barry was a mouse trap, ready to snap, and I wasn't sure how he'd take it. The dope soon flushed second thoughts from my head, and a moment later, my arms circled his chest. We sat like that for a minute or two. Then he gently disengaged himself.

"I'm going to call him now." He got up and took out his secret telephone equipment, unscrewing the telephone's casing and connecting the contraption with a jewel thief's dexterity. "I'll wire a speaker so you can hear, too."

My heart still raced from having held him. What had he thought about it?

A dial tone crackled into the little speaker. It took a while before someone picked up.

"Hello?" came Felix's hesitant voice at last.

Barry's mouth softened as he held the receiver close. "It's me."

"Oh." There was muffled laughter, silenced by a hand pressed over the mouthpiece.

"Felix? What's going on?"

"Nothing." There was more damp muffling, more giggling. "My brother," I heard him say.

Barry grew frantic. "Felix!"

"Yeah?"

"Play something for me, will you?"

"Over the phone?"

"Not *now,*" I heard a girl say on the other end.

"Please," said Barry.

There were footsteps and the scrape of a chair. "*Fe*lix," the girl said, and then a door slammed. After a few preparatory bowings, Felix began. Like thread unraveling through the eye of a needle, the sound was thin because the telephone wires carried only part of the music. Barry stared into the speaker, willing Felix himself to emerge from it.

"Can I stop now?" Felix asked after playing for a few minutes.

"All right," Barry said, barely audible.

There was a pause. Then: "I gotta go, Barry."

"How about if I visit you?"

"You mean you want to come . . . here?" He didn't sound happy about it.

"Yeah. I could ride up there. It's not that far." Barry looked at me, rings of sweat beneath his eyes.

"Maybe I should ask Dad."

"No!" Barry said. "Don't tell him! It's none of his business. I mean, let's keep it between you and me."

"I gotta go. We have rehearsal soon."

"Felix, let me come up there!"

"I don't know."

"Please! Just think about it. But don't tell him what I said, promise me!"

Barry sat still for several moments after they'd hung up. His undershirt was damp, and the receiver glistened. "Fuck!" he said, pounding a fist against his palm.

I thought of Felix putting the cello away and hurrying out to find the giggling girl.

"Could I make a call on that thing, too?"

I gave him the number I'd memorized from my mother's post card. Barry dialed, then thrust the receiver my way, disgusted. The phone rang for a long time. Finally, a sleepy man's voice answered.

"Boker tov."

The foreign words threw me for a moment. *"Shalom,"* I said. "It's Raymond, Raymond from America."

"Raymond?" the voice whispered, pronouncing my name as if it were foreign, too.

The receiver clunked down and another voice came on the phone, a woman's, slower and clearer. "Is Raymond? Ruthie's Raymond?"

"Yes."

"Good day," she said, sleepy, straining to speak English. "How you are?"

I'd gotten them out of bed, forgetting the time difference. Maybe they were religious and I'd made them break the Sabbath. I'd really messed up.

"Fine."

"Do you know who I am?"

Why did Jews have to make a test of everything?

"I am Surah, the wife of your grandfather's brother Schmiel," the voice continued, a talking stone.

I remembered a photo of someone with crooked teeth that wouldn't stay under her lips, a necklace with a heavy cameo locket, sad eyes. Jewish eyes.

"Is my mother there?"

"She is going on a trip. To Sinai Desert. You know that? She is coming back later."

My mother had mentioned nothing about a trip in her last postcard. And to a desert? She'd always shunned the beach and worn sunglasses in the winter. So Israel wasn't far enough away from my father; she had to escape even farther, to Egypt. I hadn't realized how much I wanted to hear her voice.

"How come your father is not coming?" Surah asked. "Israel so beautiful."

"I don't know." I worried that she might detect that I was high. I kept thinking of my mother in her sunglasses tramping through the desert, carrying her white pocketbook. Surah made me promise that I would come to Israel very soon.

"Shalom," I said, exhausting my Hebrew vocabulary.

"Why did your mother go to Israel all alone?" Barry asked as I handed the receiver back to him.

"My father has a girlfriend."

"You're kidding. Your father? So he bought your mother a ticket to get her out of the picture?"

"No." The task of explaining everything seemed daunting with a head full of dope. We went into the kitchen and made baloney sandwiches.

"You'll go with me up to see Felix, won't you?" he said.

"Sounds a little like kidnapping," I answered, spreading mustard on a slice of white bread. I envisioned Barry snatching up the hapless Felix, a great bird gobbling up a turtle hatchling as it scurried to the sea.

"It's not kidnapping; it's rescuing. He's my brother. He'll be glad to see me." His eyes went stern. "So, are you coming or not?"

"I don't know."

Barry held his gaze. "Do it."

I told him I'd think about it. We smoked another joint and listened to some more music.

"You can sleep over if you want to," Barry said.

Heat shot around the edges of my face and arms. In all the time I'd known Barry, he'd never asked me to stay over. I wondered why he asked now. Did it have something to do with my holding him before?

"I should call home," I said. I let it ring for a long time. Finally, someone picked up.

"Yes?" It was a sleepy woman's voice.

For a moment, I couldn't say anything. "I-is my father there?"

"Raymond? Is that you? Where are you?"

Her voice. Like those people in Israel, she sounded foreign, but in a different way. She'd pronounced my name Reh-*mund*.

"Tell him I'm over at Barry's," I blurted out and then hung up. "Jesus, it's her!"

"Who?"

"That woman." I thought of my mother's still, empty bedroom, the ghostly sheets. I saw her trekking into the wilderness, alone.

Barry motioned for me to sleep in Felix's bed, then quickly stripped down to his underwear and got into his own bed. Without clothing, he looked rigid as plumbing. A bit of black hair curled around his belly button and furred his legs, but everything else was starkly smooth.

"I always sleep in the nude," I said, heart athump, waiting to see his response. I pulled off my T-shirt, my pants. He seemed unaware as he turned over in his bed, revealing a muscular rectangle of back, and switched off the light.

"Good night."

I got into Felix's bed, staring at the ceiling, my insides churning. Barry's breathing grew consistent as a dial tone. I imagined my father and that woman fucking in the white softness of the sheeted sofa in the living room. I got up and crept into Barry's bed. He didn't move. I pressed closer against his back and stayed there, barely daring to breathe for fear of waking him. A little later, I awoke to feel him pushing against me, the round muscles of his backside thrust into my crotch.

"Felix?" he murmured in his sleep, nuzzling closer.

* * *

"Don't I know you?"

A woman across the table was smiling at me. Had she caught me inspecting the booger I'd just harvested from my nose? I looked away, convinced that her question had been meant for someone else, but a moment later, she was closing her magazine and moving over to my side of the table. "At first glance, I thought you might have been someone else," she said brightly, sitting down opposite me like a dinner companion.

"Who?"

"Someone else." Her eyes fell on my book, Faulkner's *Collected Stories,* and she sniffed. "He stole them from the family's black maid, of course."

I closed the book. I'd never read a word of Faulkner in my life until a few moments before and had gotten no farther than the second knotty page before she appeared. Her eyes were a bright blue that grew darker, like deepening water. A faint scar in the shape of a question mark hovered above her left eyebrow. I was sure I'd never seen her before in my life.

I'd begun spending my lunch hours gobbling a frank from a vendor and heading for the cool of the New York Public Library's reading room. I'd arrive there feeling as if I'd gone AWOL from the mindless boot camp of the mail room. I drank up the library's civility, soothed by the sight of people at work behind mighty fortresses of books. I would order a book at the desk and try to read, but the words slipped past, too nimble for my drowsy eyes to catch. I'd leave with no more than a few perishable handfuls of Anderson or Steinbeck that rarely survived the heat of midtown, and they were soon forgotten back in the mailroom's monosyllabic world.

"Let's get a drink outside," the woman suggested.

It was cooler here, and I would have preferred staying, but I found myself getting up to go with her.

"This is nice," she said, smoothing her skirt beneath her as she squatted down on a granite step. She looked around with the satisfaction of someone who'd just decided where to build a house.

"You're not from New York, are you?" I asked. Only a tourist would like being outside in New York during the summer.

She smiled. "Nope."

"Well, where are you from?"

She grinned. "Somewhere else."

It was like someone not telling you what their middle initial stood for.

"Did you come all the way to the library just to read a magazine?" I asked, growing piqued.

"Oh no," she purred. "I came to the library to meet you." Her earrings did a little dance, but her face grew serious. "You don't like me, do you?"

I don't *know* you, I wanted to say, but for some reason, that seemed irrelevant. She seemed capable of making everything around her conform to her way of thinking.

"You will, though. I can tell we're going to get along just fine."

This was too much. "How come you came over to my table?"

"You're smart and cute, that's why." She tossed her empty soda can into the trash, or tried to, but it hit the rim with a clank and bounced onto the pavement.

"God, doesn't that make you think of a horse jumping over a brick wall and then smashing its leg?"

The can had begun to roll across the pavement to the curb. She darted after it, shooting right in front of irritated passersby, then snatching up thc can seconds before it rolled into the gutter.

"If that happens, they have to kill the horse," she continued when she returned. "A horse can't walk with a broken leg, and if a horse can't walk, it dies. Imagine killing someone in a wheelchair just because they couldn't walk." She tossed the can into the trash, and for a terrible moment, it seemed to be the cracked bone of a horse.

"I knew that about horses," I told her. I'd seen a movie where it was mentioned. I didn't like the way she lectured me.

"Of course, in some cases, it might even make sense for people," she said, almost to herself. "In some cases," she added, leaning close, "it might even be advisable." Her earrings swung menacingly.

I edged away from her. "What are you talking about?"

She laughed. "Scared you, didn't I?"

I finished my soda but didn't throw it into the trash can. I didn't want to miss and have her see it. "You didn't scare me," I said, a little annoyed, but mostly feeling unsure.

She considered me. "Maybe not. But you're scared of something, all right," she said, "even if it's not my story. I'll say one thing, though. You have a lovely face. Nice eyes, especially." She considered them as might a jeweler. "I'm trying to figure out the color. Brown, but there's yellow in there too. Mmmm." She placed a finger on her chin. "Sort of like some semiprecious stone. Maybe agate," she decided. "Speaking of color, this morning I came upon a nest of white roaches under my sink. Albinos. They were almost beautiful."

"Roaches aren't almost beautiful, no matter what color they are." I looked at her. "Why did you tell me I was scared?"

She fixed me in a mirror-hard glance. "I'm not sure, but like most people, you're probably afraid of finding out."

This was getting on my nerves. She was like my father, who wouldn't tell me the name of that woman. I got up to leave.

Sudden exits were my customary way of handling unpleasant situations. Maybe that meant I was like my father.

She pulled me back down. "Where are you off to?"

"Quit telling me how afraid I am."

"Listen, you and I are not going to get along unless you stop flying off the handle."

"Who says we have to get along?"

"But we should, we really should. You're nice. I like you. I'm still thirsty. Why don't you get us something else to drink?" She reached for her purse and gave it to me. "My treat. I'll have a ginger ale."

"I have to get back to work." The stone step was beginning to grow hard.

"Okay. Maybe I'll see you here tomorrow around the same time," she said. "Or maybe not." She grinned, then got up and left, her earrings jiggling on either side of her, her own tiny entourage.

"What's your name?" I called after her.

"Agatha," she said without turning around.

I found her on the steps after leaving work a couple of days later. I didn't feel like going right home.

"Mail Boy," she said, waving to me.

We got sodas, and she entertained me with chatty reports on her coworkers, introduced by nickname: Sister Maude, her sour-faced supervisor, Shellac Lock, the payroll clerk with the industrial-strength permanent, or Ars Antiqua, an elderly vice president. "Your eyes look different today," she said, leaning close enough for me to see the tiny locket she wore. "Today the brown is golden, almost metallic, the color of a tarnished ducat."

I sipped my soda and listened to her say these things.

She had to go the bank, so I accompanied her to the echoing hall of the Bowery Savings Bank on 42nd Street with its great stone arches and massive chandeliers. "Welcome to King Arthur's train station," she said, heading to a counter with its deposit slips and chained pens. She filled a slip out, and as we waited on line, she recited some lines of poetry for me.

Ah, bitter chill it was!
The owl, for all his feathers, was a-cold;
The hare limp'd trembling through the frozen grass,
And silent was the flock in woolly fold . . .

"Great poem for the summer, don't you think? Keats."

Her talk was a cool wave washing over me and I let myself be pulled into its teasing and mysterious undertow, forgetting my annoyance of the other day. She took my hand and led me across the floor's elaborate mosaic to the teller, and it seemed we were enacting a ceremony to mark our new friendship.

I began to look for her during lunch or afterward. I thought of clever things to say to her and prepared snappy answers to questions I thought she might ask. I memorized lines from old movies to quote, determined to be as brilliant and as articulate as she. The thought of her waiting on the steps brightened the dull mornings in the mail room, and once eleven o'clock rolled around, my spirits rose. On the stroke of twelve, I fled the basement and zigzagged through the cars stalled on East 41st Street until I reached the library.

If she was there, my day felt complete. But when she didn't show, I wasn't just disappointed: I was puzzled. There'd been a mistake, I was sure, for in my mind, we had already become a couple. Had I gotten there too early? Too late? When I was convinced she wasn't coming, I didn't even bother getting a frank but turned around, dismayed. One rainy day I headed for the library to find the steps empty, as they should have been, but I cursed the glistening granite anyway. The frank-vendor offered me a sympathetic smile.

Days passed, she didn't reappear, and I began to think that I had seen the last of her—or perhaps that I had never seen her at all. Maybe I'd imagined the whole thing. But a day or two later, she was perched on the steps as before.

"Want a bite?" she said, lifting up her sandwich.

"No," I said, chilly on purpose. Where had she been?

"It's tuna. Don't you like tuna?"

"Where were you the other day?"

"I thought everyone liked tuna." She took another bite.

"I said, where were you?"

Her mouth pursed in irritation before she popped the rest of the sandwich into her mouth and reached for her bag. "Sorry, but I didn't think we had an *appointment,*" she said, tearing open a Wash 'n Dry.

The frank-vendor was watching the whole thing. Red-faced, I turned to go.

"Sit down," she said.

"I waited for you all week."

She thought for a moment, her eyes fixed on mine, appraising, I thought, their color. "Tell you what. Since you like ap*point*ments so much, let's make one right now. How about you meeting me after work this Friday?"

I tried not to sound too excited. "If you want to."

That Friday we headed eastward along 42nd Street's estuary of crosstown traffic. We crossed First Avenue and looked out from the United Nations promenade to Queens with its warehouses, a factory town on the other side of the river. The light was gauzy and sweet. Agatha was quiet. A threatening tangle of Spanish guys approached: three strutting teenagers, each wearing short T-shirts that exposed taut bellies. I tensed. We were trapped. I put my arm around her waist to make them think we were a couple.

"Hispanic guys remind me of little Cuban dance-band leaders," Agatha said with a grin after they'd walked away. She let herself out of my embrace.

"How old are you?" I asked.

"Probably ten years older than you."

"Do you have a boyfriend?"

"Yes. He just walked by. And now he won't speak to me again because he's seen me with you." She winked, all the while my heart blipped like a periscope sighting a target.

"Is that really true?"

"No," she said. "It was silly, just like your question."

"You don't like answering questions, do you?"

"Nope. Asking's more fun."

That summer we covered a lot of ground on those after-work strolls. Until then I'd had no idea that streets might go on so far before reaching a river or a dead end. Walking was what you did when you ran out of tokens. My calves burned by the time we reached a subway station where we said our good-byes. I had no idea of where she lived. She neither gave me her telephone number nor asked for mine. But had I asked, I sensed she wouldn't tell me.

In old novels, I always felt sad when the mother of the bride gave her daughter away. I wanted the two of them to go on peacefully baking bread together, putting up preserves, doing needlework. But always those marriages—always a feast, a hope chest, and yards of wedding-dress silk. It all came down to the same thing: a mother standing by while her daughter was bartered away. Sold. Slaved.

Me, too. Mother knew what kind of man he was; she'd married him. Women always have a choice, even if they make out as if they're helpless. She also knew about what he did to me, so why did she hole herself up in that room of hers and pretend nothing was happening?

Why didn't I scream and poke his eyes out? Why did I hurt her instead?

All women are afraid. I hate women.

New Cornwall, July 3

I haven't been home in months, I can't bring myself to go. Mattie tells me that my father's in constant pain on account of his arthritis. I didn't think cripples could get arthritis, like people with lung cancer getting bronchitis or lepers, eczema. Funny, in a way. Mattie says my father needs to speak to me.

He knows where he can find me.

NINE

August.

Stuie announced that his days at Radio Shack were numbered. Feelie's Wheel was going to have some kind of a gig downtown at the end of the summer, and after that, he'd be their techie full time. He assumed a new raunchy demeanor—leather jacket and boots, a tattoo. His sister Sharon remained at large. She'd called once or twice but wouldn't say where she was. "Now she's even weirder than she was before," he said, and all I could think of was his mother sitting alone at the sewing machine, so distraught over Sharon that she stitches the same piece over and over again.

The incident at the pool left things between my father and me somewhat reserved. We reached an unspoken agreement, whereby he stopped asking where I went at night and I stopped asking him about that woman. He seemed intent on keeping her hidden. They'd worked out a system so that I never saw her. Even so, she left her mark all around the apartment. The kitchen was always clean, the carpet vacuumed, and the glass top of the coffee table shone. My father began wearing new shirts—presents from her?—and even started shaving more often. But he still drank a lot in the evenings. In fact, he seemed to drink more.

Barry kept calling with updates on his trip to his brother's music camp.

"I spoke to Felix yesterday, and he finally confessed that he'd met a girl up there," he said early one morning. "He said that I should leave him alone."

"Maybe you should."

I heard Barry's lips tightening over the phone. "He doesn't really mean it. The girl's probably some stupid flute player or something. He really wants to see me, I know he does. He's just afraid of what Stein'll say about it. He has rehearsals every Tuesday evening, from seven-thirty to nine-thirty. Most of the camp assembles in this one building. It'll be easy to sneak in then. I have ordinance survey maps for the entire area and I've plotted a route for us." He spoke like a field marshall. I imagined his tense grip on the phone. *Us.* "There's a back entrance. We could get in there."

We.

He'd planned it out to the last detail. His thoroughness was frightening. I envisaged a tussle in the rehearsal room, Barry wrenching the cello from Felix, the precious instrument smashing down, strings snapping. Barry's idea was all wrong. It was a little crazy. Maybe Barry was, too.

"Listen, I really don't know about this whole thing. If Felix tells you that he doesn't want you to come—"

"You promised me you'd go with me."

I felt trapped in a protection ring. "I never said for sure that I would."

"I plan to go on August twenty-fifth."

"Why are you doing this?" I asked him. But I thought I knew: because Felix had accepted his new father and liked him. Even loved him. Because he liked being happy. All that was too hard for Barry to understand. He thrived on conflict. He needed adversaries.

"Be ready," he said, a warning.

* * *

One evening Uncle Lester came over. He couldn't have been paying a mere social call; he and his family never dropped in. He'd once said he wouldn't feel safe driving through our neighborhood in a tank.

"What happened to your famous card game?" my father asked. Annoyance sharpened his voice. They hadn't spoken since the news broke of my father's affair.

"Before you say anything terrible to me, let's have a drink." Lester held up a shopping bag imprinted with the name of his gourmet foods company. He strode into the apartment trailing cologne, sporty in a pastel-colored shirt, white pants and white loafers: vacation clothing. A heavy-looking watch was cabled to a bulky gold band around his wrist.

"Hey, Charger," he said to me.

He'd been calling me that since I was a kid and hadn't noticed that I'd grown older. "Bet you're glad to be out of high school."

Like my grandfather's, Uncle Lester's questions always told you how to answer them. I said it felt great to be out of high school.

"Heard you've become a working man, too. Feels good having your own money in your pocket, doesn't it?"

"It does," I agreed.

"You're looking good, Charger. Hey, don't you think the kid looks good, Paul?"

"Terrific," my father said without looking my way.

I headed for my room. It was Saturday night, and I didn't have a clue of what to do with myself. I left my door open so I could eavesdrop and soon heard an ice tray being cracked open in the kitchen and cubes tumbling into the teak bucket.

"How's business?" my father asked, returning to the living room. It was the standard way men usually started conversations. Women talked about their children or themselves. I imagined my uncle's clumsy sprawl on the sofa, glass in hand, while my father kept to the chair at his drafting table, back straight, shoulders square.

"Sucks," Lester said.

"Because it's summer?"

He gave a kind of chuckle. "It sucked in spring, too."

"How's Rhoda?"

"She's got someone fixing up the backyard. It's going to be really nice, fountains and everything. If you ask me, I think she's crazy, but you know how Rhoda is about fixing up the house. Always something new." There was a pause. "You miss Ruthie?"

"Ruthie," my father said.

The ice rattled in their glasses. Uncle Lester's tone changed. "Let's not mince words, Paul. I know you hate me after what happened."

"I don't hate you, Lester."

"All right. You don't hate me. But you don't like me, either."

My father took a moment to answer. "What I think is that you're a horse's ass sometimes. So tell me. Why'd you come here tonight?"

"I'm sorry about what happened, Paul. I'm really sorry. You know I've always liked you, you and Ruthie. I didn't mean to hurt anyone."

"Well, you did, Lester."

"I did it to get back at Alfred, once and for all."

"But it's me you screwed."

"I already said it had nothing to do with you—"

"As if you never fooled around yourself, Lester."

"Hey, wait a minute—"

"I could have said a thing or two about you long ago if I'd wanted to," my father continued calmly. Lester emitted a shout of protest, but my father cut him short. "Please. We're too old to play games with each other."

There was a pause. *Amazing*, I thought. *My uncle, too. What a family this is.*

"Does the kid know about you and her?" Uncle Lester asked.

"The kid knows, Lester. Everybody does. Isn't that what you wanted—"

"I already said I'm sorry, Paul. Can't you forgive me?"

My father didn't speak, but I imagined him replying with shrugged shoulders, his way of saying yes. My father couldn't stay angry at anyone.

I'd heard enough, so I closed the door, turned on the TV to a movie, put on some music, and listened with the headphones on, a combination I'd hit on to spice up the summer reruns. But I hardly watched or listened. I thought about Agatha. I thought about Michael. The air in my room barely moved, and my bed grew too warm to sit on.

After Lester left, I found my father stretched out on the sofa atop a rumpled sheet in the tropical squalor of the living room, a cigarette drooping from his lips. I could tell he'd had a few.

"What did Lester want?" I asked.

"He's broke," my father said, talking more to himself than to me. "He's flat-on-his-ass broke and he had the gall to ask me for money. Isn't that something? The famous Lester Loewenthal, firstborn son of Lazar Loewenthal, navy hero and boy wonder, wants to borrow money from me." He shook his head. "He must have decided to wait and ask me after your mother took off."

"He's really bankrupt?"

"Let's say that things are pretty tight for him. Damned tight. And you want to know why he needs the money? Because his wife wants to build fountains. Little fountains in the backyard. Your Aunt Rhoda wants fountains, trickle, trickle, trickle. It's the fountains that are going to kill him. And he doesn't have the nerve to tell her that they can't afford it. Trickle, trickle." One hand climbed into the air and then descended with a watery flicker of his fingers. He laughed, amused at his own little show. He'd had more than just a few.

"Are you going to give him anything?"

He laughed again and reached for the bottle.

"What'll happen if you don't?"

"Maybe he'll go to his father. I'd love to be there when he does. It'd be even better to see him crawling back to Alfred." His voice darkened. "I don't want you talking about this to anyone, you hear?"

"Why does everyone in the family always make a secret out of everything?" Who was I going to tell, Barry or Stuie? The strange Agatha?

"Maybe if some people'd kept a secret or two, things wouldn't be so fouled up," he said with a swallow of whiskey straight from the bottle. "Look at your old man, drunk as a lord!" he sang to himself.

It was hard to watch. "I heard Mom went on some kind of excursion to the desert in Israel."

"What? How do you know?"

I'd said it just to get a reaction from him. Now I'd have to explain.

"I got a card from her," I lied.

He sat up. "Alfred didn't mention any card." He looked at me. "What else did she say?"

"Nothing much."

"Did she say anything about me?"

He was alert now, and his eyes searched mine for an answer. I felt sorry for him. "Yes," I said, lying once more. He waited. His eyes sharpened with what looked like fear.

"She said she hoped you were fine." I hated myself for having started this.

"Enough. Go to sleep," he said, motioning with the bottle.

I couldn't sleep that night, so I got out my pack of stale cigarettes and sat by the window.

The telephone rang. I heard my father talking to someone.

"Okay, Leona," he mumbled just before he hung up. "I'll try and see you this coming weekend."

Leona.

* * *

"Mail Boy!"

I'd just turned the corner onto 42nd Street when a shiny voice came at me from the granite shade of the library. Agatha was waving, skirt swirling about her in a breeze. After the grim hours I'd spent in the basement, she looked fresh and dewy, a woman in a French impressionist painting. I should have been happy to see her. Any other day I would have been. But I'd gone to the library every day at noon for the past week and after work without seeing her.

"Stop calling me Mail Boy," I said.

The smile dropped from her face, a necklace of pearls with its string cut. "Whoa, horsie. What's going on here?"

"Where were you all last week?"

"Where should I have been?"

The answer was obvious enough to me: here, waiting on the steps at lunchtime. I shrank in humiliation: she was the popular, eight-year-old birthday girl and I was the nerd whose mother asked for me to be invited to the party.

I told her.

"And would you mind telling me *why* should I have been waiting for you?" Her earrings did a little dance, enjoying themselves at my expense. "Haven't we gone through this already?"

"I thought you liked me."

"Not at this moment I don't. But I could again if you lightened up. Tell me, what do you think of Tchaikovsky? I mean, you *do* like him, don't you? They're playing him tonight for free in Central Park."

Her arm was slipping through mine before I said another word, and we set off. She strode briskly down the street, a camp counselor on a forest path, compass at the ready. But something was wrong. I'd barely decided to put aside my own bad mood when I became aware of hers. No patter of office anecdotes punctuated the blocks we covered. She felt tense as a tightrope walker against me, and by the time we reached the park, she'd sunk down into someplace very dark. Had I ticked her off so much? I feared the next corner would find her hailing a taxi and departing.

"I'm sorry about before. I missed you."

"Okay. Just stop expecting things from me and we'll be fine."

"Is that all?"

"That's all."

But the veil over her face didn't lift. Only a scattering of people waited on the grass before the stage that had been set up in the Sheep Meadow.

"See, it pays to get here early," she said, and we found a place on the grass. The concert wasn't to start for another hour. The moment we sat down, she gazed off, tendrils of moodiness clinging to her. Something was definitely going on.

"My father's been having an affair," I said, hoping that might get her talking. Her mood had unlocked my own turmoil. "I don't know what's going to happen when my mother comes back."

"Don't expect to understand anything men do," she snapped. "They're cruel as children. So does your mother know about this?"

I nodded. "I think she's too scared to get a divorce."

"Then it's her own fault."

"Why? My father's the one who started it."

"If she lets him get away with it, then it's her fault. Women who let men walk over them deserve what they get." She took a page torn from the newspaper out of her pocketbook and read. "How nice. They're starting with the 'Serenade for Strings.' "

She bristled with an anger I'd never seen in her. Perhaps the very heavens had overheard her, for the sky grew overcast. I prayed for rain, for anything to give me a reason to flee her hostility. *Don't expect to understand what men do.* I was glad when more people started to come. Blankets carpeted the grass, the musicians took their places on the stage, and lush cadences of music swept over us as the sky brooded with clouds. The music sounded familiar: the same piece I'd put on while over at Barry's the other night. I'd stayed in his bed, unwilling to leave, yet terrified that he might wake up. But he'd kept on sleeping soundly, so I pressed against him, growing hard through my underwear, and as gently as I could, I came.

I couldn't concentrate on the music, so I asked to read the page of the newspaper. "It is often conjectured that Tchaikovsky's tortured personal life was reflected in some of his music, but one hears little evidence of this in the lilting 'Serenade,' " the notes read. I kept turning Agatha's way, hoping to meet her glance, but her eyes remained stubbornly fixed on the stage. The music dragged on, a term of imprisonment. I thought of Felix, bowing away under Barry's punishing gaze. I was relieved when Agatha decided that she'd had enough, and we headed for the street.

"Wasn't it lovely?" she said.

"No, it was boring." I was contrary on purpose. She'd ignored me during the whole concert, and I wasn't going to be amenable.

Her mouth squared. "Do you know what your problem is? You're a sulker. You're still sore at me for not having waited for you. Maybe you spend a little too much time by yourself. People who do that expect everything to go their way." She spoke loudly, and I was conscious of people listening. I felt like a fool who knew little of life; Agatha was older, more mature. I yearned to be on the train going home. We'd say good-bye for the last time that evening. I would kiss her at the subway entrance. I'd kiss her even if she didn't want to be kissed. I'd kiss her precisely because she never wanted to be kissed. And that would be that.

The light turned red just as we reached the corner. Agatha, who never waited for lights to change, darted out into the street. She slalomed toward the mall in the middle through honking cars, leaving me behind, plumes of exhaust at her skirt. She crossed over the median strip and continued into the lane of northbound traffic and might have made it the rest of the way, but for some reason, she came to a full, teetering stop in the middle of the street, narrowly missing a taxi. Her arms flew up in a gesture of helplessness, and cars careened dangerously close with a snarl of honking. Drivers shouted out of their windows as they strained to avoid her, but she seemed not to hear them and stayed perilously locked in place, a boulder lodged in a stream, forcing everything to course around her.

The light changed and I took off after her. "Agatha!" I said when I reached her. She fell into my arms, brittle and immovable, and I hustled her over to the curb. She slumped against a mail box, looking at me through glassy, vacant eyes.

"Is she hurt?" A man spoke from the back seat of a cab that had pulled over. His face was hard, jaws frozen, but his eyes burned with fear. "John?" he said, looking at Agatha.

She pulled me close and buried her face in my shoulder.

"John, please—"

"Go! Just go!" she said without looking at him.

His eyes flicked my way. I thought he might say something, but the window rolled up and the cab drove away.

"He didn't get me," she mumbled.

"Who was that?"

"My father. I knew he was in the city. I've been feeling it all week. Hold me." She fell against me, weightless and wobbly. She hadn't let me touch her since that afternoon on the United Nations promenade. Holding her felt like learning a secret about her.

"Oh!" She giggled and stepped back. I heard a trickle. A cloud-shaped stain began spreading across the pavement at her feet.

"Good thing I wear skirts," she said. "Raymond, look the other way, for God's sake!"

I turned, but out of the corner of my eye I saw her extract a tissue from her handbag delicately. "Stand in front of me while I take care of this, will you?"

"Are you sure you're okay?" I asked when she was done.

"It was just a little accident," she whispered.

"That guy was really your father?"

She nodded. "He's probably here to speak to some of Mother's relatives. Let's get out of here in case he decides to come back."

I was too confused to ask who "John" was. The subway entrance was just ahead. The air had grown thick with what felt like impending rain.

"Don't leave me alone," she said. "Please." She took my hand.

We rode downtown and emerged from her station into a downpour and hurried along the street in a giddy rush. Rain freshened the city. Bodegas strung with bare bulbs offered heaps of gleaming fruit on outdoor stands. The rain stopped soon after, sewers gurgled like mountain streams, and a breeze cooled the streets. Her building was cramped halfway down a side street, its front monkey-barred with fire escapes. Gargoyles missing chunks of their faces leered down at us from the doorway. The battered front door opened with a struggle, and the vestibule was spiked with cat's piss sharp as vinegar.

Had that man in the cab really been her father?

"Home," she said, opening several locks. The apartment's single room was thick with books and bundles of papers. Clumps of clothing were piled around a battered desk supporting a high-bosomed typewriter. An aquarium stood dry and empty beside it. Stranded in the middle of it all were a mattress and box spring on the floor.

"What's that?" I asked, stopping in my tracks before an inscription of dripping red letters spray-painted onto the opposite wall: "Only when you have denied me will I return."

"Nietzsche," she said without looking. She took a towel to her hair and then handed it to me. The letters deepened in color and grew ominous as I stared at them. My eyes fell onto an oil painting in the kitchen of a woman with a knife to her own breast.

"That's me," she said, anticipating my question. "A friend painted it."

"What happened to the fish in that aquarium?"

"They were . . . they died. Do you mind if I take a bath? To wash off the rain." She stepped out of her clothing.

I tried to remain nonchalant, but when her naked buttocks and silky pubic hair emerged from her skirt mere inches away from me, my insides churned. She stepped into the tub. A soft arc of belly hung downward as she leaned over; her ribs pulleyed beneath her skin, and her breasts swung gently. Without her clothing, she was slight, almost fragile. "Ooh, it's a little cold," she said as she sank into the water. "Sit down, you look nervous."

"I'm not nervous," I said. I was mind-boggled. An hour ago, she'd almost gotten herself run over by her father, and now this. I hardly knew what to think.

"I hope I didn't frighten you before," she said over the gentle trickle of water. "Sometimes I get so scared. Would you mind doing my back?"

She handed me the soap. Her skin was taut and fluid to my hand, and she eased against my touch. I'd never touched a woman's naked back before. I'd never touched anyone's naked back before except Barry's. It was nice soaping her. *This is why people have lovers,* I thought, listening to the soothing splash of the water.

"Was that really your father?"

She nodded.

"So why didn't he get out of the cab?"

"He knew I didn't want to see him."

"He gave me a strange look."

"He probably thought I was keeping you." She drew her hands through the water. "I can feel it every time he comes to the city. Everything shifts and gets unsteady." She paused. "It's another reason why you didn't see me all last week."

"Will he be coming here?"

"He doesn't know where I live."

"What does he want from you?"

She brought a handful of water to her face, droplets slid down and cut into the water like bits of glass. "Forgiveness."

I came across a hard lump near her shoulder blade like a coin embedded beneath the skin. "What's this?"

"A memento." She turned around, breasts gleaming. She smiled. "You're much sweeter now than you were when I first met you. There's a hard side to you, do you know that? You're not really hard at all, but you make yourself that way."

She rose and pulled a little tempest along with her. The last of the daylight darted into the gleaming curls of her pubic hair before she slipped into a bathrobe.

"You can take a bath now, too, if you want." She pulled the plug.

"No, no."

"Oh, come on. Hop in."

"Maybe I'll just wash my feet," I said, sure I wouldn't be able to undress in front of her. I unlaced my sneakers, rolled up my pants, and climbed onto the edge of the tub. It wobbled, ready to throw me off like an angry horse.

"You have nice feet," she said, watching me as she combed her hair. "Arches like my mother's. You can tell a lot about a person by looking at their feet. They're the most honest part of the body. Spritzer?" She opened the refrigerator and took out a bottle of seltzer and a lemon. "It's all I drink in the summer."

After I washed, we dragged the mattress over to the window and sat down with our drinks.

"Is all this clothing yours?" I asked.

"No, it's his. And so is that." She pointed to the inscription. She had been together with a man for about two years. She'd loved him, she said, very much. Too much, perhaps. He was tall and broad-shouldered, an angry poet, a self-styled revolutionary. He had a temper, too: the floors were seeded with the glass of countless tumblers hurled in anger. A dent in the wall marked where he'd let fly a cast-iron skillet. "This, too," she said, pointing to the question mark above her eyebrow.

"That lump on your back?"

"Right for ten points. I began worrying about him when all he could talk about was burning his brother-in-law's warehouse down."

"Why did you stay with someone like that?"

She took a sip. "I loved him. Sounds pretty sappy, doesn't it?"

"But then you kicked him out because he hit you?"

"It wasn't just that. He did something worse. He wanted to know everything about me. He wanted to know . . . too much."

"Too much?"

"Everyone has secrets. Even you, I bet. But secrets aren't bad, and sometimes they're necessary. A person without a secret is a person without a soul." She stroked my hair. "There's another reason I loved him. He also helped me."

"With what?"

She considered her drink. "With . . . certain things. But then I had to get free of him."

"Couldn't you just throw all this stuff out?"

Her eyes went wide, enclosing everything protectively. "Oh no, I can't. At least not right now. Not yet."

I waited for her to say his name, but she didn't. The rain started up again, brilliant with lightning. She leaned against me, damp and flowery from the soap. I was conscious of her nakedness beneath her thin cotton robe.

"My aunt called me at work," she said softly. "My mother's very sick. I'll have to go and see her soon. There might not be too much time left." Agatha sipped her drink. "She was always on time, never late. She always left the house early enough . . ."

Agatha seemed to be thinking out loud, then sat up abruptly. "You'd better go now."

"Who's John?"

"No one," she said, a strange flicker in her eyes. "Please." She motioned for my sneakers.

"Agatha?" I went to kiss her, but she turned away.

"Please."

I picked up my shoes. Something had just happened, but I didn't know what. Her eyes began to look like those of the man in the cab. I hurried the hell out of there.

I checked on her mailbox on my way out. J. SPRAGUE.

J. John.

So if she was John, who was Agatha?

We kept on meeting each other often, although never planning to. We'd hop on a downtown train and stop at the produce markets along First Avenue for the makings of a supper on the way to her apartment. As soon as we got home, she'd bathe. I began bathing with her. She brought the soap against my chest with sure, broad strokes as might a sculptor, shaping me. She pulled my head against her as she shampooed me, taking a long time, curious fingers working into my scalp, and when she rinsed me with the rubber nozzle, her face took on the pleased look of someone who'd finished something. After we were done bathing, Agatha pulled out a fresh sheet from a great bag of laundry, blinding-white and bearing the chilly press of bleach.

She loved fried fish, so hot weather or no, the kitchen coughed oily smoke. We pulled the mattress to the window to catch a lazy East River breeze while Sarah Vaughn sang: *What is this thing called love, this crazy thing called love?* The shouts of children swelled up from downstairs, cars blasted salsa, and fire trucks pulled garlands of siren through the streets, but Agatha's room remained tranquil. Seltzer bottles accumulated beside the bed along with a still life of paring knife, citrus press, cutting board, and lemons whole, halved, and squeezed.

I gave her gifts: shiny, perfumed bath beads, and a new paring knife from Hoffritz for our spritzers. I thought about her all the time. I decided that she was to become my lover. Each evening I followed her up the stairs—always glancing briefly at the mysterious *J* on the mailbox—wondering whether tonight would be the night we'd consummate our love so that I'd lose my virginity. But each evening, she sent me home abruptly. "Please," she'd say, setting down her spritzer with the finality of a judge's gavel. "Go."

Until one night. I'd just gotten out of the bathtub. Her aunt called. Agatha's telephone rarely rang, and it jolted me to hear it. "Yes," I heard her say in a small whisper. "Yes, of course. I'll have to check with my boss, but I don't know when I'll be able to get away." She spoke carefully, and with pain.

She returned, walking thinly. "My mother's gotten worse. She might not last the summer." Her voice was windy, distant. She placed a hand on my bare shoulder. "Stay with me, won't you?" she whispered, her voice barely more than a fingertip.

I said I would.

"Call your father and tell him where you are."

No one answered. It was a sign. My father was leaving me free to do what I wanted that evening.

Agatha put fresh sheets on the bed. Without warning, her bathrobe slid from her shoulders and onto the floor into a creamy mound, then she turned and pulled on an undershirt. She dug one out of the laundry bag for me, too.

"I'm glad you're here," she said as she shut the light. I lay down, every inch of me buzzing. Her skin sighed as she slipped between the sheets. I waited for our bodies to touch.

"I'm terrified of going to see my mother," she said.

"Because she's going to die?"

"Because—" She reached over and touched my hand. "Let's just sleep, okay?" She turned onto her side, throwing up a wall of back.

I felt adrift in the sheets' white sea. The red lettering stared down at me. Light from the street threw the dent in the wall into sharp relief until it was a ghoulish, all-seeing eye.

"Agatha? Are you asleep?"

"Almost."

"What does that message on the wall mean?"

"Nothing. Go to sleep."

I'm in a woman's bed, I thought. *Something should happen.* I wanted it to. It had to. But I was still soft. I eased myself sideways and pushed up against her as I had against Barry. Just as I was figuring out where to put my arms, she pulled away.

"You don't have to do this, Raymond," she whispered without turning around.

"Agatha—"

"It's okay. Just go to sleep."

I pulled to the far side of the bed, gripping the sheet, annoyed, defeated. How had she divined my secret? I saw Michael scratching his belly, legs stretched out, grinning at me with satisfaction. *Just who are you trying to kid, Andrew?* I followed the snowy curves of Agatha's body beneath her nightshirt, stroking myself discreetly, maliciously, and I got hard, sort of, but I stopped, confused. The apartment's undergrowth of clothing and books and papers seemed to grow and spread, the heavy leaves of a monstrous tropical plant threatening to smother me. My eyes rose to the jigsaw puzzle of the cracked ceiling. My father was with Leona at that moment, the two of them naked in my mother's bedroom. My father was fucking, humping—my father, but not me. Agatha slept.

I reached over and picked up one of the shirts from the nearest pile. The fabric was shiny and wilted from wear. I sniffed under the arms: rank.

It was his. I slipped it on over my T-shirt.

The guy must have been a giant; it billowed around me, smothered me. I checked; Agatha's back was still to me, silent and impassive. I put on a pair of pants, too, the olive-green, army-navy surplus type. I had to hold up the waist to keep it from falling, and the legs trailed along the floor.

The red lettering glowed like neon. I imagined the desk and its typewriter watching me. I began to walk around, feeling like a clown in the oversized clothing. *His clothing.* I sat down at the desk and placed my hands on the keys of the typewriter. *This is where he sat.* I peeked through the boxes and folders and the layers of papers, silt settled to the bottom of a pond, swirling up with the slightest disturbance.

Still she slept. I wondered whether she did so to give me the chance to find out what she herself couldn't tell me. I came upon a stack of books bound together with string tucked away in a corner; each with a black-and-white marbleized cover, the kind I had in grade school, with the rectangle for name and address. I undid the string and opened a book. *It's hardly four o'clock in the afternoon but getting dark. The shortness of winter days conveys a feeling of death. Amazing how in certain moods even weather can make you feel as if you've lost something precious and dear.*

A journal, I thought. *Hers.* My fingers tightened. Reading someone's journal was as low as reading their mail or snooping at them naked in the bathroom. But hard to resist. The chill in my fingertips thawed. I slipped closer to the window to sit in the blue light of the street lamp, the better to read.

When I first found out about her diagnosis, I was furious, not only because it meant that she could die, but because it would let him get away with what he'd done . . .

Everything in the room pointed its finger at me. I was sure Agatha heard the wild knock of my heart. *Close it,* I told myself. *Close it right now. Don't look at another word.* What if she saw? But I flipped ahead. *Just more one page and I'll stop,* I told myself, knowing I wouldn't.

In old novels, I always felt sad when the mother of the bride gave her daughter away. I wanted the two of them to go on peacefully baking bread together, putting up preserves and doing needlework. But always those marriages—always the feast, the hope chest, and yards of wedding-dress silk, no better than a winding sheet . . .

Her life and all the things she hadn't told me, and probably never would, lay in those notebooks. There must have been twenty of them. Hundreds of pages, words, confessions. Secrets. So many secrets.

I quickly shed that man's clothes and got back into bed, but before I did, I took one of the notebooks and slipped it into my pants to take with me.

"Wake up," a chalky voice was saying some time later.

The lights were on. Agatha was fully dressed, standing over me. The room was filmy and vague.

"What's the matter?" I mumbled.

"You have to go now."

"Go?" Had she seen me after all?

"Right now." She turned around so that I could dress. I pulled on my clothes, limbs thick with sleep, with fear.

"What time is it?"

"Almost three. Please hurry." She began pacing.

"I'm sorry I touched you before—"

She wasn't listening. "Here," she said when I'd tied my sneakers. She pressed some bills into my hand, avoiding my glance. "Take a cab."

"What's going on?"

"Please," she said turning her back to me. "You must go."

A moment later, I was standing in the hallway, her door locked. I was sure that if I knocked, a complete stranger would answer. I started down the hall, the floor thin and brittle beneath me, ready to crack, so that I'd plunge through and cut myself on its jagged edges. The notebook jabbed at me inside my pants, a child that knew it was being kidnapped. I trudged past the mailboxes. *J. Sprague.*

Outside, the asphalt was muddy from the day's heat, the humid night clotted uncomfortably against my skin. Agatha had looked at me with a stranger's eyes when she woke me up. She'd forgotten who I was. She had become someone else, but who?

I knew: J. Sprague.

John.

It happened again and again. Agatha would ask me to stay over, only to wake me up several hours later and banish me. I would call up my father to lie about spending the night at Stuie's or Barry's. He'd pretend to believe me. The apartment was always empty when I got home.

Each night I promised myself to leave after we ate, dreading the inevitable early morning eviction. Other times just the thought of waking up to see her standing over me in the middle of the night was so scary that I was determined never to go home with her again. But I always did. Bathing together, eating her fried fish, and sleeping on her fresh sheets, even for a few hours, was more remarkable than anything I'd done before. She got flip-flops so my feet wouldn't get hurt from the glass in the floor. She cut my toenails, bought me buttery-soft cotton socks, and embroidered a T-shirt with my name. She filled me with a kind of bliss, and it didn't matter that it hardly lasted long. For those few hours, I felt married to her. But no matter what, I'd awaken to see her fluttering with discomfort, a distraught angel, and I'd be banished into the night. I gave up trying to convince her to let me stay and meekly left, limbs slack with fatigue. And no matter what, I never left without one of those notebooks.

Mother skates on the Schylkill in winter, Hans Brinker-style, muffler looping up in the wind and all. I call out to warn her where the ice is soft and starting to pool, but she doesn't hear me. She drifts farther away, headed for danger . . .

The notebooks occupied me, they obsessed me. They became all I knew, a whole other world. Each notebook was an attic, hung with secrets like webs that clung to my face as I penetrated them, each one a locked dresser drawer, a hidden pocket. I went to the mail room, barely conscious of what went on around me, tumbling through the years of her life. I learned about her father, about a boy named Owen, roughly my age—she obviously hadn't always been weird about sleeping with people. I learned about that place she'd been sent to, about the woman painter who'd painted that horrible picture of her. I read about her aunt, Mathilde Johanna Sprague. Johanna. I stopped and read her name once more. Johanna. *John.* Slowly I began to understand her silences.

I began to love her, and one night I told her so. We'd just gotten into bed, which meant the countdown had begun until my expulsion.

"Be careful. Loving someone makes it easier to do them harm," she said.

"I'll never do you harm," I said.

But she had already fallen asleep.

Destruction is life. Destruction is creation. Destruction is passion, I must destroy in order to love. Havoc, disarray, dystopia.

There are so many to stifle, restrain, withhold, and pervert me.

Why am I here? What crime have I committed? I am a prisoner of my own rage.

"That's nice," Michael said when I told him about Agatha. "I hope you and *Agatha* will be very happy."

The sneer in his voice was unmistakable. I hadn't seen him since that last time. I'd avoided the terrace. But like my resolution to stay away from her, I knew it was only a matter of time until I found myself climbing the winding concrete steps up toward the top of the park.

"What especially do you like about her, Andrew?"

"She's smart," I said. "She's nice to me. I've never felt this way about anyone before."

"What exactly do you feel, Andrew? Love?"

There was the sneer again. "Fuck you."

He laughed, but only for a moment. "You're unhappy."

"I am not unhappy."

"Every time you come up here, you carry on like a little caliph."

"You don't have to sit next to me if you don't want to."

"You're nasty, too."

Agatha once told me that sometimes it seemed as though I looked at the world through a teller's window, fussy if a slip hadn't been filled out correctly. My forehead grew warm, and there was no breeze to cool it. I crossed my legs and pulled my arms in tight, a basket stubbornly clutched. Why had I come up here, anyway? Maybe for the same reason Agatha asked me over and then threw me out: neither of us knew what we wanted. I noticed Michael looking down.

"What's wrong?" I asked.

An irritated wave of his hand told me not to worry myself.

"Tell me."

"Why? Is it really so important for you to know? Do you really care? For your information, something was wrong the last time you saw me, too, but it would never have occurred to you to have asked . . . Raymond."

I pulled back. "Why did you call me that?"

"For the same reason it's embroidered on your T-shirt: it's probably your real name. And I might know one or two other things about you that you haven't told me."

Something knuckled into my chest. I longed to flee but couldn't. *Because there didn't seem anywhere to run to.* His silence held me. He lit a cigarette, pulled in the smoke, gulping it down like food before discharging it. "Do you remember you once asked me why I come up here? Well, now I'll tell you. Because it's nice. Much nicer than it is down there. It's scary up here sometimes. I've been roughed up once or twice, sure. But I've had some sweet moments up here, too, which is more than I can say for down there."

"Where's 'down there'?"

"The rest of the world. That's why I told you I didn't want you coming back here. This place was nice, but you made it as ugly as any other. You had no right. There are plenty of ugly places as it is, you don't have to ruin this one."

"Mind if I have one of those?" I asked, motioning to his cigarettes.

"You don't smoke," he said. "Go home, Andr—I mean, Raymond. Whatever your fucking name is. Just go home."

I heard the hurt in his voice. "Let me stay. Please."

"On one condition: if you agree to tell me exactly what's on your mind and not lie, okay?"

I nodded.

"Start." He folded his arms across his chest, waiting.

"My father drinks all the time," I said. "I think he feels bad for cheating on my mother."

"Do you like your father?"

"I didn't use to. But now I do. Now I think I understand him. And I want to help him, but I can't. My mother's coming home at the end of the summer, and I'm leaving for college. There's nothing I can do."

"Maybe he doesn't need your help. What else do you have to tell me?"

"That's it."

He shook his head. "There's something else, Raymond."

"Your turn," I insisted.

He stamped out his cigarette, stripped it as before. "My wife is moving to California. She'll be taking our son with her."

Wife. Son. What was he talking about? "I didn't know . . . I thought . . ."

"He's eight. His name is Ronald. Real smart. Reads a new book every week. A mind as quick as a finger snap." He bricked the words together slowly, painfully. "Bet you were like that, too." He smiled. "Ronald. Raymond. They almost sound the same."

"How come you're married?"

"How *come?* Most people are."

"But you . . ."

"She's taking him with her when she moves out next month. I'm going on a trip with him in a couple of days up to New Hampshire. It'll be my last chance to see him for a while. They always give the kid to the woman." He leaned forward, elbows on his knees, each arm carrying its weight of muscle. I moved a little closer, then a little more. The street swirled faintly below, a world apart from us.

The sadness in his voice was strangely soothing. I'd never heard a man sound that way—yearning instead of demanding, needing instead of taking. He'd almost stopped being a man and had become someone—something—else. And then he began to cry. He was the second man I'd seen crying that summer after years of dry-eyed uncles, fathers, and grandfathers. He wrapped a hand tightly around his eyes, either to hide his tears or perhaps to stop them. I pressed against him, expecting Barry's resistance, but Michael gave, soft and hard at the same time. I put my arms around him, and they stretched to include every inch, every pound, I reeled to know that I was holding a man. We sat there like this until he stopped crying.

"Look at me," he said, letting his arm slip away. He wiped his eyes with the back of his hand.

I held on. "Are you okay?"

He shrugged, and his warm bulk shifted against me.

"Michael," I said, pulling my arm back. "Can I ask you something?" But I had no question, only an intention. I flung my arm around him once more.

"Are you going to tell me something?" he asked in a husky whisper.

My fingers gripped the hard surface of his back, and I imagined his muscles softening to let my hand sink into them. I swung myself up off the bench toward him, holding on to his shoulders, and then I straddled his thighs and wrapped my legs tight around them.

"Whoa," he said with a smile. "What's this?" He went to lift me off, but I held on tighter. Something had started inside me. I pushed my face against his chest and pressed myself against him. I felt his hardness beneath his jeans and thrust against it hard as well. He gripped my arms, and I feared he might lift me off, but he merely tried to steady me. I burned with the feel of his thing against mine. His thigh muscles broadened and tightened. He lifted a leg and pressed it against me, letting me feel it, rubbing our things together harder and faster. "Okay," he whispered. "That's it. Let it go." Seconds later, I exploded. Wind blew from my mouth and through my brain, and slowly my limbs thawed and slackened.

He lifted me off him. "You're going to get us both in trouble," he said. "Is that what you do to Agatha?"

I could barely stand. I shook my head.

"Well, don't. Girls aren't as tough as guys. You might break something. Go on home," he said, giving my bicep a squeeze.

Back in my building's lobby, I glimpsed myself in one of the mirrors: face flushed, my hair matted to spikes, a wet patch between my legs, a badge, a mark. *Look at yourself,* I thought, a wet spot cooling deliciously against my thigh. *Look. See. Know. Know at last.*

Week after week, I read the journals, sitting on my bed before the open window, a cigarette burning leisurely in the ashtray. Living rooms rang with the sounds of happy people across the alley, televisions blared the canned laughter of situation comedies, but those marbleized notebooks concealed the world of Agatha and her aunt, her father and mother in a haunted suburban castle. I read those journals until I was no longer able to read, then got up the next morning and continued reading on the subway. I read constantly, obsessively. I read on even when I wasn't sure of what I was reading. It didn't matter—I had to continue. Nights when my eyes went papery with strain, when the cramped writing on the page resembled no more than a sooty window, I began to understand why people were paid to spy, why they spied, and why they listened through doorways, tapped phones, or steamed open letters: there was nothing as irresistible as knowing someone else's thoughts. Sometimes I hardly read the words at all, so giddy was I with revelation. And it was thrilling to know that she didn't know I knew.

Agatha has never forgiven him, so how can she forgive me? Her love has been tainted, so how can she love me? But I will cleanse her. I will purify her. I will teach her that love must not mean subjugation . . .

Agatha? Forgive me? Agatha forgiving herself? I'd been waiting for the train on the way home from work and stared into the jagged movie of the subway tunnel, waiting for the confusion in my head to clear.

He never liked me because I won't condone his bloodsucking ways. Will golf clubs bring the civilization forward? Tennis rackets? Badminton sets? So what if I lived in his garage for a couple of months? I will not recant what I have said, that he is a bloodsucker squeezing the lifeblood out of his employees, amassing his wealth through legal slavery . . .

Who was living in whose garage?

He has perverted my sister. Her diamonds shine with the sweat of oppression. She sheathes herself in the skins of animals slain to satiate her mean desire . . .

This didn't sound like the woman in the lab coat I'd been reading about. And Agatha had never mentioned a sister.

She who shares my birthright, half of my soul, and half of my heart . . .

In Van Cortlandt Park in her nice holiday dress, overcome by the loveliness of the day, she runs through the grass, a fluttering pinwheel, until her father calls her back to the path. Her dress is soiled; he promises punishment. Her eyes fill with tears. How can such freedom end in sorrow? It is almost too much for me to bear and I vow to avenge her misery. My beautiful sister . . .

I read that over again. Agatha wasn't Jewish. She'd never mentioned a sister.

The pages began to go flabby with ranting and long-winded whining, or else they were bludgeoned senseless by verbiage, iron prose weighting them down: bourgeois, this, oppression that. The Third World. Multinational conspiracies. *She tells me that I should stop blaming the world for imagined injustices.*

Imagined? How can she say this? The world is thorned by greed . . .

It began to sound as if someone else had written this journal, yet the handwriting remained the same. I continued reading and rereading, detective and thief at the same time.

I am my mother's daughter.

Only when you have denied me will I return.

They'd been written by the same hand, but I was sure they couldn't have been the same person's thoughts. The daughter had to be Agatha/John, but the second writer?

During those long nights when she sleeps and I cannot, when I yearn for her but cannot have her, what is there for me to do? So I have begun to read them, each and every one of them, from cover to cover.

I thought of that inscription: *Only when you have denied . . .*

I stopped reading. The train was hurtling past a string of white-tiled stations, each one terribly empty. I grew convinced that even if these journals were hers, they weren't all hers. But if she hadn't written them, who had?

Only when you have denied . . .

I felt the grungy shirt over my shoulders once more, the baggy pants trailing. He and I, insomniacs against our will, had something in common: we'd both been prisoners of her silence. He'd not only read her journals, as I now did, *he'd copied from them.* I flipped back to a passage I'd read the other day but passed over in confusion:

I will preserve the archive of her misery by transcribing it. I will help her to free herself from the manacles of her soul. I will make sure her words don't disappear.

With each station, the train gained speed, gained fury, matching the race of my discoveries. *I will do this to know her. I will find out everything.* So he thought he was cribbing everything for her own good. What a creep. But was I any better?

Art is life, life, art, and an artist must appropriate what is needed.

The train eased to a stop. How much had he himself written, how much had he copied?

And where had it been copied from?

That summer I began to see things I'd never seen before. A frail old man crossing the street in the middle of the block was sheared between a moving bus and a parked car and ground to no more than a smear on the asphalt. A woman just as old pulled her clothes off in the middle of a steaming street and began running, a terrible sack of bones and withered skin. The subway riders seemed as limp and lifeless as before, but I detected mayhem within. Days of heavy rain during the middle of August turned midtown into a bayou, followed by days of miserable heat. In the space of weeks, the world seemed to have grown dangerous. Things seemed out of balance and uncontrolled. Had it always been that way, or had the journals allowed me to see it?

The Anguished Poet—my name for the writer—was angry at a world heavy with something called "weltschmerz." *The world is a sewer,* the AP wrote. *People are ignorant because they are too lazy or too fearful to be wise. If knowledge is power, then wisdom is always courage. But most people are idiots and cowards.* He might have been a bad-tempered lunatic, but maybe he was some kind of visionary who saw things others wished weren't there. *The world needs a cataclysm to cleanse itself, and I will help create it.*

The next page bore a single chilling sentence: *She came home from the hospital bearing my scar, a defiant purple slash across her cheek . . .*

I closed the book, frightened.

Once after leaving her apartment at two in the morning, I turned a corner and a shadow shifted behind me: I hurried along, scanning the dark pockets of doorways for danger, keeping to the middle of the street as I'd been taught to do. Avenue B looked empty but safe, and I'd walked that stretch of street several times that summer late at night without anything happening. But moments later, a figure darted out from the moldy-smelling darkness beneath the Charles Theater's corroded marquee.

"You," growled a dark face. Seconds later, a big guy was pushing me up against the wall, his grip handcuffing me, throwing me backward into what had been the niche for the movie posters.

"Leave me alone—"

"You little snipe," he said. "You arrogant little farthead! You fuck-dog-asshole. What are you doing here?"

I struggled to free myself, but he was very strong.

"I've been following you. I know what you're up to."

Up close, he was even larger and wilder. "Let me go," I said, unable to break from his iron hold.

One hand clamped around my neck while the other worked down my body to get the notebook free.

"You little shit," he said, snatching it up and wielding it like a weapon. "Where did you get this?" I tried to make a run for it, but he threw me against the wall. "I should trash you right now, slimebag! I should break your head and stomp your brains!" He grabbed hold of my shirt, ripping it off and hurling me once more against the wall. "The next time I catch you up in her apartment, I'll kill you," he said. "Now get the fuck out of here!"

I ran all the way to the station. A light rain had begun to fall, and, without my shirt, I shivered. My neck stung from where he'd grabbed it. When the train came, I remembered the money Agatha had given me for a cab, but the doors closed and I sat down, wet, naked, and unprotected. Fatigue laced my brain like liquor. I was an egg with its shell broken, insides puddling out. All around me, wrinkled heartbreaks of people lay asleep in foul corners of the car. And I felt like one of them.

Only when you have denied me will I return. That guy had seen me going over there with her. He'd been waiting downstairs when I left. My stop came and I trudged home.

"Raymond!"

My father opened the door, a limp undershirt half out of his pants. He looked worn, used. The television squawked in the background. It must have been almost four in the morning. He'd been waiting up. I'd always called from Agatha's to say I'd be coming home late, but this time I'd forgotten. He threw a heavy arm around me that was sticky with sweat. He'd been drinking. His face sank against the side of my head.

"Where were you? What happened?" He fingered my face as my mother would have. The door was still open, and his cries multiplied in the hallway.

"I'm okay," I said, anxious to free myself. I was conscious of being shirtless. I was about to lie about being over at Barry's when a woman I'd never seen emerged from the living room. She was tall, perhaps even taller than my father, barefoot, and wearing a brightly patterned dress. When she smiled, a trident of wrinkles formed at the corners of her eyes. She was black.

"Oh," I gulped.

"This is Leona," my father said.

She smiled shyly. "Hello, Ray-mohnd."

I wondered whether I was supposed to shake her hand and decided it would be better to just smile and say hello. I didn't quite look at her. Her brown, naked feet pressed into the carpet, large and confident. *Is this Paul?*

"I waited until midnight, and when you still didn't come home, I called your friends," my father said.

"We didn't know where you were," Leona said.

We.

"What happened to your back, Raymond? Where's your shirt?"

"I got into a fight. In the park."

"What were you doing in the park at this hour?" Without waiting for an answer, his heavy arm squeezed me close once more. "Don't you ever pull this again, you hear?" His eyes were fierce and fluid.

I swallowed. "Yes, Dad."

"Let's get that bruise looked after before we do any more talking," Leona said. She took my hand and led me into the bathroom, sat me down on the toilet seat, and dabbed a stinging coat of iodine onto the wound. Her brown fingers worked in the iodine, looking as if her own skin color were pouring onto mine.

This is her, I thought. *The woman.*

"Tonight your father tell me he don' understand you," she said, lips pulled tight. Her fingers worked with force, trying to pump some sense into me. "He tell me he don' understand notin' anymore about you. I tell him boys your age are in they own world, so there's no point tryin' to make no sense."

Her voice was like pieces of marble, smooth here but jagged there. Even if my father was confused about me, she wasn't. She knew where my bruises came from, or could easily guess, her fingers divining things about me that very moment.

"Are you ungry?" she asked, putting away the iodine.

It had been a long time since anyone asked me that question in the bachelor pad our apartment had become. I nodded yes and followed her into the kitchen. She took out a frying pan, eggs and milk, and began to cook. For the first time in weeks, the kitchen held the smell of real, fresh food. I watched as she used my mother's utensils, her cookware, her old stoneware bowl. Leona wore my mother's frilly apron, but her bare feet made her seem just a little . . . untamed. My father took a bottle of whiskey from a kitchen cabinet and headed for the living room.

"Paul, you put that away now," she called after him. "Raymohnd is back."

He kept on going. I ate ravenously. The eggs were fluffy, and there was toast, and fried potatoes flecked with a surprise of red pepper. Leona sat on the other side of the table and beamed to see me eating food she'd cooked.

"Your father is sad because you leavin' home soon," she said.

It was odd to hear a stranger talk about me. Her accent was like a woodcut, made of edges and gullies.

"He tell me how he miss you all summer when you stay out late."

"Sorry." I tried to figure out her age, but sometimes it's hard to tell with a black person. She looked young but spoke like someone older.

"Your father a good man," she said. "He drink too much, that's all. He work himself up into a *steyht* all the time. He just want to be stone-cold drunk when your mother come back so he don't have to face her. I been married, and my husband was a drinker, too. Men, they don't want to face tings."

"He never used to drink."

"He never used to *tink,* neither. Your mother goin' away force him to." She looked at me. "You smart. I bet you tink no one understand you."

Leona was like some people I knew: if you said nothing, they would go on talking.

"Did my father tell you when my mother's coming back?"

She rubbed her hands together, giving herself comfort. I'd hurt her without meaning to.

"Yes. I know. Did you like the omelette?"

From the living room came a crash. Leona shot up. "Paul?" she cried.

We hurried over. My father stood near the couch. The bottle of whisky had dropped onto the coffee table, shattering its glass top.

"What you doin' here, Paul?" Leona said.

"Get away from here," my father mumbled, pushing her away with limp hands.

She picked up the whiskey bottle to survey the damage. "You done it now, Paul," she said, looking at the star-shaped crater in the glass. "You and your drinkin'. Raymond, get me a rag and a dustpan."

"Why is it women always have to clean things up?" my father asked. "Why can't they just leave things dirty? There's nothing to fix, Leona. Nothing." His speech wobbled around him. I went for the dustpan.

"Your mother called at the press today, Raymond," he said, his voice trailing after me. "All the way from the Promised Land. The Holy Land. Your mother's holy, too. That's why she went there. She's holier than the rest of us. Sure didn't want to speak to me, though. Guess she thinks you're pretty holy, too. How about you? You think you're holy?"

I got the dustpan and a rag. He didn't take his eyes off me as Leona and I swept up the pieces of broken glass. "Oh no. It's you she misses, Ray. You're the apple of her eye. You're the golden boy. Me, I don't mean shit to her!" He swayed as he spoke. Drinking left him flimsy. Every syllable sent gusts of liquor my way. "But you like me, don't you, Leona?" He leaned over and threw his arms around her middle.

"Paul!" She pushed him away.

"You'd want to go into the desert with me, too? C'mon. Let's go—" He lurched forward again, grabbed her from behind and pinched her. She swung around and smacked his face, and he slumped halfway across the sofa, curled up like an insect. He began weeping softly.

"Dad!" I said.

Leona fled. She appeared a moment later in her shoes and her jacket, holding a shoulder bag.

"How's his face, Raymond?" she asked me.

"Leona, you're not going?" my father said. "Please—"

"I have to be at work tomorrow."

"Don't go, Leona."

"Raymond's here now, he'll look after you." She looked at me. "Get him to bed, you hear?" She turned to go, dress swaying around her. The front door opened and closed, and her shoes clacked in the hallway.

We sat like that for a while, then he pushed himself up.

"Dad?"

"Shut up, okay? Just shut up."

I've always pitied Mother. Pity is a female cottage industry, like piecework and taking in laundry. Marys draped with Jesuses dripping sympathy, hookers with hearts of gold, etc. Women throw themselves into another's misery, eager to get dirty. Compassion is men's work. Philosophical, detached. Clean. What man would marry a woman in a wheelchair? Only a woman would have married a cripple, especially one she didn't love. But Mother wasn't that stupid, so if she chose a cripple, she must have wanted a man who wouldn't make too many demands on her.

New Cornwall, October 3

He wants to leave. He wants to take me with him. In a weak moment, I told him that if I left, he could stay with me for a while, but only for a while. I told him I still wasn't sure. He says he loves me, but I know what he's looking for: forgiveness. He knows what the world knows: no one can forgive like a woman.

TEN

I had finally reached the last two journals. I worried that Agatha would notice how the stack had diminished, even though I took pains to throw clothing into the corner to cover it. Yet I couldn't figure any way of returning them. I told myself she was always so anxious for me to leave that she probably never saw anything stuck down the front of my pants. She would have felt it, had she let me hug her, but that was out of the question. I vowed to get them back somehow.

Those last two volumes were crammed with details of what the Anguished Poet referred to as The Plan. All references to Agatha disappeared. Pages were as densely written as the unreadable political tracts I'd seen pasted onto lamp poles in her neighborhood. The handwriting grew stern, it grew scary, the script of one possessed. The first entries describing it were dated from the year before. Details changed, but the main goal was to avenge what the AP called his brother-in-law's crimes against humanity. He'd cowed his wage slaves into submission. Unionless, they were unable to stand up for their rights, so he would do it for them. In reality, however, the AP's motives were clear enough: he was supremely pissed off at the guy and wanted to get back at him.

The Plan was simple: he would sneak into his brother-in-law's sporting-goods warehouse in Long Island City and burn it to the ground. He had it all figured out. It would take but a small container of benzine to douse a carton of basketballs, a match would be lit, and the job would be done. Pages were crammed with floor plans of the warehouse and maps of the surrounding streets. Routes of approach and escape were indicated, written with chilling detail. There was even a timetable of the N train. I had to laugh: the AP was probably the only revolutionary who'd ever planned a getaway on a subway train. It was to take place on August 25, the anniversary, it was noted, of Nietzsche's death. "Nietzsche, 1844–1900," written in heavy block letters and framed with an ornate border that took up half a page, a kind of memorial.

Agatha's name came up unexpectedly. *She'll help me. She'll do it for me if she loves me. She'll do it because she knows what it is to have a monster as a father*. I thought of Agatha's scars, the dent in the wall, the broken glass. Now it made sense. She'd refused to help him and he'd struck her. I thought of the mound of clothing in Agatha's apartment, the piles of books and papers like a fortress built around her bed with its spotless sheets. She'd let herself be surrounded by him, even if she could no longer bear to be with him. She still loved him. Him, and not me.

August 25. It was a week from today. Why did that date stick in my mind? Then I remembered. It was when my mother was due back from Israel.

Barry suggested meeting in Rockefeller Center during my lunch hour. He'd swing by during one of his messenger runs. We arranged to meet on the steps of St. Patrick's Cathedral, across the street from the huge statue of a bronze man holding up the world. Weekends he was off on one of his long-distance jaunts, training for that crazy scheme of his to kidnap Felix. Otherwise, he worked. I got myself a can of soda and studied the statue. Monstrous bronze bulges of muscle exploded from his arms and legs, and he looked ready to hurl his globe onto Fifth Avenue for no reason at all. A man's body was power, by its very nature dangerous. No wonder men scared me, even if I yearned for their sweaty press.

After leaving Michael that night, I'd gone home, stripped down to my underwear and smelled what had gone sticky and stiff all over my skin. There was a lot. I still didn't know what made me do that with him, except being sure that he wouldn't hurt me. He was strong but gentle, and for that reason, irresistible.

Barry appeared several minutes later, sweating and sheathed in a tight-fitting cyclist's jersey. He'd grown even thinner than before, almost delicate compared to the bronze man lurching above us. He set his bike against the sidewalk—racers had no kickstands—and squirted a stream of water into his mouth from a bottle.

"Great day," he said, even though it was almost ninety degrees. Barry loved heat and exertion.

"I have to show you something." I removed one of the journals from a plastic bag.

"You found this?"

"I sort of borrowed it." There was so much I hadn't told him: Agatha, Michael, Leona, but I didn't feel like going into it. "A friend of mine lent it to me."

He looked at me. "What kind of friend?"

"A girlfriend," I said. It was true, in a way.

"Oh yeah? What's her name?"

I told him.

His eyes sharpened. "You do it with her yet?"

"Yes," I said, rationalizing my lie by telling myself that I referred to Michael, not Agatha. Michael was right: I was a liar.

"Yeah?" he said, eyes wide. "How was it? Was it her first time? Did she just let you, or did you have to make her?"

I smiled confidently. "Ask Felix."

His face turned cold. "Listen, whoever that girl is, she's probably just a twit. By the way, her name's Patricia. I made Felix tell me all about her. She plays the goddamn harp. Can you imagine anything as lame as a harp? Felix doesn't have time for someone like her." Barry looked ready to keep on talking about her until he remembered the journal and began flipping through the pages of diagrams and explanations.

"Whoever this guy is, he looks dangerous. You can tell by the handwriting." He shook his head and pointed to a block of script almost too dense to read. "This kind of penmanship is the mark of an obsessive-compulsive personality. I once read a book about it. And these diagrams . . . the guy looks off the wall."

"Who was Nietzsche?"

"Some German. Probably a Nazi. Maybe this guy is one, too." He grinned. "Know what? I think we should just go to this place and see if it's on the level." He pulled out a street map from his back pocket. "Looks like it should be near the Sunnyside rail yards. We can take Broadway as far as Seventy-second Street, cut through Central Park—"

"You want to go to that warehouse? On August twenty-fifth?"

"Yeah. It'd be fun to see whether this guy actually shows up."

"And then what?" I thought of that crazy encounter on Avenue B, the wild face snorting close to mine, the rank of his body and breath.

"I don't know. Watch, I guess. Anyway, we can wind our way down Fifty-ninth Street and then pedal over the bridge."

"Pedal?"

"A bike ride like this'll be good training for you when we go up to get Felix."

I let it pass. If he still thought I was going to help him

kidnap his brother—and on a bicycle—he was crazy. "I'm not biking through Harlem, Barry."

"Broadway's no problem. There's plenty of people. It's during the day. I've gone up and down Broadway tons of times and nothing's ever happened to me."

"But it's so far to Long Island City. And it's hot. Let's take the subway."

"We should be able to do it in three hours or less," he said, as if I hadn't spoken. "We'll bring water, food, take our time. You'll be able to do it—" He stopped. "Wait, this thing is supposed to happen on August twenty-fifth? Fuck! I was planning to go up to Felix on that day."

Great, I thought. *That takes care of that.*

"I suppose we could go a day or two later." He jotted something down in a pocket calendar. "Okay. We do this on the twenty-fifth, then go up to Felix on the twenty-seventh." He looked at his watch, squirted another stream of water into his mouth, and got up. "Let's meet at my house this Saturday." He gave the journal back to me and flung himself onto the saddle, slicing into the traffic.

What if he got up to the music camp to find Felix and that girl making out? Would he slash her like a jealous lover? I opened the journal, glancing at the pages freighted with their ominous messages. Barry was right. The guy wasn't all there. Yet I had begun to like him.

Agatha and I stood before fragrant slabs of sea bass and snapper, smooth and buttery on a palette of ice. The eyes of the fish glistened like mica. Agatha's hand gripped mine when it came to rest on the counter.

"I like you," she said. "You've finally become soft. Now we can be friends."

I'd become less of a jerk in her eyes, less of a bank teller. But I was a sneak thief, pillaging those notebooks week after week as she slept, then spiriting them away. They collected in a dark corner at the bottom of my closet like library books too overdue to return. Once I'd justified my snooping as revenge for Agatha not making love to me; now I was simply nosy. But no matter how miserable I felt about what I did, I'd kept on stuffing those notebooks down my pants and sneaking them out of the apartment. I was no better than the AP. He'd fashioned himself a poet/revolutionary, but he was simply a hot-tempered freeloader, a plagiarist, a fake.

The scar above Agatha's eyebrow warned me that my fate could be similar making off with the journals, but I didn't care. I started slipping the paring knife I'd bought her into my jeans each time I left her apartment and dared the AP to catch me. One time he tried, but I outran him, clutching the latest journal tight against my groin all the way to First Avenue, where I hailed a cab and escaped, movie-style, seeing him fume in the rearview mirror.

"A pound and a half of the flounder, please," Agatha was saying to the guy behind the counter. She turned to me. "Let's get some wine tonight, too, okay?"

We took a long time to reach her building. School started in less than ten days. She'd made up her mind to go to Philadelphia and visit her mother in the coming week, which meant that I would be gone by the time she returned. Things were about to end.

"I'm going to miss you, Agatha."

"You'll be back for winter break. I'll see you then."

It wasn't what I wanted her to say. I wanted her to tell me not to go, to stay in the city and move in with her. I'd begun to have second thoughts about going away. My father was becoming an alcoholic and carrying on with a woman who'd practically moved in. There was Michael, too. I couldn't leave in the middle of it all. But mostly, I couldn't leave Agatha, who cared for me as no one else ever had. We reached her stoop.

The weird man was at the window across the street, as always, someone I always thought might take pleasure in pinning down live moths.

"What's wrong with him?" I asked.

"Just another soul living a life of quiet desperation, what else?"

We walked up the stairs slowly.

J. Sprague.

She bathed—she asked to do so alone this time—and changed into a white nightgown. When I finished my bath, I stepped out of the tub, and stubbed my big toe on a carton rock-hard with books. The cartons loomed even larger than usual that evening, heavier, more immovable.

"Fuck!" I cried. Each throb was a Morse-code message of anger. The AP was taking silent revenge. It would be just a matter of time until he cornered me on a night I didn't have the paring knife. "I've never understood why you keep this stuff. Why don't you just give it back or let him cart his stupid junk away?" I hobbled to the bed.

"It's not junk, Raymond," she said, frighteningly calm. I knew I'd said the wrong thing.

Agatha was pulling wobbly slices of flounder across a sandy floor of bread crumbs as I nursed my toe. Moments later, the fish sizzled in the pan, the sound painful. *Who fries fish in this heat?* I thought. Everything annoyed me. I felt like throwing things around. I was pissed at having to go away. Letters from the college arrived welcoming me and assigning me to my dorm. There were forms to fill out: Meal plan? Proposed major? Athletics? Yet nothing seemed to matter except staying in this crowded, broken apartment with Agatha.

"Getting hungry?" Agatha stood with the spatula in her hand, oblivious to my animosity.

We put on fresh sheets and ate sitting by the window as usual, but that night no breeze cooled us. Agatha stared into space, never looking my way. A thick canopy of fume hung just above my head. The fish tasted too heavy to eat. The streets were uncomfortably still; I missed their urgent calamity. The air was like plastic, difficult to breathe. I eyed the corner where the journals had been. The AP was right: I was a snipe and a fart-head.

"You okay?"

She nodded.

"You angry?"

She didn't answer. The phone rang. She set down her plate. "I can't come any sooner," I heard her say. "I can't." There was a pause. "Yes. All right. Yes."

"I really have to go see my mother," she said when she returned. "I can't put it off any longer."

"Won't your boss let you take off?"

"It's not that." Her hand fell to the sheet. "My aunt says that if I wait until the end of the week, it might be too late."

I set down my plate.

"I don't want to go," she whispered to an empty space in the middle of the room, hardly aware I was there. "I can't."

"Why not?"

"If I wait until the end of the week, then she'll be dead by the time I get there. It will be all over."

"Agatha?"

"I'm bad," she whispered. "I'm so very bad. But I didn't mean to be. I didn't mean to hurt you, Mother."

The news changed her, it flicked a switch. She spoke as she did when waking me up in the middle of the night, half herself, half not. I sensed something about to happen, and the room seemed to shift. She rose and walked to the corner where the journals would have been.

I stood up. I had to stop her from going there. "You can go to Philadelphia tomorrow," I said. "I'll go with you—"

"They're full of my secrets," she said, ever closer to the corner. She began picking through the clothing. My heart chugged. "He knew what I did. I didn't tell him, but he knew. He found out. He *spied.*"

"Who?"

"He knew everything. There is nothing worse than someone knowing everything about you. It means there's nowhere else for you to go. It means that no matter what, you'll always be watched, you'll always be . . . naked."

"Agatha?"

She smiled, looking right at me once more, back from wherever she'd gone. "Yes, Ray?"

"What are you talking about?"

"He stole my secrets, don't you see? It went on for months: the creak of the wheelchair outside my door, his eyes fingering me. Mother knew what he was up to but wouldn't do anything. She was too afraid. 'Tell him to stop,' I said. She asked me whether I had anything to hide. 'Look me right in the eye and swear that you don't. Swear you've always been a good girl.' At that moment, I hated her, and so I told her the truth. I said I let those boys do it to me. I said I wanted them to make me bad."

She no longer looked at me but spoke as if talking in her sleep.

This was what the AP heard while in bed beside her.

"I planned to leave after high school. I couldn't stay there with him. I had to get away. But she wanted me to stay. She didn't want to be left alone with him. One night I threw open the door and he was there in the wheelchair, hands between his legs. I should have hurled him down the stairs. I should have broken him. But he was too strong. I ran to Mother's room off the kitchen with a pair of scissors and . . . I went at her."

"John," I said to myself.

Her head snapped around, suddenly alert, eyes flaring. "What did you say? Don't call me that," she snarled. "That's his name, not mine. I have nothing to say to him. All he wants is forgiveness. He wants things to be settled before my mother dies."

"That man who lived here with you, did he know all this?"

She shook her head. "He wanted to. He was going to put it all in a book about me. He said he loved me, but he only wanted my secrets."

"Is your name really John?"

"Johanna. Named after my aunt. So that she'd leave money for me in her will."

"Your Aunt Mattie, right?"

"What did you say?"

"Mattie. Your aunt—"

"How do you know her name?"

"On the mailbox—"

"It's *not* there. It's not anywhere. How do you know her name? Tell me!" She threw herself at me, grabbing my shoulders. "You listened too, just like he did. You heard me while I slept. You snooped. You robbed, you took!"

"No, I didn't—"

She yanked me up to my feet. "Leave," she said. "Get out. Get out now. Go!" The red inscription glowed fiercely on the wall behind her. *Only when you have denied me will I return.* She threw open the door and pushed me toward it, and I stumbled over boxes and clothing on the way. "Get out! You stinking pig! Get out!"

"Look who's here," my father said as I opened the front door. "Staying home for a change?"

"Yes. Where's Leona?"

"Home," he said, weight in his voice. "You okay? You look bad. What's the matter?"

"I'm hungry," I lied. "Let's go someplace. How about the cafeteria?"

"Worst food in the Bronx. Sure."

I smiled. It was great seeing him.

"Seems like years ago when I ran into you here," he said,

holding open the glass door. We filled up our trays and got a table.

"Not as good as what Leona makes," I said, examining the roast beef under its pasty mat of gravy.

"She's breaking things off," my father said. "How did she put it? 'I tought we were having a little vacation, but a vacation that don't end is work.' "

I could just imagine her saying that. I was going to miss her. She had all the advantages of my mother without taking everything so seriously. Leona knew how to be happy; I wasn't sure my mother did, or else she didn't think it was necessary.

My father hardly touched his food but held his fork, looking ready to letter with it.

"She's leaving the press, too. Moving to Florida to be with her children. But she's coming over one more time. We're going to have a kind of farewell party." He looked at me. "You're going away soon, too, aren't you?" I nodded. "You don't seem very excited about it."

I was never going to see Agatha again.

She would never forgive me for what I'd done.

"I'm not," I said.

"You should be. You're going to college. It's a big deal. Wish I'd gone to college. Maybe I'd have amounted to something."

"You have amounted to something."

"Knock it off and eat this slop. We got to give you some money for clothes. Your mother'll go shopping with you when she gets back."

I quickened. It was the first time he'd mentioned her in a while. He slid some peas from one side of the plate to the other.

"I want to give it another try with your mother," he said. "I hope things work out. I know I can be a pain sometimes. But sometimes your mother is . . ." He put down his knife and fork. "She means well, but she just tries too hard."

"To do what?"

"Everything. She's never been able to let things be."

I understood. Any time my mother didn't know what to say, she said something else. For her, not talking was a sign of not knowing.

"And Leona?"

"Leona," he said, and his voice drifted off, carrying her name with it.

I tried to eat more of the roast beef but couldn't. My father and I had both ventured far from what we'd known, we'd been cast off, and now we had to find our way back. The fans droned around us. Time seemed empty for the moment while our lives waited before starting up again.

I noticed Michael standing just beyond our table.

Where had he come from? For all I knew, he'd been watching us the whole time. He wore sneakers and a pair of jeans and held the hand of a little boy who looked a lot like him. Our eyes met and he smiled, looking ready to come over until my glance shot down to the grey mess of my mashed potatoes. From the corner of my eye, I saw him and the little boy head toward the counter.

"You know that guy?" my father asked.

I caught my breath. Something told me that I had better not deepen the lie. "Yes," I said.

He studied Michael's retreating form and looked ready to say something. I recognized the look on his face from those mornings when my mother had wanted us to go to Brooklyn, when she'd tried to convince him to go on a vacation, or when she'd attempted to persuade him to do anything he didn't want to do and he'd resisted because it upset his routine or took him too far from himself. It was a look that peered out from behind a curtain, keeping him not hidden, but veiled. His was the face of a man who wasn't sure he wanted others to see him, since they might ask something of him that he'd have to refuse, and that might lead to conflict.

Michael and the boy walked by our table once more on the way out.

"Make sure to tell your father how much you love him . . .

Andrew," he said sharply. They left. The glass door blew a gust of stale air into my face as it opened and closed.

"Who's Andrew?"

"Let's get out of here."

He pushed his plate away. "We don't really know each other that well, do we?" my father said. "And now you're going off."

He spent the rest of the evening as he often had since my mother left: first with lettering, then with drinking. Just before I went to sleep, I found him slouched on the sofa in his undershirt, looking like a statue taken off its mount. I roused him so that he could undress and brush his teeth, but he shoved my hand away. As always, drinking put him in a foul mood.

"I knew about you. I even told Leona. I knew." His eyes fixed me in a sloppy gaze. "You never thought I knew anything about you, did you?" He laughed darkly. "What you don't know . . ."

"Dad—" I didn't want to hear anything else.

"You and your little secrets. *Andrew.* Jesus! Everybody and their stupid little secrets . . ."

"Dad, go to sleep."

"Stop playing mother, for God's sake. You already have a mother." He slumped back into the sofa. "Andrew," he mumbled.

"I cook something nice for you and Paul," Leona said, her words hammering pleasantly off-kilter as always. An oily sweetness filled the kitchen. She'd spread a tablecloth and folded the napkins to look like flowers. She'd done all she could to make the evening festive, but the inevitable loomed: my mother was returning tomorrow. I sensed Leona handling the dishes and utensils with special care, striving to return them to their rightful owner undamaged.

"Put on som-ting nice tonight, Ray-mohnd," she said. The

light danced on the gold cross around her neck. I was going to miss her.

"Hello, Ray," my father said, coming into the kitchen. He wore his usual shiny-seat pants but had on a fresh shirt. He carried a glass of whiskey.

"No, Paul," Leona said.

"I'm diluting it," he said, pouring in a splash of seltzer.

We sat down. The trio of Sabbath candles sat on their shelf unlit, shunning everything until my mother's return, ready to tell her all they knew about what had transpired in her absence the first time she lit them. The meat tasted spicy, but I wasn't sure what kind of meat it was.

Leona kept flitting back and forth from stove to table, just as my mother used to do.

"Sit down already, Leona," my father told her.

"You really driving trough Harlem on a bicycle?" she asked. "How come a smart boy like you tink up such a ting? You crazy!"

"There'll be plenty of people out on the street," I told her, repeating Barry's assurance, even if I didn't buy it completely. I would have thought that black people wouldn't have considered other black people dangerous, but had I said that, Leona would have replied, 'I'm not black, I'm from Antigua.' "

"She's right," my father said. "Take the subway. By the way, Leona, what is this I'm eating?"

"Do you like it?"

"Tell me what it is, and I'll tell you whether or not I like it."

"Goat."

My father set down his fork. "Very good," he said, not touching his food again.

Leona pretended not to notice. "Tell Ray-mohnd he shouldn't be going trough no Harlem on a bicycle, Paul." But her face admitted defeat.

"I'll give you both money for the subway, Ray." He got up.

"I made dessert, too, Paul."

"Ray'll eat it."

She watched him go. "You like what I make?" she asked.

"Is this really goat?" I thought of their whiskers, their little horns, the shiny turds shaped like coffee beans I saw on a hike once.

"What difference does it make? Just eat." She edged my plate closer to me.

I forced myself to have some more for Leona's sake. I had to make up for my father's uneaten portion. It wasn't all that bad and might have tasted like my mother's rotisserie chicken if not for the spices. When I was finished, she brought out a dish of coconut-flavored tapioca, which was terribly sweet, but she was watching me, so I ate all of it.

"Go to your father," she said when I was done. She sounded tired, but I recognized it as another kind of weariness. She must have felt that her job in the house was done. She sat before the plates of half-eaten food like a general surveying an army's defeat.

I kissed her on the cheek.

"Go to him," she said, giving me a gentle push. "Tell him he drink too much. He don't listen to me none. He don't listen to nobody."

My father was at his worktable. He lifted his pen when I approached.

"I've decided to pick your mother up at the airport tomorrow. She doesn't know. It'll be a surprise. What do you think?"

"And then?"

"Then your mother will have to decide what she wants to do." He set down his pen to examine his work and blew on the ink.

"What about you?"

"What *about* me?"

"What are you going to decide?"

"Your mother was the one who took off—"

"She took off because of you."

He continued writing, the pen scratching against the paper. His silence seemed stubborn. *He don't listen to nobody.* My mother had slammed doors, preferring noise to his silence. I understood why.

"Leona loves you."

"I know."

"So now you're just going to kick her out? Maybe she really doesn't want to go. Maybe she wants to stay—"

"I'm married to your mother. What are you suggesting, a three-way?" He set down his pen. "Leona knew I might go back to your mother."

I thought of Leona at the kitchen table, alone. "How can you just throw love away?"

"You haven't stopped talking about love all summer, Mr. Casanova. Tell me. Who have you loved recently?" Without waiting for an answer, he said, "That guy in the cafeteria? Seems a little old for you."

I headed for my room and threw myself down on my bed, feeling a chill like air over a torn scab. It sure was easy to do a lot of wrong to someone in a very short time. Maybe it was impossible to go through life without leaving a mess behind. Maybe there were things that would never get completely worked out but would always drag behind you, like an exhaust pipe scraping against the road and giving off sparks. My father and I were both scared. From the kitchen came the peaceful trickle of water as Leona did the dishes. I imagined her large and careful hands setting everything onto the rack. More than anything else, she yearned to take care of my father, but he was an unlikely candidate for anyone's ministrations. He could stash his entire life into a single suitcase—one change of clothing, pencils, a bottle or two of whiskey—and he'd be content to carry it around from place to place, hardly worrying about where he landed. If I'd learned one thing that summer, it was that love and need often had little if anything to do with one another.

It was time for another of my stale cigrettes and some far-off music on the radio. I took out a journal I'd read the week before. I imagined Agatha sitting beside me in the fading light through her window, fragile as a dream upon the bleached bed linen. I heard her whispering my name, a thousand tears crowding each syllable. She had loved me, I thought. I might have said that to my father, and it would have been true, but it would have meant an explanation I didn't yet have.

. . . into her room . . . I would find her, see her and her abominable dolls. I find her . . . pick up the scissors . . . see the crazy look in her eye, love and fear, love mangled/tainted/obliterated by fear, obliterated by her fear of him, his shackle, his marriage, the cripple he'd made of her, hate her, hate her, strike—

Later, whispers and moans began to sift into the room, soft as vapor. I couldn't tell from where. They gained form and shape, crowding around me: the sound of love coming from across the alley. The sounds grew and heaved, the coiled breath of a woman, a man's groans, almost mocking. I grazed the soft pulp of my tit with my finger until it tautened, then let my finger slide down my belly. Soon I was hard and straining. A woman uttered a sound—high, sharp, almost a yelp, almost a laugh—

"Paul . . ."

The man replied with a single, deep gust, then another—and then there was silence. My frantic fist pumped and strained—I threw my head back and let everything break free.

A moment or two later, I heard someone walking into the bathroom and the toilet flushing.

Inexplicably, a cat chose just that moment to yowl in the alley, making a sound large enough to contain all the yearning in the world. The house grew silent. The trees whistled in the park across the street, metallic, a sound like the fall. I couldn't sleep.

Agatha would be leaving tomorrow. She would hate me for the rest of her life.

I tiptoed into the kitchen and dialed her number. The phone rang for a long time.

"It's me, Raymond."

"What do you want?" The ice in her voice jabbed my ear. She hung up.

I dressed in a hurry. Just before leaving, I looked at the notebooks in my closet, a pile of accusations. How would I ever get them back to their owner? But who was their owner?

Not tonight.

I took a cab downtown, a twenty-dollar bill in my pocket to pay for it. Across from Agatha's building, the man in the grimy undershirt was at his window, the poison-glow of a cigarette between his fingers. The bottom door of her building was locked, and there was no buzzer. Agatha's light was on, but calling up was a waste of time: she would never let me in. I had to wait for someone to come out. I sat down on the steps. *I am here on this stoop and it is my reality.* The man kept smoking, eyeing me ominously. No one came or went. How long would it take to get in there? When someone finally left the building, I slipped in, and minutes later, I stood before her door, knocking softly.

"Agatha? It's me, Raymond."

Something inside stirred, but barely.

"Agatha?"

"What do you want?"

"Can I come in?"

The door opened a crack.

"I'm sorry," I said.

She moved from the door without saying a word, leaving me to enter or not. I tripped over a shoe, then a broken desk: the apartment was in shambles. I stood knee-deep in clothing, books, and other soft rubble. The window with the gate Agatha often forgot to lock was thrown open. My eyes fell on the red inscription, now circled in fresh black paint. Something had been added: "My books are mine, you little *Schwein!*"

"He was here," she said. "He came for his journals." Her face was limp, shapeless. For the second time since I'd known her, she looked terrified.

Destruction is life. Destruction is creation. Destruction is passion. I must destroy in order to love.

"They're gone. He didn't find them. They weren't here the other night. I looked for them after you left." She kicked away papers and books from the empty corner where the notebooks had been stacked. "Why did you take them?"

"I wanted to know," I said. "I wanted to know about you. Also about him. But I'll bring them back, Agatha. I'll bring them all back."

"Not here. I don't want them. They're not mine anymore." And then she turned off the light and slipped into bed.

What was I supposed to do? Get into bed with her? No. But how could I leave with so much still unsaid, so many questions unanswered? Except that it had been like that all along. There was going to be much I would never know, and much I would never be able to understand. I'd always thought that if things went wrong, they might be fixed. I'd assumed that after a while, all things returned to their natural state, dust settled. A pond always lost its ripples and grew smooth. But maybe not always. Some things were irretrievable, irrevocable, permanent. Some things stayed broken. Maybe lots of things. Agatha had fallen into one of her impossibly deep sleeps. Staying there any longer would change nothing. I left, closing a door that snapped shut the moment I pulled it.

"I told my father I'd be back by five," I said when I got to Barry's house. "We're going to the airport to pick up my mother."

"No problem."

We started out, cool sunlight burnishing the ornate cornices of the buildings along Pelham Parkway. It had rained the night before; the streets smelled rich and leathery. We took Jerome's journal and headed over the Macombs Dam Bridge, fussy and ceremonial with its two different spans. On

Lenox, a solitary bus blustered down the broad avenue, a great boar rooting for food. The sun burned away the damp morning air, leaving a dry smell of concrete. I wouldn't have minded a little break just then, but Barry was tireless, sailing sleekly ahead, driven by obligation.

The tiny grocery stores, windows crammed and dirty, crude hand-lettered signs announcing check-cashing places, and buildings with cinder-blocked windows all told me I was in Harlem. The side streets looked ominously empty. Any time we stopped for a light, I kept my glance down, since even looking at black people might be provocation. I imagined unforeseeable terrors lurking behind parked cars, gangs of kids ready to spring out and topple me. But nothing happened. The dirty brick fronts of the buildings began to look old and kindly. Rows of windows burst with the brilliant red of geraniums, and children hooted at us as we whizzed by. The doors of a church opened to let out a flurry of women who spilled down the steps in pastel-colored dresses and hats. Did that kid from the Parks Department with the big gold cross live around here? I wished he might see me so that he'd know I wasn't afraid to be there.

At 96th Street, the city lost its dry torpor. Mountains of produce dripped with the spray of a hose before large corner groceries, the pears and peaches being busily picked over by dozens of hands. I imagined Leona there. "Good-bye Raymohnd," she had said that morning before I left the house, emphasizing the second syllable of my name as usual. "College give you time to tink about tings. You gonna be all right."

We took a break in Central Park. Barry looked at his watch. "Not bad," he said.

I gulped down water. My legs burned, and the saddle kept pressing against me even after I dismounted. The day had grown hot, and I was dizzy. I thought of that concert with Agatha. It seemed like years ago. "How much farther?" I asked.

Barry studied the map. "Less than an hour."

A thought occurred to me: if the AP was for real, then

he'd be heading out there today, too. *Burn it to the ground, every tennis racket, baseball bat. Burn it to the ground, every account book, every ledger, every office memo. Burn it to the ground* . . . I could see the headlines: "Long Island City Blaze Kills 7." I imagined turning a corner to see a city block in flames, fire engines blaring past, great billows of smoke. But I was certain nothing like that would happen. The AP's madman face flickered before me. His plan was nothing more than revenge on an unfair universe.

"Let's go," Barry said, taking a final squirt of water.

It was too late to turn back, but I vowed not to have anything to do with his plot to kidnap Felix.

We headed eastward, toward the clunky span of the Queensborough Bridge, window gates stretched across the river. I struggled up the ramp, and each pump of the pedal brought me higher and higher over the water like the relentless crank up the first peak of the Cyclone in Coney Island. Riding through the girders was like being within the teeth of a great machine grinding out traffic. The sky opened up around me, blue and white and soft.

In Long Island City we pulled into the shade of the El tracks, where Barry checked the map once more. "Northern Boulevard, then a left on Steinway," he announced. Above us, planes scraped the air over LaGuardia. The street stretched on, dusty and motionless. Harlem had been cool and shady, but Queens was bleak. I remembered the miserable taxi ride my mother and I had taken to the airport earlier in the summer.

"Hang a right," Barry shouted.

A service road brought us beside the deafening traffic of the Grand Central Parkway. Cars and sixteen-wheelers roared past. Expressways locked all around us. The air boomed with a relentless noise, heavy with fumes. We came to a stop before a gate. "St. Michael's Cemetery," read a sign. We were lost.

"That asshole," Barry said, crumpling up the copies of the journal pages. He threw them over the fence onto the highway, where they danced merrily, waltzed along by the traffic. The plans were completely bogus, a bad joke, or a stupid miscalculation. I thought of all the diagrams and the subway schedule, and suddenly the whole thing seemed very funny. Or maybe that guy had made no mistake. The AP was a *schmendrick,* no more able to commit arson than I was, so he'd destroyed the showroom on paper only. Or else he'd transformed it into a cemetery. His brother-in-law was dead to him, he was saying.

"I'm hungry, Barry. Let's eat." Like all cemeteries, this one was green, inviting, and nearly empty, the perfect place for a picnic. We walked through the open gate and ditched our bikes in a tangle of bushes. The moment we were inside, a hush descended, and we were quickly far from anything else. After so much concrete and asphalt, the green lawns were soothing.

"We made OK time, at least," Barry said. "My odometer clocked fourteen-point-three miles. It's now just after two, so that means we did about ten miles an hour."

A plane flew overhead. My mother would be coming home that night. What would happen next? Was my father serious about picking her up? Staying with her? But did it make a difference either way? I'd be going off to college. I was about to become their grown child, so it hardly mattered what my parents did. Another plane flew overhead. From the air, the cemetery was only a random green spot, nothing more. Barry and I weren't even visible. Things changed depending on where you were.

I unwrapped my sandwich, took a bite, and then stopped. Leona had made me a goat sandwich. I looked at the meat, at its bright mantle of sauce, and was almost unable to take another bite. But I was hungry. And I couldn't throw it away, since Leona had made it.

"Feel like eating some goat?" I said to Barry.

Barry leaned over and smelled my sandwich, sticking his big nose between the bread and sniffing, like some kind of carnivorous animal.

"You eat that?"

"Why not? Goat's great."

He gave me a funny look, deciding whether or not to believe me. I had the urge to provoke him, just to see what he'd say. I'd begun to feel free and open that afternoon. Maybe it had to do with winging through Harlem, going over the bridge, and winding up in a cemetery. Or maybe it had nothing to do with anything.

"Tuna fish is lame," I added.

Barry shook his head and turned away. Like an appliance, if you didn't follow instructions, he didn't work. He took off his shirt, balled it up for a pillow and stretched out. "This is nice," he said, turning onto his side.

"What do we do now?"

Unbelievably, he'd fallen asleep. It was broad daylight. A moment ago, he'd been wide awake, but not anymore. I looked closer. His chest rose and fell, and his breathing sent a flutter through the grass beside his mouth.

I didn't know what else to do, so I took off my shirt, pillowed it and stretched out beside him. The grass felt cool and damp, smelling of water. Cars zoomed past, churning up a warm wind.

"Barry?" I whispered and moved a little closer. I began to think that he wasn't asleep but only making as though he were. He must have known I'd kissed him that night in his room—how could he not know—and he was telling me to do it again. My heart was going like mad, planes flying, cars dive-bombing down the highway. Suddenly everything in the world was happening at once. *You know why you come here, Andrew.* I leaned closer. Nobody would see, nobody would know. *I can do whatever I want.* I kissed Barry's shoulder, his skin fluid against my lips. I waited. Still, Barry slept. I kissed him again—

This time he spiraled around, taut with fury. "Get away from me, you!" he shouted. "Just get the hell away!"

"Barry . . ."

"Keep away."

"You'd let Felix, I bet."

"Shut up!" He threw himself on top of me, machine-gunning me with fists. I tried to throw him off, and we locked into a standstill for a few seconds before we disengaged and he got to his feet and started collecting his things.

"Where are you going?"

"Pervert!" He threw on his shirt and dumped stuff into his backpack.

My throat had dried to bark when I tried to speak. I was ashamed, but the next minute, I was angry. "Moron!" I shouted. And then I did the unthinkable: I grabbed his precious, featherlight Crescent and flung it into the air, a lopsided bird that landed with a muffled *cloink* inches from the maul of the expressway.

"You crazy fuck!" Barry shouted, running after it.

I watched Barry check the bicycle for damage and realign the front fork. He trundled the bike to the gate of the cemetery and left without another word. I had the whole cemetery to myself.

It was almost three. My mother would be getting in at six. It seemed like a nice idea to meet her plane. JKF couldn't be that far away. When I got my bike, I saw that Barry had let the air out of the tires, so I decided to leave it where it was and proceed on foot. I'd never really liked bicycles that much, and after today, I liked them even less.

I made it to the airport by five, grimy and worn out, and headed for a bathroom. My face was a sunburnt red and my hair plastered with sweat. My shirt peeled off to reveal a bright patch of red stopping at the collar line.

I bought a *Times*. The news squib on the second page mentioned an Israeli tourist bus disappearing on the way back from the Sinai. Israeli police suspected terrorism. I'd heard of planes hijacked, but buses? It was almost like hijacking an elevator. I folded the paper under my arm and made my way to the International Arrivals area, just in case my father was already there. People clustered around a roped-off circle beneath a gigantic American flag. Every fifteen minutes, another batch of passengers arrived: couples from India overloaded with luggage, the women fluttering by in saris; clumps of backpackers; the elderly with suitcases on wheels; the legions of short-legged Japanese; a stately delegation of Africans. Private-car drivers in suits held up signs printed with foreign-looking names. There was no sign of my father, so I found a seat in another terminal and read my paper.

Every so often I looked up at the Arrivals board, names and numbers flipping like slot machines. When "Landed" flashed beside my mother's flight number, I returned to the Arrivals area and waited. More Indians, more Japanese. Everyone was coming to America. But where was my mother? My father? Uncle Alfred? I thought I recognized the three priests still in their black coats, I'd seen the evening my mother left. I waited a full hour after the arrival time before asking someone at the counter and was told that all who'd been aboard that flight had debarked.

I called home.

"Where the hell are you?" my father said, voice slippery with whiskey. "Get home!"

"Where's Mom?"

"How the hell do I know!" he said and slammed down the phone.

"Why didn't you tell me you were going to the airport?" he said when I got home.

"I thought I'd surprise you."

"Great surprise."

Uncle Alfred was there. "Sit down," he told me. "Something's happened."

"She was on that bus?" I sputtered.

"How did you know?"

I showed him the paper. "You mean they really hijacked her?"

"Nobody's talking hijacking, Ray."

"Let me see that," my father said. His face was a battlefield, red and furrowed with worry as it had been that night he'd waited up for me. "This could only happen to your mother," he said.

"It's not her fault, Paul," Uncle Alfred said.

"Yes it is. Who told her to fly her ass over to Israel in the first place? Who told her to go into the desert?" His angry glance found me. "And where were you, at the beach? Your face is sunburnt. Have a goddamn beer."

"I took the bike trip, remember?" I said and snapped open a can. It was warm: he hadn't waited for it to get cold before drinking it.

My uncle started making phone calls: the Israeli embassy, the American embassy in Israel, our family over there. We listened. My father and I avoided looking at each other.

"No news," he said, hanging up after the last call. "I'm taking off, Paul. I'll keep calling the family over there later tonight and let you know if I hear anything important." He glanced at the crack in the coffee table, resembling a great bloodshot eye.

"Try to keep him off the sauce, will you?" he said as I walked him to the door.

"Come over here," my father called after Uncle Alfred left.

I hesitated. I didn't like talking to him when he was drunk.

"I said to come over here, goddammit!" He grasped his beer can, looking ready to throw it. I sat down. "You're going away," he said. "I haven't hardly seen you the whole summer."

"Leona told you not to drink so much."

"Leona? Leona! When a vaca-shun don't end, it start to be work, mon!" he said, mimicking her. "What do you know about Leona? What do you know about women? What do you know about anything? No, I take that back. You're smart. You know a lot. Probably more than I give you credit for. Take after your mother. But what do I know? What the hell do *I* know? Nothing! I'm one stupid ass!"

"Dad—" He stood up with a Mr. Gumby wobble as he went for the bottle underneath his worktable and took a long swig from it.

"Dad, stop."

"I'm one stupid asshole. That's why your mother left. It's why Leona left, too. Even you," he said, pointing with his free hand. "You're leaving." He took another swallow.

"Put that down, Dad." I went to take the bottle from him, but he pulled it away, a child refusing to give up a toy. He teetered, about to fall. I stepped toward him, and he toppled over. His head hit the broken eye of the coffee table with a thud. He crumpled, limp, and moaned loudly. I ran for a towel and pressed it around his head as I lifted him up. He was heavy and shapeless, too big for me to carry alone, so I stretched him out on the carpet. Flickers of glass glistened in the pulp of the wound. I got tweezers to pick them out with.

"Oh, Jesus," he said with each probe.

"Take it easy, Dad," I said.

"Raymond," he murmured.

I looked at him. Bloodied and cut, clothing grimy, he might have been a bum on the sidewalk. But no: he was my father. When I finished, he dozed off right there on the floor.

I went over to his worktable. *One Hundred of the World's Favorite Poems* lay beside a sheet lettered with lines addressed to my mother:

Shall I compare thee to a summer's day?
Thou art more lovely and more temperate:
Rough winds do shake the darling buds of May
And summer's lease hath all too short a date . . .

The phone rang, and my father stirred.

"Still no word," Uncle Alfred said to me. "How's your father doing?"

"Asleep." I didn't mention what had happened.

"You should go to sleep, too."

I looked in at my father. The bottle lay on its side in a dark pool on the carpet. My father's bruise brooded, a volcano still smoking. He'd refused to lie and so he'd gotten hurt. Not me. *The scissors leave a scar like a slit across her left cheek. It moves when she speaks, half-moon-shaped, like a smile* . . . Agatha's rage had blazed at me as she'd thrown me out of her apartment, but my black soul was fireproof, and I'd escaped untouched.

5

Jerome

New Cornwall, October 8

She came home from the hospital bearing my scar, my purple slash across her cheek. It looked like I'd tried to tear another mouth into her after her first one had kept silent for too long. I'd disfigured her. She had been so beautiful before; I had made her ugly.

ELEVEN

The kid said he had something for her. A *little present,* he'd said, all that Jerome had heard in the din of the Union Square subway stop. After Loewenthal dropped him off, Jerome headed for the station, backpack groaning with purloined canned goods. He waited near the turnstiles, peering like a gargoyle just beyond the gate, all the while hordes of hollow office functionaries poured forth from the downtown express—over-coiffed, heavily earringed, buskined Dianas in corporate dress and running shoes, or bloated barristers, briefcased, suited and necktied, pretenders with paychecks all, salmon fighting to reach the end of the day, to feed, perchance to spawn. (That day he'd remembered to get prawns for Dwight instead of more shrimp.)

The ambush beneath the marquee of the Charles Theater confirmed all Jerome had feared: not only had someone else taken his place, but someone was prying into his journals. He'd seen that little horn-rimmed brat prowling around her building late at night more than once. The sight of one of his notebooks halfway down the kid's pants had made him want to rip him in two and barbecue him. *A little present.* The crudface wore a

Bryn Mawr T-shirt and suspenders. Suspenders to hold up his goddamned *jeans!* Jerome knew where that T-shirt had come from, all right.

The moment she appeared, Jerome's knees turned to jelly. She'd unfolded like a flower through the car's opening doors, neck visibly soft, an enticing churn to her skirt as she hurried up the stairs, little Lord Fauntleroy tagging behind. *A present? For me?* She'd giggled that patent-leather-pumps, Daddy's-best-girl, *Chaste Maid in Cheapside* giggle. *For me? No one ever buys me presents.*

Jerome yearned to throw them both down to the ground and let the rush hour's stampede pulverize them. *No one else buys me presents.* When she and Jerome had lived together, he was always bringing home little things for her: raspberries, silk scarves, gray wool gloves she promptly left on a bench in Central Park. *No one ever buys me presents.* Crudface was lapping it all up and feeling gallant. And what did he get her? Some overpriced party favor paid for with his allowance, no doubt. The tortoiseshell glasses—to say nothing of those suspenders—marked him as the type who'd buy a *meaningful* gift. A book, no doubt. *Poetry.* In hardcover. The crudface. What did he know about poetry? He probably penned fetid little stanzas dripping with enjambment in expensive notebooks with cloth covers, lines coiled and caked in their own self-reflective ooze. "I'll give you a hint," the kid said, pleased with himself. "It's something sharp."

But that was all Jerome had heard. His stomach pains froze him in place. He grabbed hold of a grimy stanchion, a buoy in tidal waves of gastric distress, and he stayed put until the painful wrench of his stomach wall relaxed. All for the best, he told himself as the two of them drifted away. What would he have done had he caught up with them? She'd sic her lawyer father on him again, and this time he'd be hit with a fine instead of just a warning. But he'd confront her soon enough. *It's something sharp.* He'd use whatever it was to cut off that kid's marble-sized balls, then throw him in front of a Seven

Santini Brothers moving truck, ridding her house of him, cleansing and purifying it, Odysseus returning in triumph to Ithaca. And he would get her back. *Rage kneaded his resolve,* he thought, mentally writing the lines in his journal. *He'd let it dry brittle, hard, and impervious.* Not bad.

"Forget about the elevator, Governor," Louis said as he let Jerome into the building. "Broke. You there, what are you doing?" He turned to a heavy-set man pulling his sleeping mat toward a dark corner.

"Relocating. The corner's warmer."

"You can't go there. That spot's reserved." He closed the door behind Jerome, squeezed the padlock shut, and took off after the man. "You can't just move around whenever you please," he said. "We have rules here."

On hot days like this, the ground floor was especially ripe, and the groundlings—Jerome's name for them—were nearly motionless on their mats, bundled in their layers as if it were January. Maybe they'd reached a point where they no longer felt the change of season, too tired to even feel weather.

"I tell you, someone's coming in here this afternoon," Louis railed at the man.

"So? I got seniority."

The argument continued as Jerome headed for the stairwell. Hierarchy flourished even in squalor, even when there was little more to fight over than a patch of damp, dirty floor. The powerless sought power. He tried the elevator with his key, but no amount of jiggling got it moving.

"I *told* you it wasn't working," Louis boomed from behind.

Jerome guiltily pocketed his key. This dingy cave was Louis's domain. Dwight said Louis had been a merchant marine all his life; now his ship was in permanent dry dock. Jerome began the long ascent. The stairs were straight from an M.C. Escher drawing, cruelly endless. The cans clanked merrily on his back. He imagined Agatha and that kid up in the apartment, eating fish she'd cooked, drinking a cool glass of wine by the open window. He pictured her, fresh from the shower, sitting on the bed on one of those sheets she so maniacally bleached. He'd never understood her laundry fetish until one night when she'd explained it in her shorthand of dreams. *To lie down where it's pure, where he can't see.* Agatha was more articulate in dreams than awake.

I never wanted to hurt her, he thought, mentally repeating what had become his mantra since she'd thrown him out. He'd always had a temper, true, but she knew what it was to live with rage. She knew that the examined life was lived *in extremis.* But she'd pushed him, prattling like a schoolgirl one minute, only to pull herself mute mid-sentence the next. At night, her body's silence suffocated him. Asleep, however, she spoke, and he'd listened, thirsty for all he might hear. And he'd drunk.

By the time he reached the top floor, Jerome was famished, but Dwight wasn't home yet. Jerome unloaded his pack and climbed out onto the fire escape. The sun had begun to slip below a nearby building, its wall a semaphore of lighted windows. Far below, people rummaged in and out of buildings as trucks rumbled over cobblestoned Greene Street. A dumpster overflowed with convolutions of a flouncy pink material resembling the entrails of some slack-bellied beast. (An ulcerated stomach lining in full flame?) Passersby looked small enough to need either pity or protection. Humanity always appeared nobler from a distance. No wonder Dwight liked towers.

A nasty pinch to Jerome's stomach jerked his gaze back up to safety. He'd always been a little acrophobic, and it was easy to imagine the curlicued fire escape wrenching free and hurtling earthward, Apollo's scrap-metal chariot . . . *oh, to hell with those lousy classical allusions,* he heard Maurice Rose say. Strange: Rose had been on his mind more and more during the past couple of days. *I hadn't really copied anything from her, Maurice, believe me. I'd just let myself be inspired by what she'd said in her sleep.* But Rose had been stern with him. *It's still plagiarism, Jerome. Stealing. Copying down someone else's stories. No wonder she threw you out. I would have, too.*

That last remark had hurt, and the pinch in his belly deepened. His bottle of Mylanta was a country mile distant in his cubicle, reachable only through a maze of concrete pillars and coils of electric cable, entrails spilling from the guts of the building. *Stop thinking about her,* he commanded himself. *Stop—*

An angry boom, the howl of a trapped beast, broke from deep within the building's core. They were starting again, those grungeholes in Dwight's garage band. Garbage band was more like it. Their guitars' every strum sent set wavelengths of menace into motion. They pounded on the front door until Louis opened it. He'd seen them toss beer cans at the sleeping people, and once even a cigarette butt. Jerome seethed but held his tongue, for Dwight counseled coexistence. But what was a self-made aesthete like Dwight doing with the dregs of Feelie's Wheel? He claimed to be fascinated by their "brutal wisdom." Jerome figured it was mostly the coke.

"Sorry I'm late," Dwight said, coming in, a loaf of Italian bread under his arm.

"What happened to the elevator?"

"It's stuck."

"Can't it be fixed?" Jerome asked, tearing off a piece of bread.

"Locking mechanism's busted, and that's a major repair. But I'm not telling Gottlieb about it, he might give me flak, so it looks like we'll be getting a lot of exercise from now on."

"He's going to find out about it sooner or later."

"I'll be out of here by then." He found a pair of candles, fixed them between the metal slate of the fire escape as usual and lit them. "There."

"It was those Neanderthals in the band who busted it, right?" Jerome persisted. He could just see them stumbling back to the building late at night, primitive nervous systems swamped in Colt 45, forcing the elevator door open and tearing the whole thing free of the lock. The band was always grumbling about having to walk up the steps because Dwight kept the elevator locked.

"I think we forgot the glasses," Dwight said. He went to get them.

"Don't you think you're carrying this gourmet number a little too far?" Jerome asked when he returned. Dwight set down the glasses with care. The bottle of wine made a playful pop when he uncorked it.

"Have some of this and you'll feel better. Cheers. A very *translucent* Merlot," Dwight crooned.

What else is wine supposed to be, opaque? Jerome wanted to say. He considered getting drunk.

"Don't you think it's strange having these little banquets of ours, considering all those people downstairs?"

"Why shouldn't I enjoy what you bring?" Dwight cranked open a tin of paté and spread a lavish dollop on a heel of bread. "Besides, I give them a roof over their heads. I share food with them."

"You don't invite those guys from the band up here."

"We have a business relationship, not a personal one. By the way, I've been thinking about that tower." He took another sip of wine and paused for effect. "I've decided to stage a mammoth reading."

"Open mike?"

"Not completely open," Dwight said. "Just for those who usually have no public voice: the people downstairs. You always see them walking down the street talking to themselves. That's because no one listens. This way, they will. I'll sell tickets. The band will play in between readers. It'll be an *event.*"

Jerome tried to imagine the groundlings struggling up some Tower of Babel, crumpled papers in hand, all the while that rat pack of grubby, ball-scratching grease monkeys blasted everyone's eardrums.

"It's one thing to get a hundred well-fed college students to sit around all night in an abandoned factory reading from the phone book but another to have homeless people performing like dancing bears. What if they're in no mood to spout poetry? What if they'd rather sleep and guzzle Thunderbird? I think it's what most of them would rather do anyway."

"I'll be giving them an audience."

"Dwight, I don't like this. It's crude. You're turning those people downstairs into objects. And why a tower, for God's sake? Towers are fascist."

Dwight faced him. "Sometimes I think you're jealous. Sometimes I think you're frustrated because your art's not happening."

Jerome set down his glass. Dwight was right, in a way. Losing the journals had set him back, and he hadn't written anything substantial all summer. Seeing Agatha with that kid earlier hadn't helped, either. But who was Dwight to say? What did he know about feeling, longing, yearning? about despair? He delegated and directed, and then he obliterated his mind with coke. What did that have to do with art?

"You never fall in love, do you, Dwight?" Jerome countered.

"You make it sound like an accusation."

"Do you?"

"Maybe the problem is that nobody falls in love with me." He held up the wineglass. "I'm not like you, Jerome. I'll never . . . submerge myself in someone else like you do. Maybe I can't. Or else I don't want to—"

"So you build towers."

"My phallus. Isn't that what you're thinking? The dick I can't use to fuck anybody with?"

"You think I'm silly carrying on about a woman."

"You create your kind of theater and I create mine."

"Hello," a voice intoned.

It was Sharon, pointing a cautious ballerina's toe onto the

fire escape as she might to test the water before a swim. As usual, she'd sifted into view out of nowhere, insubstantial as breath. She made Jerome uncomfortable. Her strangeness clung to him like humidity. Talking to her was like walking on a trampoline; there was no secure footing, no proof that his words were understood. He worried about her. Most nights, she left the building—barefoot—and stayed away for hours, returning early in the morning, the soles of her feet black and bloodied.

"Better not come out here," Dwight said. The fire escape had become shakier in the past couple of days, loosened, Jerome feared, by the band's vibrations. "You know you're afraid of heights."

"I'll be all right," she said. She collected the folds of her gown and carried them through the window, settling in a corner. "Why do you hate me, Dwight?"

"I don't hate you, Sharon."

"You shouldn't wear black all the time. It's the color of death."

"Here," Jerome said, offering her some bread.

"Death has no color," Dwight said. "Have some of this, too." He pushed the paté her way. She spread some on her bread, but her tiny bites hardly consumed it. Her head jerked backward. "I hear them," she said.

"What?" Jerome asked.

"She means the band," Dwight said, spearing a stuffed grape leaf.

"In the walls," said Sharon. "They're everywhere. Make them go, Dwight. Make them go. They're evil. They killed my father."

"The guys in the band didn't kill your father."

"So who did?" The knife in her hand fell and hit the grating of the fire escape with a sharp *ping* before plunging through the air. Jerome watched with horror: a straight pin dropped from a roof could split someone's skull. A nearly imperceptible ring sounded from below.

"So this is where you're hiding." A man with a clown's fringe of wooly hair held down by a baseball cap appeared at the window, a little out of breath. "We're waiting for you, man."

"I'll be right down, Bong," Dwight said.

Sharon pulled close to Jerome. "Get them away from here," she murmured.

"Who let you out of the loony bin, Goldilocks?" Bong said.

"Killer!" she shouted at him.

"You are one twisted sister, anyone ever tell you that?"

"Get out of here," Jerome said.

"You talking to me, buddy?"

"Bong, take it easy," said Dwight.

"Are you talking to fucking *me?*" Bong persisted.

Jerome pulled himself up. "I said get out of here."

Bong lunged, they fell over each other, and Jerome pinned him against the brick. His baseball cap fell off, his hair bushed out into a shaggy halo, and the cap sailed off the fire escape.

"I told you to leave but you didn't," Jerome said, hands in a choke hold around Bong's neck. Bong's face began darkening, his eyes pulsed.

"Jerome, let him go!" Dwight shouted.

"You shit," Bong gasped, still struggling. They waltzed perilously close to the edge of the railing. Sharon started screaming.

"I said let him go, Jerome!" Dwight shouted.

Jerome pulled away, and Bong staggered back toward the window. "You're going to pay for this," he panted, his hand feeling for his lost cap.

"Tell everyone that I'll be right down," Dwight said.

"You're gonna fucking pay!" Bong said as he climbed back through the window.

"Why did you have to go and do that, Jerome?" Dwight said after he left. "I have to work with him and the rest of them. They're a temperamental bunch, especially him. It's not going to be very cool if you create friction around here."

"You don't *have* to work with them, Dwight. You *want* to. For some reason, you *like* them." Jerome turned to Sharon. "Are you all right?"

"Killer," she snarled at him. "You're just like them."

Dwight took a final sip of wine, shot Jerome an I-told-you-so look, and stood up. "I'll be in the basement," he said. "Stay out of trouble." He climbed through the window and left.

Sharon brooded in her corner, arms clutching her knees. Jerome felt the man's warm, sinuous neck between his fingers. He hadn't been able to stop himself from going at him. And it had felt . . . good. He could have done more. The old poison still flowed within him. He needed to walk off what pulled and twisted inside him, except that the fire escape hemmed him in. He was Rilke's panther pacing back and forth behind rusting iron bars.

"I didn't mean to do that," he said.

"You killer. Men like you murdered my father."

Jerome struggled to connect the dots of her thoughts. "Did what?"

"My father's life meant nothing to nobody."

Jerome began dumping leftovers into a paper bag. Dwight was right. She really was in another zone.

"I'm not a killer. I just have a bad temper, that's all." He slid near her, but she pulled away. "If you're so damned scared of everything in this place, then why did you come here?"

"My father told me it was time to leave home."

"Your father?"

"Yes."

"Your dead father?"

"Yes. And Dwight . . . I thought . . ." Her gaze drifted over the balcony, carrying the rest of her sentence with it. "When I first met Dwight, he seemed as clear as a drop of water. But not now. Do you know why he hates me? Because I confront him with his own evil. I've heard those songs he writes. He has evil dreams, evil hopes. Look at what he's building. He's hurting. You're hurting, too. I can feel it."

Jerome bristled. He hated to have people try to tell him how he was feeling. They'd done that at New Cornwall. Psychology was the science of excuses and second-guesses.

"It's getting dark. Let's go inside," he said.

She locked her arms around herself.

"Please." He extended a hand, and she let herself be pulled up from the dirty nest of her gown, but the moment she was back inside, she broke into a run down the dark hallway.

"Where are you going?" he called, following her. Jesus, she was fast.

A rumble of drums sounded through the stairwell just as he caught up with her.

"Get away from me!" she shouted, and a propeller of hands fended him off. She fled to the next floor and down a corridor into a room where she began throwing things into a shopping bag, then lunged past him and back into the corridor, fleet as a mountain goat, gown and shopping bag billowing behind her.

"Sharon, stop!" With his last bit of energy, he reached her as she opened a door to the stairwell. She was about to take a step forward, but there were no stairs—she'd mistakenly pulled open the elevator door. Music howled up from the guts of the building—Jesus God, it was the empty shaft—

Her scream lashed into the abyss just as Jerome pulled her to safety. The shopping bag lurched free. A book flew open, a heavy bird struggling to fly. Clothing became lopsided stars, and papers softly spiraled.

Jerome fell against the wall, spent. "Why did you do that?"

"What happened?"

"Elevator's broken. The cab's stuck somewhere. The door wasn't supposed to open, but it did."

"I thought it was the stairwell."

"You thought."

"I have to get my things."

"To hell with your things. You almost goddamn died!"

"Don't yell at me."

"Let's get out of here." They walked down the stairs, the music growing louder at each landing.

"I still have to get my things," she said when they reached the ground floor.

"I know, I know. The bottom of the shaft is one flight down. Wait here and I'll get your stuff."

"No, I can get it myself," she said. The music came at them from all directions.

The basement elevator door wouldn't open.

"Forget about it, Sharon. Let's go back up. I can't take this noise."

"But my things!" She began pounding on the door.

"Going in there is dangerous. The elevator's hanging all the way up in the shaft. It could fall at any minute."

"I want my things!"

Jerome remembered the key Dwight had given him. He jiggled it into the lock and the door opened. The shaft was dark, the air oily. A monstrous coil lurked at the bottom of the shaft. Sharon hopped down and began collecting her belongings with the calm of someone picking mushrooms.

"Hurry," Jerome shouted over the din of the music, holding the door open. "That thing could drop down at any minute." He thought of the massive elevator cab twelve stories above, held by an aged, fraying cable ready to snap.

"I found it!" she said. "It's still in one piece."

"What is?"

She held up something barely visible. "My father's fountain pen. He gave it to me just before he was killed—"

"Hurry up!" *A fountain pen,* he thought.

She threw her arms around him. "Kiss me! Kiss me now!"

"Sharon—"

"Kiss me. Dwight never has. Please. Here. Now. Because now I know you're not a killer."

"Let's get out of here first," Jerome said, leaning down to give her a hand. "Then I'll kiss you."

She pulled out of his reach. "No. Kiss me first. You saved my life. Come."

He sensed that she wouldn't budge unless he did as she asked, so he hopped down to her and planted a hasty kiss on her lips.

"Okay, now let's go!"

But she held him in a grip surprisingly strong, and her lips—clumsy and wet—pursued him. The music bellowed louder, the walls of the elevator shaft shook, and he imagined the cab above them swaying like a bell, its cable loosening strand by strand. Sharon was one-hundred-percent certified Good-Housekeeping-Seal-of-Approval crazy, and she'd drawn him into her own private suicide pact. But the press of her body was firm and soft, and he could not resist.

"Why did you just start running like that?" he asked after they'd climbed back out.

"I was scared. You scared me."

"You weren't scared of risking your life just for a fountain pen?"

"It was my father's fountain pen."

They made their way past the groundlings on their blankets and newspapers, the humid air so thick with human emanation that the candles threatened to ignite it. Each time he saw them, the scene took on a fresh dimension of horror in Jerome's mind—sometimes Fagin's den of street urchins, sometimes an almshouse straight out of Tolstoy. He tried not to look their way, knowing what Dwight had in store for them. *You ransacked my dreams*. But Jerome was no better, another vulture picking at carcasses.

Sharon seemed oblivious to it all, delicately sidestepping piles of rubble to let fall a dozen hellos, part flight attendant, part Florence Nightingale, her gown's dirty satin ashimmer in the candlelight. "How's it going, sweetheart?" one of the men greeted, while another blew her a kiss. "Who's the new gentleman, darling?" a woman asked, nodding in Jerome's direction.

They understood Sharon. They might fight over a plastic milk carton; in their world of scarcity and loss, rescuing a fountain pen was understandable.

"Don't stay out too late," Louis called after them as they left.

The streets were dark, and they headed down Mercer, quiet as a village lane. Sharon walked barefoot in the gutter.

"Aren't your feet cold?" he asked.

"Not if I keep to the cobblestones. They stay warm after the sun goes down."

She balanced herself delicately, step after careful step, her dress billowing in time to her own airy music. It was hard to imagine someone as soft and amorphous as Sharon tolerating a world of corners and edges. Life turned people into cobblestones, hard enough to endure what pounded against them. Anything too soft got squished in between.

"You said I was a killer," Jerome said.

"You were ready to kill that man, weren't you?"

"I was angry. But I wouldn't have killed him."

"Maybe. Or maybe not. Something went wild in your eyes."

"How old are you?"

"A woman's age. Sometimes I feel older than my mother, sometimes I don't."

The steady *plap* of her feet against the cobblestones was soothing. The city felt at rest.

"Tell me about your father," he said.

"I sensed it before it happened. I sensed it like a sneeze coming. I can feel things. I knew that the old lady down the hall from us would slip on the ice and crack her hip. I knew when the identical twin boys from 12C would drown in the Hutchinson River one summer day when there wasn't a cloud in the sky."

The carousel of her thoughts swung around several times before he was able to jump on. "And your father?"

"My father," she said, each syllable dusty.

It had happened one evening on his way home from work. She was coming back from the store with a jar of Noxema and a bottle of blue ink for the beloved Montblanc Meisterstück fountain pen, carried by her father all the way from Hamburg, Germany, as he fled the Nazis, who were burning the Jews. When the building's elevator came, she was absorbed in the prospect of the confident, broad lines her pen would make on her loose-leaf paper as she did her homework. *Words strung together without rhyme or reason,* Mrs. Barmbrack, her English teacher, complained. But the pen's glide was too lovely to resist, too free to limit. She hadn't seen the men crowding behind the elevator's circular window, wire-honeycomb through it like hat veil. Two men sprang out like the lid of one of those trick jars releasing cloth snakes. One gripped a knife, the other a limp bouquet of bills. Sharon fled up the stairs and got the elevator on the second floor. It arrived bearing the soft, bleeding heap of her father on the floor. The ink dropped and smashed into a blue-colored star, the Noxema bombed to earth, and the red blood, white cream, and blue ink formed a gory banner at her feet.

For weeks after that, Sharon saw nothing but the picture of her lifeless father in its frame of blood. The prospect of leaving the house iced her veins in terror. The hallway became mined with fright, the elevator a guillotine rising and falling with its deadly chop. She stopped going to school.

"Then I began seeing him right outside my window, standing on the terrace, except that there was no terrace," she said. "He sat on his flying carpet at a terrifying height.

" '*Röschen,*' he said one night. It was his name for me. Little Rose. The Rose of Sharon. He looked normal, not a scar anywhere. It was like one of those slates I had where you peel up a sheet and the writing disappears. 'Where are your pins?' I asked him. His mouth was always stuck with upholstery pins."

What's the matter, you don't think I've earned the right to retire?

"He returned a couple of times a week. *Röschen, there are one or two things you should know. For instance, that with your mother, it wasn't the first time. I was hers, but not the other way around. A man has needs, men more than women. Do you still love me, Röschen? Do you know why I'm telling you this? Because you're keeping yourself cooped up. You're such a beautiful girl. Go out. Love is no crime. Meet some nice gentleman.*

" 'I can't go out,' I told him. 'Not after what happened.' "

Ach, you hardly went out before it happened, either. And besides, what does one thing have to do with another?

" 'Speak louder,' I would tell him. 'I can't hear you above the racket from Stuie's room.' "

I said, what does one thing have to do with another?

" 'All men are violent.' "

You're too young to make generalizations. You don't look good, Röschen. Not a drop of color in your face.

" 'You should talk.' "

Röschen. Listen. Time is passing, You only live once. Believe me. Go out. Mix. Nur ein Stein soll allein sein.

" 'Stop talking in German. You know I can't understand.' "

She sighed. "It took me weeks before I could finally venture outside the apartment, and then only with my mother. I climbed up and down eleven flights of steps to avoid the elevator."

Your mother's tired, Röschen. She can't keep climbing steps. Start acting like someone your age. Go out with a fella. Come to think of it, maybe you should think about getting a job, too. And please—enough already with the wedding dress.

Her father stopped coming. As if in his place, a friend of her brother's began visiting. He wasn't anything like her brother; he was quiet and a little slithery, brooding in a corner any time she came into Stuie's room to ask him to turn down the stereo. His dark eyes made her think of Victor Mature in *Kiss of Death,* her favorite movie. He seemed frightened, but for some reason, seeing him sent a prickle through her. She was, she told herself, in love. It wasn't long before her father reappeared.

" 'You see, I'm trying to make a move,' I told him."

Move, schmoove. He's all skin and bones. Looks like a worrier. He'll have piles before he's thirty, mark my words. Pick someone else.

"Stuie and that boy—his name was Barry—had a fight, and Barry never came back. I waited, I couldn't sleep. I wasn't the same after that. I began to want something. Then there was Dwight, another Barry, except skinnier. The same thing happened all over again. I was ready. I put on this wedding dress and vowed to leave it on until I found a husband."

Taste in your mouth you have, Röschen. Stranger than him, they don't come.

"But I didn't care. I followed him. That was the last I heard from my father. I knew he was angry at me."

"Your father was right," Jerome said. "Dwight isn't the one for you. He's seriously shut down." Ichabod Crane without the horse, he thought. Someone in a Henry James story. "I don't think that Dwight likes people very much. Not individually, anyway."

They bought cold noodles and sesame paste in Chinatown and ate on a bench in the Mulberry Street playground. It was good being away from Dwight and his building, and to Jerome's surprise, it was good being with Sharon, too. He had the urge to tell her everything about his silly, miserable life, and he was sure she had the power to set it to rights. He told her about Agatha.

"It doesn't sound as if you love that woman," she said, sucking up a long noodle through her lips. "More like you wished that she might save you from yourself. You wanted her to think that you weren't a bad person."

"And you? What do you think?"

She handed the container of noodles back to him. "If you listen closely, you can hear the stream under here," she said, letting his question fall away. "It whistles. But you have to be very quiet." She closed her eyes and for a minute or two assumed bonelike stillness, face and hands ghostlike in the light of the street lamp.

"There," she said.

"Where do you go at night?"

"I walk. I look for my father. You don't think that strange, I mean, talking to someone who's dead?"

Jerome remembered Loewenthal in the cemetery. "I guess not. Let's head back, okay?"

He pounded on the door—three times, once, then twice, the signal—and Louis answered it. Jerome steeled himself for the plunge into the reek, for the lineup of the wasted, the sore, and the miserable.

"Evening," said Louis. The ground floor was usually quiet at that time of night. Most of the groundlings dozed after a day of scavenging, but Jerome knew that they could never stay asleep for long once the band started.

Tonight a group of people clustered in the back around the glow of a *botanica* candle.

"People got to give up they notions of possession," a man was saying.

"Private Property. Private Driveway, Keep Out. Private everything," someone seconded. "Pretty soon there'll be private air and private water, too."

"Already got dat. You can buy bottles of it in de store, and fools are ready to pay for it."

"We already have private parts, that's enough," someone else said, and they all laughed.

"You can't expect people to willingly sacrifice their own comfort for some abstract idea such as the public weal. That's what all these socialists don't understand. Socialism is an abstraction, but not human—"

The last voice rang with a familiar clarity. Jerome hurried toward the back. A man in a blue-serge suit was speaking, perched on a pile of grimy blankets.

"Maurice!" Jerome shouted. "Maurice Rose!"

The man squinted. "Who's that?"

"It's me, Jerome!" He threw his arms around him, and the tiny man nearly disappeared in his hold. He smelled of the street, sour and close. He smelled of the bottle. Something pulled at Jerome's heart. "What are you doing here?"

"I sort of live here now."

"Since when?"

Maurice looked to the others for help. "A week, I'd say. And you?"

"I guess I live here, too. Upstairs. What happened?"

Rose gave a philosophical shrug. "I could tell you that one day Kroszak came with her hand out for the rent and that I didn't have it, and then another day she came with the same hand and I still didn't have it, and then another day she came, there was no hand but the order to leave. I could tell you that the Social Service lady promised me this and promised me that, but nothing happened. I could tell you that Tabachova tried to get me into the nursing home where she works, but they did business like Kroszak, and so that didn't work, either. So here I am."

What about his pension? Social Security? The brother who was supposedly sending him checks these many years? But it was all too late, at least for the moment. Rose had already been uprooted, cast off, set adrift.

"And you, by the way, snuck out like a rat deserting a sinking ship. Don't think I didn't notice," Rose said, an accusing finger wogging at Jerome. He smiled and his face became a mosaic of wrinkles. He winked in Sharon's direction. "So who's the lady friend?"

But Sharon was already throwing her arms around Rose. "Father!" she cried.

"Father?" Rose said.

Jerome looked. Could it be? No, it couldn't. But did it matter? Probably not.

* * *

Jerome set up a place for Maurice in a far corner away from the others, where a wide chink in the cinder block admitted a dependable beam of afternoon light. He would have taken him upstairs, but Rose couldn't make the climb. Sharon arranged the nook for him, fashioning a bed out of salvaged boards, milk cartons and foam saved from a dumpster. Jerome lugged in a more or less serviceable chair and a day later, an old office desk, since Rose had announced his intention of dedicating the remainder of what he referred to as his retirement to the craft of poetry.

Sharon presented him with the fountain pen. "Giving it back" was how she put it.

Early in the morning after she returned from her all-night walk, she took him to Washington Square Park, where he composed poems on steno pads Sharon had pinched from Woolworth's. Afternoons, they went to the Jefferson Market Library, and evenings, he read to the others by candlelight. His unconventional diaspora inspired him, he said, and the poetry accumulated, page after page ivied with Rose's delicate hand. Sharon washed the little clothing he had and hung it out to dry upstairs. She was always surprising him with gifts that appeared out from under the folds of her wedding gown: fruit, or a pocket dictionary or—to his utter delight—a bottle of Yardley aftershave, which he splashed on his silvery whiskers. In his soiled suit and crumpled hat, he was a short, wizened Whitman.

"Thank you, my child," he would say with each gift.

"I love you, Daddy," she'd answer.

"What's all this father-and-daughter stuff?" Jerome asked when she wasn't around.

"*Shah,*" Rose told him.

"This is perfect," Rose said, motioning to his little corner of the ground floor as Jerome set down a bucket before a plastic basin so Rose could wash.

"You call this perfect?" Jerome muttered.

"Well, a window wouldn't hurt. And some indoor plumbing. Maybe a nice snake plant, too."

The dampness of the ground floor had the old man wheezing all the time. The whole of his tiny body battled to cough up what he spat out, dangerously pink, into a grimy handkerchief. It hurt Jerome to see Rose like this. He hated to admit it, but it was strange to see an elderly Jewish person living in squalor. Squalor was something he associated not only with the less fortunate, but with those less . . . connected with society, those with less at stake, or those who'd become too disenchanted to even care. Jews weren't like that. They forced themselves into society, even if not wanted. They held on. Rose had tried, but couldn't. Jerome knew that he had to get him out as soon as possible. But how, and where to?

"Listen to that," Jerome said to Sharon as Rose suffered through yet another coughing fit. "We have to do something for him."

A librarian found the number of the Social Services Office on 14th Street, and Sharon made an appointment for Maurice. When the day came, she put on shoes and a normal dress, a caseworker saw them, and they emerged semi-triumphant: something might be done for Maurice if he came up with a little documentation and a mailing address.

"You know, come to think of it, I gave Tabachova a suitcase with some papers," Rose said.

"I'll pick it up this week," Jerome promised.

Jerome returned in the evening to find a circle of groundlings reading their own verse in urgent, rushed voices. The concrete walls echoed with ceaseless recitation as the others dozed or sipped from pocket flasks or smoked or watched the wax drip from candles. Maurice had organized a kind of literary salon on the ground floor. Soon others heard about it and came, shopping carts of junk parked outside like motorcycles before a downtown club. And, of course, many stayed, so the ranks of the groundlings swelled.

"Good poetry must create corners and ends, leaving the reader to imagine the spaces in between," Rose lectured one evening.

"The city is a poem. Its blocks are verses. Its corners are rhymes," someone responded.

"Being poor is a poem," offered someone else.

"A bad poem," a voice concluded.

After supper on the fire escape, Dwight worked in the sub-basement nonstop, stripped to the waist, grimy and blackened as a miner in the ghostly incandescence of his welding torch. The tower grew ever taller as people trudged into the building, rusty delivery in tow, scraping along the concrete floor and banging down the steps like a giant's footfalls, all of it stacked, soldered, lashed, banged, or simply thrown into place.

"A funeral pyre," Jerome told Sharon, watching from the top of the staircase one day. "That's what they're building. This isn't going to end nicely, believe me. Do you know what Dwight has planned? He's going to make a spectacle out of this. He's going to charge admission and open up his little shop of horrors to the public. He's rigging up lighting to illuminate the tower. That band will play, there's going to be dancing, and he's going to sell drinks. He figures that he's going to be thrown out of here soon anyway, so he doesn't care if the cops bust him for overoccupancy or selling alcohol without a license. He's going to cash in on this. Know what he said the other day? 'I need to disseminate my vision.' Goebbels could have come out with that, too."

Sharon listened without alarm. "Maurice is happy," she said simply. "It will be good."

Dwight appeared, dirty and sweating from working on the tower.

"Can't you tell those boys in the basement to play a little softer?" Jerome urged.

"Yes, Dwight," said Sharon. "Can't they?"

"I'll see. How's the poetry coming along, Maurice? Are you going to have something for us to read?"

"Us?" Jerome said.

"Maurice is going to read from the tower."

"No!" Jerome roared. "He can't!"

"Why not, Jerome?" Rose said.

Jerome couldn't say. A dark premonition held him.

"I'll talk to you when I get back from work," Jerome said. He left, vowing to get Rose the hell out of there as soon as he could.

P-A-R-K. Kroszak's street lay in its usual brain-dead torpor of early evening. The aluminum-clad houses emitted dusty heat. Kroszak's dogs were about to lurch into their reflex howling the moment he climbed over the backyard fence until a whiff of recognition had them pawing and tonguing him. Weariness filled their heavy, dark eyes. Jerome uncoupled himself from their furry hold. *I understand,* he thought.

"What you doing here?" Tabachova said when he appeared at her door. "When Misses see you, she call police!" With a damp hand, she pulled him into a room cramped with doilies and plump wooden dolls, a plump wooden doll herself.

"Sutcase? Yes, I chev. I keep when Mr. Rose move out." She reached down under her bed. "Misses want to throw away," she said, red-faced as she pulled out a dark blue valise with brass corners. She stood up and looked at him. "Chow are you, Bernstein? You okay? You too smart to get in trouble. Why not become professor, scientist? Get married, chev femily. How old you are already, twenty-five, six?"

"Twenty-five."

"Too old. Chev femily. How is Rose?"

Jerome couldn't bring himself to tell her, so he made up a story about Maurice staying with relatives.

"Is good. I worry. In this country, they let you die in street. This is America, promised land, so!"

He thanked her and left. How little the suitcase weighed! Light as an insect's carcass it was, even if it contained the remains of Rose's whole life. *A burial urn weighs more.* On the way out, he caught sight of Linda's house, TV on in the living room. He smelled the attic stacked with her dead brother's mementos. He thought of Linda's face, her breasts, her snowy legs. She hated him now, no doubt. He'd be a black spot in her memory now.

Jerome opened the suitcase on the train. There were the tea-stained poems he'd left with Rose that last day at Kroszak's. Rose had marked them up with his delicate hand. *("Imprecise!" "Stop whining!" "Enough with the Rilke already!")* Jerome found outdated insurance forms, outdated leases from apartments long since vacated, outdated Social Security papers. The suitcase was filled with useless documents. Why had Rose held on to it all? Maybe to remind himself that his was once a stable existence. Newspaper clippings, theater programs—the random ephemera of a faded lifetime, the rest lost, forgotten, abandoned, become memory itself. The empty space was filled with ghosts: no baby pictures, no children's grammar-school notebooks or baby shoes, no day-camp awards. Childlessness had been the single, great tragedy of his life, he once told Jerome. He'd given reckless sums to charity and prayed to a god he couldn't be sure he believed in, all because he yearned for a child. His wife even went to a Haitian woman on Marcy Avenue. "A sin fooling around with that," Rose had said, recalling his wife fiddling with a doll made of straw and whispering to it in a strange heathen language. Deep down, Rose sensed that all was hopeless. Both he and his wife had been only children, he'd reasoned; theirs was a union of solitary people, so what else was to be expected? Perhaps certain things were so for a reason, but what might ever explain this heart-crushing absence? Rose spoke of his grief at not having children as rarely as he spoke about his drinking, but Jerome knew the two were linked. Tiny, slender, and fragile, Rose had come to resemble the child he never had.

The train rumbled on. Perhaps this one overweening disappointment made all the others seem endurable by comparison—Rose's fall from life's grace, first into Kroszak's, and then into the hole of Dwight's groundlings, were hardships but not defeats. Loss of possessions paled beside childlessness. Jerome closed the suitcase with a heavy heart.

He felt the train's mad lurching through the tunnel, through time, a wild slide over the mirrored tracks without stopping. Since leaving college, he'd been living here and there, and this year he'd lost two homes in a row. What did it mean to live somewhere? Or nowhere? It hadn't even occurred to him to peek into his old room while at Kroszak's. In the space of two months it had become the set of a revolving theater stage, already out of view and dismantled.

He clutched the suitcase tightly.

"What do you think of the tower?" Dwight asked one evening when they were on the fire escape. They'd just eaten and finished a bottle of red wine.

"When will you finish it?"

"Soon."

Dwight's spectacle was planned for August 25, less than two weeks away.

"Recognize the date?" he asked with a smile.

"Nietzsche's birthday?"

"Mine, too. So I'm going to have a party. You know, your elderly friend is quite the bard. He's organized a little adult-education program down there."

"His stuff is bad and you know it."

"It does have a mordant romanticism to it. Listen." He pulled a piece of crumpled paper from his pocket.

The Broadway bus carries a young girl from City College
and a man in overalls
downtown

past Columbus in his circle and the smoking rings of
Times Square
past the gritty palace of the Met: a caravan sailing
into the breeze blowing up
from South Ferry.
Their faces meet for a moment
and worlds collide . . .
and worlds collide . . .

"Quaint, no? A combination of bad Hart Crane and good Ferlinghetti," Dwight said.

"If you think his stuff is bad, then why do you encourage him?"

"Rose interests me. He's the reincarnation of sentiment, a curlicue on a building, a figure in a genre painting. He's a symbol of—"

"Rose isn't a symbol of anything! He's a person, a very sick, very frail *person*, in case you hadn't noticed." The fire escape creaked. The wine had left Jerome edgy. He could just imagine the monster spectacle Dwight was planning in that basement horror chamber of his, and there was no way in hell that he was going to let Maurice Rose take part in it. It would be too much for him. It would kill him.

"Rose is going to add something important to what I'm doing."

"He's in no condition to be doing this, Dwight, and you know it. The man is ill. You should hear him coughing."

"But he *wants* to do it. He asked me about reading."

"A seventy-four-year-old man with asthma shouldn't be climbing towers."

"He's working all the time to prepare for it. This is going to be his big chance."

"It's going to be his *last* chance if he does it. He can't take all the excitement. He's always complaining about the band as it is. Even the dogs barking in the yard where we used to live drove him crazy."

"By the way, we're running low on food," Dwight said. "I was thinking. A friend of mine has a van. We could go over to where you work and fill it up."

Jerome shook his head. "That's out of the question now. Loewenthal might go bankrupt. I know it sounds stupid, but I just can't steal from him anymore. I've been meaning to tell you this."

"If he's almost bankrupt, another case less or more won't make a difference either way, will it? If you won't have a job there much longer, now's the perfect time for a nice haul before you get the pink slip."

"I can't."

"You once said that it felt good to steal from him."

"That was in the beginning. I like him now."

"We need food."

Jerome looked down. "No."

"You've been here almost the whole summer and you've hardly done anything for the project, Jerome."

"Who helped bail out the basement two nights ago after that leak flooded everything?" An old water main ran along the building's foundations. The damp wall had grown damper and they'd started to notice several trickles. Then one day after a rainstorm, the basement lay under four inches of water.

"But you've never helped with the tower."

"No."

Dwight looked at him. "You think I'm self-absorbed, don't you?"

"Maybe you shouldn't take this whole thing so seriously," Jerome said, hearing the voice of Mr. Rose.

"You're the one who once talked about turning one's life into art."

"I said one has to make use of one's life in order to create art. Besides, I've been thinking."

"About what?"

"That maybe there might be things in life more important than art. Or at least as important."

"Such as?"

Jerome thought of the suitcase of useless papers. He imagined two old people sitting on a sofa in a handsome room furnished with a burgundy carpet and thick drapes. They sat very still. Neither spoke, and it looked like they might sit in that stillness for the rest of their lives. It was, he thought, a picture of abiding love, heavy with the realization that all love ends in loss.

"I don't know," he said. The wine had begun to leave him tired.

"Do you understand my sculpture?"

Dwight looked eager to thrash out the tower's significance for a good hour. But what was there to understand? It was a statue of Dwight himself, or *to* him. Other than that, it looked like someone had picked up the George Washington Bridge and dropped it.

"Maybe not."

"Will you get the stuff from the warehouse? One last time? I'll never ask you for anything again." His tone of voice carried a chill of finality to it, not so much warning as leave-taking.

"Sure," Jerome said, feeling a twinge in his stomach.

On the day of the hoist, Jerome awoke as usual, breathing the dust of his lightless vault. What time was it? He didn't know; time hardly existed in the dark. Sleeping in his room was like being cinder-blocked alive inside a tomb, but it was the only place to escape the band's electric tentacles. He could just make out Sharon's shopping bags and Rose's suitcase nearby on the floor: the unmatched luggage of the transient and uprooted. Sharon had moved into his room several days before. Sometimes they made love.

He put his ear to the ground. Yes, they were down there already, or maybe they were still going from the night before. Their rumblings pulsed upward floor after floor, pumped by a ceaseless metal heart. As the day of Dwight's event approached, Feelie's Wheel was always playing, an army forever in the midst of a charge.

"Sharon?" He looked over to the other side of the room. He often woke up to find her on her mattress, asleep for no more than an hour or two after her nightly wandering, her dress suspended on a hanger looped through a knotted cable dangling from the ceiling. He wanted her to be there today but she wasn't.

He washed his face at the large plastic sink. Through some miracle, the water hadn't been shut off, although Dwight said that Gottlieb warned him not to turn on any other faucets, because the old plumbing couldn't withstand much pressure. Jerome filled a bucket for Mr. Rose and began the climb downstairs.

"Just in time," Sharon said, smoothing the sheets on Mr. Rose's bed. She often seemed pale and worn in the morning after her wanderings but had begun to look fresh and rested. There were times he was sure he was falling in love with her.

A single beam of light through a cinder-block chink silvered the tips of Rose's beard. As usual, he wore his suit, tie and all. A wheeze like a muezzin's call spiraled up from his chest, and he began to cough. His face ran an angry red, and he thrust his mouth into a mound of tissues pulled from his pocket and spat.

"Drink this!" Sharon said, giving him water.

His lips struggled at the rim of the glass, and water dripped down his shirt.

Jerome looked at Sharon.

"Don't say anything," she whispered. "I know what you're thinking."

Rose set down the glass. "You don't want me reading down there, I know, Jerome. Well, you're not going to make an invalid out of me." His tiny fist beat upon the armrest. "How many other chances am I going to have people hear my poetry?"

"They're not going to *hear* anything, Mr. Rose. The cretins in that band are going to be blasting away on their amps the whole time."

"Dwight promised me they'd stop when I read. He said we'd all have a microphone."

"You should see what he's building down there."

"So let him build. As long as there'll be a place for me to sit down and read, I'll be fine."

"Remember how you used to tell me about Flaubert, Mann, and the others, Mr. Rose? Those guys in the band wouldn't know Flaubert from a beer can! They don't *sift!*"

"Jerome, calm down or your stomach'll start acting up," Sharon said.

"I'm going to read, and that's that," Rose said. "Besides, they're expecting me to read." He motioned to the other groundlings. "They say that because of me, they've started to write poetry themselves. I can't back out now, now can I?"

Jerome turned to Sharon. "What if something happens, Sharon? What if the police come?"

"Enough!" Rose said. "Maybe you really don't believe I have any talent. *Aha*, now we have something. You're jealous." His white eyebrows arched steeply.

Jerome sighed. "I thought you didn't like Dwight, Sharon. You used to carry on about how evil he was."

"He is. But if Maurice wants to do this, we should let him."

Rose patted her hand. "Thank you. At least someone around here believes in me." He turned to Jerome. "How much longer do I have, anyway? Tell the truth. Do you think that reading a couple of poems is going to make a difference either way?"

This whole thing was crazy, Jerome thought. But maybe Sharon was right; if this was what Rose wanted to do, he should do it. But if anything happened to Rose up on that scaffold, he'd never forgive himself. Or Dwight.

"You're coming with us when we get the food," Jerome said, a last effort to dissuade Rose, who'd volunteered to go along to the Seven Wonders heist. "Won't that be enough excitement for you?"

Rose waved him away. "That's life. The reading's art."

Dwight came up from the basement. "Ready?"

Mother floats on a chilly cloud above me. "Evil daughter," she says. "I will absolve you if you want me to." "Yes, Mother," I say. "Yes. Please." And then she rains herself upon me. "Cry," she commands. "Do what I found it so hard to do. For once in your life, cry."

TWELVE

Loewenthal's face glares down, cheeks red to bursting, a badly shaven countenance corona'ed with blinding sunlight and writ large with fury: Moses shouldering a pair of tablets to hurl, Jove in eyeglasses wielding a thunderbolt. (*Enough already with the allusions, Jerome,* Maurice Rose says.) Jerome cowers low in a putrid swamp of caviar steaming up from the hot asphalt. Pigeons circle above, hungry for a peck at Jerome's overfed carrion. Rose in his blue suit surveys everything calmly from the loading dock where he sits in judgment, a tiny Lincoln in his memorial. *Dope.* He shakes his head with all the melancholy of the Levant. *You had a good deal with Loewenthal and he liked you, so now you have to go and louse it up.* Wait, Jerome wheezes, struggling to point at him. You wanted to come along, too! You didn't say we shouldn't do it. So why do I get the rap? Rose smiles. *You shouldn't have gotten caught.* A pigeon swoops in close to Jerome, eyes gleaming meanly. Jerome tries to get up, but he's stuck in the caviar like a mastodon in a tar pit, and the filthy bird pecks at Jerome's innards, Prometheus-style. As the crimson beak tears and pierces his soggy flesh, the bird's face becomes Loewenthal's, then Agatha's, and then his brother-in-law's. Get away, all of you, Jerome moans, leave me alone . . .

Jerome rubbed his eyes and saw the cinder-block walls around him once more. The incident in Loewenthal's parking lot the week before burdened him nightly, daily. *Lowlife, scumbag, rat bastard*—the names Loewenthal had called him! *And you get an old man to help you steal, you lowlife.* The day before, Loewenthal had finally told Jerome that he would have to let him go. "You're a good kid. I'm going to miss you, but I have to do this," he'd said, slipping another hundred dollars into Jerome's pay envelope. In spite of everything, Jerome had grown to like Loewenthal. He'd begun to see how they were alike, each carrying his own shopping bag of miseries. But Jerome had betrayed him.

Jerome threw himself onto his side. The mattress barely softened the concrete floor. Unbelievable: he had a guilty conscience from committing the most time-honored and justifiable of larcenies—stealing from his employer. Jerome was on one side, money-grubbers like Loewenthal on the other. But suddenly the old equations of them and us, righteous and foul, had fallen apart, a bridge of wet paper under life's complicated traffic. Once slogans and catchwords had helped him clarify the world's moral ambiguities, but now he saw how they'd merely simplified them, oversimplified them, thinned the soup to broth and the broth to hot water.

Lowlife, scumbag, and rat bastard—

Jerome remembered with a jolt that Dwight's horrible spectacle was to be staged that very night. It was to be videotaped and the music recorded. Dwight had sent out fliers to radio stations and newspapers, written press releases, made phone calls. The neighborhood was wheat-pasted with hundreds of posters. The affair was going to be important, significant, and necessary, Dwight said. It would be analyzed and discussed, and most of all, it would be remembered. *Like Altamont,* Jerome thought. Those guys in the band had asked some of their friends to act as security guards.

Jerome dressed. After his chilly, concrete vault, Dwight's loft was warm and sunny. Stacked along one wall was the loot of the heist: cases of canned shrimp, Vienna sausage, boxes of pasta and biscuits, and several cartons of caviar. Let loose in the warehouse, the groundlings had gone haywire, tearing cartons open and eating things right there instead of carrying boxes to the truck as they'd been told to do. They'd stuffed cookies in their mouths and torn open sleeves of crackers and breadsticks and croutons and *pain grillé*, crumbs caking their lips. Wine bottles were uncorked, and fingers worked into jars of pâté as if it were putty.

Loewenthal had appeared on the loading dock out of nowhere—it had been a late Saturday afternoon, when Jerome didn't expect him—arms raised in biblical rage at the desecration of his temple. Jerome had ducked down behind the shelves, but Loewenthal found him out. "Jerry! Why, Jerry?" he'd shouted. "How could you do this to me?" It was a cry in the wilderness, piteous to hear. "Lowlife, scumbag, rat bastard!" Loewenthal had shouted. "Here, take all of it, you bloodsuckers!" he'd said, pulling boxes down from the shelves, one after the other, glass smashing, packages ripping open. Then he'd broke down and started crying right there in the middle of everything. His son—the famous/infamous Stevie—was with him, and he'd started crying, too. But Loewenthal had come to an utter and complete standstill when he saw Rose carrying off a small carton of oysterettes.

"Why oysterettes?" Jerome had asked Rose on the way back.

"They're delicious with tomato soup."

Jerome's punishment had already begun on the return trip. Traffic in the Queens Midtown Tunnel had stalled, the van stewed in the heat, and the groundlings festered, damp and foul-smelling. Rose had suddenly slumped forward in his seat, face white, lips dry. Jerome poured a bottle of mineral water over his face to revive him, and one of the groundlings, taking his cue, followed suit but with a bottle of wine, dyeing Rose's silver beard purple. Rose blinked. "What's going on?" he'd mumbled, startled at seeing his stained white shirt.

"Salve, O Poeta!"

Rose smiled as Jerome came downstairs with the water for washing. Stubborn pink splotches remained on his white shirt, despite all of Sharon's scrubbing. Without his hat on, he looked even smaller than usual. Or had he grown shorter? Age shrinks you, Jerome thought. The body grows weary of carrying itself around and lets down its load bit by bit.

"Look, Jerome." Sharon held up an immersion coil, which she set into the water, then plugged it into the socket at the end of a wire running toward the basement. "Hot water for shaving."

A tiny rumble rose in the bucket as the water heated, and Sharon began shaving him. How did she get the shaving cream and the coil? Her resourcefulness always amazed Jerome. How much she'd changed since the first time he met her. She no longer lurked around the stairwells, afraid and suspicious, but had become Rose's social worker. She'd arranged everything for him at the welfare office: he'd be getting retroactive benefits as soon as they provided a fixed address for him. Because of Sharon, Rose would be able to get out of there. Perhaps the biggest miracle was that she'd helped him cut back on his drinking, holding him nights when his tiny limbs shivered with need for a drink. Jerome had begun to think of the three of them as a kind of family.

"Can you get this?" Rose asked, pointing to the fuzzy undergrowth in his ears. "And what about you, Jerome? You look like you could use a shave, too."

Jerome smiled as he sidled over to Sharon. "Are you really going to let him go through with it?" he whispered.

"I've made him promise to read no longer than twenty minutes."

Inch by inch, the beard came off, revealing his skin's rough archive. His suitcase had held precious little, Jerome thought, but his face documented everything. The razor clicked gently against the metal bucket each time Sharon rinsed it. She worked expertly, like that tiny haircutter in *David Copperfield.* How quiet everything was: the band wasn't rehearsing. The silence was delicious.

"What do you know, a lady barber," Louis said, passing by. "How much do you charge?"

"You can be next after Jerome," Sharon said, splashing some Yardley onto Mr. Rose's neck and face. Freshly shaved, in his white shirt, hair freshly combed, Rose might have been a bar-mitzvah boy on his way to read the Torah.

"Now you," Sharon said to Jerome. "Why don't you read one of the poems you'll be doing tonight, Maurice?"

Rose beamed and reached into his pocket.

I am the singer
I am the bringer of song and illusion
a face held in light
someone who tells you their stories one night
or another . . .

Jerome listened, first happy, then puzzled, and finally uneasy.

I am the singer
I am the stranger
Sometimes it's easier to talk to a stranger—

" '*Than to a friend,*' " Jerome muttered.

"Have you heard that one before?" Sharon asked.

Know it? He'd written it, that one and perhaps others Rose

would read. The poem had been among the papers in the suitcase. Rose wasn't even aware of his plagiarism. This was getting sadder by the minute.

Yet had Jerome himself done any differently while in Agatha's bed?

"Morning, everyone."

Dwight appeared, furiously awake, grimy, and looking like he'd slept in his clothes. His glasses had finally broken completely, so he wore none, squinting and staring, which gave him a look of perpetual suspicion.

"You won't forget the microphone, will you?" Mr. Rose asked.

"Already hooked up."

Dwight and Jerome nodded at one another only briefly. After returning from the heist and settling Rose in bed, Jerome had lashed out at Dwight. "I can't believe I let you sucker me into doing something like that. The old man could have died!" Dwight wouldn't listen and stormed down to the subbasement. They didn't speak for a whole day.

"You'll be able to help tonight taking tickets, Jerome, won't you?" Dwight asked.

Jerome nodded once more.

The front door scraped open and several men emerged, dragging something large and bulky.

"What do you think?" said a large black man leading the group. "Got it on Twelfth Avenue. Ain't it a beauty?"

The shell of a Chevy Impala convertible thrust through the doorway, looking like it had jumped the curb and crashed. Dwight turned, stunned.

"*Yes,*" he said. "That's it. Someone get the guys from the basement up here."

"What are you going to do with that?" Jerome asked.

"Put it right on the top of that tower!"

Bong and Jake appeared, and they exchanged wary glances with Jerome. There'd been tension since the incident on the fire escape, and for a moment, Jerome expected trouble. But everyone grabbed onto the car and dragged it the rest of the way along the floor toward the stairs, edges sparking against the concrete. Some of the groundlings started to pick up the rear, and soon a procession had formed.

"Just tip her the fuck over!" Bong said when they reached the stairwell. They heaved it up and let it fall with a sonic crash that boomeranged through the basement. The groundlings applauded. It had rained the night before, the walls were damp, the air chilly and smelling of mineral, and the basement felt like a murky, primeval swamp. The tower rose in its midst, a ragged castle.

"Awesome," Jake breathed.

"Get some more of the guys down here," Dwight ordered. "We have to hoist it up."

He rigged a large piece of piping over the stairwell railing, the others wrapped the Chevy's carcass with cable, and slowly a dozen hands began to heave the piece into the air, a battered star straining at the rope as it ascended. The groundlings followed its course like medieval peasants witnessing some celestial phenomenon. Dwight scampered up the tower, ready to receive it.

"Okay, lower it down," he said, beckoning to the car as he might to help someone park it. But the Chevy remained stubbornly in the air. Bong and Jake hadn't heard. Dwight looked up expectantly from his crag on the side of the tower, but the car swung gently from its ropes. Jerome thought of the elevator cab, stuck in limbo in the shaft. Maybe the whole summer was like that: a great weight at a dangerous height, ready to fall, crush, damage, and destroy.

"Come on, lower it!"

The car began to descend directly above Dwight's head. From where Jerome stood, it was easy to imagine that Dwight was some Isaac who'd led himself up this crazy mountain to be sacrificed. He moved to the side as the vehicle descended further, touching down with a great creak and causing the tower to teeter precariously. Dwight began securing the car with cable. The thing swayed, and for a moment, it almost looked ready to topple until settling with a heavy chink.

Jerome left, two things on his mind: talking to Loewenthal and trying to see Agatha. He had to make two apologies. He had to mend what he'd broken, if it could be mended at all. Outside, water pooled at clogged sewers all along Mercer Street. The sky hung heavy with rain. Soggy posters announcing the spectacle clung to building fronts, each one with the haunting silhouette of a figure vaguely human, but faceless. Who was it? (*It's me, who else?* joked Rose.) The poster bore the name "House," Dwight's title for his event. With each poster Jerome passed, the figure grew in menace. Dwight had built a monster, and that night, people were going to pay to come and worship it, hundreds of them. *House.* Well, now there was a car as well. All that was missing was the backyard swimming pool, but if there was another flood, they'd have that, too.

I am the singer . . .

He visualized Rose scaling the face of Dwight's artificial mountain, holding on for dear life, the smooth leather soles of his shoes uncertain against the jagged terrain. Perched up in that car—Rose had never driven a car in his life—gasping for breath, minutes from a sputtering, asthmatic death, he struggles to be heard above the mind-pulverizing music. *I am the singer . . .*

It was madness. It was cruelty. He couldn't let it go on. He would stop Rose from doing it, no matter what Rose or Sharon said. He would get him out of there that afternoon. Where would he take him?

The week before, Loewenthal had mentioned that his wife and daughter were going to Los Angeles. "Now that you're not going to be working, maybe you'd like to come up for a couple of days and relax," he'd said to Jerome. "Keep me company."

Yes. No. Jerome couldn't ask him that, not after what he'd done.

Maybe. It was worth a try. There was nothing more to lose. He searched for a pay phone. His stomach curdled as he picked up the receiver.

"Mr. Loewenthal? Hello?"

"Who's this?" Loewenthal's voice dragged Jerome back to the parking lot's melting asphalt.

"This is . . . are you . . ."

Loewenthal exploded into the receiver. "You sack of shit," he roared. "You sack of slimy horse shit! Go to hell!" The receiver crashed down. Jerome slumped against the side of the booth. Loewenthal was going to hate him forever. Breath failed him, and for a moment, he felt as if he had ceased to exist.

He headed for Agatha's building.

Midway he stopped. Why? Why go there when he was in love with Sharon? A surge of feeling had raced through him like brushfire that morning, to see her shave Maurice. She was disconnected from the world and . . . a little strange, but a year in New Cornwall had taught him that even madness was a matter of degree—and often of choice. It could be self-protection. Somehow, he was sure that Sharon knew what she was doing. She'd be good for him. Her calm was strong enough to withstand the broadest of his rages.

Only when you have denied me will I return.

But even if he loved Sharon, he still had to ask for Agatha's forgiveness for what all he'd done, including having trashed her apartment. And he'd try to get back his journals.

When he reached Agatha's building, something caught his eye among the row of broken-down garbage cans lining the curb: an old, beat-up bookbag. With shaking fingers, he opened it. *J. Sprague*, in perfectly formed letters stamped onto the leather's rough skin. Agatha had given it to him back in New Cornwall. But what was it doing in a garbage can out on the street? And what about that pair of fatigues and those shirts? Had Agatha decided to unload more of his things? His heart began to race. Perhaps that punk in the suspenders had something to do with this, usurping Jerome's rightful place in the apartment by divesting it of his belongings. Except, Jerome realized, he no longer belonged in that apartment.

He began digging into the garbage, frantically pulling out more of his belongings, unable to stop, his every limb thundering, fearful of what lay beneath the pile. Yet what exactly was he looking for? *My past, my foundation.* But was it here? In a garbage can on the Lower East Side? He picked further, restless as one of those Puerto Rican ladies rummaging through the bargain tables on 14th Street. Now that he'd begun his search, he could not abandon it. *But you have to.* Who spoke? He didn't know. These days, it could have been anyone: Agatha, Miriam, Rose. Even Loewenthal. Maybe even the universe: Sharon had told him that anything might speak to you if you paid attention.

"Jesus fuck!"

He pulled out a notebook half-buried beneath an empty package of frozen broccoli and opened it. *June 12. I am here on this stoop and it is my reality. It offers me its space, its chill. I must be humble in its damp, chilly presence . . .* He kept on reading and didn't stop until he'd come to the last page. He read until he smelled the sting of pine in the winter air of New Cornwall, the heavy sweetness of fish frying in oil, the warm breath of Agatha's skin on the side of her neck. He imagined Agatha in her apartment, looking down at him, watching him, waiting to see what he'd do. *I'll leave you alone,* he thought. *I'll accept what happened and let you heal.* He closed the book.

Something moved in a window across the street. Jerome knew it had to be the cretin, mealy undershirt, scrawny arms and all. He didn't want to look, so he didn't see him lifting up a gun and aiming it through the snake plants. He didn't look as the man pulled the trigger, nor did he duck when the bullet was fired. So it struck, first the window glass, then Jerome's finger, breaking away part of his right pinkie with a wet snap. The journal fell into the garbage can not far from the finger's mottled stump of the finger itself, a bloody slug sunk into the garbage can's unweeded garden.

"Jerome?"

A face like Sharon's peered down at him, and a hand lightly touched his arm. Where was he? The heat of an entire sun flared in his hand. *Where did it fall? It couldn't have gone far . . .* What had happened? He recalled tumbling into the garbage can and thrashing around, trying to locate the missing digit. *A needle in a fucking haystack.* Two barking dogs sniffed around for a treat. *Finger food.* What were Kroszak's dogs doing there?

"Did you find it?" he whispered.

"Find what?"

What's missing, for chrissake. Sharon didn't understand, so he tried to feel through the padding of gauze and bandage, then gave up. Those dogs probably got it, gnawing his flesh from the bones as though from a drumstick.

"Mr. Bernstein?"

Another face, a man in glasses.

"Can you see me? If you can, nod your head."

The man leered at him from behind the snake plants. *Such ugly plants, Miriam.* But no matter what, any time a leaf broke off, Miriam set it in water, unable to throw out a living thing.

"Mr. Bernstein? Can you tell me how many fingers I have up?"

Jerome whimpered. Why was this stranger tormenting him?

"Jerome, it's okay. It's me." Sharon touched the side of his face.

"Sh-Sharon?"

She tried to smile. "You're okay, Jerome. You're okay . . ."

"Where am I?"

"Bellevue. When I couldn't find you, I asked Dwight, and he said you might have gone over to that woman's apartment."

"Maurice . . . don't let him . . . please."

"Shh. Take it easy."

"Get me out of here."

"Soon. You need to rest first."

"Maurice," he whispered. Maurice had to be plucked from the jaws of Dwight's torture chamber, his shop of horrors, his subbasemented hell complete with giant Dis, its three-way mouth fitted with the shell of an aquamarine 1959 Impala, the one with the ugly back fins, tribute to crass materialism . . .

As soon as everyone left, Jerome threw himself out of bed, but the first step he took landed him on the floor, falling against the bandaged stump of his pinkie, ramming it into spasms of unfathomable pain. It took several minutes for him to recover.

It was dark by the time he finally left the hospital. The air was hazy, and puddles mirrored the streets. More rain. He carried his bandaged hand, burning like a lantern, Diogenes searching . . . for what? Someone had stolen his work boots, so he had no choice but to make his way barefoot. The street was mined with broken glass, pieces of metal, dog doody. How did Sharon do it night after night?

Were those really his things in that garbage can? Had he seen that journal? The rain had surely washed his words off the pages by now, unlooping them into meaningless lines. He almost felt ready to turn around and try to salvage something. But he didn't. It was gone and far away, all of it. And that was okay. Agatha's window had been closed, mute. She'd never given him any answers, right up to the very end, except that now he realized that he no longer needed them. Go, the empty window seemed to be saying. Not "Get away," but "You can go now." She was no longer throwing him out, she was letting him leave. He began to walk.

Across La Quatorce to Second Avenue, then Third. Con Ed's clock, a silent, low-hanging moon. Almost ten. Dwight's event started at midnight. He made up his mind: as soon as he got back to the building, he would collect Maurice and Sharon, go to the bus terminal and head for Loewenthal's house, where he'd throw himself on Loewenthal's mercy. Even if Loewenthal turned him away, he'd at least hear Jerome's apology first.

The air had grown thick; another downpour was imminent. Once he crossed Houston Street, he began to see clumps of people heading south, the crowds ever thickening as he neared Dwight's building, people clustered on the corners as though it was the entrance to a high school before the first bell. The street was tense with anticipation, a thousand switches ready to be tripped.

"Get in line!" a guy with a fringed leather jacket and tattooed forearms barked at him when he tried to enter the building.

"I live here," Jerome said.

"I don't care where you live. Get in line." He blocked Jerome but made way for a man garbed in the grubby apparel of the street and clutching a handful of paper: one of Dwight's readers. Jerome tried to follow him, but the thick arm came down like a turnpike.

"I told you to get the fuck in line."

"I said I *live* here!" Jerome used his good hand to push the guy out of his way, but an arm clamped around his neck from behind. Jerome freed himself and swung his fist—the bad one this time—into the man's mustachioed face, and his hand broke into a million shards of pain. Jerome plunged inside.

No trace of the encampment remained on the ground floor. The crowd filed in, funneling toward the basement stairs in the murky light of bulbs strung from the ceiling. Music surged up from below. Where was Sharon? Rose? Jerome strained to reach the stairs, hand held tightly against his chest, a million heels punishing his bare feet.

Down in the subbasement the band played under a pool of cold halogen light, while at the other end, Dwight's sculpture loomed, imperious and daunting. The wet splotches on the wall had grown larger, ominous runes of warning. The floor was damp under his feet as he struggled to make his way to the tower in search of Sharon and Maurice.

"Get back."

A kid in a black leather vest who looked no older than eighteen tried to block Jerome's way, his tattooed upper arms soft and floury.

"I'm part of this show," Jerome said.

"Get the fuck back—"

Dwight climbed down from the tower just then, electric cable roped around his shoulder.

"Where were you, Jerome? You were supposed to help with the tickets."

Jerome held up his fraying bandage. "Extenuating circumstances. Where's Rose?"

"Over there somewhere." Dwight pointed to a cluster of groundlings huddled in a corner near the tower.

"Dwight, don't make him go up there, please. It'll be too much for him. He'll collapse from the strain."

"I'm not making him do anything. I can't talk now. I have to fix one of the cables."

"Jerome!"

Sharon waved to him from the groundlings' corner.

"Where were you?" he asked, throwing one arm around her and kissing her. "I woke up and you were gone."

"The doctor said the painkiller would knock you out for a while, so I figured I'd check in here to look after Rose and then get back before you woke up." She touched his cheek. "Sorry."

"I want to get the hell out of here, okay? You, me, and Rose. Let's go now."

But Sharon's attention was elsewhere. "Stuie? Is that you?"

The kid in the leather vest turned. "Jesus, shit. What are you doing here?"

"You know him, Sharon?" Jerome asked.

"He's my brother." They looked at each other, then Sharon leaned over and kissed him on the forehead.

"Mom's ready to go off the deep end, she's been so worried about you," Stuie said. "Who's this guy?" He nodded at Jerome.

Sharon smiled and answered slowly. "A friend. What's that?" She pointed to his tattoo.

"Mars, God of War, on this arm. Thor, God of Thunder, on the other."

"Also of crops," Jerome added quickly. "Sharon, we have to get out of here—"

"Jerome Bernstein!"

Maurice Rose sat nearby against the wall in a chair, a folder on his lap, legs crossed, looking calm in his hat. "What happened to you?" He pointed to Jerome's bandage.

"You're not going up on that thing. I won't let you."

Rose pulled his papers close. "Respect your elders, young man."

"I'll ask you one more time: don't."

"You talk like I've never given a reading before."

The music suddenly ceased, Dwight took the stage, and the lights lowered to a single spot holding him in a circle.

"Welcome to *House,*" he began in a low voice. Dwight seemed even skinnier and slighter than ever. He seemed less real. "House is where you live, a domicile. Listen to the words of those who have come to this house this summer from no house. Like words themselves, floating without the shelter of sentences, these poets have built houses with their words, shelter with syllables—"

Jerome couldn't bear to listen to any more of it. "Sharon, please. Get him to leave."

She fired him a helpless look. "I can't."

Jerome remembered something. "I thought he was your father."

"Yes, and I want him to be happy."

For the next hour, Jerome had no choice but to watch as the groundlings and their colleagues began the long trek up the tower's steplike projections to the battered Chevy Impala on the summit. Each ascended slowly, unsteady hands grasping for random outcroppings of debris. What did it mean that Dwight had immersed them in garbage to provide entertainment for the curious? They'd brought offerings to Dwight's altar, and now they were to become its sacrifices. Each time someone ascended, the tower swayed, metal skin creaking and scraping, a cranky snake dangerously close to shedding.

Once reaching the summit and inside the Chevy, they stared down in fright and relief, not knowing what to make of so many people staring at them after years of being invisible to passersby. Some forgot about reading at all, enjoying the view from the battered convertible, recuperating from their climb. "Come on, now!" Louis shouted from below to rouse them from their torpor. Some of the crowd listened, but most seemed to be waiting for the music to start up again. *Everyone has come,* Jerome thought, *just to be here.*

Several of the readers got through a poem or two and then retreated, spent from the strain of so much attention on them, but one woman kept on going, ad-libbing, then lecturing, and finally shouting at the crowd. She screamed into the microphone, emitting deafening shards of distortion, then stood up and gripped the sides of the car so that it swayed on its perch, and the tower swayed with it. She reminded Jerome of that crazy painter friend of Agatha's from New Cornwall, but with a shock, Jerome recognized her as the woman who'd offered him the Rolaids on the subway the day he'd escaped from Linda. "I am your mother," she was saying. "I am the one you've taken from and used and then discarded. I am your source of life, but you have exiled me!"

"Yeah, Mom!" someone shouted.

"You've sucked from my breasts and taken my nourishment, but now that I am dry, you have no use for me!"

Jerome noticed Sharon staring upward, lips fallen softly open. He'd seen the lines across her face when her brother mentioned her mother's sadness at her absence. Once or twice, Jerome had tried to find out something about where she'd come from, but Sharon had always slipped behind a veil of silence.

She'd been vague about how she'd wound up at Dwight's house. Jerome began to understand. She'd run away.

The band started up again—Dwight's signal for the woman to stop—but she only tried to shout it down until the music finally devoured her and she had no choice but to retreat.

"The old man's next," Stuie said to Sharon.

"Mr. Rose—" Jerome began.

"Shah," he said. "Nothing's going to happen to me." Sharon gave him a kiss on the cheek and brushed off the sleeves of his suit jacket. Rose approached the tower, frail but unmistakably dignified. Jerome thought of Moses going up the mountain to get a glimpse into Canaan before breathing his last. In his suit and hat, papers under his arm, slow but not hesitant, Rose was a pilgrim on a journey he'd always yearned to make. He had endured. A tear formed in Jerome's eyes. *Don't let anything happen to him,* he prayed to whomever.

It took a long time before Rose reached the Chevy. Then the door wouldn't open and he struggled with the handle. He stopped, and the crowd let out a gasp.

Jerome grabbed Sharon's arm. "He's going to fall!"

"He won't," she said, her eyes never leaving him.

Rose righted himself. The door finally opened, Rose got in, and soon he was confidently adjusting the microphone.

"Ladies and gentlemen," he began.

His is a voice from another era, Jerome thought, *from another world.* Behind the wheel and the microphone, Rose had returned to his prime of authority and respect, a time of offices and telephone calls, urgency and responsibility. His silver hair shimmered regally in the bright light. High above the rabble—for that is what they seemed by comparison—he was once more what he had been: a repository of knowledge, culture, and tradition. His was a world of men in hats and women in gloves, of thank-you notes and timepieces needing to be wound, a more deliberate time of streetcars and strolls. It was one unable to forget the tyranny that had slashed through its middle, making its pursuit of poetry that much braver. His generation had argued sitting around tenement kitchen tables, studied history with the fervor of scripture, and believed in utopias. It saw sacrifices—even when blind—as ennobling. His was an age of sentiment, unable or unwilling to view itself with irony, since to do so meant to abandon the pursuit of truth. His age still believed in beauty. People like Rose still allowed themselves to be horrified, indignant, enraged, impassioned. They understood the value of shame. Perhaps for all those reasons, Rose's generation seemed innocent, since it was in its core idealistic, and all ideals risk taking themselves too seriously. Worse, all ideals risked being corrupted. But at least Rose's generation didn't need spectacles such as this—loud, uncomfortable pinches to make sure they were still alive.

I am the singer
I am the bringer of song and illusion . . .

"Go, Grandpa," someone shouted.

The sight of him up there hammered at Jerome's heart. He closed his eyes and began to cry.

Sharon touched his shoulder. "You okay?"

He half-nodded and brought up the mitt of his bandaged hand to wipe his eyes. He no longer knew what he felt, except that he was feeling it for the first time, and like all first things, a little scary.

When Rose finished, he descended with slow precision, one tiny foot after the other, and the band machine-gunned at the crowd once more.

"Okay, let's get him out of here, Sharon—"

Just then, a great iron boom shook the building, buckling the floor, the walls, and the very air. The sculpture shifted and creaked, and the Chevy tilted down precariously, ready for a nosedive. There were screams, and the crowd erupted into panic. People began pressing toward the exit.

"Look!" Sharon said, pointing to the wall. The wet splotches had grown noticeably larger and darker.

"The water main," Jerome said. "Come on!"

Stuie rushed past them, heading for the stage.

"Wait!" Jerome grabbed him.

"I gotta go to the band!"

"Come with us!"

But Stuie had already meshed with the crowd starting to press toward the stairwell to leave.

"You and Rose get out of here!" Jerome shouted to Sharon. "And get the other groundlings to join you. I'll go after your brother."

"What's going on?" Rose asked, hardly unsettled.

"I said go, Sharon!"

"What about Dwight?"

Jerome hadn't even thought about him. Who knew where he was?

"I'll look for him, too. Now go." He kissed her.

Water started pouring from a crack high up along the wall. Jerome pushed through the crowd toward the far end, hand throbbing, bare feet squashed to pulp. People slammed at him in their crazed struggle to reach the stairwell; all the while, he searched for Dwight and Stuie. It shamed him to think that he'd completely forgotten about Dwight—or else he'd already struck him from his mind.

The water was spouting through new cracks. *What had caused that boom?* He remembered the elevator hanging in the shaft. Maybe the reverberations from the band's amplifiers had snapped the cable and the cab had fallen, which was enough to rupture the old water main. The tower kept swaying dangerously, creaking like a rusty Ferris wheel, the Chevy slipping ever closer to the edge.

"Stanley!" Jerome shouted. The kid was charging up the stairs along with the guys in the band.

Then all went dark. Shouts went up as people packed toward the stairs, buffeting against Jerome as he headed in the opposite direction toward the stage.

He found Dwight fiddling with some electric cables in the feeble beam of a flashlight. "Let's get out of here!"

"I can't. I have to fix the lights."

"Fuck the lights! Come on!" This was crazy. Everything was falling apart, the basement was about to become an aquarium, and Dwight was fooling around with electricity. "The band's already split, Dwight!"

"Maybe it's a fuse," Dwight said to himself.

"You're going to get electrocuted!" Jerome shouted, grabbing Dwight's shoulders.

"Get away," Dwight hissed. "This is fucking mine."

A great creak shook the basement, coming from the direction of the tower. The phantom bulk of the car plunged earthward, landing with a splash and an iron thud. There were more screems.

"I'm taking off, Dwight."

"Go."

Something fizzled and flickered, holding Dwight's face in a moment of hellish light.

"Dwight, get away from there!" He grabbed Dwight once more, but Dwight threw him so that he fell backward into the foul-smelling water. He pushed himself back up as fast as he could. At any moment, hundreds of volts might come surging from those wires into the flood. He sloshed toward the stairs, passing the dim form of the car, now filling up. When he reached the top of the stairs, he looked back down, trying to make out Dwight, who stood still and immobile. He looked trapped. For the second time that evening, Jerome muttered a prayer to himself, this time for Dwight's safety.

He saw Sharon's brother on the ground floor. "Come with me. Your sister's looking for you."

"I gotta drive the guys in the band away from here."

"You aren't driving them anywhere, Stanley. You're taking me and Sharon." He pulled Stuie toward the front door.

"Hey you fuckhead!" Bong grabbed Jerome, his boot came down hard on Jerome's bare foot, and Jerome swooned in pain, toppling backward. He clutched Stuie's arm for support, and they fell to the ground together.

"Please, Stanley," Jerome whispered into the kid's ear. "Help me."

"Get up," Bong shouted down at Stuie. "We gotta get a move on."

"Wait at the northeast corner of Broadway and Mercer," Stuie said before getting up. "And my name's Stuie, not Stanley."

"Governor!" Louis shouted, running to help Jerome to his feet.

6

Lester

My father is everywhere, even when I don't see him, even when I know for sure that he can't be here. He is calm and imperturbable, a forest creature invisible in the cool shadow of a leaf, jeweled lizard eyes holding me in their liquid gaze. He still lives locked within me, dangerous.

The one thing worse than fear is being afraid to show it.

THIRTEEN

Stevie slept peacefully on the couch in the den. The cast jutted out stiffly from under the blanket, a plaster anchor holding him fast. The boy's clothing and things lay in clumps around him—the den had become his bedroom so he wouldn't have to climb stairs—and Lester often found himself sitting there late at night as he did now, watching Stevie sleep. The first couple of nights, the new cast had kept Stevie up crying. It itched. It was heavy, but mostly it was there. Tonight he slept at last, and Lester was grateful. Tonight he, too, would be able to sleep.

Rhoda's departure with Deborah was clouded with suspicion in Lester's mind. She had grown distant, dissatisfied in the past couple of weeks. *What did I do to them to make her leave?* He wondered whether Stevie hadn't hurt himself on purpose, out of spite, since the very day they'd gone to Los Angeles, he'd stumbled into a hole in the backyard and twisted his ankle.

"How come you didn't keep an eye on him?" Rhoda had demanded when Lester called with the bad news. "How could you just let him run around?" Hadn't Stevie always run around? he'd tried to say. But it was impossible for him to convince

Rhoda of anything. "You always let things get out of control," she said, angry in a way he'd never heard before. Her voice chilled the room long after he'd hung up. It warned, it condemned. Lester shivered and pulled one of Stevie's blankets over himself and sat a bit longer.

Satisfied that Stevie would stay asleep, he went into the bathroom to brush his teeth. The empty vial of Stevie's pills waited in the medicine cabinet. He still hadn't refilled the prescription for the sedatives. Rhoda had reminded him about it the morning she left, and he'd kept meaning to drive over to the pharmacy. But he hadn't, and he realized he didn't want to. Stevie would do just fine without any pills, Lester had decided, and by the time Rhoda returned, he would be able to announce that the boy no longer needed medication. Then the accident happened. He'd fill the prescription in the morning.

On the way upstairs, he was aware of how long it took him to cross the house—of how big it was, with its acres of closets and window glass. There was so much space walled up, shut in, painted over—a big, bloated box dug into the dirt. Heavy, too. How much did a house weigh? Artie had once talked about jacking up Eddie's house and rolling it onto a vacant lot in Nyack.

He stopped and listened. Yes, Stevie still slept, and the sound of his breathing was a wordless voice of reassurance.

Next morning, Lester had already begun making his coffee as usual when he realized he was wide-awake, even if it was barely past seven in the morning. Anxiety was a natural stimulant. He wasn't used to having a whole day to fill up as he chose. He needed something to do, saw the dirty dishes piled in the sink, and told himself to load them in the dishwasher. Instead, his gaze retreated to the yard, which had become a labyrinth of spontaneous moats and gullies. The pyramid of white gravel stood untouched and solitary, almost stately. Mounds of earth had greened with weeds, and birds drank from pools of rainwater. The whole thing looked like a ruined civilization. The yard was slowly returning to its origins.

Lester had finally confessed to Rhoda the full extent of his business troubles. "Shot full of holes and ready to sink," was how he'd put it. The image of a ship made of Swiss cheese came to mind, funny, almost. "Why didn't you tell me the truth before?" she'd asked him. "Why did you wait so long? Why did you *lie?*" She'd been right. Withholding information was a type of deception. The very next day, Rhoda had announced she was going to the coast. Her sister was redecorating and needed some help, she claimed. But Lester understood.

She'd called a day later. They were having a wonderful time. Deborah loved the beach. Lester imagined her, gleaming, oiled, nubile on her towel, a ring of muscled youths ogling her. Rhoda hadn't stayed on the phone long. He'd told her he loved her. He felt he had to say it, had to say something to soothe the dryness of their conversation. "Yes," she answered. But that was all she said.

The same day, Lester had called up Roger Henderson and asked him to put the work in the backyard on hold. "Of course," Roger had said. "But why?" Lester had an answer prepared. "Rhoda's out of town for a few days. I'd rather she be here while the work's going on."

"Dad?"

Lester hurried into the den. Stevie was up, eyes no more than slits.

"When're Mom and Debbie coming back?"

"Another five days."

"How come they went away?"

Lester sighed. How many times could Stevie ask the same question? "To visit Aunt Hannah."

"I want to visit Aunt Hannah, too. If Debbie can go, why can't I?"

Lester sat down beside him, and all the fatigue of the past week settled into his legs like sand in an hourglass. "Debbie went along to help your mother."

"I can help, too."

"Not until your leg's better. You can go the next time."

Stevie fixed him in a stare. "There won't be a next time. Mommy won't come back. She's going to stay there forever."

Stevie's prophecy left him winded. "What do you mean?"

The telephone rang.

"It's her!" Stevie cried, pushing out of bed, letting the cast crash against the floor.

"Stay here!"

But the little boy had already grabbed his crutches and was hobbling toward the phone in Lester's bedroom.

"Hold the wire," Lester heard Stevie say, his pet phrase of the moment.

It was Artie. "What are you doing home on a Saturday morning, Lester? I thought you always went into work on Saturdays. I figured I'd get the machine."

Lester thought quickly. "I took off because the kid's sick."

"I just want to let you know that we're presenting the petition to the town council on Monday. We're giving your friend Erhard sixty days to get rid of the chickens and the septic tank. It's up to him to do it or not."

Your friend. "You know that Eddie's not going to go along with any of this."

"I know."

He waited.

"I'm not signing it, Artie."

"You're stubborn, Lester. Just about everyone else in the subdivision signed it. People know you haven't. It doesn't look good." He paused. "It looks like you support him."

"I support everyone's right to live and let live, Eddie's included. He's never done anything wrong to me. Besides, Rhoda signed. Isn't that enough?"

Artie took a deep breath, the way he did when he was about to put in his final bet during a card game. "You want to stick up for the underdog, is that it? But we were willing to settle with him. We even offered him money to move."

Lester imagined Eddie's house on rollers sailing down

Route 9 in a hail of chickens, swinging around the curve and then crashing. Not signing now was going to cost him, so why stick out his neck, especially after his last unpleasant dealing with Eddie? The man could be as unpleasant as mold. His anger foamed right below a thin skin of contempt just about to rupture. Who was to say he wouldn't empty a rifle into Stevie the next time he let the chickens out of the coop? Yet Lester knew he wouldn't, and for that reason, he wasn't going to sign anything. Maybe it was something in Artie's voice, the demand, the assumption of being right, like the dogma of some religious people. He began to sweat.

He said no.

"You're sure about it, Lester?"

Lester imagined Artie arrayed in his midtown office, leather chair squeaking, corner windows, artwork. Artie wasn't accustomed to not getting what he wanted.

"Yeah, Artie."

There was an ominous pause.

"Well, see you at the game tonight," he said. "Don't forget the brownies." He laughed.

Lester laughed, too. He hung up and looked around the kitchen. Not only were dishes piled in the sink, but the floor bore muddy traces of Stevie's crutches. The windows were grey and a dirty dish towel hung from the refrigerator door handle. The bathrooms were grimy, and the living-room carpet needed vacuuming. He'd have to tackle all of that before the game. Ever since Rhoda left, he had neglected the house, until it resembled his own grimy mood of despair.

Stevie clunked into the room.

"Daddy, take me to Eddie!" Stevie sprang up into the air and landed on the bed as he might have on a trampoline, cast swinging out like a pirate's wooden leg. "Eddie *said* I have to help *him* unload the new chick*en* feed," Stevie said, punctuating his speech with bounces.

"Stop that."

"Chick-en *feed!* Chick-en *feed!*"

Lester grabbed him around his waist, warm and sinewy as clay, and held him down. "You'll hurt your leg again that way."

"When do we go for the ride?"

Lester had promised to take him along to the office when he went there next. "Promise me you won't act up and we'll go," Lester told him.

Stevie pulled away and started bouncing again. "Act *up!* Act *up!*"

They looped downhill toward Eddie's dark little forest. Lester braced himself for the sweetly nauseating cloud of chicken dung. The smell bothered him, but knowing how Artie and the others felt about it made it seem as funny as a fart during a dinner party. Once the subdivision was rid of Eddie, they'd straighten the road, fell the trees, and put in another big box. The air would clear, and Eddie would be forgotten.

No.

He'd told Eddie what Artie and the others were up to and urged him to get a lawyer, but Eddie pretended that nothing was happening. People like Eddie let themselves be chewed up and spat out, he thought.

As if summoned, Eddie stepped out of the chicken coop just as they drove by. Lester gripped the wheel, determined not to stop—it would mean an hour's visit. But Eddie might be offended. Should he honk and keep going, risking Eddie's displeasure by not stopping? Pretend he hadn't seen Eddie? Things between them had become strained since the night of the card game.

"Eddie! Eddie!" Stevie cried, rapping on the window.

"Be quiet!" Lester shouted. He was about to look away when his eyes met Eddie's. He braked, indecisive, and the car swerved onto the shoulder. Stevie shrieked as Lester struggled to gain the road again.

"I told you to behave!" Lester scolded.

"Why can't we see Eddie?"

They drove on. Lester was too exhausted to answer. Now Eddie would be angry at him for not stopping. Lester sank into his seat, defeated. As he headed over the Tappan Zee Bridge, he was overwhelmed by the feeling of last things and failure. In a week, he would be forty-eight. Forty-eight wasn't that old, but it was an age when your projects were supposed to start coming to term, bearing fruit, and prospering. Once he'd hoped to have become a major distributor, part-investor in a winery or an olive grove. He'd had dreams, plans. Now he was going to close up shop. It was hard not to think that he'd done some things that were very wrong. It was hard not to think of what was happening as some kind of divine punishment.

Strange, it was Jerry he found himself thinking about these days. They'd gotten to know each other that summer. He'd wanted to fire him a week after taking him on. The guy was moody and sullen, angry at the world. He acted like he was too good to be doing manual labor, always scribbling away in some notebook. Plus, he didn't believe in deodorant. But Lester had slipped him some Ban, and with time, the guy lost the chip on his shoulder, and they'd become friends. Something about Jerry reminded Lester of himself. He'd felt badly, knowing that he'd have to let him go.

Lester pulled into the parking lot. It was too large for such a small operation, but there was a time when he'd planned to expand. A school once stood adjacent to it; after it was torn down, his building seemed isolated and set adrift. His heart choked. This was all he had after fifteen years, and he was losing it. Della had accepted things graciously, if sadly; Maribel, the Spanish girl hired the year before, didn't bother to mask her disappointment. "You just let me go, like that!" she'd said with a snap of her fingers, looking almost ready to break into a dance. She was right. But now it was too late.

Lester braked quickly. A beat-up van was parked near the loading dock, one he didn't recognize. Its doors were open. People he'd never seen before were running out of the warehouse carrying cartons. They looked . . . like bums.

They were his cartons. People were stealing from him!

"Stay here," he told Stevie.

He got out. The back door of the warehouse was open. Cartons were stacked on the loading dock. A great black man in overalls heaved a large box onto one shoulder. Inside, people in ragged clothing were running up and down the aisles opening boxes, uncorking bottles, eating, drinking.

An old man in a suit and hat who reminded him of his Uncle Asa was trying to get a box of oysterettes off the shelf.

"What's going on here?" Lester shouted.

"Ask my boss," the old man said politely, continuing toward the truck. "He's inside."

Boss, Lester thought weakly.

A pair of men appeared on the dock, each heaving cartons of Scottish kippers, the ones with less salt than the others, big seller.

"Hey!" he shouted at them, realizing he had to act. But no one seemed to notice him. A younger man, skinny and dressed completely in black, lugged a carton on one shoulder, glancing at Lester but continuing toward the parking lot.

"Hey!" shouted one of the kipper-carriers. "The old man's fainted!"

The box of oysterettes lay on its side, the old man crumpled beside it, hat upturned.

In the midst of it all, Lester caught sight of Jerome hurrying toward the old man, a large crate hoisted upon his shoulders. Lester knew from a distance what it contained: beluga caviar in six-ounce jars with silver-colored lids. The labels on the jars bore an intricate design and something written in what he figured was Persian. The carton was large, but Jerome was strong. The second kipper-carrier disappeared into the warehouse and returned with a couple of bottles. Lester knew which kind: Staatliche Bad Rhoenigen, retail price fifty-nine cents a bottle. He pried off the cap on the edge of Loewenthal's fender—European seltzer didn't have screw-tops yet—then splashed the water in the old man's face, where it bubbled silvery over the ashen cheeks.

"Hey, Jerry!" Lester finally shouted.

Jerome came to a sudden halt and the carton lurched off his shoulder, landing with a terrible crash on the asphalt. The box ripped open and the jars tumbled out, some breaking, the caviar rupturing through the broken glass like innards. Retail price: $5.99 a jar.

The old man came to and looked up. "What gives?" he said.

Lester didn't take his eyes off Jerome, who started backing off, gesturing with his hands.

"Mr. Loewenthal, wait—"

The jar of caviar was already in Lester's hand, scooped up like a baseball. He threw it, Jerome ducked, the jar smashed on the side of the building and began to ooze. Lester went for another, another, taking potshots as Jerome sought shelter behind the van. When Jerome ran up onto the loading dock, Lester followed, keeping right behind him until he caught up with him.

"What the hell are you doing here?" he shouted, grabbing Jerome by the shoulders.

"Stealing from you," Jerome answered, eyes wide in terror.

The metallic reek of caviar steamed up from the asphalt. For a moment, Lester thought he was going to pass out. Instead, he gave Jerome an angry shove. "Get the hell out of here, all of you!" he shouted. "Get out!"

The men in their rags scrambled down from the loading dock, stuffing handfuls of food into their mouths. They scampered into the van, pockets bulging with merchandise. Jerome and the skinny guy dressed in black helped the old man into the back seat. Soon the doors were closed and the van was rumbling toward the street. Lester turned his back to wait until he was sure it had left.

"Daddy," Stevie said, hobbling past the broken jars and packages toward Lester, throwing his arms around him.

Lester let the little boy support him. He told himself not to cry in front of the child, but the tears had already begun. The sun burned down on his shoulders and through his thinning hair to his scalp, and Lester imagined the very asphalt—heating, melting, and starting to bubble—cooking him in its caviar-laden stew.

"Let's go," he said. He locked the doors to the warehouse. He couldn't stay there another minute. He'd deal with it later, or maybe never.

They stopped at a Wendy's on the way home. Stevie chose a seat by the window and ate while reading out the license plate of each car pulling into the lot. Lester ignored his food. The scene behind the warehouse replayed itself in slow motion over and over again. Jerome had spoken in the slurred voice of a record played at a slow speed: *Stealing from you. I'm stealing from you . . .*

A message from Moe was waiting on his machine at home. They'd decided to cancel the card game for the coming Friday night. There was no explanation, but Lester understood: they'd given him a last chance to sign the petition, he'd refused, so now they were banishing him. What they were canceling was his membership in their little club. The game would continue, only somewhere else. Probably at Roger's, he figured. Roger was eager to curry everyone's favor, and since he had connections to the town supervisor, they were eager to curry his. He was sure to mention Rhoda's landscaping having been postponed, and they'd draw their own conclusions as to why. Roger's information was sure to earn him points, since prestige grew by attacking the right people. Lester's name would be mud. *Mud,* he thought, just like in my backyard.

Later that evening, Lester cooked a pan of salami and eggs, Stevie's favorite, and they watched television together in the den, Stevie nestled against him. For the first time in his life, Lester had the feeling that there was little he could do about anything, except perhaps to wait, even if he didn't know for what. He leaned over and kissed Stevie on the forehead, grateful beyond all measure that he was there.

The doorbell rang. Eddie? More eggs?

"You," Lester Loewenthal growled when he opened the door to see Jerome. "What the hell are you doing here?"

"I'm sorry."

"You're sorry," Lester answered.

"Please—"

"Well, I'm sorry, too."

"I have the money you gave me. Most of it, anyway." He reached into his pocket for a fistful of bills. "Here."

Lester's arms remained crossed over his chest. "What happened to your hand?" The bandage was still on, frayed and dirty.

"It's a long story."

A lopsided clack against the floor meant that Stevie was coming. "That lady's wearing a wedding dress!" he said, pushing behind his father and pointing. A young woman was approaching from the driveway, an old man on her arm. "Hey, you're one of the pricks who stole from me!" Lester said.

"A carton of oysterettes. Forgive me," the man replied meekly.

"Did all you of make the trip just to apologize?" Lester asked.

"Sorry we've bothered you so late at night," the young woman said.

"More apologies." The whole world felt pity for Lester Loewenthal. He looked at her. "What's with the wedding dress?" He noticed her bare feet, and Jerome's. "Doesn't anyone wear shoes anymore?"

The old man began coughing.

"Please," the woman in the wedding dress said, "could we come in? Just for a moment? Mr. Rose needs to sit down."

"He needs to sit down," Lester repeated, opening the door. "Maybe he needs some more oysterettes, too."

"Thanks, Mr. Loewenthal," Jerome said.

Lester eyed him. "You're a son of a bitch, Jerry. Remember that: A son of a bitch. So what happened to your hand?"

"Someone shot me."

"Hey!" Lester shouted into the driveway at an approaching figure. "Who are you?"

A kid in a leather vest walked up to the door.

"Her brother." He nodded toward Sharon.

"Is anyone else coming?" Lester asked. He winced to see the woman in the dirty wedding gown sit down on Rhoda's off-white sofa. The man's suit was dirty, too. So was Jerome. All of them looked like they'd been living on the street.

Lester couldn't remember the last time anyone had sat in the living room.

When everyone was inside, Jerome introduced them.

"Pleased to meet you, Lester," Mr. Rose said, joining the woman on the sofa. "Do you think I could possibly have a cup of tea?"

"A little tea," Loewenthal said, in a daze. "First he steals my oysterettes, then he wants my tea. Very nice. Would any of the other weary travelers care for a spot of tea as well?"

"That would be nice," Sharon said.

"You have any Southern Comfort?" the kid asked.

"He's underage. Don't give it to him," Sharon said.

"Shut up," said Stuie.

"How come your dress is so dirty?" asked Stevie.

Loewenthal noticed that Jerome couldn't take his eyes off the little boy.

"Come with me," he said to Stevie. They went into the kitchen. His hands shook as he reached for cups and saucers. What were Bernstein and the rest of these not-so-merry pranksters doing coming over to his house? And what was even more frightening, what was Lester doing letting them in and then serving them? Nothing made sense anymore. In the short space of a couple of days, everything had changed. Ordinarily he would have been asleep early to get up the next morning for work. Rhoda would have been there, and Deborah, too. Stevie wouldn't be in a cast. The backyard wouldn't be torn up. He wouldn't be serving tea—tea?—to people who'd stolen from his bankrupt business. And he'd be getting ready for the card game.

"A nice place you have here," Mr. Rose said when Lester returned. "Very nice."

Loewenthal set down a tray with boxes of *Gallettes de Province, Biscotti di Parma,* and some *ciambelle.* "Have some of each. You're probably familiar with them, Jerry. You took four cartons of each. Enjoy."

Jerome nodded miserably.

"Is she getting married?" Stevie asked, pointing to Sharon.

"Time for bed, Stevie!" Lester said. He handed him his crutches. "Let's go."

"No, Stevie," Sharon replied. "I'm not getting married yet. I told myself I would wear my bridal gown until I found someone to marry."

"Is *that* why?" Stuie said.

"This tea is just what I needed," Mr. Rose said. "What a night."

"You were wonderful, Mr. Rose," Sharon said. "I was so proud of you."

"Thank you. Tell me, Mr. Loewenthal, do you like poetry?"

"That's Jerry's department," Lester said, nodding at Jerome without looking at him. He noticed Stevie lingering in the doorway. "Go to bed."

Stevie gripped his crutches, watching as Maurice Rose drank his tea. "You like chickens, Mister?" Stevie asked.

"Mostly in soup."

Stevie's face soured.

"I said go to bed!" Loewenthal shouted.

"Let me help him," Sharon said. She rose and walked with the boy toward the den. "How did you hurt your foot?"

"I fell. Doesn't it hurt to walk barefoot?" Stevie asked as they left the room.

"Not if you walk softly."

"Delicious, these cookies," Mr. Rose said.

Sharon had just returned when the sound of the television came from the den.

"Stevie, shut that off!"

"Hey, look. The whole thing's on the news," Stuie said.

Jerome and Sharon hurried into the den, leaving Lester and Rose alone.

"Did you say you liked poetry or not?" Mr. Rose asked. "I have some here if you'd like to hear it."

"You're my father's age," Loewenthal said, disbelieving.

"I'm probably older. People tell me I look younger than I am. So how about it?"

"Go ahead," Lester said, spent. Poetry made as much sense as anything else now.

Rose fumbled for a sheet of paper in his pocket.

I am the singer
I am the bringer of song and illusion . . .

"Oh my God," Sharon said from the den.

"Excuse me." Loewenthal joined the others. A loft building, surrounded by police and firemen, was shown on the screen. People were being carried out on stretchers.

Sharon touched Jerome's arm.

"Bad scene," Stuie said. "Jake and Bong are going to kill me if they ever see me again."

"Stay away from them, they're creeps," Sharon said.

Loewenthal tried to make sense out of what the reporter said: an illegal party in a loft-building basement, an elevator crushing someone to death, people trampled . . . "Where is this?" he asked Jerome.

"Where I used to live."

"You didn't see Dwight, did you?" Jerome whispered to Sharon. She shook her head. "He was still in there when I left. He wouldn't leave. I tried to get him to come along."

"Who's the babe?" Stuie asked, pointing to a framed photograph on the wall.

"My daughter," Lester said.

He found beds for them and brought a stack of towels. "There are two bathrooms. You can all take showers if you want to. Most of you should. Oh, do me a favor," he said to Sharon. "Put this on tomorrow," he told her, handing her one of his wife's cotton shifts. "We can send the gown to the cleaners."

"Do you have something for my stomach, Mr. Loewenthal?" Jerome asked.

Loewenthal took a bottle from a hall closet and gave it to him.

"You're a son of a bitch, Bernstein," he said. "Remember that."

"It's all in the papers," Stuie said when they ate breakfast in the morning. "Look."

Sharon scanned the front page. "I tried to get as many of the groundlings out as I could. Louis left. He said he has a sister somewhere in Brooklyn. But some of the others wouldn't go. They said it was their home and they were staying put."

"Did you know Louis was a bird-watcher? He said that any time he was on leave from the merchant marines he went birding," said Rose.

"What kind of a place was that?" Loewenthal asked, pointing to the paper.

Sharon thought for a moment. "A kind of house, I guess."

"You should call Mom and tell her where you are, Stuie."

"Look who's talking."

"How come she's wearing Mommy's clothing?" Stevie asked, pointing to Sharon.

"Has anyone ever told you what a nice figure you have?" Mr. Rose said.

"Where's Jerome?" Lester asked.

"Out back," Sharon said.

He'd thought of Jerome and his frayed bandage all morning

and was tempted to go out and talk to him. But he couldn't. He would be civil to Jerome as long as he was under his roof, he'd told himself the night before. But no more. The image of Jerome and his compadres carting away Lester's property wouldn't go away. It was more than a matter of ethics. It was a slap in the face, a stab in the back. During those drives into the city, he'd spilled out his life to Jerome, told him everything, held back nothing. Jerome had hardly reciprocated. He hadn't shared, *he hadn't played along*. He'd made up his mind not to trust Lester. He'd decided that Lester was the enemy, and that was why he hadn't felt the least bit bad about stealing from him, even if he knew damn well that the business was in the red. Lester wondered why he'd agreed to let Jerome stay on. He must have been crazy. Naive. No wonder Artie and the rest of them laughed at him. He was more of a simpleton than Roger. He'd deserved everything he'd gotten.

He peeked out the window. Jerome walked along the edge of the property, picking up a small stone and tossing it, a breeze playing at the frayed edge of his bandage. He'd given Jerome a pair of his old chinos and a T, and from that distance, Jerome might have been a younger version of himself, surveying the property and wondering what had happened to all the trees. Lester couldn't stop looking at him.

During the next couple of days—Lester had agreed to let them stay until Rhoda returned—the house bustled with activity. Sharon tackled the dirty dishes in the sink, mopped floors, and did several washes in the machine. Lester walked into the bathroom to find it gleaming. Jerome bundled up all the old newspapers for recycling, and the kid washed Lester's car. The old man took it upon himself to alphabetize the books in the den. The annoying crackle vanished from the hi-fi speakers—the kid must have done something—and the TV's reception improved. (Lester had seen the kid fumbling with the antenna.) The bags of clothing in the basement destined for Goodwill disappeared, as did the books for the town library. Sharon and Jerome took turns cooking supper.

He's trying to say he's sorry, Lester thought. Yet he still couldn't bring himself to say a word to Jerome, not even while they ate. *Not now,* he told himself. *Maybe not ever.*

More bad news followed about the disaster in Jerome's building. The bodies of two homeless people were found in the basement—drowned. The police were looking for the person responsible for giving the party. The building owner had been arrested on his return to the country.

There was no mention of Dwight.

The next day, Lester went out back and saw Jerome by himself tossing stones into one of the large puddles, waiting for the ripples to disappear before tossing another stone. The fresh bandage was bright in the sun. Lester's doctor had agreed to see him. When the old bandage came off, Jerome saw that he'd lost half of one pinkie, and since then, he'd grown even more quiet than before. Lester thought back to the first times he'd given Jerome a lift after work. He'd mentioned a woman. Had it been Sharon? For some reason, he didn't think so. A bird fluttered down onto the pyramid of stones, surveying the yard's chaos. The piles of dirt and holes reminded him of the funeral of Rhoda's mother, of Moe's swimming pool, of all his humiliations. Maybe there was something to the idea of fate, of bad luck, of being born under a bad star. There was a word for his situation: *schlimazel.*

Yet the backyard looked peaceful in its decay. During the past few days, alone with Stevie, away from the business, and now, surrounded by this strange encampment, Lester approached Jerome, thinking he might talk to him at last, but he was unable to shake the image of those men carting his boxes across the Seven Wonders parking lot. He noticed Jerome turning to look at something on the ground that had caught his attention.

"Remember him?" Lester said, pointing to the statue of

Mercury lying on its side, face sheathed in a fine film of dirt. Jerome nodded and smiled, and slowly their eyes met. Lester noticed Jerome struggling to return his gaze, to allow Lester to look at him, and accept whatever anger Lester felt. He saw that something in Jerome had changed, a sharpness blunted. He seemed ready to receive something instead of pushing it away.

"Does it still hurt?" Lester nodded at Jerome's hand.

"A little."

"I'm sorry about it."

Jerome shrugged. "Guess I won't play the piano in Carnegie Hall."

"Tell me. What exactly was going on in that building of yours? Was it some kind of commune?"

They pulled over two rusty garden chairs, sat down, and Jerome told him everything.

"I should have stopped Dwight," Jerome said. "I should never have let him go through with this. I knew it would end badly."

"He sounds like some kind of crackpot."

"He was a misguided visionary."

"So you were stealing that stuff for all those people?"

Jerome looked away. "Yes."

"How long did you do it?"

Jerome answered in a whisper. "All summer."

"I know."

"What—"

"With the racket from your backpack? How could I not have known that something was going on? I started watching you. I saw you sneaking into the warehouse after you'd clocked out."

"So why'd you let me keep on doing it?"

"At first I hoped you'd stop. Then I wanted to see how long you'd have the balls to keep it up."

Jerome fiddled with the ends of the bandage.

"Who shot you, by the way?"

"This guy. I threw a can of sardines at his window."

"You threw a can of sardines at someone?"

"It's a long story."

"I have plenty of time, or haven't you noticed?"

So Jerome told him about Agatha, too.

"And that girl?"

For the first time since being at Loewenthal's, Jerome smiled. "Oh, I don't know."

They kept on sitting.

"I have no reason to let you and your gang stay here, do I?"

Jerome shook his head.

"So why am I doing it?"

"I don't know, Mr. Loewenthal."

"I don't know either."

Jerome looked at him. "I've fucked up. I've really fucked up. Everything I touch turns to shit. What makes me want to destroy everything?"

"Don't talk like that," Lester said, beginning to feel uneasy. How many times he had asked himself the same questions, thought the same things? He noticed Jerome's hand massaging his belly and remembered that Jerome had stomach problems sometimes.

"I'm a failure," Jerome concluded.

"I said don't talk like that. People always bollix up the things that are most important to them. They wouldn't bother with anything that wasn't important. Maybe they do it *because* they're so important."

"What do you mean?"

"I don't know what I mean." He reached for a stone and picked it up. "Maybe because they think that if they don't mess up their own lives, something or someone else will, so they'd rather be the one to do it." He kicked at the moist earth and scanned the ruin of the yard, like a cemetery with its waiting holes. Beyond it, the house stood lemon-colored, calm, unaffected, imperious. Rhoda's. Stevie came to mind, a clash of perfection and error, joy, and confounded expectation: his first-born, his only son. Stevie's outbursts had once seemed momentary, terrifying glimpses into the infinite, the incomprehensible, the *uncontrollable*—in short, into the workings of a vengeful God. But this summer, Lester had begun to look at it differently. Maybe there was actually very little over which one had control. This summer, as life reached a new low point and it grew clear that nothing would work out as he'd hoped no matter what he did, he'd begun to understand that most of the time, things didn't go either wrong or right, they just went. He'd never thought much about destiny or fate before—ruminations he'd always felt were for the weak and the lazy—but with the earth shifting quite literally under his feet, he'd begun to reconsider. Reason made sense only as long as things went well. When they didn't, the rules no longer held, conventional wisdom no longer applied. It was like trying to keep warm when one of the walls of your house was missing. Being inside didn't help, since there was no true inside anymore.

"Half of what we do in this life has to do with what we mean to do, and the other half just happens," he heard himself say.

"So why bother doing anything?"

"To try and get it right. That's hard enough. And it's all you *can* do. Most plans that work out are either coincidences or luck." Why, were Artie or Moe geniuses? Did they command some magical power? Roger Henderson's wife's colostomy bag—was that really supposed to mean anything other than a bum gut? Lester held the pebble between his fingers, enjoying its smoothness. "I'm filing for bankruptcy at the end of the month, Jerry."

"Mr. Loewenthal—"

Lester raised a hand. "No. It's good. It's very good. Maybe it's the first good thing I've done in a long time. Things'll either work out or they won't." He paused. "I'm not ashamed," he said, answering his father's unspoken charge. "Not one bit."

"People make mistakes," Jerome said, rubbing his side again.

Lester nodded. "What about this new girl?"

"I don't know."

Lester looked at him. "You're afraid you'll mess this up, too, is that it?"

"Maybe."

Lester gave the pebble a final rub and then tossed it.

"It's nice out here," Jerome said after a while, motioning toward the yard. "It reminds me of where I lived after I left college."

"Glad you think so because it's going to stay just how it is. I don't have a red cent to finish it. A pity. I bet it would look great. It would certainly make my wife very happy."

Jerome turned to him, eyes wide. "Let me do it," he said. "Please."

"What do you know about landscaping?"

"Nothing. But I can learn. Oh, do you happen to have any Milk of Magnesia?"

If the garden was to be finished, they'd need the plans, but Lester couldn't find where Rhoda had put them. (He wanted this to be a surprise and didn't want to call her.) He asked Roger for a copy, and to his surprise, Roger told him to come to his office and pick it up. He'd been friendly, no trace of malice whatsoever. But Roger always had been polite, and besides, Lester's banishment from the card game meant that Roger had moved up one rung of the ladder.

Roger's office was all the way to the back of his garden-supply store. Stevie's crutches made a bouncy thud as he swung himself past the rakes and lawn mowers. Having a house filled with people for the past couple of days had energized Stevie. He and Jerome had become friends, both of them invalids with their casts and bandages, and Stevie had fallen in love with Sharon, who delighted him with stories of her father talking to her from outside the window. Lester paused before Roger's door. He hadn't seen Roger since the last card game. There was a time when he thought they might become friends. He waited outside the door for a moment before knocking, readying himself for the ordeal. This wasn't going to be easy.

I'm going to lick your pussy clean. I'm going to work my tongue right down your tight little cunt . . .

Someone inside was speaking.

I know you want it. I'm going to lick your pussy clean.

Lester drew back. That voice.

. . . I'm going to work my tongue right down your tight little cunt . . .

Lester let out a whimper.

"Dad—"

Lester clamped his hand over Stevie's mouth and pulled his head against him. The easiest thing in the world would be to push the door open and strangle Roger with the telephone cord. He could knock him senseless with one of Stevie's crutches, step on his face and crush his horn-rimmed glasses under his foot. But no—

"Come on," he whispered to Stevie.

"Right down your tight little cunt," Stevie said with glee. "Right down to your chicken titty!"

"No problem," the kid was saying, eyes bright with anticipation as Lester explained what he had in mind. "We can just record it. I have the band's Nagra, and that'll pick up everything. You got a camera? It'd be great to get a shot of him as he does it, too. This is going to be cool!"

Lester returned the next day at around the same time and took the kid with him. They left with ten minutes of tape filled with Roger's obscenities, plus some Polaroid shots. Roger had gripped the phone in his hand, too frightened to replace it as the kid jumped out from behind Lester, snapping a camera over and over again. When he finally did, he reached into a drawer for what Lester assumed might be a gun, but he didn't even flinch.

"Too late, Roger," he said, holding up the tape recorder. "Too goddamn late."

"That's one damn sick dude," Stuie said on the way home.

Later that night, Lester headed over to Eddie's house. Eddie sat on the porch, as he often did at that time of day.

"Mind if I join you, Eddie?"

Eddie motioned to his beer cooler, and Lester took a can.

"It's nice here." He listened to the rustle of the leaves. It occurred to him that if Eddie'd had children, a son or two might have been sitting there with them.

Eddie's gun lay beside him.

"When's Rhoda coming home?"

"Tomorrow."

"Quite a crowd you got over there at your place these days," Eddie said. "The girl's pretty. Is that old man her father?"

Eddie takes notice of everything, Lester thought. "Not exactly." He sensed Eddie waiting to hear the rest of the story, but when he said nothing, Eddie said, "That's all right, you don't have to tell me."

Lester tightened. It didn't take much to tick Eddie off. People like him had such a hard time in the world because they painted themselves into a corner.

"He's an old guy who had nowhere to live," Lester began.

But Eddie was already too miffed to be interested. "Susan used to like this time of day," he said. He hadn't mentioned his dead wife in a while. "Do you know how long I've been living here? Take a guess."

"Longer than I have, so it's more than twelve years."

"Twenty-one. They still hadn't finished Route 303 when we bought the place. This whole area was different then." He drank his beer. "Nothing like it is now. Nicer. Quieter." He looked right at Lester. "Better, if you ask me."

Lester nodded.

"Twenty-one years," Eddie repeated.

"That sure is a long time, Eddie." He had some more beer.

"Got a little notice today," Eddie said. "Hand-delivered."

Lester set down his can.

"The town supervisor's office wants me to get rid of my septic tank. They want me to get rid of my chickens, too. Said they violated some kind of county law. I want to know the last time a chicken hurt anybody. I want to know the last time a chicken ran over a kid or bit someone. You know how many chickens I got in there?" He nodded toward the coop. "Take a guess."

"I don't know. Fifty? Sixty?"

"Try a hundred and ten. Ninety-five hens and fifteen roosters. And they want me to just take all of them and throw them away."

"You could probably sell them—"

"I ain't doing nothing to any of them, do you hear me? Nothing! They're *my* chickens!"

"It has nothing to do with chickens, Eddie. It's just how some people think this subdivision should look, the way it should be."

"Well, how the hell should it be?"

Lester didn't know what to say. The sunlight had spread out and dimmed. The breeze through the leaves made an ancient, melancholic sound, carrying fall along with it. Rhoda came to mind. He missed her. Her absence forced him to think about things. He realized that Seven Wonders no longer mattered anymore. He'd even stopped worrying about what his father or Alfred might say about it. But the trees swaying softly—they mattered. Stevie mattered. Strangely enough, Jerome's lost pinkie had begun to matter, too. And Eddie being thrown off his property mattered.

"I want you to listen to something, Eddie," he said taking the kid's tape recorder from his pocket. He flicked a switch.

I want to eat your pussy . . .

Eddie sat forward. "What the hell's that?"

"Listen."

I want run my tongue all the way inside your fresh, hot pussy . . .

"Now have a look at this." Lester took out an envelope containing Polaroid pictures of a middle-aged man in tortoiseshell glasses, wearing a white shirt and tie, sitting behind a desk, telephone receiver in his hand, looking surprised.

"Roger Henderson," said Eddie.

"Since Rhoda's been away, he's been calling up other women in the subdivision." Lester slipped the pictures back into the envelope. "And before that, he was the one who'd been calling up Rhoda. So let's say I pay Roger a little visit and show him what I have. And let's say that I ask him to remove his name from the petition and urge the others to withdraw it. Maybe he'll do it. If not, I tell him that I'm ready to go visit his brother-in-law in the town supervisor's office."

Eddie pulled away. Threatening someone like Roger frightened him.

"No," he said. "Whatever's going to happen is going to happen."

"But this might really change things, Eddie. It might be the only thing that can." Then he thought of the gun. Maybe Eddie planned to take care of things in his own way, a posse of one, a madman's kamikaze mission.

"Think about it, Eddie."

Eddie's eyes narrowed. "Why would you want to do something like this, anyway? You're one of them."

"Not anymore. They've thrown me out of the card game."

"Thrown you out—"

A moment later, a cluck and clack of the chickens broke the evening's calm.

"Jesus!" Eddie cried. "Someone let them out again!" He sprang up and ran toward the coop. He took his gun with him.

Lester hurried after him. A dense cluster of feathers and claws and pecking heads had begun spreading like foam out of the coop and moving downhill through the open gate toward the road. The creatures cut a frenzied path, hardly knowing where they were heading, terrified and unable to stop. Lester had witnessed escapes before, but Eddie had always been able to get them under control. This time, a perverse determination had seized the animals, and the road drew them to its danger. Eddie tried to shepherd them back inside the gate, but they fanned out around him, water around a rock in a stream. Who had done this? Artie and Moe?

In the distance, a car was sweeping around the curve with terrible speed. A screech of brakes ended in a hot-sounding skid just before the chickens. The car slowed and drove on, leaving a twitching mass of feathers behind.

"Get back!" Eddie shouted at the animals, now pleading with them, but they didn't heed him, no longer his. In desperation, he began kicking at them and batting them with his rifle. "Stupid chickens! You stupid, stupid things!" He raised the gun into the air and began shooting. The birds swept up from the ground in terror and fluttered around in a cloud of feathers.

Jerome was running toward them, his bandage a dim beacon in the darkness. "Stevie's lost!"

"Oh my God," said Lester.

Another shot went off. Another car passed, striking a pair of birds that let out a miserable cluck as they were flung to the side of the road. By now, the chickens were everywhere, crowding the night with jittery-clawed confusion.

Another shot.

"Stop, Eddie!" Lester shouted, keeping his distance.

A pinpoint of light appeared just around the curve. Like a cat drawn to any sudden motion, Eddie turned his gun toward it. The light grew larger. Lester squinted, trying to make it out. It was too small to be a car, but moving very fast. Then Lester saw: a bicycle taking the curve at tremendous speed. The brood of chickens came to a halt for a moment or two, waiting to see what would happen next, a stiff meringue of feathers frozen on the dark asphalt. Seconds later, Lester made out a helmet, bicycle pants, a shiny striped cyclist's shirt. He imagined the bicycle's tires slicing through the flurry of chickens like the top of a coconut custard pie. Eddie fired again.

Lester noticed Jerome creeping up behind Eddie. In the same moment, he spotted Stevie hobbling down the road, crutches doing a knitting dance.

"Stevie, stay back!"

But the boy hadn't heard or hadn't listened, and he kept coming. The bicycle met the cluster of chickens with a squeal of brakes just as Jerome wrestled Eddie to the ground. The gun went off, and the bicycle plunged into the frothy commotion, torpedoing its rider onto the shoulder, helmet rasping against gravel.

"Get away from me, you!" Eddie cried as Jerome grabbed the gun.

Lester ran toward the fallen cyclist just as another car appeared, coming from the other direction. It slowed around the curve but not quickly enough to avoid the bicycle stranded in the middle of the road, snapping it in two before braking to a halt on the shoulder. The driver, a young guy, jumped out into a mess of broken wings and bloody feathers.

"I didn't even see him, I swear," he said.

"Chickie, chickie!" Stevie cried, eyes filled with terror at the sight of the slain fowl. He tried gathering up one of the wounded birds, still gripping his crutches, but the bird fluttered from his grasp and limped along the ground.

Lester spotted yet another car in the distance. "Stevie, get back!" he cried, advancing toward the boy, marooned in the middle of the road, crutches uncertain in the midst of so many tiny feet and flapping wings.

Eddie freed himself from Jerome and lunged toward Stevie but couldn't reach him. Moments before the car came upon them, Eddie grabbed a chicken and flung it at Stevie, hitting the boy's face with a cluck and a wet *thwap* and knocking him backward so that he tumbled out of harm's way.

7

Raymond

Instead of going crazy, mother stayed unhappy, a cloth washed too often, gone stiff, frail, and bleached. Sometimes I think I hear her crying in a far room, long and hard, almost in another language.

I will always be my mother's daughter.

FOURTEEN

"What are you doing here?"

I spun around. I'd been in Agatha's empty apartment for no more than a minute or two when someone pushed through wearing a pair of baggy pants and a T-shirt that said "Seven Wonders Gourmet Food." It was him: the AP. I stepped back, ready to bolt, except that he blocked the doorway. *Only when you have denied me.* The red lettering on the wall behind me—both lines of it—glowed ominously, responding to his presence. I was trapped. He looked a little less frightening than he did that night under the Charles marquee, since he'd shaved and didn't seem as grungy or as crazed, either. But I remembered his ambush, the feverish grip around my neck, and I was ready to make a break for it.

"It's cool," he said, coming in. "Take it easy."

I kept my distance. The floor creaked as he stepped around, tracing a rough perimeter of each room. He seemed to be looking for something, although nothing remained. The bare floors shone, and the emptiness echoed. Without heaps of things, Agatha's apartment had grown. I'd never understood her need for clutter until then, when the relentless sunlight on so many empty walls and floors left them hard and inhospitable. Clutter keeps you from feeling lonely.

When he'd finished his survey, he turned to me. "How'd you get in?"

"The door was open."

"She's gone," he said.

"I know. Philadelphia."

"Her mother?"

I nodded. Earlier this morning, I'd called, only to find the number disconnected. Directory Assistance supplied me with several Spragues in Philadelphia, but the sole M. Sprague hadn't answered. I wasn't so surprised to find the apartment empty when I got there, for I knew she had to disappear. She had left my life as she'd entered it—unexpectedly, unreasonably, even painfully—but above all, inexplicably, and nothing that unstable could last. It was almost easy to believe that she hadn't entered it at all, so that when I'd look back on this summer, all that would remain would be a luminous sheet of light through those dirty windows. The empty apartment was a message, silent as her sleep but as full of meaning. I knew it would be a long time before I met someone like her again, if I ever did, and it might be even longer until I learned to love or let myself be loved.

Agatha was not the only person who was gone. Michael had left, too, off to a new job in Chicago.

The AP's fingers ran along the wall and stopped at his inscription, tracing its letters with his fingers. *Only when you have denied . . .*

"By the way, I'm not a swine," I told him.

He studied me. "No, I guess not. Sorry." He started a circuit around the apartment once more, and this time it seemed like pacing, and he couldn't stop, determined to find something, even if nothing was there. I grew uneasy. I knew his temper. I tensed as he approached the corner where his journals had been.

"So how'd you meet her?"

"In the library." I thought back to that first puzzling encounter. She'd been looking for him that day, I realized. Perhaps she had been looking for him the whole summer.

"Be honest. Didn't you think she was a little strange?" He shot me an uncomfortable smile. His question felt like a trap.

"She was scared."

He nodded his head in what look like approval. "How old are you?"

"Seventeen."

"You like older women."

I thought for a moment. "Older men," I corrected him, although I didn't know Michael's age for sure. Why had I just said that? But why not? Everyone could know it now for all I cared, including my father, although I sensed he already knew. Leona had probably figured it out, too. Telling my mother was going to be another thing, however.

"Oh," he said.

"What's your name?" Agatha had never mentioned it, nor was it written anywhere in the journals, and suddenly I wanted to know. "I'm Raymond."

He introduced himself and extended his hand, and I shook it. One of them had only four fingers. So this was the AP. He had become something of a myth to me that summer, indestructible and powerful, fighting against a world determined to ignore him.

"Are you in college, Raymond?"

"Just starting."

"Know what you want to major in?"

"Psychology, maybe." Being with Agatha had given me the idea.

He faced me squarely. "So tell me. What are you doing here?"

I had wanted to see Agatha once more before she left. I wanted to tell her how bad I felt about what I'd done. And I wanted to return the journals. But when I reached her stoop,

I knew there was another reason, and perhaps it was the most important one: to thank her. I told him this.

"You wanted to thank her? For what?"

For everything, I thought, *even for things I had no notion of.* Most of all, I wanted to thank her for what I'd learned from her that I'd one day discover to be true.

"Oh, for liking me, I guess," I told him. "How about you?

"I'll be moving upstate for a while and wanted to ask her about some things of mine that she had." His eyes held me. "Some notebooks."

I slipped off my backpack and set it down between us. "Here," I said.

All his composure vanished as he knelt down and began removing the journals one by one. He examined each cover for a long time, as he might have a child returned from a kidnapper. I expected him to at least flip through one or two of them, but he merely set them down in a neat pile, and when all had been removed, he sat staring at them.

I felt very tired. I'd slept little the night before. A call had come from Israel just after midnight with the news that my mother was safe. Her bus had broken down in the middle of the Sinai Peninsula, and it had taken a while until they got it towed to the nearest village and repaired. The telephone lines—never all that reliable in Israel, I'd been told—were down in a sandstorm, so it took several days before the driver could call. My father and I had finally reached her at my relatives' house. "They told me you called before, Raymond," she'd said softly. "Come the hell home already, Ruthie, will you?" he'd yelled into the receiver.

"So tell me," Jerome said. "Did you read them?" He remained on his knees before the pile of notebooks.

I struggled to figure out the right answer. I was sure that part of him wanted them to have been read, but the chill in his eyes told me he was angry.

"Yes." The apartment's echo added ice to my guilty voice. "But at first I thought they were hers. I thought they would tell me how to make her love me as much as she loved you."

"They weren't all hers," he said quickly. He ran a finger around the edge of the pile. "Did you like them?"

"Yes. I liked them all a lot." It was true. He was dangerous, but his every breath was full and emphatic. "You shouldn't have come in here and messed things up that night," I ventured.

"I wouldn't have if the journals had been here." He looked down. "There's a bunch of things I shouldn't have done. But sometimes you do things without thinking about them. You do things you really don't want to do, but something makes you do them anyway."

Both of us were saying good-byes that afternoon, taking leave, departing. I was beginning to learn that even harder than leaving someone you'd loved was the ache of not being sure you'd loved them enough or in the right way. There was a word for it: regret.

We found a large shopping bag in a closet for him to carry his journals in.

"I guess that's it," he said, picking up the bundle. "Wait. Tell me one thing. You and her . . . I mean, if you like guys, then how come you and she—"

"We didn't."

"Never?"

I didn't look at him when I answered, still a little ashamed. "No."

We walked out. I was about to shut the door, but something made me want to leave it open as I'd found it.

"How come you like Nietzsche so much?" I asked him on the way down the stairs.

Jerome shrugged. "I don't know. He seems kind of cool. Rilke, too."

I saw him glancing at the building across the street. The man wasn't there. The window was empty, the snake plants gone. Who knows what might have happened to him? Suddenly it seemed as if everyone was leaving the place where they lived. It was a summer of no fixed addresses, of shifting homes and uncertain residence.

"Are you in a hurry?" he asked. "Would you mind if we made a little detour?"

I'd told my father I'd be back by five so we could leave for the airport at six to pick up my mother. It was just after three. I had some time. Besides, I liked this guy. "Sure," I said.

He took me to a loft building on the corner of Prince Street and Mercer. The ground-floor windows were bricked up. Workmen were putting up scaffolding. The cobblestones had been dug up from the street in front, and a dusty trench revealed a great, rusty conduit. Homeless people sat on the sidewalk along the side of the building, some clutching large plastic garbage bags protectively.

"I used to live up there," Jerome said, pointing to a fire escape on the top floor. He went to a metal door plastered over with posters and knocked three times, once, then twice. Nothing happened, so he tried it again. He stood back and looked at the building, studying its details as if to memorize them.

"Fuck!" he shouted suddenly.

"What's wrong?"

"Dwight, you fucking asshole! Why did you have to be so fucking hard?"

"My, my," said one of the homeless men, dressed in two blazers, Bermuda shorts, and running shoes. "I'll thank you to keep a civil tongue in your head."

"Let's just get the hell out of here," Jerome said. He strode off, leaving me to hurry after him.

"You said you're moving upstate?"

"This guy is letting me and some friends of mine stay at his place."

I remembered that I had brought a present for Agatha. "Here," I said, reaching into my backpack. "This is for you."

He tore off the wrapping paper to reveal the book with its

marbleized cover. "Thanks," he said. "You know, you don't really act like some gay boy."

I didn't know how to, not yet. But I was ready to learn. I'd hoped Michael might teach me or Barry. Now I'd have to wait until college.

We walked as far as Houston and were about to hang a left, but he came to a sudden stop before a poster that was half-peeled off a wall. I had only a glimpse of the letters *ouse* before he pulled it the rest of the way off and tore it up into a couple of pieces that he let fly away on a breeze.